W9-BPC-977

Leaving
Blue Bayou

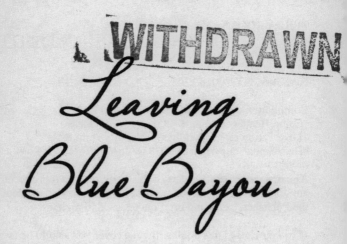

Leaving
Blue Bayou

JoAnn Ross

ZEBRA BOOKS
KENSINGTON PUBLISHING CORP.
http://www.kensingtonbooks.com

ZEBRA BOOKS are published by

Kensington Publishing Corp.
119 West 40th Street
New York, NY 10018

All Kensington titles, imprints and distributed lines are available at special quantity discounts for bulk purchases for sales
promotion, premiums, fund-raising, educational or institutional
use.

Special book excerpts or customized printings can also be created to fit specific needs. For details, write or phone the office of
the Kensington Special Sales Manager: Kensington Publishing
Corp., 119 West 40th Street, New York, NY 10018. Attn. Special
Sales Department. Phone: 1-800-221-2647.

Zebra and the Z logo Reg. U.S. Pat. & TM Off.

ISBN-13: 978-1-4201-3084-3
ISBN-10: 1-4201-3084-6

First Printing: October 2012

10 9 8 7 6 5 4 3 2 1

Printed in the United States of America

WITHDRAWN

<u>CO</u>NTENTS

CAJUN HEAT

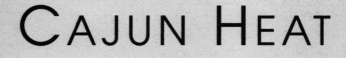

One

If anyone had told him, back in his hormone-driven teenage days, that a guy could get paid sinfully big bucks for making love to the world's sexiest women, Gabriel Broussard would've hightailed it out of South Louisiana's bayou country a helluva lot sooner.

The morning after what would permanently be etched in stone as the worst night of his life, he'd loaded up his truck, just like the Clampetts had done in that old sixties sitcom, (though in his case it'd been a black Trans Am), and moved to Beverly.

Hills, that is.

Swimming pools.

Movie stars.

Okay, so technically this house wasn't actually in the Hills, but on the beach at Malibu, which in Gabe's mind was a lot cooler and still included its share of swimming pools and movie stars. Of which, though it still blew his own mind to think so, he just happened to be one.

Which explained the panties. Sort of.

"Six pairs," Angela Moreno announced as she dropped the lacy undies in front of him.

Gabe morosely eyed the pile of silk and satin lace. They were all just like all the others this week—either red or black. Whatever happened to girly pastels? A soft, feminine pink? Or even a sweet virginal white? Though it'd been years since he'd had any interest in virgins, with the right woman, it could make a nice fantasy.

These were flat out forward.

Big fucking surprise. Like throwing underwear with pinned-on telephone numbers over his gate wasn't?

He plucked a black triangle with two strings the width of dental floss from the pile and held it up to the scant bit of sunlight that was managing to slip through the storm shutters he'd closed to keep out of the range of the vultures—tabloid photographers—who'd been circling ever since Tamara Templeton had tearfully announced on *Inside Edition* that she was breaking their engagement because she could no longer deal with Gabe's "addiction to kinky sex."

That's when the panty attacks had begun. This particular pair was as transparent as Tamara's ploy. When the sight of his hand showing through the sheer black fabric didn't strum a single sexual chord, Gabe wondered if he might be getting old.

Christ, wasn't that a fun thought?

"Six pair are less than yesterday," he said.

"The day's still young." His assistant had to raise her voice to be heard over the *whump whump whump* of the rotors from the helicopter circling overhead. It was as if he was under siege. She dropped a blizzard of pink messages atop the underwear.

"Diane Sawyer's already called three times this morning, Katie Couric twice, and Barbara Walters didn't exactly come right out and say so, but I got the distinct impression that if you'd throw your interview her way, you'd be a shoo-in for one of her celebrity shows. If I were you, I'd hold out for the Oscar special."

"If you were me, you wouldn't be in this mess," Gabe muttered.

"Good point. And one I was too polite to mention." She ignored his snort. "Oh, and Leno's producer called and suggested that coming clean on *The Tonight Show* could really help your damage control campaign."

"I don't have a damage control campaign," Gabe ground out. Not being nearly as wild as his bad boy reputation made him out to be, he'd never needed one.

"Maybe you ought to get one. I vote for calling Barbara. Hardly anyone makes it through her interviews without crying."

"And how would me crying like a girl on national television help my image?"

"It'd make you look sensitive. Women love that. Besides, you might pick up some sympathy."

"I fail to see how accusing America's sweetheart of lying would gain the sympathy vote."

Tamara Templeton had literally grown up in viewers' living rooms. She'd made her first appearance as a plucky orphan sent from New York to live with her aunt and uncle and numerous cousins on the family farm somewhere in the nameless Midwest when she was nine years old.

Amazingly, in a competitive business where the average television show had a shelf life between milk and yogurt, bolstered by its saccharine "family value" stories set in "simpler" times, *Heartland*—which, in Hollywood high concept terms, had initially been dismissed by critics as *Little House on the Prairie* meets *The Waltons*—was still running strong twelve years after its debut.

And Tamara was a multimillionaire several times over.

She had her own clothing line, a perfume label, a series of best-selling books about her fictional character's adventures,

and a doll whose period prairie dresses probably cost more
than the average parents spent on their own kids' clothes.

Her movies, which to Gabe's mind were even more likely
to give their young audience cavities than the damn TV show,
were guaranteed blockbusters, and Gabe had heard tales of
studios refusing to set a release date for their summer movies
until *her* opening weekend was set in stone.

She was young, beautiful, rich, and appeared, to her le-
gion of fans worldwide, to have everything any young woman
could wish for. But there was one thing she was lacking. The
respect of her acting peers.

Which is where Gabe had come in.

"Your mistake was letting her announce your engagement
in the first place," Angela pointed out what Gabe had been
telling himself over and over again since this mess had
started.

"Like I knew she was going to pull a stunt like that." Gabe
clenched his jaw. "Hell, we'd only been out twice." Both "duty
dates" set up by the agent they shared.

Angela shrugged. "Sometimes it happens that way. People meet, heartstrings zing, and the next thing you know,
you're in some Vegas chapel, pledging to love and honor
until death do you part, while an Elvis impersonator belts
out 'Burning Love.'"

Knowing that Angela had actually done the Elvis impersonator wedding bit, Gabe refrained from pointing out that
he'd rather go skinny dipping with gators.

"Read my lips. Nothing went zing. Nothing fucking happened. Period."

Not that Tamara hadn't tried. And she was a fine one to
talk about kinky, leaning over and telling him, just as they'd
left the limo to do the red carpet walk into the Golden
Globes, that she wasn't wearing any underwear.

There'd been a time when an announcement like that
would've given him a boner the size of Alaska, but ever

since his first movie, where he'd been cast in the starring role of the rogue pirate Jean Lafitte, a virtual Aladdin's cave of gorgeous, available women had opened up to him. In the beginning, he'd done what any healthy male would do when gifted with such a scrumptious smorgasbord of female dessert—he'd feasted.

Unfortunately, it hadn't taken him long to discover that even the sweetest desserts could become boring. And it was hard to value anything that came too easily.

"Hell." He dragged his hand through the shaggy hair he'd been growing for an upcoming role as a borderline crooked, New Orleans cop. "I've got to get out of town."

"Like there's any place on the planet the paparazzi won't find you."

He'd spent a sleepless night thinking about that.

"There's one place."

Gabe had never planned to return to his hometown of Blue Bayou. Then again, he sure as hell hadn't planned to end up in a mess like this, either.

Besides, it wasn't as if he had anywhere else to go.

Two

It was funny how life turned out. Who'd have thought that a girl who'd been forced to buy her clothes in the Chubbettes department of the Tots to Teens Emporium, the very same girl who'd been a wallflower at her senior prom, would grow up to have men pay to get naked with her?

It just went to show, Emma Quinlan considered, as she ran her hands down her third bare male back of the day, that the American dream was alive and well and living in Blue Bayou, Louisiana.

Not that she'd dreamed that much of naked men back when she'd been growing up.

She'd been too sheltered, too shy, and far too inhibited. Then there'd been the weight issue. Photographs showed that she'd been a cherubic infant, the very same type celebrated on greeting cards and baby food commercials.

Then she'd gone through a "baby fat" stage. Which, when she was in the fourth grade, resulted in her being sent off to a fat camp where calorie cops monitored every bite that went into her mouth and did surprise inspections of the cabins, searching out contraband. One poor calorie criminal had been caught with packages of Gummi Bears hidden beneath a loose floorboard beneath his bunk. Years later, the memory of his frightened eyes as he struggled to plod his way through a punishment lap of the track was vividly etched in her mind.

The camps became a yearly ritual, as predictable as the return of swallows to the Louisiana Gulf coast every August on their fall migration.

For six weeks during July and August, every bite Emma put in her mouth was monitored. Her days were spent doing calisthenics and running around the oval track and soccer field; her nights were spent dreaming of crawfish jambalaya, chicken gumbo, and bread pudding.

There were rumors of girls who'd trade sex for food, but Emma had never met a camper who'd actually admitted to sinking that low, and since she wasn't the kind of girl any of the counselors would've hit on, she'd never had to face such a moral dilemma.

By the time she was fourteen, Emma realized that she was destined to go through life as a "large girl." That was also the year that her mother—a petite blonde, whose crowning achievement in life seemed to be that she could still fit into her size zero wedding dress fifteen years after the ceremony—informed Emma that she was now old enough to shop for back-to-school clothes by herself.

"You are so lucky!" Emma's best friend, Roxi Dupree, had declared that memorable Saturday afternoon. "My mother is soo old-fashioned. If she had her way, I'd be wearing calico like Half-Pint in *Little House on the Prairie*!"

Roxi might have envied what she viewed as Emma's shopping freedom, but she hadn't seen the disappointment in Angela Quinlan's judicious gaze when Emma had gotten off the bus from the fat gulag, a mere two pounds thinner than when she'd been sent away.

It hadn't taken a mind reader to grasp the truth—that Emma's former beauty queen mother was ashamed to go clothes shopping with her fat teenage daughter.

"Uh, sugar?"

The deep male voice shattered the unhappy memory. *Bygones*, Emma told herself firmly.

"Yes?"

"I don't want to be tellin' you how to do your business, but maybe you're rubbing just a touch hard?"

Damn. She glanced down at the deeply tanned skin. She had such a death grip on his shoulders. "I'm so sorry, Nate."

"No harm done," he said, the south Louisiana drawl blending appealingly with his Cajun French accent. "Though maybe you could use a bit of your own medicine. You seem a tad tense."

"It's just been a busy week, what with the Jean Lafitte weekend coming up."

Liar. The reason she was tense was not due to her days, but her recent sleepless nights.

She danced her fingers down his bare spine. And felt the muscles of his back clench.

"I'm sorry," she repeated, spreading her palms outward.

"No need to apologize. That felt real good. I was going to ask you a favor, but since you're already having a tough few days—"

"Don't be silly. We're friends, Nate. Ask away."

She could feel his chuckle beneath her hands. "That's what I love about you, *chère*. You agree without even hearing what the favor is."

He turned his head and looked up at her, affection warming his Paul Newman blue eyes. "I was supposed to pick someone up at the airport this afternoon, but I got a call that these old windows I've been trying to find for a remodel job are goin' on auction in Houma this afternoon, and—"

"I'll be glad to go to the airport. Besides, I owe you for getting your brother to help me out."

If it hadn't been for Finn Callahan's detective skills, Emma's louse of an ex-husband would've gotten away with absconding with all their joint funds. Including the money she'd socked away in order to open her Every Body's Beautiful day spa. Not only had Finn—a former FBI agent—not charged her his going rate, Nate insisted on paying for the weekly massage the doctor had prescribed after he'd broken his shoulder falling off a scaffolding.

"You don't owe me a thing. Your ex is pond scum. I was glad to help put him away."

Having never been one to hold grudges, Emma had tried not to feel gleeful when the news bulletin about her former husband's arrest for embezzlement and tax fraud had come over her car radio.

"So, what time is the flight, and who's coming in?"

"It gets in at five thirty-five at Concourse D. It's a Delta flight from L.A."

"Oh?" Her heart hitched. Oh, please. She cast a quick, desperate look into the adjoining room at the voodoo altar, draped in Barbie-pink tulle, that Roxi had set up as packaging for her "Hex Appeal" love spell business. Don't let it be—

"It's Gabe."

Damn. Where the hell was voodoo power when you needed it?

"Well." She blew out a breath. "That's certainly a surprise."

That was an understatement. Gabriel Broussard had been so eager to escape Blue Bayou, he'd hightailed it out of town without so much as a good-bye.

Not that he'd owed Emma one.

The hell he didn't. Okay. Maybe she did hold a grudge.

But only against men who'd kissed her silly, felt her up until she'd melted into a puddle of hot, desperate need, then disappeared from her life.

Unfortunately, Gabriel hadn't disappeared from the planet. In fact, it was impossible to go into a grocery store without seeing his midnight blue eyes smoldering from the cover of some sleazy tabloid. There was usually some barely clad female plastered to him.

Just last month, an enterprising photographer with a telescopic lens had captured him supposedly making love to his co-star on the deck of some Greek shipping tycoon's yacht. The day after that photo hit the newsstands, splashed all over the front of the *Enquirer*, the actress's producer husband had filed for divorce.

Then there'd been this latest scandal with Tamara the prairie princess . . .

"Guess you've heard what happened," Nate said.

Emma shrugged. "I may have caught something about it on *Entertainment Tonight*." And had lost sleep for the past three nights imagining what, exactly, constituted kinky sex.

"Gabe says it'll blow over."

"Most things do, I suppose." It's what people said about Hurricane Ivan. Which had left a trail of destruction in its wake.

"Meanwhile, he figured Blue Bayou would be a good place to lie low."

"How lucky for all of us," she said through gritted teeth.

"You sure nothing's wrong, *chère*?"

"Positive." She forced a smile. It wasn't his fault that his best friend had the sexual morals of an alley cat. "All done."

"And feeling like a new man." He rolled his head onto his shoulders. Then he retrieved his wallet from his back pocket and handed her his Amex card. "You definitely have magic hands, Emma, darlin'."

"Thank you." Those hands were not as steady as they should have been as she ran the card. "I guess Gabe's staying at your house, then?"

"I offered. But he said he'd rather stay out at the camp."

Terrific. Not only would she be stuck in a car with the man during rush hour traffic, she was also going to have to return to the scene of the crime.

"You sure it's no problem? He can always rent a car, but bein' a star and all, as soon as he shows up at the Hertz counter, his cover'll probably be blown."

She forced a smile she was a very long way from feeling. "Of course it's no problem."

"Then why are you frowning?"

"I've got a headache coming on." A two-hundred-and-ten pound Cajun one. "I'll take a couple aspirin and I'll be fine."

"You're always a damn sight better than fine, *chère*." His grin was quick and sexy, without the seductive overtones that had always made his friend's smile so dangerous.

She could handle this, Emma assured herself as she locked up the spa for the day. An uncharacteristic forty-five minutes early, which had Cal Marchand, proprietor of Cal's Cajun Café across the street checking his watch in surprise.

The thing to do was to just pull on her big girl underpants, drive into New Orleans and get it over with. Gabriel Broussard might be *People* magazine's sexiest man alive. He might have seduced scores of women all over the world, but the man *Cosmo* readers had voted the pirate they'd most like to be held prisoner on a desert island with was, after all, just a man. Not that different from any other.

Besides, she wasn't the same shy, tongue-tied, small-town bayou girl she'd been ten years ago. She'd lived in the city; she'd gotten married, only to end up publicly humiliated by a man who turned out to be slimier than swamp scum.

It hadn't been easy, but she'd picked herself up, dusted

herself off, divorced the dickhead, as Roxi loyally referred to him, started her own business and was a dues paying member of Blue Bayou's Chamber of Commerce.

She'd even been elected deputy mayor, which was, admittedly, an unpaid position, but it did come with the perk of riding in a snazzy convertible in the Jean Lafitte Day parade. Roxi, a former Miss Blue Bayou, had even taught her a beauty queen wave.

She'd been fired in the crucible of life. She was intelligent, tough, and had tossed off her nice girl Catholic upbringing after the dickhead dumped her for another woman. A bimbo who'd applied for a loan to buy a pair of D cup boobs so she could win a job as a cocktail waitress at New Orleans' Coyote Ugly Saloon.

Emma might not be a tomb raider like Lara Croft, or an international spy with a to-kill-for wardrobe and a trunkful of glamorous wigs like *Alias*'s Sydney Bristow, but this new, improved Emma Quinlan could take names and kick butt right along with the rest of those fictional take-charge females.

And if she were the type of woman to hold a grudge, which she wasn't, she assured herself yet again, the butt she'd most like to kick belonged to Blue Bayou bad boy Gabriel Broussard.

Three
_____

There was no way she could have missed him. Emma supposed that he'd chosen the plain white T-shirt, faded jeans, scuffed cowboy boots, red Ragin' Cajun baseball cap and RayBans in order to blend into the locals crowding the terminal, but there was no way Gabriel would ever blend in anywhere.

He was six feet one before tacking on the added height from those wedged heels of the boots and his body beneath that tight shirt appeared as lean and hard as it'd been when he was eighteen. The shaggy black hair curling at the nape of his neck was as black as a moonless night over the bayou and the thin white scar running across his cheekbone added a dashing, dangerous look reminiscent of the pirates who'd once used the bayou as a home base while raiding merchant ships out in the Gulf.

A sexy stubble of beard darkened his jaw, and his mouth was set in a firm, no-trespassing line designed to discourage anyone who might recognize him from speaking to him. He made his way past the newsstands, take-out Cajun food counters, and souvenir stands selling Tabasco sauce and plastic alligators on the loose-hipped predatory stride of a swamp panther.

Emma was wondering if Nate had informed Gabriel about the change of plans, that she'd be the one picking him up, when he honed in on her like a heat-seeking missile.

"Hey, *chère*."

His drawl was as rich as the pralines being sold next to those grinning plastic gators. Emma had read that when he'd first gone to Hollywood, he'd been told to sound more "American," to which he'd responded that the last time he'd looked at a map, Louisiana *was* in America, and besides, having an accent sure as hell hadn't hurt Antonio Banderas, Pierce Brosnan, or Sean Connery.

After *The Last Pirate* was released, and all those earlier detractors realized how sexy moviegoers found that bayou drawl, Gabriel Broussard's name rocketed to the top of every A list in town.

Case closed. As they say in the movie business, *A Star Was Born.*

His sensually chiseled lips tilted into a weary, all-too memorable half smile that hinted at dark secrets. The smile that made women want to take him into their arms, coddle him, and make the pain go away. The smile that had coaxed more than one willing female into the backseat of the Batmobile black Trans Am he'd roared around the bayou in back in high school.

Then, even as she braced against it, he folded her in his strong arms.

Because the feel of that hard, male, built-for-sin body against hers made her want to hold on, Emma stiffened.

If he noticed her resistance, Gabe didn't show it as he put her a little away from him, keeping his long dark fingers curved around her shoulders as he subjected her to an openly masculine appraisal, from the top of her dark head, down to her Sunset Poppy lacquered toenails. The little toe was smeared a bit from putting her brand-new sandals back on before it dried, but from the way his gaze lingered on her breasts, Emma didn't figure he'd notice the flaw.

"Damned if you haven't turned into one hot female, you."

The intimate growl was more suited for a bedroom than the crowded concourse in Louis Armstrong International Airport. As for the words . . . well, they shouldn't have given her such a secret thrill.

They shouldn't.

But, heaven help her, they did.

They also gave her a rash, reckless idea.

While Emma wasn't one of those people who actually believed those tacky supermarket tabloid stories about bat boys and alien babies, and who in Hollywood was sleeping with whom, it was more than a little obvious that while he might no longer be the town's bad boy from the wrong side of the tracks, one thing about Gabriel Broussard hadn't changed. Seduction still came as naturally to him as breathing.

So, what if she turned the tables? What if *she* seduced *him*?

After all, he owed her. Big time.

Emma was proud of how she'd moved on after her divorce from Richard, the adulterous, tax-dodging, embezzling dickhead. But some old habits died hard, and in many ways, although there were times when she aspired to be promiscuous, she was still a good girl. Sometimes too much so, if her best friend could be believed.

Roxi, who could have written a modern girl's guide to hooking up, had taped all six seasons of *Sex and the City* and every Wednesday evening, while Richard had supposedly been at his Rotary Club meetings, she and Emma had gotten together to watch them. Unfortunately, while Roxi memorized Samantha's pick-up lines, Emma identified with the hopelessly romantic Charlotte.

It wasn't as if Roxi hadn't tried to liven up Emma's life, encouraging her to push the sexual envelope, to act on impulse.

Ha! Easy for *her* to say. Emma didn't do impulsive. She made lists. Lots and lots of lists. All of which were color coded by day of the week, month of the year, and whether they were business or personal.

Not only was she diligent about crossing items off as she accomplished them, if she did something that wasn't on one of those pieces of yellow lined legal paper, she'd add it to the bottom of the list, just for the satisfaction of drawing a line through it.

After going back to school to become a professional masseuse, she'd worked on her business plan for Every Body's Beautiful for eighteen months before buying so much as a towel. Much to Roxi's frustration, most of Emma's evenings were spent alone, poring over the day spa's books and spreadsheets, looking for ways she could improve her cash flow.

Reminding her on an almost daily basis that you didn't have to be in love with a man to sleep with him, Roxi was all the time also repeating her favorite bumper sticker slogan: Well-Behaved Women Seldom Made History. But being mostly content with the life she'd made for herself after the divorce debacle, Emma didn't feel a need to make history.

Still, what woman didn't have a few things in her past she might have done differently? Like marrying the dickhead.

Or believing, back when she'd been a naïve eighteen-year-old wallflower, that Gabriel Broussard would eventually grow tired of all those nymphets who were only attracted to his bad boy aura and tragically beautiful good looks.

Having harbored a secret crush on him for years, Emma had spent long lonely hours fantasizing scenarios where he'd suddenly recognize that there was a gleaming pearl amidst all the flashy cubic zirconium he'd been wasting his time with.

That pearl being her. A nice, caring, good girl who truly loved him for the sensitive, emotionally wounded heart that dwelt inside that devastatingly sexy body. For the man she'd known he could become.

A helluva lot of good that did you.

Maybe it was time, just for the few days he'd be in town, she ditched Emma, the good girl. And tried being Emma, the *good-time* girl.

Besides, part of Gabriel's appeal was that he'd always been a forbidden pleasure. Like all things forbidden, the fantasy undoubtedly surpassed the reality. Maybe it was time to find out if the bad boy of Blue Bayou could actually live up to his reputation.

And then, once she'd gotten a long overdue satisfaction, she'd just leave. The same way he had.

Later, when she was thinking clearly again, Emma would remind herself that her own reputation wasn't exactly that of a wild-woman seductress. And her body certainly wasn't Hollywood tucked, buffed, and toned.

But it was hard to even think at all when her mind was being bombarded by pheromones from a damn testosterone bomb.

Feeling uncharacteristically reckless—not to mention light-headed—she backed two steps away to give him a good look. Trying not to teeter on the ridiculously high fuck-me stilettos that had seemed like a good idea when she'd seen them in the window of The Magic Slipper, and resisting the urge to lick her suddenly dry lips, Emma smoothed her palms over the hips of the brand-new flowered silk skirt she'd bought after closing up today.

She hadn't bought the outfit for Gabe. The timing was only coincidence. No way would she risk maxing out her AMEX for any man.

Apparently the money, which could have paid Every Body's Beautiful's electric bill for six months, had not been wasted. Emma experienced a sudden surge of feminine power as his gaze followed the provocative gesture.

Channeling her inner Samantha, Emma checked him out in turn, drinking in the mouthwatering sight of broad male shoulders, bulging biceps and the strong V-shaped torso that arrowed down into lean male hips. Allowing her gaze to linger suggestively on the button placket of his jeans, she watched his penis flex beneath the worn denim.

Oh. My. God.

An illicit thrill zinged through Emma. Hot damn if Roxi wasn't right.

Men were easy.

Wishing she'd known this feminine secret back in high school, Emma lifted her eyes back to his, which were still shaded by those damn sunglasses, and treated him to a bold, sultry look hot enough to melt steel.

"You're not looking so bad yourself, sugar," she said on a throaty let's-get-naked drawl Emma figured Samantha would use in this situation, if New York City's most famous bad girl had been born in bayou country.

When Gabe's lips twitched in a faint smile, Emma's rebellious mind conjured up an X-rated fantasy of them tugging at her suddenly sensitive nipples.

"Nate called me just as I was leaving for the airport this morning," he said.

In Emma's fantasy, his mouth was moving south, trailing wet hot kisses over her naked flesh. And she'd begun to tingle in places she'd forgotten *could* tingle.

"I wasn't real thrilled when he started in explainin' about havin' to go out of town, since that meant I was gonna have to rent a car, me," Gabe continued.

In her fantasy, he was nudging her dampening panties down with his beautiful white teeth. His words were beginning to be drowned out by the thundering hoofbeat of stampeding hormones.

"Which wasn't real high up on my Top Ten things to do right now since I'm trying to stay under the radar. Then he told me he'd found a stand-in."

"That stand-in being me."

Standing in. Standing up. Lying down. Against the wall, on the floor, the ceiling. Emma didn't care how. Or where. She just wanted him. Any which way.

"*Mais,* yeah." His slow, lazy gaze traveled slowly, erotically, down the length of her again. "If I'd known certain things about Blue Bayou had gotten so appealing, I'd have come back a helluva lot sooner."

What on earth would Samantha say to that? Emma's mind stalled; her breath caught.

Think!

Since her brain seemed to have crashed, more vital regions leaped into the breach. "Some days a guy gets lucky," she heard herself cooing in a very unEmma-like way.

Emma realized she'd hit the bull's-eye when an ebony brow lifted above the frames of those wraparound shades. "You sayin' this is going to be one of those days, *chère*?"

Emma had spent most of her teenage years—and later, even after a marriage that should have been declared dead at the altar—dreaming about Gabriel looking at her this way, as if she were the most desirable woman he'd ever seen. As if she were a whiskey-drenched bread pudding smothered in whipped cream he wanted to eat up.

Amazingly, this reality was proving even more exciting. She took her time, pretending to think it over, while, relying on age-old feminine instincts she hadn't even realized she possessed, she slowly trailed her fingers along the V-neck of her silk blouse.

"That's for me to know."

His shielded gaze followed the deliberately languid gesture, honing in on her cleavage.

Easy.

"And you to find out."

He moved closer, the pointy tips of his boots touching her bare toes. "Sounds like a treasure hunt."

His deep, rumbling voice caressed every nerve.

"It just might be." She cocked her head. Electricity was sparking all around them. "Do you enjoy treasure hunts?"

He rubbed his square jaw, drawing her gaze to that cleft just beneath his lower lip. "That depends on the treasure."

He moved even closer, so that there wasn't a breath of air between them, and toyed with a strand of auburn hair, wrapping it around his hand in a way that had her imagining him dragging her by the hair below deck to his pirate captain's quarters, where he'd force her to do all sorts of wicked, wild, wonderful things.

His hand—his large, dark hand—skimmed down her neck, sliding over her shoulder like warm silk. "If I have enough motivation, I can be very, very good at them."

Emma gave him the fluttery Scarlett O'Hara smile Roxi used to practice in the mirror back when they were thirteen. "I'll just bet you can."

Emma was hot, hot, hot.

So blisteringly hot she was on the verge of melting into a pitiful puddle of need right here in front of a display tower of Mean Devil Woman Cajun Hot Sauce.

"What do you say we blow this place and get started?" Gabriel suggested, lowering his head until his mouth was hovering just above hers. So close she could feel his hot breath against her lips.

Some faint vestige of reason in Emma's mind managed to break through the hormones that were jumping up and down, screaming yes, yes, yes! to remind her that this was no longer her own private erotic fantasy.

The game she was playing with Gabriel Broussard was all too real. What on earth made her think she was up to playing in this man's league?

Still, the part of her mind that was still functional asked, what was the worst that could happen? That he might reject her? So? Wasn't it better to have loved and lost than to never have loved at all?

Not that they were talking about love.

It was lust. Pure and simple.

What would Samantha say?

It'd be his loss.

Good answer.

"So," she asked brightly, with renewed confidence, "do you have luggage?"

"Just this." He held up a scuffed leather duffle bag that looked as if it'd been around the world at least a dozen times. Emma wondered if it was the same one he'd packed before leaving her sleeping in his bed.

You're a survivor. You can do this.

"I'm parked outside," she said.

Duh! Where the hell else would she be parked? A blonde with a cotton candy mass of frosted and over-teased hair and a dangerous spark in her overly made-up blue eyes was headed toward them. If they hung around here any longer, any opportunity to escape unnoticed would be lost.

"We'd better get going before we draw a crowd and you end up on the front of some tabloid." She turned and started walking toward the exit.

"Wouldn't be the first time." He smiled like an unrepentant sinner and fell into step beside her, shortening his stride to match hers.

His response brought to mind Tamara Templeton's alleged reason for breaking her engagement to Gabe. Which, in turn, had Emma wondering what kind of kinky situation she was getting herself into, driving this man out to that isolated camp in the bayou.

This was insane.

Amazing.

Insanely amazing.

Heat, thick with moisture, hit like a fist as they left the terminal. Emma could feel her hair, which she'd spent twenty minutes this morning blow-drying to a smooth, auburn sheen, spring into a mass of wild, unruly curls.

It figured. Even her hair couldn't control itself around Gabriel Broussard.

Four

What the hell had he been thinking? Coming on to Emma Quinlan that way? Christ, Emma, of all people.

As he'd followed that magnificent J.Lo butt out of the terminal, to the sporty, cherry red Miata convertible that fit the bold, adventurous female Emma Quinlan seemed to have metamorphosed into, Gabe was having trouble reconciling this lushly curvaceous, sexy, incredibly hot female with the shy, plump girl who'd so openly adored him back in high school.

That Emma had followed him around like a puppy, and although it probably had been selfish of him, he'd let her. Emma had been the only person he could talk to. The only person he could share his impossible dreams with. The only person, besides Nate Callahan—who'd been struggling to start up his construction business and take care of his dying mother in those days—whom Gabe trusted.

And, although there'd occasionally been times when he'd felt a little sexual tug, and known that she would have been more than willing to let him do anything he wanted, getting naked in the backseat of his Trans Am with a friend would've been just too weird.

Like their one night together hadn't been?

Shit.

"What are you going to do for a car out at the camp?"

"Can't see that I'll need one. Nate stocked the place with groceries and the pirogue's there. It's not like Blue Bayou's got a lot of nightlife I'm going to be missing out on."

"You might be surprised. We're celebrating Jean Lafitte Days this weekend."

"Yeah, Nate mentioned something about that. But as much as I hate to miss all the fun, I think I'll pass."

"You don't have to be sarcastic. A parade and a dance probably don't seem that big a deal to a jet-setting movie star," she said. "But people enjoy it. And the money from the tickets goes to an after-school recreation program for the kids of the parish, so it's all for a good cause."

"I'm not sayin' it isn't. In fact, I'll write you a check. I'm just not feelin' real sociable right now."

"Speaking as deputy mayor, I'll be happy to accept any contribution you'd like to make," she said stiffly, sounding, Gabe thought, uncomfortably, like her mother.

"I've gotta admit to bein' surprised you're not still pissed off at me."

"About what?" Her tone was casual enough, but the slight tightening of her fingers on the steering wheel gave her away.

"My last night in town. The one we spent together."

"It may come as a huge surprise to your movie star ego, but it's been years since I even thought about that." She kept her gaze directed out the windshield. "Besides, it wasn't as if anything happened."

"That's not the way I remember it."

Her skirt, colored in a bright tropical print, was calf-length. Which was the bad news since it had him salivating like one of Pavlov's pups for a look at her long legs.

The good news was that it was cut like a sarong. As she stepped on the gas to pass a minivan, the silk parted, giving him a view of thigh that caused his insides to tingle and heat up.

Speaking of heating up . . .

"I recall you bein' hot as a Mardi Gras firecracker, you."

"You were so drunk I'm surprised you remember anything about that night."

"I might have been tanked, sure enough. But it's hard to forget giving a girl her first orgasm."

Her deep, rich laugh sent the heat in his belly traveling south. "You are so full of yourself, Gabriel Broussard. What makes you think that was my first?"

He'd tried to forget most of the things that had happened that night, but one thing had remained vividly etched on his mind: the memory of Emma writhing beneath his plundering mouth, her bare back bowed off the soft, Spanish-moss stuffed mattress, the breathless cries—almost like keening—that were ripped from her ravished lips as he drove her higher and higher until she'd come, screaming his name.

Even now, ten years later, the mental picture of her, flushed and uncharacteristically wanton, was so vivid, it was all he could do to keep from licking the pale flesh exposed by that sexy slit in her skirt.

"Solo flying doesn't count," he said.

A corner of her mouth turned down in a frown, but she didn't deny his point that he'd been her first. First man. First orgasm.

"Speaking of flying, along with all that booze, you also had enough Demerol in your system to fly to the moon." She tossed him a look. "Solo."

She'd warned him against mixing drugs and alcohol. But had he listened? Hell, no. He'd been on a crazy, self-destructive binge that night and by the time they'd reached the camp after the emergency room visit, he'd had to lean on her to stagger into the cabin.

He'd fallen onto the bed, taking her with him in a tangle of arms and legs. Her dress—an unflattering, black taffeta—had crackled when he'd delved beneath it. That sound had, for some inexplicable reason, generated such a hot spurt of lust that years later, while filming the scene in *The Last Pirate*, where Jean Lafitte attends a ball in the French Quarter, the sound of all those rustling petticoats the costume designer had put the actresses in caused him to walk around with a boner for two days.

His reaction had not gone unnoticed; several conservative religious groups had had a field day posting close-ups of his groin on the Internet as yet another example of the erosion of the national morality.

"I sure as hell wasn't feeling any pain, me." Not when he'd left the ER anyway. And certainly not later, when he'd been rolling around on that fragrant mattress with Emma. "Like I said, I don't remember much about that night. But I've got the feelin' I never thanked you for all you did."

"We were friends," she said simply. "You would have done the same thing for me."

The bitch was, Gabe wasn't real sure he would've. He'd been a pretty self-centered bastard in those days. A '90s James Dean retread. Rebel without a clue.

Gabe sighed.

"So," he said, deciding to change the topic, "I guess you heard about the little mess I'm in."

"Which mess is that?"

"Excuse me. I hadn't realized you'd been away on Mars the past week." Of all the topics he could have chosen, why the hell had he brought that one up? What was wrong with the weather? That was always a safe topic. Or sports.

"So, do you think the Saints are going to be able to capture the NFC South this season?"

"I've no idea." Her tone suggested she didn't give a rat's ass, either. "Football isn't real big up on Mars—it's hard to mark the yardage lines in all that red dust—so I'm a little out of the loop." They were crossing the old iron bridge over the Mississippi. "So, what mess are we talking about?"

"The one about my so-called engagement."

"Ah." She nodded in a way that told him she'd known exactly what he'd been referring to. "The one your little television star fiancée called off."

Gabe ground his teeth and felt his penis, which had gotten semi-hard at the memory of Emma lying beneath him, deflated like a three-day-old balloon. Timing, he thought, was effin' everything. "Tamara Templeton was never my fiancée."

"I see." She nodded again, obviously not buying his denial. "And you bought her that ten carat Tiffany diamond why?"

"I didn't buy it."

That captured her attention. She glanced over at him. "Mary Hart said you did."

"Mary Hart may be one helluva television personality. She's also fairer than most of her breed." Because for some reason it was important that Emma understand he wasn't a total son-of-a-bitch, he yanked off the shades and looked her straight in the eye. "She's been known to get her facts wrong."

He watched the wheels turn around in her bright head as she processed that little bit of information. Then she turned her attention back to the narrow road. "If Mary Hart's so fair, why didn't you tell her what you've just told me? That you weren't really engaged?"

Good question. "Dammit, because it's fuckin' complicated."

"You don't have to shout at me, Gabriel. After all, you're the one who brought it up," she reminded him.

"You've not only gotten damn sexy, *chère*. You're a helluva lot tougher than you used to be." Sassier. And damned if it didn't look good on her.

"From necessity." She shot him another look. "Do you have a problem with tough women?"

"Actually, I like them." He especially liked picturing Emma wearing only a pair of black leather thigh-high boots and a wicked smile. "Under the right circumstances." Like in his bedroom with flames crackling in the fireplace, and some slow, sultry tenor jazz flowing from the Surround sound speakers. "When they play fair."

"And your fiancée didn't?"

"She wasn't my goddamn—"

"Right. Tamara Templeton wasn't your real fiancée. Just your fake one. Which is funny—"

"There's nothing funny about this."

"Funny odd. Not funny ha-ha," she corrected calmly. "Although I'm admittedly no expert on precious gems, that Texas-size rock weighing down her left hand sure didn't look like a fake diamond."

Gabe could tell from her tone that she wasn't ready to suspend all disbelief. Hell, he didn't blame her.

"You're right. It was real. But I didn't buy it." He yanked off his Ragin' Cajun cap and dragged his hand through his hair. "Hell, we'd only gone out twice. Both times set up by our agent to maximize press coverage."

"I wouldn't think you'd need that."

"It wasn't really my choice. But Tamara was hot to change her image—"

"So she figured the best way to do that would be to go out with Hollywood's bad boy?"

Okay, now they were back to dealing with major disbelief.

"That reputation is overrated," he ground out through clenched teeth. "It's typecasting. Because I tend to choose roles that look at the dark side of human nature, people figure I'm a son of a bitch in real life."

"If you say so."

He still wasn't convincing her. Gabe mentally added a whip to the image of her wearing those dominatrix boots. "My agent asked me to accompany Tamara to a couple public events. Since Caroline was the first person in the business to take me seriously, and stuck with me when I refused to play the teen idol card after the pirate flick, I figured I owed her one."

"I can see why you wouldn't want to be typecast as a teen hunk. But *The Last Pirate* was a very good movie."

"You saw it?" Gabe found himself liking that idea.

"Of course. It played to a packed house at the Bijou for five weeks. I doubt there was anyone in the parish who didn't see it at least once."

"Which is surprising, since I'm sure as hell not Blue Bayou's favorite son."

"Jean Lafitte was from around here. That gave it a local connection. Plus, I think a lot of people were curious to see how Blue Bayou's favorite juvenile delinquent turned out." Her plump, made-for-sin mouth curved in a smile that sent a lightning bolt of heat straight to his groin. "You were very good. Not that I ever had any doubts."

"That made three people in town who thought I might have a future other than landing my ass behind bars."

He wondered what she'd thought while watching the erotic scene where the pirate ravished the Spanish ship captain's wife. Had she gotten turned on by the forced seduction? Had she watched the pirate take a jeweled dagger and cut open the woman's bodice to gain access to her breasts and remembered when he'd torn open her dress and taken her soft and yielding flesh in his mouth?

And when his dark and dangerous character had surged between the woman's fleshy white thighs that had opened willingly for him, had Emma remembered how he'd pinned her to the mattress and, using his mouth, his teeth, his tongue, made her come?

The view outside the window became hazed with the red lust shimmering before his eyes as he imagined lashing Emma's wrists and ankles to his bed and fucking her hard and fast and deep. But only after he'd driven her crazy enough to beg for it.

Jesus. If he kept on this runaway sex train of thought, he was going to come in his jeans before they even got to the camp.

"Three people," he repeated, his voice raspy with pent-up lust. He would have cleared his damn throat, but didn't want her to realize that somehow, when he hadn't been paying close enough attention, she'd captured control over not just the situation, but his damn mutinous dick, as well. "You, Nate, and Mrs. Herlihy."

The high school drama teacher had rescued Gabe from detention when Raul Dupree had come down with flu. She talked him into auditioning for the role of Sweeny Todd in the spring musical, and literally changed his life.

"She's retiring this year," Emma said conversationally.

"No shit? Isn't she a little young to quit teaching?"

"She's sixty-eight. And she's not retiring, exactly. She's going to volunteer at the Boys and Girls Club after-school program."

"That sounds like something she'd do."

Rescuing more at-risk kids. They might not grow up to be Hollywood stars—which to Gabe's mind was a mixed blessing—but they also might avoid going to prison, which is where he probably would've ended up if it hadn't been for the teacher's intervention.

"We're giving her an award after the Jean Lafitte parade on Saturday," Emma said.

Gabe tensed, sensing what was coming.

"A plaque isn't all that much to pay her back for all she's done for the town." She paused another beat. "It'd probably make the ceremony a lot bigger deal if you were the one presenting it."

This time it was he who paused. "I don't think that'd be a real good idea, *chère*. Seems I'd be taking the spotlight off the person who really deserved it."

It was a not so artful a dodge. "And we both know how you hate the spotlight," Emma murmured. "Which is undoubtedly why you chose a low-profile career like acting."

"Got me there," he said.

"You just want to hide out from the press. Which brings us back to those dates—"

"They weren't dates, in the traditional sense of the word." The woman was like a damn pit bull. Why couldn't she just let the thing go? "And I was a perfect gentleman."

She laughed at that idea.

"Hey." He held up three fingers in the sign of a pledge. "Scout's honor."

"Funny. I don't remember you being a Boy Scout."

True enough. Even if he had been able to afford the uniform, which he hadn't, there's no way the other parents would have allowed the kid of the town drunk to have anything to do with their churchgoing sons. Thinking back on the wild, angry kid he'd been back then, Gabe couldn't really blame them.

"I don't remember you bein' so sarcastic." Or offering him anything less than her unwavering support, including, that one night, when he'd opened a forbidden door he should've just kept locked.

Hell, maybe she was holding a grudge. He couldn't deny she had every right to.

"I'm sorry. The scout remark may have been hitting below the belt. So, don't leave me hanging."

"Like I did that night?" Gabe decided there was no more point in beating around the bush. "When I left you a virgin?"

A soft flush, like a late summer rose, filled her cheeks as she realized her inadvertent double entendre. "I meant I want to know the rest of the story that brought you back home."

The woman wasn't just hot. She was damn pretty. And, since he didn't believe people really changed all that much, Gabe suspected that beneath her sexy new attitude, Emma was still that sweet, caring girl who had, for one suspended night in time, made him feel things he'd never thought he'd feel. Wish for impossible things beyond his reach. Ache for the kind of love he hadn't thought a guy like him could ever have.

"Gabe?"

She was looking at him again, her expression quizzical.

"Sorry." He shook his head, like his old retriever, Beau, used to do when climbing out of the water with a duck. Emma wasn't the only one puzzled by the feelings bombarding him. She'd stirred something in him. Something he couldn't quite put a name to. "Looking at the color in your pretty face got me sidetracked. I can't remember the last time I've been with a woman who blushed."

He took hold of her hand, which smelled a bit like almonds, and nibbled on her knuckles. "Watching your cheeks go all pink makes me wonder what it'd take to make the rest of you blush all over."

She shivered. Not, Gabe suspected, because she was suddenly finding the air-conditioning blasting from the dashboard vents too cold.

"You were telling me about those dates that weren't really dates." She tugged her hand free. Her gaze fixed on a mirage shimmering like a phantom pool on the black asphalt ahead.

"Anyone ever tell you you've got a one-track mind, *chère*?"

"Why am I not surprised an actor would have something against linear thought?"

"Hey, I can do linear thought. In fact, my mind's been pretty much runnin' on a single track since I walked off that plane and saw you standing there lookin' like you'd stepped out of a Gauguin painting."

The blush he'd found so appealing in her cheeks bloomed across the magnificent cleavage revealed by her neckline. The blouse was silk. Remembering all too well that her perfumed flesh was softer, Gabe was suddenly burning with the need to touch. To taste. To cup those lush breasts in his hands, to stroke her nipples, which, he couldn't help noticing, were pressing against the flowered silk.

They weren't the only thing that had gone hard. No friggin' doubt about it, his cock had taken on a mind of its own. And if it had its randy way, they'd be pulling over to the side of the road, and he'd be lifting that skirt while her long legs straddled him, while she took him deep inside her wet, slick womanly warmth. He fantasized nipping at those pebbled nipples, sucking on them hard enough to make her body tighten around him, as she rode him hard and fast.

"That sounds suspiciously like a line from some movie," she accused.

"It's no line." He'd never been one to pretty sex up with sweet words and silken promises. Never had to. But damned if she didn't remind him of the painter's lushly feminine Tahitian subjects. And he should know, since two of the paintings were currently hanging on his bedroom wall. "You ever have anyone film you, *chère*? While you're making love?"

"Of course not." Her eyes widened; she sounded properly scandalized. But perhaps intrigued?

There was a half beat of silence. Then . . .

"Have you ever?" she asked. *Oh, yeah,* Gabe thought,

definitely intrigued. "Filmed someone while you were making love?"

"Not yet. But there's always a first time." He nodded in the direction of the duffle bag he'd thrown into the backseat when he'd climbed into the car. "I brought along my video camera." Unable to resist the lure of her soft, fragrant skin, he slipped his hand into that enticing slit in her skirt and began trailing small, concentric circles just above her dimpled knee. "I've been thinkin' of getting into directing, me."

That was true enough. Although he enjoyed acting, he was beginning to tire of living in some other character's skin for weeks, sometimes months, at a time. And then there was the issue of control. It wasn't that he was a control freak or anything—hell, damn straight he was.

There wasn't much in the movie business under anyone's control. It was, he'd often considered, like playing one of those flying trapeze artists without a net. But directing offered more opportunity for calling the shots than acting ever would.

"How would you like to star in my first film?" Encouraged that she hadn't yanked the slit in her skirt closed, he trailed his fingers up petal-soft skin.

"You want me to star in a porno film?"

"An erotic film," he corrected huskily, getting turned on by the imagined sight of a nude Emma in his viewfinder. "One with limited distribution. Just the two of us."

"I don't think—"

"I'll take a page from Gauguin's book and film you outdoors," he said reflectively, overriding her refusal as creative wheels started turning. The more Gabe thought about it, the more it seemed like a perfect way to while away the days he was going to be stuck out in the bayou.

"Maybe on that old swing at the camp, lying on your back, your hair loose, flowing over your breasts, your rosy pink nipples thrusting through those long wild curls."

With his free hand, he plucked the clip from her hair, allowing the curls to tumble riotously free, shining like a bright copper penny in the stuttering rays of sun managing to break through the gathering clouds.

"Gabe." His name shuddered out from between glossy pink lips. "Don't."

"Don't what, *chère*? Don't touch you?" When his fingers continued their sensual quest, she trembled, but did not pull away. "Don't imagine how you'd look, with the sun setting at your back, your long sexy legs spread over the wooden arms of the swing, your lower lips all lush and wet, and—"

"Dammit, Gabriel," she complained. "Please."

"Please, *oui*?" He skimmed a feathery touch back down to her knee, this time on the inside of her thigh, and watched her unconsciously rub her thighs together.

Gabe wanted to be there.

Between those long, wraparound legs.

Inside her.

"Or please, *non*?"

"How am I supposed to think when you're doing that"— she arched her back against his touch as he lightly scraped the warming flesh with a fingernail—"let alone drive."

Realizing that if he wasn't careful, he could be responsible for them ending up in the water, Gabe reluctantly reclaimed his hand and turned back to the idea of filming Emma in the throes of passion.

"You'll need to be eating something. An apple fits Gauguin's *Eve in the Garden of Eden* theme, but it's too clichéd," he said thoughtfully, getting into the idea as creative juices stirred along with sexual ones. "A ripe peach." He nodded, pleased with the notion. "I'll feed it to you. Then lick the sweet, sticky juice off your sun-warmed naked flesh."

She actually moaned. The same way he imagined she would if he were trailing his tongue down her torso, over the soft feminine swell of her stomach. Then beyond.

He was about to tell her just to pull over to the side of the road, when the front tire suddenly started going *thump thump thump*.

"Damn." The mood was shattered. Emma hit the steering wheel with the palm of her hand as she pulled over to the side of the road. "That's all we need," she complained. "That storm's getting closer, and this time of day, it'll take the auto club at least an hour to get out here from the city."

"No problem." It took all his acting talent to keep his tone even when what he wanted to do was bang his head against the dashboard at the way she'd been yanked out of the sensual spell his seductive words had wrapped around them. "You've got yourself a spare, right?"

"Well, of course, but—"

"I haven't changed a tire since my old days working at Dix's Automotive. But I'll bet it's one of those things you don't forget. Like ridin' a bicycle." He winked at her. "Or sex."

Now that the moment had been lost, the thing to do was get the damn tire changed so they could get to the camp.

Where he and the luscious, soft-skinned, sweet-smelling Emma Quinlan could begin driving each other crazy.

Five

As Gabe took the jack from the Miata's trunk, Emma tried to remember her former husband ever doing anything more physical than swinging a golf club and came up blank.

Richard had been too busy stealing money from his employer—who just happened to be his father-in-law—and screwing the bimbo to help out with any chores.

Now, watching Gabe work, she decided that there was something to be said for having a male around the house to do those manly things. Like change a tire. Mow the lawn. Tie you up.

Tie you up? Where had that come from?

From that damn Jean Lafitte movie. Emma had known she was in trouble the minute it had come up in the conversation and was vastly relieved that there was no way Gabe would ever know she'd sat in the dark of the Bijou, popcorn going uneaten, as she'd watched his larger-than-life character throw that woman over his shoulder, then leap from her husband's Spanish galleon to his own ship that was flying the bloodred flag feared throughout southern waters.

His captive had fought like a wildcat, kicking, biting, scratching, her nails leaving a scarlet trail down the dark skin of his back. But she'd been no match for the rapacious rogue. Nor her own rioting female desires. By the time the actress was bucking beneath him, opening herself up to his invasion, Emma's panties had been drenched and her legs so weak, she'd had to stay seated until long after the credits had rolled and the theater emptied.

That night she'd dreamed of being held hostage by a pirate, who, unsurprisingly, looked exactly like Gabriel Broussard. Dressed in a pirate's black shirt, tight trousers, and high black leather boots, he'd tied her to the mast of his ship, his strong hands claiming her body at will, while his low, rumbling voice told her all the things he intended to do to her.

Wicked, outrageous things. Things that shocked her. Shamed her. And, dammit, excited her.

Just remembering that movie, and the dream, along with the scandalous way she'd allowed him to touch her in the car, was enough to make her so hot she was surprised she wasn't liquidizing from the inside out.

Watching him work wasn't helping. Who'd have guessed that changing a flat tire could be such a turn-on? As he crouched down and loosened the lug nuts with a speedy efficiency that a NASCAR pit mechanic might have envied, the faded denim pulled tight against strong, muscular thighs in a way that had Emma imagining naughty things. Kinky things.

She was used to seeing men without clothes on. Her days, after all, were spent with nude men who wore nothing but a towel and a blissful expression as her hands brought them to ecstasy. Or, as close to it as a person could get without having sex.

But, Emma was discovering, there was a huge difference between nude and naked. Nude was when a man wasn't wearing clothes. Naked was when he wasn't wearing clothes and was up to no good.

And, heaven help her, naked was how she wanted Gabe.

When he bent over to jack up the wheel, any lingering desire to kick his butt evaporated. It was a gold medal, world-class butt and what Emma wanted to do, was aching to do, was bite it.

Do it, that devilish Samantha perched on her damp shoulder, advised.

I can't just maul him!

"What world do you live in, chica?*"* A new voice, sounding a lot like Gabrielle, from *Desperate Housewives,* chimed in.

Terrific. Now they were ganging up on her.

"It's not that easy, dammit." Emma was appalled when she heard the words come out of her mouth.

"Something wrong?" Gabe glanced back at her.

"No." She forced a smile. "I was just saying that didn't look very easy."

He shrugged. "Like I said, some things you never forget. Who'd have thought a past working as a grease monkey would ever come in handy?"

Thunder rumbled ominously on the horizon; black clouds raced in from the Gulf. The dense air was thick enough to drink. As he returned to work, sweat dampened his shirt, causing it to cling to his back, revealing every corded muscle. More muscles bunched in his arms as he pumped the jack.

Lightning crackled across the darkening sky. Emma could taste the electricity on her tongue, beneath her skin, scorching along her nerve endings. She'd lived in south Louisiana all of her life. She was accustomed to the heat and constant humidity. But never had she been so hot she felt on the verge of fainting.

Her head grew light. White spots, like paper-winged moths,

fluttered in front of her eyes. She placed a hand against the back fender of the Miata to steady herself. Gabe, who'd replaced the flat with the spare and was tightening the lug nuts, glanced up at her.

"You sure you're okay?"

"Of course."

If you didn't count the fact that she was on the verge of falling flat on her face. Her hair was clinging to her forehead; more unruly curls had escaped to stick to the back of her damp neck. Swaying a bit, she tried to brush it away with the hand that wasn't holding onto the car for dear life, but her fingers were shaking.

Deep blue eyes framed by long, sooty lashes that would have appeared feminine were it not for the lean, hungry lines of his face, studied Emma with an intensity that did nothing to help clear her head.

"You look as if you're about to pass out, *mon ange*."

He'd called her his angel that night. When he'd drawn her down onto that mattress and kissed her. A deep, searing kiss that had scorched away a lifetime of inhibitions. A kiss she'd been fantasizing about since she'd been twelve years old. But the reality had far surpassed those romantic, junior high school daydreams.

"I've never fainted in my life." The spots swirled like snowflakes as she tossed her head.

"There's always a first time for everything."

He tossed aside the jack, stood up and curled his hands around her upper arms to steady her.

The wind picked up, rattling the sugar cane in the fields on either side of the road. "You're tremblin' like a willow in a hurricane, you."

Emma was far from willowy, but at this moment, with this man, she felt strangely, uncharacteristically fragile.

"You scared of storms, *chère*?"

"No." She swallowed.

"You're not scared of me?" His hands were moving up and down her arms, the gesture, which was meant to soothe, made her ache with the need to feel them everywhere.

"No." She shook her head.

Emma was afraid of herself. Of this dizzying, hot way only this man had ever made her feel. Despite her little internal pep talk about rejection being no big deal, the truth was that while Richard's very public affair had wounded her pride, Gabe's taking off without so much as a good-bye kiss had been like an arrow shot into the center of her heart.

It had taken her a long time to get over that night; now, what she feared was risking her foolish heart again.

She lifted her hand, skimmed her fingers over his face. Even with that scar cutting across his cheekbone, it was beautiful, the face of a fallen angel which could have been washed off the ceiling of a cathedral.

"Should I be? Afraid of you?"

"Mais, non." He touched her in turn, his fingertips feeling like sparklers as they traced the line of her mouth, brushed her cheek, her temple, into her hair. "I'd never hurt you, Emma."

But he would. Oh, he honestly wouldn't mean to. But she could see the heartache coming as clearly as the storm barreling toward them across the bayou.

As she felt herself drowning in the midnight blue of his eyes, Emma suspected that the pain could be well worth the risk.

Lightning forked across the sky, sparking inside her. The rumbling answer of thunder was echoed in Emma's own heart as she stood there, looking up at him, knowing that her wildly foolish heart was glowing, unguarded, in her eyes.

He framed her face with his hands. "I'm going to kiss you

now, *chère*." His deep voice was tender, yet roughened with arousal.

Emma had to remind herself to breathe as his mouth, slowly, inexorably, moved downward, toward hers.

Having never forgotten the last time they'd been together, she braced herself for the heat.

Six

Prepared for an invasion of teeth and tongue, Emma was surprised when he began kissing her gently—little licks and nips up her cheek, over her eyelids, which closed at the touch of his lips, her temple, the hollow beneath her lower lip—which no other man had ever taken the time to discover—was somehow directly connected to that hot, damp place between her legs.

"Gabe?"

"What, *chère*?"

The tip of his tongue touched hers, then retreated, while he trailed a hand down her throat, to where she knew he could feel the out-of-control beat of her blood.

Her arms felt heavy as she lifted them, linking her fingers together behind his neck. "I thought you were going to kiss me."

"That's what I'm doing."

"But I want . . ."

Her voice trailed off as his caressing touch dipped into the warmth between her breasts.

"What do you want, Emma?"

Taking hold of her hair, he pulled her head back, to give his mouth access to her throat.

"I want you to *really* kiss me."

She felt his smile against her tingling lips.

Then his tongue thrust between her lips, sweeping deep to mate with hers, and his mouth, which had been so gentle only a moment before, ground against hers hard enough to bruise, the plundering kiss one of raw, sexual possession.

"*Mon Dieu*, you taste good," he rasped as he pinned her between the hot metal of the car and the even greater heat of his body. "I could eat you up."

She wrapped a leg around his; her skirt fell open, baring her thigh all the way up to her panties and she managed to get a hand between them, curving her fingers around his length.

"You're killing me here, Emma," he groaned when she began stroking the erection that swelled even larger, hotter, against the denim.

He yanked his head back just long enough to look down at her. The masculine hunger darkened, like molten cobalt flowing over obsidian.

"Where the hell have you been hiding?" His voice was low and guttural, his hands thrillingly rough. Relentless.

"I wasn't hiding. I've been right here. In Blue Bayou." Waiting for him, Emma could have said, but didn't because it would be too hard to explain how that could be true when she didn't understand it herself.

Gabe might have been her first man, but he hadn't been her last. She had, after all, been married.

But she'd never forgotten their night together and now she was discovering that some secret, hidden part of her heart had been awaiting his return.

As for her body . . . it wanted him. Everywhere. In every way.

"I've been here," she repeated breathlessly beneath the

plundering mouth that had branded her on a stormy night ten years ago.

A clap of thunder caused the ground beneath them to tremble. The black sky overhead opened up.

As a hot, stinging rain pelted down on them, Gabe dragged her hand from his groin. Her body might be lush, but her bones were narrow, allowing him to wrap his fingers around both slender wrists. Lifting her hands, he held them against the roof of the car, forcing her body into a taut, trembling bow.

She didn't fight against his dominant male behavior. Didn't try to free herself. Yet there was nothing submissive about the way she was rotating her pelvis against his, or the way, somehow managing to stand on those spindly little fuck-me-big-boy high heels, she lifted her leg even higher, wrapping it around his waist.

He ran his free hand up her smooth bare leg. The crotch of her panties was soaked. And not from the rain.

He felt her suck in an expectant breath as he pushed the elastic band of the high cut leg aside.

He paused.

She whimpered.

"Dammit." She arched her hips even higher, straining, seeking. "Touch me."

Obliging Emma, pleasing himself, Gabe stroked the slick, hot flesh.

One of them trembled as he slipped a finger into the welcoming wet warmth. Gabe wasn't sure whether it was Emma. Or him.

He slipped another finger inside her, at the same time flicking her swelled clitoris with a searing stroke of his thumb.

"Oh, God." She rolled her head against the window as he swallowed her moan with a long deep soul kiss.

"Tell me." He bit her bottom lip, then soothed the sting

with the tip of his tongue. "Tell me that you want this as much as I do."

"Of course I do." A sound, somewhere between a laugh and moan was ripped from her throat as he thrust deeper. Harder. "Can't you tell?"

She was flowing over his hand. Her avid lips ate into his, her breasts pressed against his chest.

"*Mais*, yeah." He ripped open the top button of his jeans, wondering why he'd never before noticed that the 501s he'd worn since high school were like a fucking chastity belt.

Maybe, he conceded, as his fingers, which were not nearly as steady as he was accustomed to, struggled with button number two, the reason he'd never noticed was that having always preferred to be the one in control, he'd never been so desperate, so damn needy to bury himself inside a woman. Up to the hilt in one hard, deep thrust.

But then again, he'd never known a woman as uninhibited as Emma. It wasn't that he wasn't accustomed to good sex. He always made sure the woman came, at least once, before he gave any thought to his own satisfaction; but there was always a part of him that remained an uninvolved observer, watching how the women beneath him moved, the expressions on their faces as he urged them higher and higher, the breathy little sounds they made when they came. The man in him was proud of his ability to satisfy; the actor in him recognized a performance when he saw one.

It wasn't that they were faking, exactly. Since practice made perfect, Gabe had been able to spot a phony orgasm before he was legally old enough to drink. But there was a certain artificiality about the way they arranged their bodies so as to always ensure they looked good, the way they never expended enough energy for their carefully coiffed hair to get sweaty, the way their faces, while portraying passion, never went lax with spent lust.

Emma was nothing like that.

Her eyes were closed, squeezed so tightly, lines fanned out from them, nearly into her hair. Her head was flung so far back, the tendons in her neck strained and her mouth was open, encouraging erotic thoughts of what those voluptuous ripe lips would look like surrounding his cock.

She was totally into the moment. Into him. Oblivious to the rain pelting down on her expressive, upturned face like stinging needles, oblivious to the fact that they were parked along the highway, risking discovery at any moment.

A sudden, ear-splitting blast of an airhorn blared through the rain.

Emma's eyes flew open as the eighteen-wheeler rumbled by. Her leg slid back down his to the ground.

"I can't believe I . . ." Her face, her lovely, flushed, wet face was bemused. "On a public road . . . Out in the open." She looked up at the sky. "In the pouring rain."

"Yeah." Timing, Gabe thought again with a frustration that did nothing to soothe his still rampant hard-on, was everything.

He released her hands. When she used one to cover her mouth, he braced himself for tears.

Emma surprised him yet again.

She laughed. "That was the most reckless thing I've ever done."

She put her freed hands against his chest. Then her eyes, which had begun to clear, started turning all sexy and soft focused again.

"Talk about reckless," Gabe groaned. "If you don't stop looking at me that way, I'm going to take you right here and now, and believe me, darlin', once I get inside you, not even an entire convention of long-haul truckers leaning on airhorns is going to be able to make me stop."

Her face lit up. "Even better."

It was Gabe's turn to laugh. Although his erection was still throbbing painfully, her unmasked excitement at the sexual threat was the first thing in a very long time he'd found to laugh about.

Her hair had tumbled down around her shoulders. The tangled curls looked like wet copper silk and smelled like peaches. Gabe ached with the need to feel them draped over his chest. His thighs. His penis.

"We're all wet," she murmured, seeming surprised at the discovery.

"Seem to be."

The flowered skirt clung damply to her womanly convex stomach, rounded thighs, and mound. Her blouse was rendered nearly transparent by rain. Beneath the silk she was wearing a white lace bra that matched the panties he'd nearly ripped off her. Her taut nipples were the same raspberry pink hue he hadn't even realized had remained imprinted on his memory all these years.

"But it sure as hell looks better on you," he said.

She tilted her head. Her lips tilted in a faint, somewhat indulgent smile. "What is it about men that whenever they see a woman they imagine her naked?"

"I don't."

She folded her arms beneath those amazing breasts. "Of course you don't." Her tone was a great deal drier than the weather.

"When men look at women they picture them in garter belts, silk stockings, and mile-high stiletto heels."

She rolled her eyes. "That is so chauvinistic."

"What can I say? Men are pigs," he agreed easily.

Gabe cupped her breasts, watching her eyes widen as he pinched those nipples. Hard.

She exhaled a short, surprised breath; the yielding flesh swelled in his hands.

"You are, without a doubt, the most responsive woman I've ever met."

Struggling against the urge to drag her into that little red car, rip their wet clothes away, throw his naked body on top of hers and devour her, Gabe lowered his forehead to hers and drew in a deep, painful breath that was meant to calm.

But damn well didn't even come close to tempering the male need to mate that was rampaging through every pore of his body.

"I'm going to put the jack in the trunk," he said. "Then we're going to the camp, where I'm going to take a long time to finish what we started ten years ago."

She shuddered against him; there was so much heat emanating from both their bodies, he was amazed they weren't surrounded by clouds of steam.

"After I have you, I'm going to feed you." He'd always liked to cook. The idea of cooking for Emma was nearly as appealing as making love to her. "Then we're going to spend the rest of the night seeing just how reckless we can be."

"I don't have any clothes with me."

"Don' worry 'bout it. You won't need any for what I have in mind."

"What if I have plans?"

"Do you?"

"Yes." She hooked an arm around his neck, went up on her toes, and gave him a quick, hard kiss. "I'm planning to spend the night with you."

Seven

Gabe offered to drive the rest of the way, but feeling the need to maintain some vestige of control over the situation, Emma declined.

"Just as well," he said agreeably. "This way I can play with your leg."

"Just my leg," she said.

"Spoilsport."

"Unless you want to end up in the bayou."

"Good point." He sighed. "And one I'd reluctantly already thought of myself right before we got that flat."

As she drove away from New Orleans, deep into bayou country, a comfortable silence surrounded them, the quiet of the night broken only by the metallic percussion of the rain on the roof of the Miata, the hiss of waters beneath the rolling tires, the music flowing softly from the car speakers.

They'd gone about two miles when Gabe unbuckled his seat belt, turned around and went up on his knees, giving Emma an up-close-and-personal view of threads beginning to unravel beneath his right cheek.

Down, girl.

Needing a distraction, she glanced up into the rearview mirror and watched him unzip the duffle bag, and figured he must be getting out a dry shirt. Which was a shame, because she really, really loved the way that white knit T-shirt clung to his chest, defining pecs and six-pack abs that had instilled lust in female moviegoers from Seattle to Shanghai.

It turned out he wasn't after a shirt, after all. But a CD.

"Thought we could use a change from the snooze stuff," he said, pressing the eject button on her dashboard player.

"That's Celtic Grace." The Irish group was hugely soothing as background music to her massages. "They're very popular."

"If you happen to like New Age." His dismissive tone put them right up there with polka bands and Barney tunes.

"A great many people do." Including her. "Life's become very hectic. New Age is relaxing."

"There's a difference between being relaxed and comatose."

He exchanged her CD with his, pushed play, leaned back in the leather bucket seat, stretched his long athletic legs out in front of him and laced his fingers behind his dark head.

Cutting him a surreptitious sideways glance, Emma found the sight of those dark biceps bulging anything but relaxing.

A smoky, female voice drifted out of the speakers.

"Now, that's music," he said approvingly. "Doesn't get any better than Lady Day."

Although they'd been about as intimate as two people could be only minutes before, being alone with him, in this dark car in the rain, with Billie Holiday's sultry, sex-tinged voice singing about how she couldn't help lovin' that man, caused Emma's stomach muscles to knot.

Did he remember playing that exact same CD on another drive to the camp ten years earlier? The night before he'd left for California?

Emma had never been so nervous. Not even the night before her wedding to Richard, when she'd tossed and turned, futilely chasing sleep, afraid that she was making a terrible mistake.

The next morning she'd told her mother that she wanted to postpone the ceremony, to give herself time to sort out her confused feelings, but Angela Quinlan had briskly pointed out that with five hundred of their "closest friends" arriving at the Church of the Holy Assumption within the next six hours, canceling was not an option.

So, behaving like the dutiful daughter she had always been, with the exception of those stolen hours with Gabe, Emma had walked down that long white satin runner on her father's arm, feeling like a condemned prisoner being led to her execution.

That was before she'd learned the hard way to stand up for herself. To make her own decisions.

Decisions like spending tonight with Gabriel Broussard.

Emma might feel like putty in his hands, but she didn't want Gabe to mistakenly believe that she was still that fat red-haired girl who would have done anything to get him to notice her.

To want her.

To love her.

No! This wasn't about love. Gabe was talking about sex, pure and simple.

Could she actually go through with it? Could she throw caution to the wind and share a night of mind-blowing passion, knowing that it wouldn't lead to anything but multiple orgasms?

And your point is? the Samantha inside her head asked.

It was the right thing to do, Emma assured herself. The way to get the man out of her system once and for all. In fact, looking at it that way, having sex with Gabe wasn't so reckless, after all. It was eminently logical.

But, for the time being, if she didn't stop thinking about getting naked with him, she really was going to risk driving into the bayou.

"You know, I never doubted that you'd be a star," she said. He'd always had charisma, what Roxi had called his red-hot aura. "But it must have been difficult, breaking into a business as competitive as the Hollywood filmmaking industry."

"I doubt anyone has it that easy. And I know damn well I wasn't the only wannabe actor to live in a car my first month in L.A.," he said.

"That sounds terrible."

"At the time it didn't seem like that big a deal. The weather was nice and I just kept driving around to different beach parking lots to stay ahead of the cops.

"My first place was a seedy apartment on Hollywood Boulevard, which is not, by the way, anywhere near as glamorous as it might sound. There were four of us crammed into a space not much bigger than the Trans Am."

"Were they actors, too?"

"Two of them were. The third was a wannabe screenwriter who moonlighted as a waiter at this trendy Rodeo Drive restaurant five nights a week. He also pulled in a few extra bucks making porno films under the name of Stone Mallet."

A laugh burst from her. "Stone Mallet? Really?"

"My hand to God." He grinned as he raised his right hand. "Porn names aren't exactly subtle. But, I suppose it looked better on credits than James Klozik, which was his real name. He offered to help me break into the business. Promised me that with all his connections, I could be a big star."

"Did you? Make any of those movies?"

"And have my dick turn green and fall off from some STD? Hell, no."

"I'll bet you could've," she said. "Not have your—uh—penis fall off. But be a porn star."

It was dark inside the car, but she could feel his smile. "Seen a lot of porn flicks, have you, *chère*?"

"No." She could feel the heat rise in her face. "But I have a very good imagination. . . . So, I remember reading that you got a job in construction?"

"As a day laborer." Gabe liked that she'd cared enough to read about him. "The work was hard and dirty, paid peasant wages, and most of the guys on the crews tended to take off running whenever *La Migra* showed up looking for aliens to deport; but the upside was that it gave me time to make the rounds of casting calls."

Where he'd discovered that the legendary casting couch did, indeed, exist, and women weren't the only ones having to dodge sexual harassment.

He'd managed to dodge the females with the bad boy grin that had charmed the panties off more than his share of females back here in Blue Bayou. Usually they'd shrug off his rejection, give him their home phone number, in case he ever changed his mind about tangling the sheets, show him the door, then call in the next guy.

A big-shot agent famous for his A list parties, had not been so easily put off. Gabe hadn't been real comfortable with the way the interview was conducted in a circular conversation pit built into the office floor, but had already figured out that Californians weren't exactly like the folks he'd grown up with in Louisiana. And movie people were even more skewed than most.

His instincts had proved right on the money when, after glancing through the black and white glossies, Gabe had spent three weeks building a rock retaining wall. It was meant to keep a popular sitcom star's Pacific Palisades mansion from sliding down onto the Coast Highway and to pay for it, the guy lunged for Gabe's crotch.

Gabe left the agent rolling on the glacier white carpeting, hands cupping his balls, cursing like a drunken sailor and screaming that he might as well go back to the fuckin' swamp because the redneck trailer trash son of a bitch sure as hell wasn't going to ever work in this town.

Having been threatened by a lot tougher guys than the pervert wearing a pink and lavender paisley shirt, mauve leather pants and a toupee that looked like roadkill, Gabe hadn't been exactly trembling in his boots.

"So," he said, "how about you? Nate tells me that you run a massage parlor."

"Every Body's Beautiful is a day spa. Roxi Dupree's my partner. We offer massages, manicures, pedicures, Tarot card and palm readings, love spells—"

"I'm not real familiar with spas, but are palm readings and love spells usually part of the business?"

"Not as a rule," Emma allowed. "But Roxi's grandmother, Evangeline, who owned Hoo Doo Voo Doo—"

"That place on Magnolia, over by the cemetery, with all the gator heads and teeth in the window?"

"That's the one. Evangeline died about six months after we opened up. Roxi got rid of all the heads and teeth and was going to dissolve the business, but all these people kept showing up at the spa wanting spells like the ones they'd bought from her grandmother.

"She didn't want to turn them down, so she started studying Evangeline's shadow books—they're sort of like a witches' cookbook—and decided to concentrate on mixing up the lotions and oils, since they fit in nicely with the spa concept."

"Where do the spells come in?"

"A lot of our business comes from people who book massages for relaxation. Since romance tends to be one of the things that seems to stress people out, it only made sense to include Hex Appeal into our menu of treatments."

"You actually believe in magic?"

From his disbelieving tone, Emma suspected Gabe didn't. "I suppose everyone has their own idea of what magic is. I believe there's some invisible force that connects everything in the universe. And that everything we do affects that force, like ripples in the water. And I believe in destiny . . ."

She paused.

"And I'll bet you don't," she said, reading his silence.

"Sure. I just believe we all make our own destiny."

She wasn't surprised, given his own personal history. Gabe had not only grown up on the wrong side of the tracks, his father had been the town drunk.

According to Charlotte Cassidy, the day checkout clerk down at the Cajun Market, who served as Blue Bayou's unofficial town crier, Claude Broussard had once been considered the person in Blue Bayou most likely to become famous.

Supposedly—and the photographs in the trophy case at the high school backed Charlotte up on this fact—he'd been a mouthwateringly handsome quarterback on the Blue Bayou Buccaneers state high-school championship football team.

He'd been recruited by every major football program in the SEC, and from other colleges as far away as Notre Dame and UCLA. Athletic shoe companies were salivating for a chance to sign the charismatic Cajun kid to an endorsement contract.

Then, on Homecoming Day, 1956, a tackle from Houma had broken through the offensive line and slammed into Claude while he was searching the field for a receiver. The hit the Baton Rouge *Advocate*'s headline referred to as "The Sack Heard Around Louisiana," not only shattered the promising quarterback's knee, it brought his entire world crashing down around him.

Things went downhill from there.

He began to drink. His cheerleader girlfriend, Angeline Beloit, got pregnant; rumor had it that it had taken Angeline's daddy's Ithaca 12-gauge to convince the high school dropout to marry the girl. Gabe was born six months after the shotgun wedding; he was eight months old when Angeline ran off with an oil rig worker from Houston.

Everyone knew Claude beat his son, but since a lot of people in the rigidly Catholic, conservative bayou town believed in that old maxim about sparing the rod and spoiling the child, authorities were never called in. Besides, no one in their right mind wanted to get on the wrong side of Crazy Claude Broussard.

So, he continued to drink and brawl, until that New Year's Eve, two years ago, when he drove his truck off the bridge leading into town. There was no funeral since the only people who might have shown up would have been those wanting to see for themselves that the bully of Blue Bayou really was dead.

No one, least of all Emma, had been surprised when Gabe didn't return home for his father's interment in the far corner of the cemetery once known as Paupers' Field.

Eight

While so much had changed in both their lives since the last time they were together, the cabin was exactly as Emma remembered it.

Like most other bayou camps, it had been built on stilts to allow for rising water to pass underneath; the cypress had weathered to a soft silver hue and a dark green metal roof slanted low over a front porch.

The narrow oyster shell road ended by the front door, but since land and water were always warring in this part of the country, one good storm could turn the road back into a waterway. Which was the reason for the flat-bottomed boat tied to the floating dock.

"This rain's going to have the ground more boggy than usual," he predicted. "No way you're going to be able to walk to the camp in those spindly shoes."

He was right. They'd also be ruined by the mud. "No problem. I'll take them off."

"You'll get your feet muddy."

"You have running water, right?"

"Yeah. Nate checked on that when he brought out the groceries." He rubbed his jaw. "I've got a better idea. I'll carry you."

It had not been easy, growing up a chubbette with Bayou Barbie for a mother. Emma had struggled against self-esteem issues most of her life, which, she'd realized with the twenty-twenty vision of hindsight, was how she'd ended up agreeing to marry Richard against her better judgment.

It wasn't that her mother had loved her ex-husband's slick southern charm. (Though she had.) Nor was it because her father had been impressed by his Vanderbilt degree. (Which, the FBI discovered during the embezzlement investigation, had turned out to be a forged document.) It was because a man who looked a bit like Brad Pitt—if you closed one eye and squinted just right with the other—professed to love her. A fat, shy wallflower who'd only gone to the graduation night cotillion because she'd been assigned to take pictures for the year-end edition of the school paper.

No, it hadn't been easy, but the good thing that had come out of her divorce was that she'd vowed never to let anyone—especially a man—make her feel insignificant again.

Still, for the first time in ages, she found herself desperately wishing Roxi had some magic spell that could make her instantly lose ten—okay, make that twenty—pounds.

"You can't carry me."

"Why not?"

Emma looked him straight in the eye. "Because I'm fat." There. She'd said it. It was a test and they both knew it.

"You're lush." Emma hadn't realized she was holding her breath until she noticed his gaze had drifted down to her breasts, which were in danger of popping out of the neckline of her blouse. "Voluptuous. Hell, darlin', if you'd lived back in pagan times, you'd have been declared a major goddess."

Well. That was definitely not what she'd been expecting to hear.

"Here's how we'll do it," he said with the absolute self-confidence she suspected had allowed him to believe a bad boy from the wrong side of the tracks in Nowhereville, Louisiana, could become the hottest hunk in Hollywood. "I'll come around to the driver's side. You'll get out and wrap those long gorgeous legs around my waist."

He skimmed a hand up her leg in a slow, hot path. "Then, if I can resist takin' you against the car, in the rain, like we almost did back there along the road, we'll make it inside without messin' up those pretty girly shoes or gettin' hit by lightning."

Feeling as if the lightning scenario had already happened, leaving her tingling from the inside out, Emma agreed.

Scarlett O'Hara, eat your heart out. Emma had always thought Rhett sweeping his unruly wife into his arms and up that famous movie staircase, was one of the most erotic moments in movies. But if Rhett had carried Scarlett the way Gabe was holding her—pelvis to pelvis, his hands digging into her bottom, the rock hard bulge of his erection thrusting against her crotch, her legs twined around him as the rain came down so hard and hot she feared she might dissolve from lust—they'd have never made it to the bedroom because Rhett would've taken Scarlett right there on those stairs. And she would have helped him.

Emma felt a momentary stab of loss when he put her back on her feet once they got to the porch so he could retrieve the key from above the lintel.

After warning herself that it was her last chance to back out, she took the hand Gabe held out to her and walked through the open door.

Gabe flicked the light switch by the door. Nothing.

"The electricity's out." Which wasn't any big surprise. Power was iffy this far from civilization. Especially during a storm.

It had been out that night, he remembered. When Emma

had brought him here after the doctor had stitched up the slice made to his cheek by his father's state football championship ring. Having been drunk as usual, Claude had tracked him down after the graduation ceremonies. Having never made it out of Blue Bayou himself, he was damned if he'd let his kid get away.

If Emma, who'd been taking pictures at the cotillion, hadn't come along when she had, Gabe probably would have killed the bastard. Which would've landed his father in Paupers' Field years earlier, and him in Angola.

"Fortunately, I came prepared." He dug a lighter from the pocket of his jeans and began lighting the candles kept on hand for just such contingencies. Then, once the living room and adjoining bedroom were bathed in a flickering yellow glow, Gabe turned toward Emma, drinking in the sight of her rich, ripe body, showcased by the clinging silk.

Because his mouth was hungry for the once forbidden taste of her luscious lips, his hands desperate to explore every inch of her plush breasts, and his throbbing erection aching to bury itself deep inside her, he forced himself to back away. To take his time. To this time, do things right.

Gabe realized she'd mistaken his hesitation for second thoughts when she dragged a hand through her tangled hair.

"I must look like a drowned cat."

Something in his heart turned over. "There you go, being too hard on yourself, *chère*."

Gabe had never considered himself a particularly sensitive person, but he would have had to have been dense as a stone not to understand some of what Emma was feeling.

Knowing that the lingering bit of insecurity was a legacy from that stick-thin, ice-hearted bitch of a mother who'd threatened to have his "trailer trash Cajun ass" thrown in jail if he ever so much as laid a finger on Emma, Gabe vowed that before tonight was over, Emma would realize exactly how desirable she was.

He pushed some wild curls away from her face, then lifted her round chin. "You look wet, you. And fuckin' hot."

"This is too fast," she said on a quick, shuddering breath as he bent closer. "Too much."

"No, *ma belle.*" He touched his mouth to hers. Her lips were soft as thistledown, as potent as whiskey. "It's not nearly enough."

The blood was pounding in his head. His cock.

God help him, he'd tried. She was right about things having gone too fast. Emma wasn't some one-night stand he'd picked up in a Melrose Avenue bar. She deserved better than a quick, hard, anonymous roll in the sheets.

After nearly taking her against the car, Gabe had vowed to slow things down. To take his time; do things right.

But he hadn't counted on her twining her arms around his neck. Or smashing her breasts hard against his chest as her hungry mouth opened beneath his.

Half crazed, desperate to touch her, he peeled away the wet silk from her skin.

"Lift your arms."

She did as instructed, allowing him to yank the blouse over her head and onto the floor.

Lacy cups framed her voluptuous breasts. Forget the Grand Canyon or Victoria Falls. Emma's breasts were the true natural wonders of the world. And even more amazingly, unlike all the ones he'd come across the past few years in California, they were real.

"Damn, Emma." He cupped her breasts in his hands, embracing the warm weight of them. "You're wearing white lace."

"Colored would've looked tacky beneath the blouse."

"You couldn't look tacky if you tried." Well, there *was* that fantasy of her wearing those black boots. Which wasn't so much tacky, he decided, as hot. Hot and wicked. "Do the panties match?"

"Of course."

"Thank you." He rocked forward on the toes of his boots, kissed her. "I fantasized about this," he murmured as he skimmed a fingertip over the white lace flowers covering her taut nipples.

"You fantasized about me?" Her eyes, which had fluttered down to half-mast, opened.

"Kinda." His touch circled, teased. Her nipples were the color of ripe strawberries, which brought up a fantasy of spreading chocolate on those amazing breasts and licking it off.

"After my fictional fiancée broke our fake engagement by telling the world I had certain, uh, predilections of the kinky kind, women started bombarding my house with panties."

He slipped the straps over her shoulders. "They came FedEx, UPS, in the U.S. mail." While his hands stayed busy with her breasts, his lips nuzzled her neck. "Some ladies were more direct and just tossed them over my gate."

"Those weren't ladies."

He chuckled. "At least not proper Southern ones," he agreed. He kissed her collarbone. "Most of the panties were black." Her shoulder. "The rest were red." The crest of her breast and inhaled her scent. "I was thinkin' it'd be nice if just one of those women had decided to show off her softer side." His lips dipped into the cleavage framed by the white lace. "And talk about soft."

Emma trembled as his tongue stroked over her straining nipple.

"*Bon Dieu*, you are one tasty female."

"It's the lotion." Emma gasped when his teeth closed around a tightened nipple and tugged. "Roxi blended it especially for me. From essential oil of peaches, vanilla, and coconut."

"What I'm tastin' sure isn't peaches. You taste like temptation, you. And sex. I've a mind to lick you all over."

Her skirt had an elastic waist, and fastened with a hook-and-eye and zipper in the back. Proving himself to be a man who definitely knew his way around women's clothing, he dispatched the hook with a simple twist of the fingers.

Emma drew in a sharp breath when his knuckles brushed against the bare skin of her back.

The sexy sound of the zipper, slowly lowering, tooth by tooth, had her wet with wanting.

The silk skirt whispered over her skin as it slid down her thighs to pool on the floor at her feet, leaving her standing there, in the center of the cabin, barely clad in a bra that was clinging to the tips of her breasts, a pair of panties, and those shoes, which must make her look like a porno actress in one of those Voluptuous Vixens DVDs she'd seen for rent in the back room of the Video Express.

Some women—like Roxi—might be able to get away with wearing barely there underwear and high heels. Emma had never believed herself to be one of them.

"Don't," he murmured when one hand instinctively went to her breasts, the other to conceal her crotch. "Don't cover up anything. And don't move. I want to see you."

Well, that was sure as hell going to blow her midnight-stuck-in-a-cabin-with-Gabe-Broussard fantasy right out of the water.

He was standing there, taking her in, studying her slowly, silently, as if memorizing every curve.

"I don't think this is such a good—"

"Shh." He touched a finger to her lips, forestalling her complaint at being looked at like a . . . what?

A sex object.

Which was impossible. No one had ever looked at her in this scorchingly hungry way Gabriel was looking at her. If even the smallest percent of what the tabloids were always saying was true, Gabe had slept with some of the most beautiful women in Hollywood. In the entire world. Women with "buns of steel" asses, Bowflex-tight stomachs, and pert, perfect breasts.

Emma didn't even want to think about how she might compare to all those past lovers.

It had been hard enough to make the decision to throw caution to the wind and sleep with Gabriel. To stand still for such an intense study from a man whose beautifully formed physique could have been immortalized in marble and gleaming bronze, chipped away at Emma's hard-won confidence.

"You are," he said, "without a doubt, the most—"

Fat, her mind jumped ahead of his words. Though she doubted it'd help all that much, Emma sucked in her oh-so-not-flat stomach.

"*Female* woman I've ever seen." His eyes, which lust had darkened to nearly a midnight black, looked into hers as he fondled her heavy breasts. *"J'aimete faire l'amour avec toi."* His deep voice was as thick as gumbo. "I wanna make love to you the way a woman like you deserves to be made love to."

Emma trembled when he ran those treacherously clever hands down her sides, then back down her spine, over the curve of her bottom.

"You've got a great ass, you." He splayed the fingers of both hands over each cheek, began kneading her flesh. Her white, abundant flesh.

"A big ass, you mean."

Emma wished she could take the words back the instant she'd heard them escape her lips. Talk about ruining the mood!

His fingers tightened. "I don't ever want to hear anyone put you down." He pressed her against him, hard. The bulge straining against the faded denim had the metal buttons pressing into her stomach. "Not even you, *chère.*" He thrust his hand between them, breaching the white stretch lace of her panties to tangle in the moist curls. "I wanted to take things slow. But I'm afraid this first time's going to be a hard, fast fuck." His free hand tangled in her hair, pulling her head back. "So if that's not what you want . . ."

She was burning from the inside out. If he didn't take her soon, Emma feared she'd self-combust. "Oh, God, yes."

Nine

Gabe's mouth took hers in a hard, claiming kiss, his tongue sweeping deep, mating with hers as he lifted her off her feet and carried her into the adjoining bedroom. The sweet-smelling mattress, stuffed with Spanish moss and herbs, gave way as they tumbled onto it, mouths fused, arms and legs entwined.

His mouth left hers to blaze a path down her throat, her breasts, her torso, with hot, openmouthed kisses that scorched her skin and made her blood flame.

Outside the cabin, the rain beat a strong, steady percussion on the tin roof. Inside, a storm swirled.

The last of Emma's clothes, and all of Gabe's, were ripped away, as if by gale-force winds. He proved to be a ruthless lover, forceful, demanding. His teeth scraped against her inner thighs, drawing a ragged moan from deep in her throat. He brushed a thumb over her swollen clit, then parted the wet pink folds of her ultrasensitive labia, spreading the moisture, exciting her, preparing her.

There was thunder. Emma could hear it in her heart,

which was pounding so hard and so loud she was certain he must be able to hear it. There was lightning, blindingly bright, but she couldn't tell whether it was outside the cabin or inside her mind.

Another tempest, more dangerous than the one conjured up by Mother Nature, swirled in the dark eyes that were watching her face intently as he slid first one finger, then another, deep inside her.

And when his hands dug into her hips, and he lifted her to his mouth to feast, the already all-consuming storm intensified.

Around Emma.

Inside her.

She writhed beneath him, her wet hair whipping across the bed as her head thrashed back and forth.

"More." The ragged word was half plea, half demand as she ground her mound against his ravenous mouth. "Please. I need . . . I want . . ."

Before her passion-hazed mind could fully form the coherent plea, Gabe's fiendishly talented tongue took one last, long, lascivious swath. She screamed his name, a full-throated scream of release that echoed out over the bayou.

Her tremors had not yet subsided when Gabe yanked open the condom he'd taken earlier from his jeans pocket. On some distant level, as he rolled the latex over his straining penis to the crisp dark hair at the broad base, Emma was grateful that one of them had thought of protection.

Taking hold of her ankles, he spread her legs wider, exposing her more fully. He was poised over her like a sleek jungle cat, every muscle taut, his dark flesh gleaming with a sheen of sweat, his sheathed erection jutting out with primal intensity.

He lifted her legs, hooking them over his shoulders.

Emma had never felt more exposed. Nor more aroused.

"Do you have any idea what I want from you?"

"No." She could barely hear her whispered answer over the hammering of rain on the roof and the pounding of blood in her ears.

His smile was swift. Carnal.

"Everything."

Gabe plunged into her with one strong swift stroke, slamming up against her cervix with a strength that ripped a hoarse cry from her ravished lips.

"Damn." He sucked in a deep, shuddering breath she could feel inside her. The muscles in his arms stood out in rigid relief as he braced himself above her body. "Are you okay?"

"I'm fine." The brief sharp pain had become an even sharper need. Her hips bucked, urging him on. "Oh, God. Don't stop."

"As if I could," he muttered between clenched teeth.

He began to move, thrusting, withdrawing, thrusting, pacing his movements with a perfection of power and timing that had her coming again. And again.

Outside, thunder boomed; the night wind wailed. Inside, bedsprings squeaked; the iron headboard pounded against the cypress wall. Rhythms matched. Breathless, Emma clung to him as they raced into the storm.

Finally, giving into the demands of his body, Gabe allowed his own release on a long, shuddering groan that echoed deep into Emma's bones.

Afterwards, they lay amidst the cooling, tangled sheets, arms and legs entwined, his large body sprawled over hers. He felt heavy, but not uncomfortably so. As she twined her still-unsteady fingers through his damp hair, Emma wondered if Gabe could feel her body's continued pulsations.

He could. The way her inner muscles kept clenching around his still throbbing cock was the sexiest thing he'd ever felt.

"Wow." Her breasts were a pillowy cushion, soft and bountiful. He turned his head and kissed the fragrant flesh. "That was more incredible than in my fantasies of you."

"You fantasized about me?" *Why?*

"*Mais,* yeah." He shared a reminiscent smile. "There was this one summer, when I was filming up in northern Ontario, in the lake district. The temperature was in the '90s, with a humidity just as high."

"I never thought of Canada being as hot as the bayou," she managed as his lips caressed a nipple.

"Neither had I. We spent seven weeks there making this movie about a guy who escapes from prison when the transport bus goes off the highway. He carjacks an SUV, takes the driver hostage and falls in love with her."

"*Ransom,*" she murmured. It had been an edgy, yet romantic movie about two unhappy people who'd found each other at the impossibly worst time. Unfortunately, the screenwriter hadn't gone for a happily-ever-after ending, instead having Gabe's character killed in a hail of bullets.

When the Bijou's lights had gone back on, all the moist eyes in the theater revealed Emma hadn't been the only moviegoer who'd cried at the tragic final scene.

"That's the one, all right." He nodded. "There was this one scene, where she was cleaning the bullet wound he'd gotten during the breakout and the strangest thing happened."

His gaze took on a faraway look as if he was picturing the moment in his mind. "I had this flashback to when we were here at the camp. When you were putting the ice pack on my stitches."

The emergency room doctor had given Emma the gel pack, instructing her that keeping the wound iced would help keep down the swelling.

She lifted her fingers, traced them along the white scar which, rather than detract from his devastating good looks, only added to his rakish appearance, keeping his features from being impossibly perfect.

"That never should've been necessary. Someone should have done something to stop your father years earlier."

Gabe shrugged his broad shoulders. "You know how it is down here. Everybody pretty much minds their own business."

"A child being abused should be everyone's business." She smoothed a hand over his temple, and down his neck. The tightened tendons told her that he wasn't as nonchalant as he was trying to sound. "If you knew a father was beating a child—"

"I'd want to kill him," he responded on a deadly primitive tone that had goose bumps prickling on Emma's skin.

It was as if a bucket of ice water had been thrown on the warm, afterglow mood. With a muttered curse, Gabe rolled off her, left the bed, and went into the adjoining bathroom.

Ten

Gabe leaned a hand against the wall as he flushed the toilet, watching the condom swirling down the drain. Just like his life would've done that night if Emma hadn't come across him and his father beating each other's brains out. From the time he'd grown taller and stronger than Claude Broussard, Gabe had thought about killing him. But, not wanting to end up in prison, he'd mostly stayed out of his way as much as he could.

Nate's dad, who'd been Blue Bayou's sheriff, had tried to get him moved out of the house, but then he'd been killed in the line of duty. Nate had helped out by giving him a key to this place, where Gabe had essentially lived on his own from his thirteenth birthday.

Although he hadn't gotten drunk again since that long ago night of the showdown he and his father had been building toward all his life, Gabe suddenly wanted a stiff drink now. Jack Black, straight up, hold the ice. And keep them comin'.

Shit. How old did a guy get before he finally escaped the ghosts of his past?

He'd never thought of himself as a coward. But as unpalatable as the idea was, while he'd spent his entire life struggling not to grow up like his drunk of an old man, he'd ended up a lot like his mother.

Like her, he'd run away from Blue Bayou. Now, having also run away from Hollywood, he was right back here where he'd begun. Which meant that he'd spent the past decade running in circles.

Dragging his hand down his face, he took a deep breath and left the bathroom.

"Sorry about that," he said as he sat down on the edge of the mattress and ran a hand down her tangle of hair. "Guess the topic just hit a little too close to home."

"That's okay," she said with that unwavering loyalty that he now realized he hadn't fully appreciated when he'd been younger. The corners of her lips tilted in a faint, reassuring smile, but her eyes were as grave as they'd been that night.

"I'm glad you didn't kill your father, Gabe"—she smoothed a caress over his knuckles which, that night, had been bruised and bloodied—"not for his sake, but for yours."

"The bastard wasn't worth doing hard time for, that's sure enough," Gabe agreed. "But if you hadn't come along when you did, I'd probably be in prison and he'd have been in the ground ten years ago."

And not a soul in the parish would've mourned Claude Broussard's passing. Gabe hadn't felt so much as a twinge of regret when Nate's wife, Regan, who was now the sheriff, had called to tell him about the accident.

"You hungry, *chère*?" He didn't want to talk about his father anymore. Didn't want to think about him. "Since the power was on when Nate stocked the fridge this morning, things shouldn't have spoiled, and we've got plenty of wood for the stove. How does some crawfish jambalaya and dirty rice sound?"

"Wonderful."

"*Bien*. So, we'll have ourselves a little supper. Share some conversation." He nipped at her bottom lip and ran his hand down the silk of her bare back. "Then we'll go back to bed."

Her answering smile could've lit up the bayou for a month of Sundays. "That's the best idea you've had yet."

Deciding that things were definitely looking up since he'd come back to Blue Bayou, Gabe paused in the act of buttoning up his jeans. "I don't suppose you'd like to save me the trouble of ripping off your clothes later, by just stayin' naked?"

That soft, lovely color he was beginning to love bloomed in her cheeks. Who would have suspected that a sexy, multi-orgasmic woman who could turn him every which way but loose, was capable of blushing? When choosing roles, Gabe had always been drawn to contradictions in character; Emma was a gorgeous, walking, talking tangle of intriguing contrasts.

He vowed by the time he left the bayou, he'd have explored every one.

"I am *not* eating without clothes on," she insisted.

He shrugged, even as he decided that Emma was going to make one bang-up dessert. "I had a feeling that's what you'd say. Though it's a damn shame, because you sure do pretty up the scenery, *tite chatte*."

He retrieved his duffle bag out of the car. Since he was a great deal taller than her, the oversize black and gold New Orleans Saints T-shirt hit Emma about mid-thigh. He heaved a deep sigh of regret when she put her panties back on.

"Spoilsport." He knew he should've just ripped the damn things when he had the chance. He liked the idea of Emma bare-crotched and bare-assed, available to him whenever he felt the urge to touch her. Take her. Pleasure her.

And she would be pleasured, Gabe vowed. In more ways than she'd ever imagined. Again and again.

Just thinking about all the ways he was going to have her, all the things he planned to do to Emma, *with* her, had sweat breaking out on his forehead and a hard-on of Herculean proportions straining against his jeans.

He was considering giving into the rampant testicular urge to drag her back to bed when his stomach grumbled.

If he was going to spend the rest of the night ravishing the delectable Emma Quinlan, he'd need to keep his strength up.

Food first.

Then, one hunger satisfied, he was going to claim her. Physically. Emotionally. Completely.

Emma was surprised at how well she and Gabe worked together. He gathered up the ingredients, assigning her the job of peeling the boiled crawdads while he started the rice.

"There was another time, up in Canada," he said, as he heated the oil in a large, cast-iron skillet, "when this actress and I were rollin' 'round the bed, supposed to be makin' love."

"I seem to recall a lot of that," Emma said.

"The couple were hot for each other, sure enough. But the time I'm talkin' about was when it was like I got zapped by a time machine and instead of bein' with her, it was like I'd ended up back here, with you.

"Jus' thinkin' about how pretty you looked, and those soft little sounds you made when you came, I got such a boner, me, that Clint had to call a break in action so we wouldn' end up with a triple-X rating."

"Things like that happen," she said with a brief, knowing nod. "To men."

His lips quirked in a smile as he added some flour to the oil, whisking the roux with smooth, deft strokes she couldn't help but admire. Although Emma had grown up in a part of the country known for its Cajun and Creole cuisine, since her mother's cook had never let her in the kitchen, her own culinary skills were self-taught and marginal, at best.

"Been with a lot of horny men, have you, darlin'?"

Hearing the laughter in his voice, Emma refused to look up from peeling the red-shelled crustaceans. "One of the first things you learn in massage school is not to take a male client's erection personally." She cringed inwardly as she heard her mother's prim tone coming out of her mouth.

"Sounds reasonable," he said easily. "Though, fair warning, Emma—any erection I get around you, you oughta take real personal."

The decadent smile he flashed her way was rife with sexual promise and sent a shiver of primitive awareness shimmying up Emma's spine. Carnal fantasies, each more kinky than the previous one, tangled hotly in her mind.

He turned down the heat beneath the pan and began dicing a fat yellow onion. "Nate left beer and wine in the fridge. Why don't you get something for us to drink while I finish peeling those mud bugs?"

Having been caught up in a fantasy of being dragged by rough-handed brigands before Jean Lafitte, Emma was momentarily disoriented to find herself in the camp kitchen, rather than in the pirate's private quarters.

"What would you like?"

"Now there's a tempting question." He put such blatant sexuality into the growled response that for a fleeting moment, Emma was back on the pirate's private galleon, naked, on her knees, forced to satisfy his every erotic demand.

"We seem to have Voodoo Beer," she reported in an uncharacteristic stammer. "And Chardonnay."

"I'll take the beer. For now." The timer he'd set for the rice dinged. "Then perhaps I'll drink the wine off your lush body for dessert."

As she opened the wine with the corkscrew she found in a drawer and unscrewed the cap of Gabe's beer, Emma couldn't decide whether to take his words as a promise or a threat.

The wine sparkled in the candlelight like sunshine on water. The robustly spiced jambalaya and dirty rice could've easily been served at one of the finest New Orleans Cajun restaurants.

While the south Louisiana culture could admittedly be accused of being chauvinistic from time to time, cooking had always been a rite of male passage for Cajun men, dating back to when they'd had to feed themselves during those long, lonely months at their camps when they'd supported their families by hunting and trapping.

As if by mutual, unspoken agreement, they kept the conversation casual over dinner. Gabe entertained Emma with anecdotes about the movie business, while she caught him up on the local gossip.

"Remember Dorothy Pettijohn and Pearl Duvall?" she asked as he cleared the table. She'd offered to help, but he'd refused, insisting that he'd rather she just stay in one place so he could enjoy the scenery while he worked.

"Sure. God, they must be at least seventy, by now."

"Seventy-three," she confirmed. The two women had lived together in a little house on Bayou Pettijohn for as long as Emma could remember. "They went off to Canada last year for a vacation and came back married."

"Good for them," Gabe said as he poured the coffee he'd turned on before they'd sat down to supper.

"A few people were scandalized." Emma's mother being one of them. "But most just figured it was their business." She smiled her thanks as he placed the heavy mug in front of her. "Turns out the ceremony took place on their fortieth anniversary."

"That's a helluva long time for any couple to be together," he said.

"Isn't it?" Emma remembered how happy they'd looked when they'd returned home from Toronto. Their faces, lined and weathered from seven decades of living, had been glowing. "I hate to admit it, but I envied them. Just a little."

"No shame in that." He took a drink of coffee, eyeing her over the rim of the earthenware mug. "By the way, in case you were wondering? That picture of me with that actress on that tycoon's yacht was a cut and paste. I don't fool around with married women. And I don't screw around on women I'm with."

Unlike some people. The unstated words hovered in the air between them.

"Nate sorta filled me in on what's been happening with you."

"It's not exactly a secret." Her fingers tensed on the mug's handle. She forced them to relax. "Given that Richard's in prison."

"For embezzling from your daddy."

"Yes. The ironic thing was that he'd married me to get in good with my father in the first place."

"Now, that's hard to believe."

"It's true."

Strangely, it didn't hurt now because it hadn't hurt then. Not really. Oh, Emma's pride had been wounded. But her heart had remained unscathed because while she'd been promising to love, honor, and respect, her heart hadn't been hers to bestow on her husband. Because she'd given it to Gabe years ago.

"He told me, the day he left me for Chandra, that he'd never really loved me."

"I'd call the guy a prick, but he'd give a bad name to penises everywhere." Gabe leaned back on the hind legs of the chair. "So, did you love him?"

"I thought I did." She'd almost managed to convince herself that she had. "I certainly wanted to."

"So, why did you marry him if you weren't sure?"

Because I finally gave up on you. "It's hard to explain."

"Was it the sex?"

Emma nearly choked on her coffee. "What?"

"The sex. I guess it was pretty good, huh?"

She was amazed to discover that she could laugh about something that had been so painfully embarrassing. "It wasn't anything to write home about." She dragged a hand through her hair and pretended a sudden interest in the well of darkness outside the window. "I wasn't his type."

"*Chère,* a woman like you is definitely the type of every male who has even one workin' nut."

Emma felt the heat—the bane of redheads—flood into her face. "That's nice of you to say—"

"It's not nice. It's the truth."

"I wasn't very good. You know," she said at his arched brow, "with the how-to part."

What was it about Gabe that had her telling him things she'd never told anyone but Roxi. Couldn't she just keep her mouth shut? Apparently not. She kept pointing out her flaws. Her big butt, her lack of sexual expertise, next she'd be telling him about the D she'd gotten in high school geometry and the bad perm that had caused her hair to break off at the roots two days before her wedding.

A rich, deep, sexy laugh exploded from him. "Emma, darlin', if you were any better at the how-to part, I'd be laid out on a slab down at Dupree's funeral parlor after dying from havin' my head blown off by that last climax."

She thought about the way he'd shouted her name as he'd come with a force that had driven her deep into the mattress and decided that even Gabe wasn't that good an actor.

"It was good, wasn't it?" she murmured.

"Better than good. It was gold-medal, world-class sex, and if I were a more generous man, I'd drive myself up to

that prison and thank your dickless ex-husband for not bein'
man enough to handle a woman of your vast sexual needs."

She might have laughed. Or argued. But for some reason,
the hot and hungry way he was looking at her made her almost believe him.

"It was a good thing, in a way," she said, taking another
sip of the chicory flavored coffee. "I'd gotten complacent,
working as a bookkeeper down at Nate's construction company. I'd thought about opening my own business for a long
time, but Richard didn't believe two careers were good for a
marriage."

"Sounds like the guy was intimidated by strong, confident, sexual women."

"That's the same thing Roxi said."

"You should listen to your friend, you."

"Well, once he left—taking our joint bank account with
him—I decided to open Every Body's Beautiful. We began
as pretty much a typical fluff and buff operation, then I
started expanding services. One of our most popular packages is the Rose Body Booster. It's an aromatherapy treat-
ment that includes a rose petal massage. We get a lot of
requests for that at Valentine's Day and Mother's Day. And
just last week we did an entire bachelorette party."

Gabe tilted his chair back on its rear legs. "Maybe I'll
sign up for one while I'm here. Just the idea of getting naked
and having you rub rose petals all over my body makes me
hot . . . But you know what makes me even hotter?"

Emma was already turned on by the mental vision of herself straddling his hips, crushing the scent of rose petals
against his oiled, muscular back. The naked hunger in those sultry dark eyes had her breath catching in her lungs, and heat
dampening the crotch of those panties he hadn't wanted her
to put back on.

She swallowed. "What?"

"The idea of me rubbing those rose petals all over your

luscious body." His eyes drifted from hers, to her lips, then lower, lingering on her breasts. "Everywhere." The molten heat in his gaze had an answering warmth uncurling deep inside her.

"Do you have any idea what it does to me, when you look at me that way, *chère*?" he murmured, leaning closer, until his lips were just a breath away from hers.

Unable to respond, Emma shook her head.

"It makes me want things." He brushed his knuckles around her jaw. Up her cheek. "Hot things." His fingers slid into her hair. "Pelvis-grinding, dirty, blow-your-mind things."

The fingers of his other hand circled her wrist and he pressed her palm against the front of his jeans, where his swollen sex backed up his claim. Then he stood up, pulling her with him, his strong hands cupping her bottom, his pelvis grinding, just as he'd promised, against hers.

"Unfasten me," he said against her mouth as his hands delved beneath the T-shirt and cupped her breasts.

The top button was already unfastened. He was gloriously naked beneath the jeans. Emma unfastened two more metal buttons, exposing the ebony hair that continued from his chest to his groin.

Anticipation curled hotly between her thighs as she finished with the last two buttons, then, feeling a great deal like the captured woman in *The Last Pirate*, Emma knelt on the hard, heart-of-pine floor and slowly drew the jeans down over Gabe's lean male hips.

Then she sat back on her heels, devouring him with her eyes. Until this moment, Emma had not realized how beautiful the male penis could be.

"Touch me." His voice was thick with need.

"*Mais,* yes," Emma borrowed a bit of his Cajun French which, to her ear, sounded sexier.

Gabe bucked his hips forward, into her touch as she explored the satiny length. Holding her rioting hair back with one hand, so he could better view the action, she stroked his erection from base to knobbed tip.

A tiny drop of moisture gleamed like a pearl in the plump cleft. Leaning forward, Emma gathered it in with a swirl of her tongue.

He swelled in her hand. A groan, somewhere between a curse and a prayer, was ripped from his chest when she took the sleek silk into her mouth. Loving him with her tongue, Emma reveled at the power thrusting between her parted lips.

"Not that way." He grabbed her hair, urging her back to her feet. "Not this time."

His hand delved beneath the black T-shirt, tearing away her panties as if they were made of tissue paper.

"I'll replace them," he growled against her mouth as he plunged his fingers deep inside her.

"They're not important." She gripped his shoulders and sagged against the hard wall of his chest and she was rocked by a sudden, molten wave of pleasure. "Oh, God, what are you doing to me?"

"I'm taking you." Balancing her on one knee, he swept the coffee mugs off the table, and laid her on her back and pressed his palms against her inner thighs, spreading her legs apart on the pine planks. "And you're going to love it."

Eleven

The kitchen was compact enough for him to keep one hand on her mound while grabbing the pair of wooden handled shears stuck in a wooden knife block. After using the shears to snip the hem of the shirt, he tossed them aside and ripped it open.

He was standing over her, looking down at her with the dark, hungry eyes of a conqueror.

"Christ, you've got some amazing body, *chère*."

He cupped her breasts, then bent his head to scrape his teeth against a straining nipple.

Emma couldn't hold back the moan his caressing touch dragged from her throat as he rolled the turgid peak between his thumb and forefinger; nor could she stop her body from arching upward, offering his wickedly clever hands and mouth better access.

"You are so beautiful." His words vibrated against her burning hot skin as his mouth moved down her torso.

His caresses continued their treacherous trail downward,

over the swell of her stomach, down her inner thighs, his fingers kneading the flesh that made swimsuit shopping such an exercise in masochism.

"Your skin's so white." His voice was rough as an oyster shell road. "Like magnolia petals."

Even more amazing than the fact that he could make her want him with a single hot look or a lingering touch, was that where she saw stretch marks and cellulite, Gabe saw flowers.

"I've been wanting to do this all during supper."

Grabbing a condom from the box he'd brought into the kitchen earlier, he sheathed himself, then, planting his long bare feet far apart, rubbed the latex-covered tip against the swollen lips of her labia, stroking in long, wet glides, teasing the tender flesh, while refusing to enter her until she was gasping, thighs quivering, heart hammering, begging him. "Please, Gabe. Oh, God, please, take me, now."

"I thought you'd never ask," he said with a satisfied chuckle against her mouth.

Emma could taste herself on his lips as he gave her a long, slow soul kiss that had white-hot stars wheeling behind her closed eyes. Then—thank you, God, finally!—he slipped into her, as smoothly as if they'd been created to fit together in just this way.

"*Dieu,* I love the way your body feels against mine." He moved his hips, sinking deeper. "All soft and welcoming." Then deeper still. "Ah," he breathed as his entire length was surrounded and they were fully joined. "That's so good."

Her senses swam. Her mind shut down.

Gabe laced his fingers with hers, moving their joined hands up, on either side of her head. "I wish I could stay inside you forever."

He began to move, slowly at first. Tenderly. Then faster and faster, hot flesh slapping against hot flesh as Emma scissored her legs around him, lifting her hips with each downstroke, meeting him thrust for thrust as they both raced over that dark edge together.

Colors—fading from the red of a bursting star to rose to a cooling pinkish blue—floated peacefully in her mind. Gabe's mouth was against her throat. Their breathing, still in unison, gradually slowed. He lifted his head, combed the wet hair from her face. "I don't think I'll ever get enough of you," he murmured, seeming, Emma thought, a bit surprised at the notion.

She smiled at that, even though she knew it was only the pleasure of the moment speaking. What she and Gabe had shared was wonderful. Better than wonderful, it was the most exquisite thing she'd ever known.

But the man who was sprawled lazily on top of her like a satiated lion, had broken her heart once before. And would again, if she didn't guard her heart more carefully this time.

"Wait here," he said. "I'll be right back."

As if she were capable of moving. Every bone in Emma's body seemed to have turned to water. "Where are you going?"

"I promised to replace those panties."

She leaned up on her elbows. "You're not driving back into town? The stores will all be closed by now."

"I'm not going to the store." He opened the refrigerator and took out a tall red can. "I'm gonna give you a pair of whipped cream underpants, *chère*." He winked. "Then I'm going to eat them off you."

Impossibly, sexual tension sparked again, tightening muscles that had gone lax. "Is there enough whipped cream in that can for both of us to have dessert?"

He grinned. "I gua-ran-tee it."

* * *

It was dark when Gabe felt Emma slipping out of the bed. If he were the kind of man who kissed and told, which he wasn't, he would have thanked Nate for having bought that whipped cream. *Mon Dieu*, how he'd enjoyed spraying it onto her lush, rounded body. Enjoyed even more licking it off her.

And if she were worried about calories, she definitely hadn't shown it, as she'd done the same thing to him.

Which had, of course, left them so messy, they'd been forced to take a shower. Amazingly, he'd taken her yet again, up against the tile wall. He hadn't felt so horny, or been able to recover so quickly between rounds, since his high school days.

If only he'd known how hot the soft, sweet-smelling Emma Quinlan was back then. He'd gotten a hint of the passion she kept banked beneath that shy, wallflower exterior on graduation night.

Would things have changed if he'd just given into his rebellious body's demands and taken her virginity? Would his life have turned out differently? Would hers?

Gabe had never been one to lie. Not even to himself. Especially to himself. The truth was, he probably wouldn't have appreciated her then. He might have even ended up hurting her more than that son-of-a-bitch embezzler she'd made the mistake of marrying.

Although he'd never believed in destiny, the past hours with Emma had Gabe wondering if perhaps there was some unseen force working here, some fate, that had led them down separate, individual paths, only to bring them back together once they were older, wiser, and even more hot for one another.

Whatever the reason, Gabe was determined to make up for lost time. The problem was, he considered, as he heard her rustling around in the dark, gathering up her scattered clothing, Emma didn't seem to be on the same page.

The door's hinges squeaked as she opened it. Gabe could feel her tense, like a deer fearing a predator's approach.

He could stop her. He was, after all, larger. Stronger. Not that he'd have to use force. Because it would only take a slow kiss, a lingering touch, a hand to that slick hot place between her legs, to have her back in his bed.

Gabe was still weighing his options when he heard the engine turn over. Heaving a weary sigh, he climbed out of bed, flipped open the cell phone and called his best friend.

"Hey, Nate," he said, when the sleep-husky voice on the other end of the line answered. "I need another favor. Yeah, everything went jus' fine. But Emma's on her way back to town from the swamp and I hate the idea of her driving through the bayou alone in the dark. Could your pretty sheriff wife send a deputy out to meet her on the highway and follow her home? Then let me know she got there okay? Thanks, *cher.*"

That little matter taken care of, Gabe pulled on a pair of boxers, and went into the kitchen to await the call letting him know that his *'tite chatte* had made it home safe and sound.

"If she thinks we're finished," he said, as the coffee dripped into the pot, "the lady has another think coming."

Having come to a crossroads in his life, Gabe wasn't entirely sure where his future was headed. But he knew damn well that Emma was going to play a starring role.

"I gua-ran-tee it."

Twelve

Emma was not having a good day. She'd mixed up her oils, using Mr. Lamoreaux's sandlewood and juniper on Mrs. Breaux, who preferred the relaxing scent of lavender. Rather than appearing unhappy, the elderly lady assured Emma that it was occasionally a good idea to get out of a rut. While Etienne Lamoreaux, who wore a gold hoop in his ear and rode an old chopper Harley, seemed to take smelling like a little old lady's sachet in stride.

All day long she jumped every time the phone rang. By closing time, she'd been forced to wonder if she wasn't putting too much importance on what had probably been to him nothing more than a convenient, one-night stand. Especially since that polite, green as spring grass deputy had informed her that he had instructions to follow her back from the camp to her house, which meant Gabriel had been aware of her sneaking away.

How difficult would it have been to keep her there, if he'd wanted her to stay? He wouldn't even have to use force. All it would've taken was a few kisses, some touches . . .

"Are you sure you want to do this?" Roxi asked.

Emma crossed her arms. "Absolutely."

"Because I can sure as hell think of worse things than daydreaming of that hot Cajun Gabriel Broussard."

"That's just the point," Emma argued. "I don't *want* to dream of him."

Her blood began to swim at the thought of Gabe touching her. Tasting her. "He's like a fever in my blood, Roxi. I can't concentrate. He's all I think about. I want him gone."

A moonstone ring, larger than the diamond one Gabe professed not to have bought for Tamara Templeton, glowed as Roxi tossed her long black hair over her shoulder. "You do realize, of course, that most of the time people want me to bring love to them. Not send it away."

"We're not talking about love. This is lust. Pure and simple."

Although, in truth, there was nothing simple about her feelings for Gabe. He stirred her up. But at the same time, during supper, she'd felt strangely relaxed with him. Okay, maybe not relaxed. But comfortable. As if she could be herself.

"Oh, God," Roxi groaned. "You went and did it, didn't you?"

"I told you we did. Several times."

"You said you had mind-bending, multi-orgasmic sex. You didn't tell me you did a pair bonding with him."

"There wasn't any bonding going on." At least not on Gabe's part. If there had been, wouldn't he have called by now?

Hell. She really wasn't any good at casual sex.

"Haven't I told you that you have to keep your emotions and your orgasms separate?"

"Easy for you to say. You haven't had sex with Gabriel Broussard."

"More's the pity. Though unfortunately, he's not my type."

Emma snorted disbelievingly.

"Really," Roxi insisted. "I have, when it comes to men, one steadfast rule: I refuse to sleep with any guy who has the whole package. The best way to keep sex a no-strings affair is to stick to only going to bed with a man who's got a below-the-belt package."

"Gabe has that, too." Emma was feeling feverish just remembering him inside her. Filling her. Loving her. "Oh, God, Roxi." She leaned her elbows on the table and dropped her face into her hands. "I love him." So much, it hurt.

"It's too bad I'm not into black magic, or I'd put a curse on that Hollywood stud muffin for seducing you."

"He didn't seduce me." He hadn't forced her to go buy that sexy outfit, that barely there underwear, those damn fuck-me-big-boy shoes, which had definitely lived up to their name. *"I seduced him."*

It was Roxi's turn to snort. "From what I've read, the guy doesn't need a lot of convincing."

"He's not like that."

"Not kinky?"

Emma thought about the way he'd taken her on the table. And later, the whipped cream. And she hadn't even realized that some of the things he'd done to her in the shower were physically possible. "Define kinky."

Roxi shook her head. "Shit. It just gets worse." She stood up, went over to the kitchen and took out a small wooden chest. "Short of putting a stake through Gabriel Broussard's manly chest, this is the most powerful 'go away, lover' spell I know." She paused as she took a small glass vial of essential oil from the box. "So, I'm asking one last time—you sure this is what you want to do, *chère*?"

Emma had entered into their one-night stand with her

eyes wide open. She'd known Gabe would hurt her. And he had.

So, the downside was that her heart was broken. Shattered, like the white shards of pottery that had covered the wood plank floor after he'd swept their coffee mugs off the table.

The upside was that she'd experienced a night of passion few women would ever know. With the sexiest man alive.

And that was worth remembering.

Now the thing to do was to get rid of Gabriel Broussard so she could move on with her life.

She nodded. "Absolutely."

Gabe missed Emma.

And not just for the sex, which had been blow-your-mind incredible, but even before *People* magazine had named him the sexiest man alive, sex had been easy to come by. And, too often, easily forgotten.

Which was not the case with Emma. It was as if the woman had burned herself into his mind. Having given her mixed messages ten years ago, he spent all day and evening out on the *gallerie*, trying to logically sort out his feelings. Which wasn't that easy to do since his mind kept returning to last night, rerunning every thing they'd done in Technicolor and Surround sound.

Every little detail about her was scorched onto his mind: her scent—tropical flowers blended with womanly arousal—as he'd dragged her down onto the bed; the flame silk of her hair draped over his thighs as she'd taken him deeper, with more enthusiasm, than any woman had taken him before; the rosebud shaped birthmark at the base of her spine; the satin of her legs wrapped around his hips, the soft little sounds she made when he kissed that sensitive spot behind her ear; the way she screamed his name when she came.

But there was more. Much, much more. He liked the way her smile lit up her eyes; he admired the way she'd taken those lemons her ex had dumped on her and turned them into day spa lemonade. He enjoyed her enthusiasm when she talked about her business; got a kick out of knowing that she'd seen all his movies, and liked the fact that her opinions of each role were honest, even if they weren't always flattering. Such as her belief that he'd made a mistake with that comic action hero flick, something he'd figured out on the first day of filming.

He'd also been damned relieved that she hadn't seemed to hold a grudge against him for having taken off to California.

Which reminded him—he still owed her an explanation.

No time like the present, he decided.

Conveniently overlooking the fact that it was eleven-thirty at night, he flipped open his cell phone.

While Regan Callahan didn't sound all that thrilled to be awakened for the second night in a row, Nate remained his typically unflappable self.

"No problem," he said.

That little matter taken care of, Gabe left the cabin, climbed into the pirogue tied to the dock, and headed across the wine-dark water toward Blue Bayou.

And Emma.

Thirteen

Gabe admittedly hadn't formulated much of a plan about what he'd do after he got to Emma's house. The one contingency he hadn't even considered was the notion that she'd be pulling out of the driveway just as he'd turned the corner onto her street.

It was nearly midnight. Where the hell was she going? To meet another man?

"The hell she is."

He wasn't stalking her, Gabe assured himself as he took off after the Miata. Not really. Even here in Blue Bayou, a woman driving alone in the middle of the night could be asking for trouble. He was merely looking out for her; the same way he'd want to protect anyone.

"Yeah, right." And if anyone believed that, he just happened to have a bridge to sell.

Less than ten minutes later, she came to a stop in front of a pair of tall wrought-iron gates surrounded on three sides by water. Having followed at a discreet distance, just like that detective he'd ridden around with researching his up-

coming cop role had taught him to do, Gabe cut the headlights of the borrowed Callahan and Son Construction truck,
pulled over to the side of the road and watched as Emma
climbed out of her car.

The cemetery gate, badly in need of oil, squeaked as she
opened it, then it slammed shut behind her. Wondering what
the hell kind of assignation the woman might have in a graveyard in the middle of the night, Gabe followed, hiding in the
shadows.

The scent of impending rain rode a night air scented with
night-blooming jasmine and damp brick. A ring circled a
full white moon, casting a ghostly gleam over crumbling
stone angels draped in a veil of thick gray fog.

Bullfrogs croaked; cicadas buzzed; fireflies winked on
and off amidst the limbs of oak trees draped in silvery Spanish moss.

Gabe watched Emma make her way across the uneven,
shell-strewn ground to a tomb covered with Xs. He recognized the tomb, which had over the centuries faded to a
dusky pink and begun to sink into the marshy ground, as belonging to Marie Dupree, a nineteenth-century voodoo priestess and ancestor of Roxi Dupree. The Xs on the brick signified
requests for spiritual intervention; the coins, shells, and
beads littering the ground around the moss-covered stone
were offerings in appreciation of wishes granted, or in hopes
of spells yet to be spun.

Emma took a small spade from a black backpack she'd
taken from the car, and removed a bit of earth from in front
of the tomb. Gabe couldn't make out her softly spoken
words, but suspected they must be some sort of incantation.
She retrieved something else from the pack, placed it in the
shallow hole, then covered it up with the soil she'd removed.

There were more words. The glint of metal as she scattered some coins and purple, gold, and green Mardi Gras
beads onto the ground.

An owl hooted; a blue heron glided low over the night black water.

Gabe was tempted to step out from behind the broken-winged stone angel and ask what was going on. At the very least, he wanted to dig up whatever it was Emma had buried.

Later.

First he'd make sure she got home safely. Then he'd return to the graveyard and learn what the hell the woman had been up to.

The idea that she'd probably had her friend cook up a love spell had him smiling all the way back to Emma's blue and white shotgun house.

Fourteen

It was even better than a love spell.

Three times, Gabe read the piece of paper Emma had buried. The first time her words—written in that tidy hand the nuns at Holy Assumption school had tried to drill into their students—made him hard.

The second time made him ache.

The third time had him debating whether or not to yank open his jeans and take care of the throbbing hard-on himself.

He could do that.

There'd been a time he probably would've. It was a logical, practical solution to the problem.

But after being inside Emma, after feeling those silky moist walls tighten around his dick and milk him so hard he was amazed he had any fillings left in his teeth, Gabe didn't want practical. Or logical.

What he wanted was Emma. Lying beneath him. Writhing. Screaming his name to high heaven.

Mais, yeah.

He'd already discovered, firsthand, how down and dirty the lady could be. To literally unearth proof of her vivid sexual fantasy life was like icing on a very sweet cake.

He rolled the paper back up. Retied the scarlet ribbon and put the list in his shirt pocket.

Emma didn't know it yet, but she was about to get lucky. They both were.

Although she'd tried to put Gabe out of her mind after burying that list of fantasies in the graveyard last night, he'd billowed in her thoughts, taunting, teasing, and oh, God, yes tasting.

"A man with as much sexual energy as Gabriel Broussard isn't going to be all that easy to get rid of," Roxi said knowingly, after Emma had complained for the third time that day about the spell not working.

"So, what do I do?"

"Keep him?"

"Sure, that's a great idea." Emma glared over at the pink draped altar. "I don't suppose you have a spell that'll make him want to give up the high life in Hollywood, come back and live in his father's old trailer while he changes tires and rebuilds engines at Dix's Automotive."

"I think the bayou reclaimed Claude's trailer after that tropical storm hit last fall."

"Don't be so literal." Emma took a vicious bite of the shrimp po'boy sandwich she'd ordered out from Cajun Cal's. "My point, and I do have one, is that there's nothing here for Gabe."

"There's you."

"Right." Emma held up her left hand, palm up. "Let's see. Glamorous Hollywood actresses, supermodels, and wild, hedonistic parties at the Playboy mansion." She lifted her right hand. "A former chubbette living in a dead-end town where the highlight of the entertainment week is Arlan Dupree changing the movie posters down at the Bijou."

"Blue Bayou isn't exactly a dead-end town."

"Does or does not the highway end here?"

Roxi shook the bottle of hot sauce over a red and white cardboard container of popcorn shrimp. If she weren't her best friend, Emma would've envied the way she could eat fried food every day without gaining an ounce. "Now, who's being too literal? Besides, it was always obvious to anyone who wanted to notice that there was something between you and Gabe."

"We were just friends."

"Which was why you wrote Mrs. Gabriel Broussard all over your seventh grade science notebook. And why you volunteered to paint scenery the year Mrs. Herlihy cast him in Sweeny Todd."

"All right. I stand corrected. He just thought of me as a friend. While I had a schoolgirl crush on him. But that was a long time ago. Lives change. People move on. Grow up."

Roxi rolled her dark eyes. "You may as well change your name to Cleopatra Quinlan, girlfriend. Because you are definitely living in denial."

"It's not that easy." Emma wadded up the waxed paper wrapper and tossed it into the wastebasket. It was twelve fifty-five. Dani Callahan, Nate's sister-in-law and Blue Bayou's librarian, had a one o'clock appointment and unlike most of the people in town, Dani was unrelentingly prompt.

"Maybe it shouldn't be easy," Roxi suggested. Sympathy born from years of friendship darkened her whiskey-hued eyes. "Don't knock first loves," she said as she slurped down the last of her R.C. Cola. "Sometimes they're the strongest mojo of all."

It turned out to be a long day. Maybe it was because of the full moon, or some strange alignment of the planets, or perhaps someone had put something in the water supply, because it seemed that everyone in town was suddenly in need of a massage.

It was nearly eight by the time Emma managed to leave Every Body's Beautiful and with her mind focused on taking off her shoes and pouring herself a glass of wine, as she unlocked her front door, she failed to see the truck parked across the street from the house.

She stepped out of the white clogs she wore to work and padded barefoot into the kitchen, where she took out a bottle of wine from the refrigerator.

"Late day," a deep, all-too-familiar voice offered from the shadows.

Emma spun around, one hand gripping the neck of the green bottle, the other splayed across her breast. "You scared me to death."

"Sorry." The man sprawled in the kitchen chair she'd sponge-painted a cheery sunshine yellow one cold gray day last December didn't look the least bit apologetic. He was inexplicably wearing a white silky shirt that laced up across the chest, black leather pants, and high boots polished to a glossy sheen. His long legs were spread open in a blatantly male way that drew Emma's attention to his groin, where the leather cupped his sex like a lover's caress.

"What are you doing here, Gabe?"

"What am I doing?" He rubbed his cleft jaw with those long dark fingers that had created such havoc to her body and her mind.

"I believe that was my question." Emma had spent enough years being the recipient of her mother's scornful tone that she was easily able to borrow it now.

Apparently unwounded by the sharp edge in her voice, he flashed her a wickedly rakish grin. "I'm here to fulfill all your fantasies, *chère*."

A premonition had the fine hairs at the back of her neck

standing on end. Surely he didn't mean . . . he couldn't be talking about . . . he wouldn't have . . . couldn't have . . .

Oh, God. Emma's knees nearly buckled when he tossed the rolled up piece of paper onto her kitchen table.

"Where did you get that?" Surely Roxi wouldn't have given it to him?

"Where you buried it." He clucked his tongue. "You should be more careful with your secrets, *ma belle*. Think what might happen if it fell into the wrong hands. Now I don't much care what folks say about me. But you might be a tad bit embarrassed if everyone in town were to find out that you secretly want to be ravished by Jean Lafitte."

"It's only a fantasy." Still unnerved by the outrageous idea of him following her out to the graveyard, Emma refused to give him the satisfaction of knowing that her fantasy wasn't of the pirate himself, but of Gabe playing the part. "And you had no business stalking me."

"I wasn't stalking." He folded his arms and had the effrontery to look annoyed. "I was lookin' out for your welfare, me."

"Of course you were." Not.

"It's the truth. I was on my way here to talk to you, when I saw you leaving the house—"

"You had a sudden need for a midnight chat?"

"Well, actually, if you want the unvarnished truth, the more driving need was for a midnight fuck. But I figured we could talk afterwards."

"Has anyone ever suggested you may possess a few Neanderthal tendencies?"

He shrugged. "Don't know about that. I am what I am."

"No kidding, Popeye."

The thing was, Gabe's claim about being his own man was absolutely true. Emma had never met an individual, male or female, with a stronger sense of self. Or with more self-confidence. How many other men, growing up with

Claude Broussard for a father, would've taken the easy way out and become the juvenile delinquent the entire town, including her parents, had probably expected him to be? Her parents had certainly forbidden her to date him, which had been a moot point since she'd have been just as likely to be asked out by Brad Pitt.

"At first I thought maybe you were off to some assignation with another man."

"And what business would that have been of yours?"

"You know, sugar, that was the exact same thing I asked myself. And you know the answer I came up with?"

"What?"

"I don't like to share." The suddenly hard gleam in his midnight blue eyes echoed that claim.

"Even if you had any claim on me, which you don't, that attitude is *so* chauvinistic."

"Guess it's that pesky Neanderthal in me," he said agreeably. "The same old-fashioned guy who thinks maybe he ought to watch out for any woman crazy enough to be driving around alone on dark country roads in the middle of the night. Which, like I said, was why I followed you to the cemetery."

He rubbed the side of his nose. Shook his dark head. "I gotta tell you, darlin', you sure as hell threw me a curve when you pulled up outside that old iron gate. At first I wondered if maybe you were one of those females who get off doin' it in graveyards."

"I believe you're the one of us who's into kink."

"Now, see, before you got off on lickin' that fluffy white cream off my dick, I might've believed that." He untied the red ribbon, and smoothed the scroll with his palm. "You already had me tied up in sexual knots, *chère*. But reading this just made things a helluva lot more interesting."

"I'm so pleased I can provide you some entertainment while you're stuck here."

"You know, that uppity princess-to-peasant tone might

work real well when we get down to playing voodoo queen and her obedient love slave."

He tapped the second item on her fantasy list. The damn list Roxi had instructed Emma to write out, claiming that by burying it in the cemetery at midnight, she'd be rid of the hot scenes that had been plaguing her mind. Scenes starring, of course, Gabriel Broussard. "But it just doesn't fit with the number one fantasy on your personal sexual hit parade."

"You had no right reading a private document." She lunged for the list.

He raised it just out of reach. "Less things have changed in the last ten years, the cemetery's a public place. Shouldn't have left your *private document* there if you weren't willin' to risk someone coming along and reading it."

"Excuse me for not anticipating stalkers with shovels."

"*Dieu*, you sure got a sassy mouth on you." He leaned closer. Skimmed a hand over her shoulder. "I must be getting perverted in my old age, because for some reason, you abusing me this way is startin' to turn me on."

"So, what else is new?" She batted away his hand. "From what I can tell, everything turns you on."

"Everything 'bout you," he agreed. "Could've been worse if Harlan Breaux got hold of it."

Harlan Breaux was what Gabe, having grown up with Claude Broussard, might have become. A stereotypical Southern bully, Harlan had a beer belly and a bad attitude right out of *Deliverance*. He'd spent time in Angola for rape, returned with his arms covered with prison tattoos, and there wasn't a woman in town who'd want to come across him in a dark alley. Or even, for that matter, in the middle of the town square at noon.

"You're right." Emma blew out a breath. "Going out alone at midnight probably wasn't the smartest thing I've ever done."

"Lucky thing I just happened to be there when you buried your love spell."

"Shows how much you know." Emma folded her arms across her breasts. Breasts that had begun to ache for his touch. "It wasn't a love spell." Her smile was sweetly false. "It was a go-away love spell."

He laughed at that. "Like that's gonna happen." He bent down and retrieved a shopping bag bearing the name of a popular New Orleans costume shop from behind the chair. "I brought you a little present. To help you get in the mood."

Expecting some sort of barely there froth of Victoria's Secret satin and lace, she was surprised to pull out a wide leather belt and heavy brown muslin skirt.

"Well, this is certainly sexy."

"You don't need frou-frou stuff to be sexy. Besides, you're a pirate's captive." He reminded her of not only her fantasy, but the scene from *The Last Pirate*. "It wasn't as if you had time to pack before I stole you away from that Spanish captain's ship."

"That was a movie."

He shrugged. "A movie's just another way of lookin' at fantasies. How about it, *chère*? Tonight you'll be my captive." He tunneled his hand beneath her hair, cupped the nape of her neck and kissed her, a hard, predatory kiss that caused needs to well up inside her. "I'll do things to you. Wild, wicked things."

His arm curved around her, anchoring her against him; he was hard, urgent, but in no way did Emma feel truly threatened. "Impossible things." His hand bunched up the flowing, calf-length broomstick skirt she'd worn to work, caressing the back of her leg, her thigh, the curve of her hip. "I'm going to spend this entire weekend taking you places, Emma. Wonderful places beyond your most daring fantasies."

His fingers slipped beneath the waistband of her panties, reminding her that, having given up on being with him again in this way, she was—oh, damn!—wearing plain white cotton.

She sucked in a sharp breath as his teeth nipped at the tender cord in her neck at the same time his fingers tightened on her bottom.

"And then, since, despite what you consider my Neanderthal tendencies, I'm all for equality; when we get around to playing Voodoo Queen, you can call the shots."

Common sense told her that all he wanted was to fuck her.

And your problem with that is?

Good point. The truth, as much as she might like to deny it, was that Gabe had reawakened something inside Emma. Something that had remained dormant all during her marriage. Something that she'd only experienced once before.

So what if what he was offering was only about sex?

In all her nearly twenty-eight years, until the other night at the camp, she'd only experienced true passion once in her life. But for some reason she'd never truly understood, he'd pulled back, leaving her virginity intact.

Hoping to recreate that passion, she'd married Richard, who'd left her believing she'd only imagined that hot, burning-up-from-the-inside-out way she'd felt with Gabriel.

But then Gabe had come back to town. And all it had taken was one knowing look from those fathomless blue eyes, one touch of those wickedly clever hands, for Emma to realize that she hadn't imagined a thing.

And, amazingly, the fever was burning hotter than it had ten years ago.

Some things hadn't changed.

Gabriel still wasn't offering forever after.

But he was offering a sexual experience women all over the planet could only dream about.

"I can't spend the entire weekend with you. It's Jean Lafitte Days," she elaborated at his arched brow. "I'm Deputy Mayor. I have responsibilities."

She watched him process that, even as she tried to decide what she'd do about the ultimatum she feared was coming.

"These responsibilities," he said slowly. Thoughtfully. "How much time they gonna take?"

Emma blinked. "Well, Nate can open the festival by himself. And the food and carnival booth committees have those things pretty well covered." Roxi had been bubbling up potions for the past month to sell at her pink and gold Hex Appeal tent. "I'm supposed to be co-grand marshal of the parade." She had been looking forward to riding in that powder blue Caddy convertible rumored to have belonged to Elvis. But compared to having sex with Gabe, it was no contest. "But Roxi can do that." After all, she already had the wave down pat.

"But, I'm not going to miss giving Mrs. Herlihy that plaque." Emma lifted her chin, prepared for an argument.

"Which is when?"

"Sunday night."

"Well, then." He nodded, surprising her by accepting the compromise. "Sounds like we should stop wasting time and get on with workin' our way down this list."

"I have a hard time picturing you doing whatever I say." It was hard—make that impossible—to imagine Gabriel in a submissive role.

"I'll do whatever gives you pleasure, *chère,*" he said in a rough, deep voice. "They're your fantasies. If I'm doin' things right, and believe me, I intend to, you'll be pleasured, whichever one of us is callin' the shots."

Emma believed that. Because everything about Gabe gave her pleasure.

"I want to push your limits," he said. "To show you how far you can go. How far we can go together. I may command you to do things your logical mind never thought you'd do. Things that may even frighten you. But you'll do them. Willingly. Eagerly."

"You're that sure of me?"

His lips curved in a slow, wickedly erotic smile that could have been one Lucifer had pulled out to convince all those heavenly angels to join him in hell. "I'm that sure of *us*. You'll do them because you've dreamed of them, in the darkest, most secret corners of your mind and heart. You'll do them because, deep down inside that magnificently lush body, is the soul of a sexual adventuress."

The certainty of his growled words made her wet. But the part of her who'd overcome the humiliation of being the cheated upon wife, needed to get one last thing clear before surrendering power.

"If you're looking for a submissive to play French maid to your macho, sexual dominant, you've got the wrong woman."

He laughed at that. A rich, hearty, bold rumble of sound that vibrated inside her every cell.

"Lucky for me the store was all out of French maid out-fits," he said. "I want you, Emma." He skimmed his palm down the front of her top. "And, if the way your nipples harden at my touch, and watching your blood beating like a bunny in your pretty white throat are any indication, you want me, too." His words were as soft as ebony silk; his touch, as his fingers plucked at her taut nipples, stole her breath. "Would it make you feel any safer if I promised never to hurt you?"

She believed him with every fiber of her being. And that belief made her bolder than she would have ever thought possible.

She met his hot, sexy gaze with a sizzling, challenging one of her own. "What kind of pirate would that be?"

His bold, pleased grin was echoed in his eyes. "Not a very good fantasy one, that's for certain." He tangled a hand in her hair and tugged with a sensual force that sent a frisson of delicious anticipation/fear skimming down her spine. "How about I rephrase that?" The hand that was still on her breast tightened, squeezing her flesh. "I'd never intentionally harm anyone. Especially a woman. Most especially you, *mon douce ami.*"

My sweet love. Endearments seemed to come trippingly off Gabe's tongue. But tonight, for this stolen time of midnight fantasies, Emma chose to believe him.

"You've got to believe that I'd rather break my own bones than cause you any injury," he continued. "And I'd never inflict any pain that you're not willing—and eager—to accept. Or that doesn't give you pleasure."

The idea of a painful pleasure was frightening. Exciting. And impossible to turn down.

Having grown up under the disapproving thumb of her mother, it had taken Emma a great deal of effort to develop the self-esteem necessary to rise from the rubble of her marriage and reinvent herself into a woman she could be proud of. If asked, she would have insisted there was no longer a submissive cell in her body.

She was discovering she'd be wrong.

Submission to Richard the dickhead would be a waste of energy.

Submission to a man strong enough to know what to do with such a valuable gift was proving thrilling.

Emma lowered her gaze to the floor. Gathered herself inward. Then, slipping more easily into character than she would have ever believed possible, she gazed demurely up at Gabe through her lashes. Her thighs were quaking; her entire body was pulsating with need with the instinctive, eons-old biological need of a sexual female for a dominant male.

"I believe you, Gabriel."

Fifteen

A blue flame rose in Gabe's eyes. Watching him carefully through her lowered lashes, she saw the flare of masculine satisfaction.

"Now, there's a good wench." She wasn't the only one who could play a role. Then again, she reminded herself, role-playing was what Gabe did for a living.

Did he play these kinds of sexual games with his other women?

Don't go there.

His gaze was that of a predator, confident of its prey. "Your fate is ultimately in your hands, Emma. Whenever I command you to do something, you'll respond, 'Yes, my lord.' However, if there's any barrier that goes against your moral code, or which you find too difficult to overcome, you'll answer, 'If it pleases you, my lord,' and I'll understand that it's something you honestly don't want to do."

"What happens if I respond in that second manner?"

"I suppose you'll learn the answer to that, if—and when—the time comes."

It was not the most reassuring of answers. But, even as pinpoints of anxiety prickled her skin, Emma's body was electrified by the possibilities.

"Yes, my lord."

"Good answer." He yanked her against him, his arousal a long, hard ridge between them, his mouth taking hers.

The savage, claiming kiss ended far too soon. Emma's head was still spinning when he released her and picked up the skirt and belt she'd dropped onto the floor.

"Take off your clothes. Then put this on."

She was uncomfortable about going topless, but since he seemed to honestly enjoy her breasts, Emma decided she could live with that. Fortunately, the skirt was full enough to cover a multitude of flaws.

"Yes, my lord." She took the skirt and headed toward the bedroom to change. She'd only gone two steps when Gabe grasped her arm and jerked her back towards him.

"Where do you think you're going?"

"To change." Even knowing this was just a game they were playing, the disapproving male energy emanating from him turned her mouth as dry as dust. "My lord," she tacked on.

His long, leather-clad legs were braced apart, his muscled arms crossed over his chest. "Did I give you permission to leave the room?"

"No, my lord, but—"

"There are no *buts* allowed, wench. Perhaps you don't understand your position." He cupped her chin in an unyielding grip and lifted her wary gaze to his implacably stony one. "You are my prisoner." If she hadn't known better, she might have thought she was standing before the actual Jean Lafitte. "You will do whatever I say." His fingers tightened on her jaw. "When I say it." His other hand grasped her breast and squeezed. Hard enough that Emma gasped.

"If I tell you to drop to your knees on the floor and take my cock between your glossy wet lips, you'll do so without hesitation. If I tell you to bend over that chair, so I can take you hard and fast from behind, you'll say, 'Yes, my lord, with pleasure and gratitude,' then bare that smooth white ass in a heartbeat." Her thighs trembled as he ran a wide palm over her ass. "Whatever I demand, you acquiesce to. Quickly. Willingly." She whimpered as he cupped her. "Is that understood?"

Emma felt the color flame in her cheeks. She was not used to being talked to so strongly by anyone. She was especially not accustomed to being treated like some nameless sex slave.

Yet, that was exactly what she'd agreed to. What she wanted.

She ducked her head. "Yes, my lord." She risked a glance up at the kitchen fixture that was a thousand times brighter than the muted, flattering candlelight in the cabin. "May your prisoner request that the light—"

"Will be left on." His rough tone was harsh. Implacable. Exactly, she realized, like his character's had been in *The Last Pirate,* when he'd told his frightened captive that she could expect no mercy from a pirate rogue. "Looking at you pleases me."

"Bu—" Remembering his warning against arguing, she tried a different tact. "Please, my lord." She placed a hand on his forearm and felt the stony muscle clench beneath her fingertips.

"Either you take those clothes off, or I'll do it for you." He trailed a fingertip down the row of pearl buttons at the front of her blouse. "And believe me, if you leave it to me, you'll never wear them again."

The buttons seemed to have shrunk since she'd gotten dressed this morning. Emma's fingers felt large and awkward as she took an unusually long time to unbutton the blouse. All too aware of his steady stare, she dropped it onto the floor, then shoved the billowy skirt down her legs.

"There." Resisting the urge to cross her arms over her breasts, she lifted her chin and glared at him, submissiveness temporarily replaced by anger darkened by embarrassment.

Was it so wrong for a woman to want to appear beautiful to the man she was about to sleep with? Surely even a size zero, with perky, bought boobs and a spa-toned butt and stomach would feel uncomfortable bathed in such bright, flaw-revealing artificial light.

"That's a good start." He nodded his approval. "The bra has to go. I liked the lacy one a helluva lot better."

A spark of irritation flared. Emma forced it back down again. "Excuse me, my lord. Since I didn't hear from you yesterday, I had no reason to expect you to make an appearance this evening."

Gabe arched a brow. "So, my *'tite chatte* has claws." He enjoyed her little flash of rebellion. He didn't want to bring his luscious little wench to her knees. All right, perhaps he did, but only to take his throbbing erection between her pretty lips.

He had no plans to force her to obey his commands, but preferred to accept her submission as a gift. The scarlet flush spreading across her chest like a fever revealed her struggle with her redhead's temper. A temper, he suspected, she wasn't even entirely aware she possessed.

If things went according to plan, Emma was about to discover a great many things about herself. Including the depths of her capacity for hot passion.

She reached behind her back, the quick, furious gesture pushing her breasts out in a provocative way that had him wanting to thrust his hard-on between those soft white globes. Emma wasn't the only one struggling with control. Gabe was definitely teetering on a razor's edge.

The way she tossed the bra aside suggested that she found it no more appealing than he did. He was going to have to take her shopping at one of those frou-frou lingerie shops in

New Orleans. Gabe liked the idea of watching his voluptuous wench model skimpy bits of silk and lace for his approval. Of course, the trick would be managing not to take her in the dressing room.

Then again . . . That idea was unreasonably arousing. In fact, Gabe was finding everything about the lushly sexy Emma arousing.

"We'll burn those underpants," he said. "They look like something a nun might wear to keep impure thoughts at bay."

"If it pleases you to do so, my lord," she said between gritted teeth.

"Does my captive wench have a problem with my command?" He moved closer, causing her to gasp when he scraped his thumbnail across the rosy pink tips of her breasts.

"It does seem like a waste of money. My lord," she tacked on.

"Ah, but I'm filthy rich," he reminded her. "From all the plundering and looting we pirates do," he tacked on, struggling to stay in character when what he wanted to do was to drag her by that wild mass of unruly red curls into the bedroom, or hell, onto the floor, and bury himself deep into her moist, welcoming warmth. "You'll take them off. Now."

Her hands went to the elastic waistband. Then paused. She glanced up at the light again. "I don't suppose—"

"I want to see you," he repeated. More sternly this time. Both he and his privateer alter ego intended to make this point perfectly clear. "I enjoy your voluptuous body." He put his hand beneath a heavy breast and lifted it to his mouth, drawing forth a ragged moan from between her parted lips as he suckled deeply on the satiny flesh.

"It suggests you're a woman with other appetites." He moved to the other breast, dampening it with his tongue while his hand moved between them, over the soft swell of her stomach, downward over her mound, to the drenched crotch of the underpants he was tempted to feed to the gators. Who probably had enough sense in their reptilian brains not to want them, either. "God, you're wet."

Her hips were rotating in unconsciously erotic little circles, as she ground her pelvis against his caressing touch in a way that triggered primitive impulses. "I can't help it, my lord."

"Definitely a woman of lusty appetites." Growing impatient, he shoved the white cotton down, and cupped her. Which was all it took to make her come in a hard release, arching her back, practically collapsing against him.

"That's one," he said, vastly pleased with himself. And with his Emma. He'd never met a more responsive woman. Nor one whose lustiness equaled his own. Certainly not all the women he'd been with over the years since leaving Blue Bayou, women who were, according to some artificial, arbitrarily imposed standard of female looks, some of the most beautiful women in the world, who, if truth be known, more often than not failed to live up to their sexy billing.

It was, after all, hard for a woman to give a guy a blow job when she was so concerned about smearing her lip gloss or the number of calories in semen, that she totally forgot about the guy whose dick was in her mouth. And it was damn hard to have bend-each-other-into-pretzels monkey sex with a woman who was all the time sucking in her already concave stomach or clenching her nearly nonexistent butt in hopes it'd look smaller.

Once he was certain she could stand on her own, Gabe released her and lifted his hand to his mouth. "You taste sweeter than *ruiz au lait*, *chère*." With his eyes locked on her widened ones, he slowly licked her essence from his fingers, one at a time. "Now, let's try out those new clothes your lord and master bought you."

Although he'd wanted the damn ugly panties gone, Gabe nearly swallowed his tongue as she rid herself of the white cotton underwear with a sexy little shimmy of her hips. Then she stepped into the skirt and fastened the wide belt around her waist. The heavy material flowed over her hips in a way that would've obscured her smooth white thighs. If he'd left it the way it had originally been designed. Which he'd had no intention of doing.

"I had the shop sew on some extra fasteners." He reached behind her, gathered up a fistful of rough brown muslin, and attached it to the Velcro strip on the belt.

"Gabe!" Shocked, she looked back over her shoulder at her sweet, bared ass.

He glowered at her from beneath lowered brows. "What did you call me?"

"I'm sorry. My lord." She actually ducked in a cute little curtsey that had him thinking that one of these days they might revisit that French maid idea. "It's just that I'm so . . . bare."

"All the better for me to see you." He turned her around and smoothed his palm over the bared flesh. "Touch you." She yelped as he lightly smacked a rounded cheek with his palm. "Punish you if you dare to disobey my commands. Or perhaps"—he spanked her again, then let his fingers linger— "just because it pleases me to do so." He tilted his head, studying the faint mark. "Pink's a flattering color for you, *chère*. Reminds me of ripe strawberries on cream. I'm thinkin' I could eat you up with a spoon."

He splayed his hands on her hips in fine pirate fashion, turned her back to face him again, making the same adjustments with the front of the skirt. "It keeps you accessible to me at all times," he explained in a voice roughened with his own almost unbearable hunger. This master stuff was proving harder than he'd imagined. "And you've got such a sweet little pussy, you should show it off more often."

Color even brighter than that on her bottom rose in her face. "What an intriguing idea. And would my lord visit me in prison after I got arrested for flashing the good citizens of Blue Bayou?"

He laughed. *Dieu*, he loved her spunk! "We'd have conjugal visits every day, *ma jolie fille*." He tugged playfully at the gossamer flame fluff between her thighs. "And twice on Sunday." He bent his head.

Emma sank into the kiss he bestowed upon her. A surprisingly gentle, even tender kiss that was totally at odds with the out-of-control pounding of her heart.

"We'd best be going," he groaned against her lips. "Before I forget my resolution to make this last and take you here and now."

"Going?" The words sliced through her sensual lassitude. When he placed his hand against the small of her bare back, just above the wide leather belt, and began leading her toward the kitchen door, she dug in her heels. "Where?"

He tilted his head. Something hot and dangerous shimmered in the midnight depths of his eyes. "Dare you question your lord and master?" His tone was dark. Ominous, almost, Emma thought as apprehension battled hotly with anticipation in her loins.

Was he still acting? Or had they crossed a line she hadn't realized existed?

She drew in a breath and tried to sort through her spinning, tumultuous thoughts. It was one thing to act out her fantasy here, in the privacy of her own home. But to risk being caught in such an embarrassing, compromising situation . . . How would she ever live it down?

He stared at her intently. "It's not that difficult a question." With deliberate slowness, he curled his long dark fingers around her throat. "Either you trust me"—his thumb brushed a feathery caress at the hollow of her neck where her pulse leaped, quickened—"or you don't." He put a booted foot between her bare ones, spreading her legs farther apart, then pulling her tightly against him so she could feel the thick, cylindrical outline of his penis against her naked belly. "Which is it, Emma? *Oui?*"

When he lifted his knee against her mound, stimulating already overly sensitized tissue, she moaned.

"Or *non?*" The question—the challenge—hovered between them, as hot and dangerous as a thunderstorm rumbling on the horizon. A sizzle of electric charge arced between them, from him to her and back again. More heat burned between her legs.

But it was the use of her name, personalizing this game that could have, with some men, turned ugly, that assured Emma she had nothing to fear from this fallen angel in black leather.

She framed his tragically beautiful face between her hands. "There is nothing I will say no to." She went up on her toes to press a submissive kiss of surrender against his boldly cut lips. "My lord."

Sixteen

Sitting beside Gabe in the Callahan and Son construction truck, racing through the dark clad only in her wench skirt and belt, Emma was relieved when he'd shown her the shirt he'd tossed into the backseat of the crew cab, along with the suitcase he'd packed while waiting for her to arrive home. "For you to put on in case we get stopped for some reason," he'd said.

The night air was thick as gumbo and swirled with tension. Emma was quickly realizing that there was a vast difference between fantasy and reality. In her fantasies there weren't any edgy, "what am I supposed to do now" moments. Things just flowed together, erotically, seamlessly.

"You havin' second thoughts 'bout this?"

His voice rumbled in the dark, his accent even thicker than usual.

"Not at all," she hedged.

"Wouldn't be surprising if you were," he assured her. "One of the first things I learned when Mrs. Herlihy put me in her drama class back in high school is that playin' make-

believe isn't always as easy as it looks." He reached across
the stick shift, captured her hand and pressed it against his
groin. "Maybe you need a little something to occupy your
mind. Keep it from fussin' about the logistics of gettin' from
your house to mine."

The tensed steel beneath the black leather fly stirred in a
way that sent a delicious, forbidden thrill through Emma.
She squeezed the thick bulge of his erection, feeling it grow
gloriously thicker. Longer.

Although she was playing the role of a submissive, sexual
prisoner, Emma felt a surge of power that she could cause
such a reaction. Intrigued, she stroked his groin with her
palm and was thrilled by the growl that rumbled upward
from his chest.

The black pants fastened with a metal snap and zipper.
She tapped the snap with her fingernail. "May I have permission to touch?"

"*Mais,* yeah." He arched his hips up. The truck picked up
speed when his boot hit the gas.

"Thank you, my lord." Her gratitude was far from feigned.
The truth was that she was aching to rip away the barrier between her fingers and that hard male flesh.

Gabe sucked in a sharp breath as she slipped her fingertips between the trousers and his burning hot flesh, taking
care of the snap with a deft twist of the wrist. He was naked
beneath the glove-soft leather. Naked and, for now, at least,
all hers.

"I've been dreaming of this," she murmured as she lowered the zipper.

"Don't feel like the fuckin' Lone Ranger," he groaned as
she freed his penis. "I've been so hot the past two days away
from you, I thought I'd explode."

"You could have taken care of it." She wrapped her fingers around the base of his straining shaft. "By solo flying."

"What fun would there be in that?" He took one hand

from the wheel, covered hers, and began moving them together, in a slow, upward motion. "When I can command my little slave to get me off?"

"Your slave is honored to be allowed the privilege of getting you off, my lord."

A vein bulged blue and thick in the muted glow of the dashboard lights. Emma could feel the blood pulsing beneath her stroking touch, a powerful thrumming that echoed the pulsing in the wet, slick, *needy* place between her thighs.

Emma desperately wanted Gabe to pull over and take her then, but knew that by staying in the role, he'd insist on fucking her in his way. On his terms, in his time. Which made her want him even more.

"Harder." His fingers tightened on hers, increasing the pace. "That's the way." He returned his hand to the steering wheel, knuckles whitening from the power of his grip. He spread his thighs farther apart. "*Mon Dieu*, you've got my balls practically jammed into my tonsils."

"Oh, dear." She skimmed her palm over the knobby tip, experimented with a little twist at the top end of the long stroke and was rewarded when he expelled a sharp hiss between his teeth. "We wouldn't want them to feel ignored, they," she said on a fair imitation of his Cajun patois.

She delved a little deeper, cupping first one, then the other. When she lightly skimmed her fingertips between the scrotum dividing them, he cursed. But not, Emma thought, as she spread the moisture down his rampant penis, in a bad way. Snowy white oyster shells sprayed upward in a fantail beneath the tires as he jerked the wheel, pulling over to the side of the road, and cutting the engine.

He closed his eyes and arched his back, lifting his hips, grinding them against her stroking hand, encouraging her with an intoxicating guttural string of French dirty words.

And then he was erupting in an explosive orgasm that was the most amazing, thrilling thing she'd ever witnessed.

"Christ," Gabe gasped. Finally replete, he sagged against the back of the seat, eyes shut, chest heaving. "That was the most fucking amazing hand job anyone's ever given me."

Emma instinctively opened her mouth to deny the compliment. Then she realized that she had, after all, been the one who'd done that. She was the one who'd made him so dramatically lose control.

Feeling pretty damn spectacular, she fought the grin that was threatening to break free. "I merely aim to please, my lord."

Gabe opened one eye. "Oh, you do that, sugar. Spectacularly." He grabbed a handful of tissues from the glove box and was prepared to clean himself off when Emma plucked them from his hand.

"I believe that's my responsibility."

He slumped back. "I believe you're right." He shut his eyes again, but reached out with unerring accuracy and stroked her hair. *"Merci."*

"It was my pleasure, my lord," Emma murmured, touching a kiss to the still semi-erect flesh. Truer words had never been spoken.

The hours passed in a sensual blur, a stolen, fantastic time apart from reality. When she'd agreed to Gabe's proposition, there'd been a secret part of Emma that had feared the reality of acting out her long-held fantasies would not live up to the erotic images in her head.

But she'd been wrong. The reality proved amazingly better.

As soon as they'd arrived at the camp, he'd tied her to the iron bed, arms above her head, legs splayed, giving his hands, his mouth, his tongue absolute access to her most private, secret places.

Except for that unforgettable graduation night with Gabe, when he'd taken her to heights she'd never imagined possible, oral sex had always made Emma nervous. Unfortunately, the more nervous she got, the more tense she became, until it became nearly impossible for her to climax.

Once, at a Christmas party at the country club, she'd overheard Richard complain to a golfing buddy that it took so long for Emma to get off, a guy was risking lockjaw trying to go down on his wife.

At the time, instead of being furious, Emma had been suffused with shame. From then on, she'd faked orgasms to get the unfulfilling act over quickly.

There was no need to fake anything with Gabe. He was the first person, other than Roxi, with whom she didn't have to pretend to be anything but what she was. Which, if she were to believe Gabe, was damn near perfect.

His absolute appreciation of her, of every inch of the body she'd spent so many years trying to cover up, soon had the last of her self-consciousness disintegrating, like morning fog beneath a hot July sun.

She enthusiastically explored her sensuality, allowing Gabe to do as he'd promised, to take her to places she'd never imagined possible. Including the wax.

"This won't hurt," he assured her as he stood over the bed, holding a burning candle in a tall, red glass container. More candles glowed around the room, their flames flickering in dancing patterns against the walls.

She was tied up again, her wrists and ankles encased in fleece-lined leather shackles that could only be opened with the key Gabe was wearing on a black cord around his neck. "Well, it might. But in a good way."

She smiled up at him, utterly confident. "I trust you. My lord." They'd already moved far beyond that initial pirate/captive fantasy, but she'd discovered she enjoyed, in certain instances, such as now, when she was lying helpless and naked, giving Gabe the words along with the power.

"You are beyond incredible." When he bent down and

kissed her, a flare of heat scorched through her body. Smok
billowed in her mind. Then he straightened.

Although she did truly trust him implicitly, Emma couldn
help tensing as he lifted the candle. As he tipped the re
glass.

Instinct had her crying out at the feel of the melted wa
hitting her breast. Her body jerked against the restraints. A
instant later, she realized she hadn't been burned. The wa
felt warm on her skin. Sensual.

Time seemed to slow down to a crawl as Gabe continue
to dribble the wax over her helpless, supine body. Emm
never knew where, exactly, he was going to place the wa
next, moving from her left breast, to her right thigh, the
back up to her right nipple, the other breast, her nipples, he
stomach, her thighs, even the tops of her feet and the littl
round bone at the inside of her ankle. That not knowing wa
both unnerving and exciting. He also varied the tempera
ture—not allowing the wax to get hot enough to scorch he
skin, but no two drops felt the same, which added a slightl
dangerous, fantasy edge to the sex play.

Much, much later, he put the candle down atop a heav
pine dresser and stood, arms folded, studying his handiwor

"That wax looks like sperm," he said. Humor laced hi
deep voice. "You look as if your luscious body is covere
with my sperm, *chère.*"

The idea was more than a little arousing. "I can onl
hope. My lord."

The laughter in his tone gleamed wickedly in his mi
night eyes. "Your captor will take his wench's request und
advisement. Meanwhile—"

He turned his back to retrieve something from the to
drawer of the dresser. Emma drew in a sharp breath when h
turned around and she viewed the knife he held in his han
The light from the burning candles glistened threateningl
on the sharpened steel.

"We'd best clean you off."

This was Gabe, Emma reminded herself as an unwilling stab of fear struck. The man she loved. The man who'd sworn never to hurt her.

"Yes, please." It was barely a whisper, but easily heard in the hush stillness of the candlelit room. Her lids drifted closed as she waited for the touch of the blade against her naked flesh.

"You'll watch me."

It was not a request. Emma opened her eyes. The primitive sight of the rampantly aroused male, the cold steel of the hunting weapon, the taboo situation he'd created for them, had her body quaking with lust.

"Yes."

He smiled. Pressed the side of the blade to her breast, which flamed beneath the darkly dangerous touch. "You'll need to hold absolutely still, *chère*," he said gently. "So I don't cut you."

"That may be," Emma admitted on a voice thickened with desire, "the hardest thing you've asked of me, yet."

His smile promised yet more wicked delights. "A woman of appetites," he murmured. "And she's all mine."

Emma had no concept of how long it took for Gabe to scrape the cool wax off her body. She did know that by the time he'd finished cleaning her, she was nearly out of her mind with lust.

"You're wet." He slipped his fingers into her. "And hot." There was a deep, sucking sound as he pulled them back out again. "Are you hungry, *ma belle*?"

"Starving," she moaned, arching against his touch, lifting her hips as high as the restraints would allow. Had it not been for the fleece linings, she could have cut her skin, she was so desperate for relief.

"A woman of strong appetites," he murmured approvingly, as he took the key from around his neck and one by one, opened the locks. He ran his hand possessively down her body, from her throat to her knees. "And you're all mine."

"Yours," Emma said on a gasp as he surged into her.

It was the last either of them would say for a very long time.

Seventeen

"Why did you leave?" she asked, over a supper of shrimp etouffee. Not only had Gabe given her more orgasms than she could count, he'd also fed her the best meals of her life.

"I figured it was the right thing to do." When the crocodile kitchen timer dinged, he crossed the room and took a pan of bread pudding from the oven. Emma couldn't decide which made her drool more—the scent of that sweet baked pudding or the sight of Gabe's firm hard butt in those jeans he'd put back on. "I didn't have any prospects. You were going off to college in the fall. No way was I going to ask you to give up your dreams to chase mine."

"You were my dream." She was no longer embarrassed to admit it.

"Could've been a dead-end one," he said. "By the time it looked like I was goin' to be working pretty regular, you'd gotten married."

Gabe remembered Nate's phone call as if it had been yesterday. He was admittedly foggy about the next few days, having spent them in a drunken pity party of self-recrimination.

"You could have written."

"Last time I checked, the mail goes both ways," he said mildly, as he poured the hot whiskey sauce over the pudding.

"You didn't exactly leave a forwarding address."

"Nate always knew where I was."

During the past few days Gabe had come to the conclusion that Nate knew a lot of things. He also suspected that if he'd checked, that so-called construction emergency that had Emma meeting him at the airport would turn out to be as bogus as Richard the dickhead's tax return.

Not that he minded. In fact, Gabe decided, as he carried the two bowls of pudding back to the bed they'd hardly left this weekend, maybe he'd buy his best friend a case of Scotch as a thank-you gift.

"Let's not rehash the past, Emma," he said, handing her one of the heavy earthenware bowls. "We'll leave yesterday behind, worry about tomorrow when it comes." He stuck a finger into his bowl, scooped out some of the brown sugar whiskey sauce and drew a ring around Emma's plump pink nipple. "Right now, I'm suddenly feelin' hungry again, me."

Eighteen

Emma was in the bathroom, getting dressed for the presentation ceremony when the phone rang.

"I think the jig's up," Nate said without preamble. "A couple reporters from the *Enquirer* just dropped by the mayor's office, asking questions about you."

"I'm surprised it took them this long," Gabe said. He'd been half expecting the hungry hoards to descend on him since he'd first arrived. He'd also decided that if any reporter tried to intrude on his and Emma's weekend, he would've dug out Nate's old twelve-gauge shotgun. "Do me a favor." He told Nate what he had in mind.

"No problem. Just make sure you send Regan and me an invite to the wedding."

"The lady hasn't said yes, yet."

"Women can be funny that way," Nate allowed. "Lord knows, my bride, she tested my resolve when it came to settling down. But I convinced her to see the light."

That was an understatement. When they and their adopted

teenage son had visited him in L.A. last fall, Gabe had never seen two people more enthralled with each other's company.

It was then that he'd first started thinkin' that maybe that's what he wanted for himself. And, as always, whenever his mind went wandering down that path, it led straight to Emma Quinlan.

The entire town showed up for the ceremony. Even Emma's mother and father were there, looking tanned and fit after two weeks spent on a ship cruising the Greek Islands.

Neither looked all that pleased to see their daughter enter the high school auditorium with Blue Bayou's former bad boy.

"Broussard," her father said.

"Sir," Gabe responded. As far as he was concerned, the guy was nearly as much of a dickhead as Emma's ex, but since she'd been unfortunate enough to have him for a father, Gabe was going to pay him respect if it killed him. Only for her. There was nothing he wouldn't do for his lush, lusty wench.

"Gabriel." Angela Quinlan somehow managed to hold her surgically perfected nose in the air while looking down at him. Which should have been even more difficult since she was a good foot shorter than his six feet two. She was also so bony a stiff wind would blow her away. Which had him suddenly wishing for a hurricane. Or maybe a tornado.

"Miz Quinlan," he said politely, smiling as he imagined a house dropping out of a stormy sky onto Emma's mother.

"I was surprised you'd come back to Blue Bayou," she said. If her tone had been any icier, there'd be frost all over the green, purple, and gold crepe paper strung across the ceiling. "Now that you're so famous, or should I say infamous"—her teeth flashed like a barracuda's as she layered the acid scorn onto the word—"there's nothing here for you anymore."

"*Mais, oui*, there sure enough is," he drawled, rocking back on his heels as he gave Emma a look hot enough to melt the metal rafters. He put an openly possessive arm around a shoulder he knew was sporting a little love bite from this morning when they'd gotten a little frisky in bed with the beignets.

"Emma?" From her tone, Gabe figured that if it weren't for the Botox keeping her forehead an expressionless slate, Angela Quinlan's brow would've climbed into her perfectly coiffed blond hair. "What is this"—she paused, as if seeking some word allowable in public—"actor talking about?"

Before Emma could respond, Nate was calling her name over the microphone, asking her to come present the elderly teacher with her award.

Obviously torn, Emma's concerned gaze moved from the stage to Gabe to her parents to Gabe again, then back toward the stage. Her green eyes reminded Gabe of the time a bird had gotten caught in the cabin, and had been frantically trying to find a way to escape.

"You'd better go do your deputy mayor thing," he said. "I'll just stay here and chat with your *maman* and dad."

"I don't know—"

He pulled her up against him for a quick, hard kiss and was pleased when, even while her mother was emanating enough frost and ice to cover Jupiter, he could still make her blood heat.

"It'll be okay," he said. He ran a hand down her hair, which she'd smoothed out before leaving for town, but was already breaking into those bright curls he loved. "I promise."

"Okay." She breathed out a sigh.

He caught her arm as she began making her way through the crowd, which had begun talking about that hot public kiss they'd just witnessed between Emma Quinlan and bad boy Gabriel Broussard. "When you get done with your speechifying, why don't you call me up to give Mrs. Herlihy that plaque."

"Are you sure?"

"Absolutely."

Her smile lit up her face. That lovely, generous face Gabe knew would still be able to make his heart turn over when he was an old man, retired from the movie business, sitting out on the *gallerie* at the camp, making love to his Emma in that wooden swing.

"There's somethin' you both should know," he said to her parents, who were still looking properly scandalized by that kiss as Emma walked to the stage. *Mon Dieu,* Gabe was enjoying pissing off these two! "I'm gonna marry Emma, me. Now, you can make things difficult, or you can go along with the program. Which I suggest you do, 'cause, if Emma agrees we'll be making ourselves a lot of babies. Now, personally, I don't give a rat's ass if you ever visit your grandchildren or not, but I've got the feeling Emma will care. So, we may as well all just pretend to get along. For her sake."

"You haven't changed, Broussard," her father said. "You're still a bastard coonass."

"Well, that may be. But at least I'm not doin' time in prison like the dickhead."

Suddenly he heard Emma calling his name. Gabe had never heard it sound sweeter than when it came from her sweet lips.

The elderly mentor blushed to the roots of her lavender hair as Gabe told the gathered crowd how every success he had in the movie business, he owed to his former teacher. Then he kissed her, a smack right on her scarlet tinted lips. The crowd cheered. Gabe didn't care. All that mattered to him was the pride in those faded blue eyes and the love in Emma's gaze as both women looked up at him.

"I've got one more announcement to make," he said.

"And, lucky for us, we've got some esteemed members of the press, from the *Enquirer*, in the back of the room."

Heads spun around. The two reporters, thought Gabe, though those words were stretching what they did for a living, looked uncomfortable. And more than a little nervous. Which vastly added to his enjoyment of the situation.

"There's been talk about my getting engaged recently, and I'd like to go on record saying that some of that story's true."

There was an audible gasp.

"I'm lookin' to get myself married." He reached out and took Emma's hand, knowing that she'd truly trusted him when it didn't turn cold at the unexpected remark. "If the lady will accept me."

Her eyes filled with moisture as she flung her arms around his neck. "It's about time you asked that question, Gabriel Broussard."

There was more cheering. As he carried his Emma past Nate, his friend looked nearly as pleased with himself as Gabe was feeling.

"What about Every Body's Beautiful?" Emma asked.

"Roxi says she'll be happy to run it while you open up a western branch. What do you say, Emma? There are a helluva lot of ladies out there who could use a place where they can feel pretty and pampered. Even if they haven't dieted themselves down to skin and bones. And believe me, their menfolk will be real happy with the idea, too."

"I love it." She snuggled into his arms as he marched past the reporters. Wanting to make sure the entire world knew that this story was true, Gabe made a point of pausing to kiss her again. Their cameras snapped. Busy kissing him back, Emma didn't seem to notice.

"There's just one thing," she said as he buckled her into the seat of the truck.

"What's that, *chère*?"

"Are you sure you can keep a woman of my vastly voluptuous hungers satisfied?"

He laughed, feeling, for the first time in his life, as if he'd come home.

"I gau-ran-tee it, *mon coeur*."

LOVE
POTION #9

———

One

A full moon rode high in the southern sky, casting an unearthly white light over the Lowcountry, illuminating the woman who moved through the marsh with the sleek grace of a swamp panther.

The thick air, pregnant with the disparate scents of salt, decaying Spartina grass, and night-blooming jasmine, dripped with moisture.

Herons glided on wide blue wings while an alligator slid silently across water the color of burgundy wine. Fireflies glowed amidst the branches of old growth cypress, which stood like silent sentinels over the watery world, silvery moss draped over their limbs like feather boas discarded by ghostly belles.

Bullfrogs croaked; cicadas whirred; somewhere in the dark a lonely owl hooted for a mate.

The familiar scents of the southern Georgia marsh reached deep into the woman's soul; the night music stirred the wildness that dwelt in her heart. It was music from an ancient time, a time when primitive man trembled with fear against the unseen denizens of the dark.

A time when her people ruled with wisdom and power.

A time of magic.

Her hooded black cape blended into the shadows as she made her way through the swirling mists of fog. Upon reaching the sacred grove of live oak she knelt and plunged her hands into the inky water. When she brought them out again, her long, slender fingers glowed with green, phosphorescent ghostfire.

Sparks fell back into the water, like a shower of stars, as she lifted her hands—palms turned upward toward the midnight velvet sky—offering a blessing to her mother, the moon.

Her exquisite face bathed in a shimmering light, the woman began chanting the words taught to her while she was still in her cradle. Words from before time passed down from woman to woman through the generations, words that flowed warmly through her veins, along with the blood that made her who she was.

What she was.

A witch.

After completing her invocation, she untied the hooded cape and let it fall to the ground. A zephyr blowing in from the nearby Atlantic caught her freed hair, whipping it into a wild jet black froth around her face. The black bodysuit she wore beneath the cape fit like a second skin, revealing every lush curve. Black leather boots, polished to a glassy sheen, encased her legs to midthigh, while a metal breastplate shaped her breasts into two glistening cones.

A silver amulet, dating back to medieval times and suspended from a hammered silver chain, nestled between her gloriously voluptuous, magnolia white breasts.

She took a small vial from the amulet. The scented oil—which she'd blended herself on Midsummer Night's Eve—was a dark and sultry concoction of scarlet rose petals, black dahlia, belladonna, dragon's blood, and, of course, wolfsbane. Best known for its properties of protection against werewolves, few were aware that Medea had embraced the selfsame deadly plant in her many works of vengeance.

She sprinkled the pungent oil over the rowan branches she'd gathered earlier and stacked in a circle of white angel wing seashells.

With the powers of midnight vibrating through her, the woman known as Morganna held her hands out over the wood, causing it to ignite in a sudden whoosh of wind and flame.

Closing her eyes, she concentrated on the faces of her life-sworn enemies, those who would use the darkness of the night to cloak their wicked ways.

She envisioned them melting like candle wax amidst the dancing flames. Felt the fire crackle in the very marrow of her bones. Heard their agonized, bloodcurdling screams. A lethal heat suffused her, fire flashed along her every nerve; suffering the evildoers' every torment, the witch swayed.

But she did not flinch. Nor did she cry out.

Any spellmaker who dealt in the dark side did not escape such acts unscathed, but given that her fate was both preordained and inescapable, Morganna bore her pain in silence.

And when it was finally completed, when a cooling, benevolent rain began to fall to drench the scorching flames, she lifted her pale white arms again and offered a prayer of thanksgiving to the goddess moon for having allowed her to survive.

"It is done."

Then, drained from the torturous burdens she'd willingly undertaken, Morganna, Mistress of the Night, folded to the damp ground and surrendered to the darkness.

TWO

"I cannot believe you allow garbage like this comic book in your shop."

Roxi Dupree, owner of Hex Appeal, glanced up from stirring crushed lavender into a love spell potpourri at the book the older woman was holding up between two fingers, as if afraid of contamination.

"It's actually a graphic novel." She sprinkled a handful of scarlet rose petals over the mixture. "And I like Morganna."

"She works the dark arts."

Roxi shrugged and refrained from pointing out that the Morganna stories were, after all, fiction. Fiction she'd grown up devouring. Stories that had fed a young girl's imagination.

Another thing she'd only ever shared with one person—her best friend Emma—was that Morganna had been a childhood role model. Oh, Roxi hadn't grown up to turn cheating boyfriends into toads (though there had been one or two who deserved it), or burn alive wicked people who harmed children, but she had taken Morganna's independent spirit to heart.

"All of us, witch or not, have our dark and light sides." Given that patience was not her strong suit, Roxi had to work at the mild tone. "Isn't all life about striving for balance between the two?"

"That may be," the older woman reluctantly allowed, even as her narrow face remained as pinched as a prune that had been left to dry too long in the sun. She tossed the book back onto the shelf.

"But Morganna, Mistress of the Night, certainly doesn't spend a great deal of time on the light side," she sniffed. "She's an angry, vengeful creature who embarks on a crusade of blood and brimstone in every book."

Roxi found it interesting that a woman who'd proclaim the popular Morganna stories garbage seemed to be so familiar with the stories.

"Not exactly brimstone," she murmured, thinking how that very word played into detractors' misguided view of pagans as devil worshipers. "And that particular crusade, by the way, is against undead spirits of the underworld who have infiltrated the bodies of humans."

Wiry wisps of steel gray hair surrounded the woman's frowning face. Her thin lips firmed as she skimmed a finger around the rim of a hammered silver chalice. "That couldn't possibly happen."

Closed-minded old biddy. "There are those who don't believe it's possible to draw down the moon, either."

The mention of the ancient rite brought to mind last night's x-rated dream where she'd been in the sacred grove drawing down the moon when a stranger, clad all in black, had appeared from the shadows and fiercely ravished her beneath the midnight sky. Just remembering the way his teeth had tormented her nipples was enough to have heat pooling between her thighs.

"She gives witches a bad name."

Martha Corey's grim accusation had Roxi reluctantly dragging her mind from her dream of a wild, midnight sexual tryst back to their conversation.

"I believe witches had a PR problem long before Morganna came on the scene." The Spanish Inquisition and the Salem hangings were two that came immediately to mind.

The woman abandoned the chalice, moving on to the iron cauldron Roxi had filled with fragrant purple and white lilacs for Beltane. "Did you hear that some Hollywood hotshot director is going to make a movie based on the comic books?"

"Graphic novels," Roxi repeated. Her frustrated sigh ruffled her dark bangs. "And yes, I believe I heard something about that."

Not only had she heard, Emma's husband, Gabriel Broussard—a former hometown bad boy who'd been named Sexiest Man Alive—was going to costar in the movie as Damien, a rival witch who just also happened to be Morganna's lover.

Actually, the dark and dangerous male witch was the reason she'd begun reading the Morganna stories. He'd certainly fueled fantasies of an entirely different sort. Ones she hadn't even understood at the time. Now that she thought about it, the man in her dream resembled Damien with his ebony hair and piercing blue eyes.

"I also read in *People* magazine that it's going to be filmed right here in Savannah."

"Imagine that." Having not seen Emma and Gabriel since their wedding six months earlier, Roxi had been looking forward to them coming to Savannah while Gabe was on location.

"Naturally, the coven is planning demonstrations."

Oh, hell. This was all she needed. Hex Appeal had only been open a few months. She'd established the original shop in Louisiana, but after Katrina blew the building away, Roxi had decided that as tragic as Katrina turned out to be, in her case the ill wind had offered an opportunity to spread her wings beyond Blue Bayou, the provincial Cajun community in which she'd spent the first twenty-five years of her life. Savannah, with its haunted and magical undercurrents, had seemed the logical choice.

"Well, that should certainly liven things up."

Practically biting her tongue in half, Roxi took a pink candle she'd made last night down from the shelf, infusing the wax with essential oils of lavender and ginger. Both powerful love forces by themselves, recent studies had shown that the combined scent of lavender and pumpkin pie increased blood flow to the penis by forty percent.

The spell she was packaging for her customer might technically be a love spell, but any woman, witch or not, knew that lust was the fast way to get any male's attention.

That idea had her unruly mind flashing back to the way her dream lover had feasted on her hot and needy body.

"Of course you'll be there."

"Be where?" In her mind his roving mouth had clamped hungrily over her breast and his wicked hand was creating havoc between her legs.

"At the demonstration."

"The demonstration?" Roxi repeated absently, trying to keep her mind in the here and now while her body, which was on the verge of melting into a hot puddle of need, desperately kept returning to last night.

She placed the small linen bag containing the potpourri into the opening of a conch shell she'd picked up on the beach just last week.

"We're creating our schedule now." Martha radiated impatience; a dark, muddied red aura of seething anger surrounded her. "The plan is to disrupt shooting so if those damn movie people insist on making their anti-witch propaganda, they'll at least have to move to another city."

"Perhaps Salem."

"That would be more suitable."

Given that the irony had flown right over the older woman's head, Roxi tried again. "Why don't you just cast some go away spells?"

Although he was now a married man, Roxi suspected that once the local witches got a look at Gabriel Broussard up close and in person, they wouldn't be in such a hurry to send him away.

"We plan to." Martha had moved onto a group of unicorns, lifting up a crystal one to check the price sticker underneath. "The demonstrations are merely our backup plan."

"Don't you think you're jumping the gun just a bit?" Once again, Roxi tried to remind herself that patience was a virtue. "Perhaps if you were to read the script—"

A sharp chin shot up. Faded blue eyes turned as stormy as her aura. "I don't need to read any script to know that we'd hate it. As any *true* witch would."

Ah. Here it was. What she'd been waiting for. The challenging of her credentials, which somehow managed to come up in the conversation whenever the old witch visited the shop. Just because Roxi chose to be a solitary witch, rather than join Martha's illustrious coven, she was considered suspect.

Fortunately, not every Lowcountry witch was as closed minded as their high priestess, or Hex Appeal would have had to close its doors after the first week.

"We're having a planning meeting tomorrow evening at my home," the elderly witch said. "I know the others will be pleased to have you join us."

With that, she left the shop like a schooner at full sail. Without buying anything. She never did. Which was just as well, because she'd undoubtedly declare anything from Hex Appeal faulty since it wasn't sold by a "real" witch.

Sighing, Roxi rearranged the remaining unicorns to make up for the one that had walked out of the shop in Martha's oversized straw bag.

The old woman wasn't really a thief. At least not if her niece, who routinely paid her kleptomaniac aunt's monthly bills from shopkeepers all over town, could be believed. But she was definitely a trial.

Three

Sloan Hawthorne dreamed of her again. The sultry witch slipped into his sleep, into his mind, like a soft and sultry mist.

They'd been in the forest, where she'd been standing in the sacred circle, waiting for him.

Overhead the midnight sky was a vast sea of black velvet scattered with diamonds. Ice crystals sparkled in the frosty air.

Neither spoke. Words were not necessary when hearts—and souls—were in unison.

Rather than her usual black, she was clad from head to toe in white, the color of the season. But there was nothing wintry about the heat shimmering in her thickly lashed eyes as she looked up at him. Offering everything she was. Everything she would ever be.

With hands that were not as steady as he would have liked, Sloan pushed her white fur hood back. A slight gasp escaped her rosy lips, hovering like a ghost on the chilly air between them as he gathered up a fistful of midnight black hair.

She trembled, but not from the winter's cold as his free hand unfastened the silver fastener of her cape and pushed it off her shoulders. From anticipation? Or, perhaps, fear?

It's all right, he soothed as he kissed her temple, her eyes, which drifted closed. *You need to trust me.* Her cheek. *I wouldn't ever hurt you.*

Although he did not say the words out loud, he knew she understood. As his mouth covered hers in a deep, claiming kiss, he felt her body relax in soft, oh so sweet surrender.

She stood before him, gloriously naked, clad only in skin as pale and smooth as freshly churned cream. A silver amulet, carved with mysterious Celtic symbols from another time, nestled between her breasts.

Although he'd lived in sun-drenched southern California for a dozen years, had worked in the movie industry for eight, Sloan had not known it was possible for any woman to be so beautiful.

He drank in the sight of her, his gaze moving over her face, taking in her eyes with their sexy, feline slant, her nose, which tipped up ever so slightly. Having always found perfection boring, Sloan approved of the faint flaw.

Her slightly parted lips were a soft and dusky pink against her milkmaid's complexion, reminding him of late summer roses on a field of snow.

She swallowed ever so slightly as he continued his slow, judicious study. When he bent his head and touched his mouth to that soft, fragrant hollow in her throat, he felt her pulse hitch. Imagined he could taste her low, deep hum of pleasure.

Her long hair draped her breasts in a jet black curtain. He smoothed it back over her shoulders. As her nipples tightened beneath his hot and hungry gaze, it took every vestige of self-control Sloan possessed to keep from taking those pert berry tips between his teeth.

He managed, just barely, to keep a tight rein on his rampant need to ravish as his roving eyes moved lower, down her torso, over her taut stomach to the nest of curls between her smooth, firm thighs. Beads of moisture glistened in the silvery moonlight like morning dew.

No longer able to resist touching, he trailed a sensual path through those thistledown silk ringlets with a fingertip and slid a finger into her moist, hidden sheath.

The body clenching around the gently invading touch was hot and tight. And, he thought, with a burst of primal male satisfaction as he flicked a thumb over her clitoris and brought her that first, sharp release, *mine*.

She was clearly staggered. Her gleaming gold eyes were blurred. Color rode high on her cheekbones and her lush lips trembled on an unsteady breath.

Just as he was worrying that he might have rushed things—rushed her—she smiled.

A slow, sexy, siren's smile.

And the spell was upon him.

Sloan had planned, while following her to this secret witch's place, to have her. To ease the woman hunger that had been bedeviling both his mind and body for too long. But, as he'd also always prided himself on being a tender, thorough lover, he'd also intended to take his time.

As lightning-hot need jolted straight to his loins, a ravaging madness flashed through Sloan. Patience broke, intentions scattered. With a violent heat raging in his blood, he muttered a half oath, half prayer, and crushed his mouth to hers.

No less hungry, she kissed him back, her avid mouth moving beneath his, murmuring words in some mysterious, magical language Sloan couldn't understand.

His clothes disappeared, thrown to the four winds swirling

wildly around them. Her nails dug into the bared flesh of his shoulders as she arched her fluid body against him. Her heart was pounding a fast, primitive beat through her blood, against her ribs, so hard he could feel it against his own chest.

Primal need clawed. At her. At him.

As the animal inside Sloan snarled and snapped its steel link chain, he dragged her to the ground, shoved her knees up, and mounted her.

"Mine." He needed to say the word out loud. Needed to hear her response.

She didn't hesitate. "Yours," she agreed on a harsh, ragged breath.

For all time.

He pistoned his hips forward, surging into her, claiming her innocence in one deep thrust.

Her cry, born not of pain, but pleasure, tangled with feminine triumph, echoed over the winter bare treetops.

Clinging to him, her body bowed, her slender hands racing up and down his back while she chanted those musical words from an ancient time, the witch opened completely. Utterly.

It began to snow, soft white flakes drifting down like feathers shaken from some pagan god's goose-down pillow. Moving together in an age-old rhythm, steeped in the magic of the night and of each other, neither Sloan nor his witch felt the cold as the snow covered them like a pristine white blanket.

"Okay. That's it."

Damn. He'd done it again. Fallen asleep at his computer. Sloan lifted his head, relieved he hadn't drooled and shorted out the keyboard.

His head pounded, his mouth was as dry as when he'd

filmed that adventure flick last year in the Sahara, his body ached like the devil, and he didn't need to look down to know that it was still reacting to his hot and horny dream. He had, after all, been suffering from a damn near perpetual hard-on since he'd begun this frigging Morganna project. He was also getting sick and tired of icy morning showers.

It was time for action.

Time to take charge.

"Time to get laid."

He reached out and snagged the phone from beneath a pile of comic books. *Make that graphic novels*, he reminded himself.

Though, personally, having grown up devouring superhero comic books, Sloan couldn't understand why there'd be a stigma to the term, but after all the years and trouble he'd gone to convincing Morganna's creator Gavin Thomas to sell him the film rights to the sexy, crime-fighting witch, the last thing he needed to do was accidentally slip up one of these days and insult the writer's work in public.

Especially given that, having already managed to incite the ultraconservative right with that pirate movie he'd made with Gabriel Broussard, he suspected the zealots would be heating up the tar and dragging out the feathers when Morganna hit the silver screen.

He was idly flipping through the pages while the phone rang and he paused on a scene where Brianna, Morganna's virginal good witch twin—who represented the white magic side of the duo—made love to a mortal male in a sacred circle of stones.

The black and white frame depicting the snow falling on the naked lovers caused the dream to come crashing back in vivid detail, which in turn had the muscles in his belly knotting painfully.

"Hello," the familiar voice on the other end of the line answered. At least that's what he thought she'd said. It was difficult to tell with all that hot blood roaring in his ears.

"Hey, Emma, darlin'." His southern drawl, a legacy from those halcyon days growing up in Savannah, rasped with unsatisfied lust as he struggled to drag his testosterone-crazed mind back to reality. "I've got a favor to ask."

Five minutes later, Sloan was online, booking a flight to Savannah.

Then went into the bathroom for yet another cold shower. One he damn well hoped would be his last.

Four

Seven months after her grand opening, thanks, in part, to Savannah's tourism trade, business was booming. Enough so that Roxi had even been able to hire a part-time employee, a descendent of a long line of voodoo practitioners who moonlighted as the lead singer in the Papa Legba Voodoo Priestesses.

Named for the most powerful of all the voodoo spirits, who, along with all his other responsibilities was in charge of all things erotic and sexual, the pop group was starting to generate crossover appeal, which Roxi attributed in large part to Jaira Guidnard's mile-long legs, poreless dark chocolate skin, and a body that caused males from eight to eighty to trip over their tongues.

"Do you believe this?" Jaira asked ten minutes after a busload of Swedish tourists had descended on the shop, located on the city's colorful Riverwalk. "It's like a damn Viking invasion."

"They're also paying our rent for the next three months," Roxi said. "Not to mention your salary."

"Well, there is that," Jaira agreed. "And some of them are actually kind of cute if you go for the hunky blond Scandinavian type."

She flashed a blindingly bright smile at one of the Vikings, who immediately walked into a display of pewter wind chimes hanging from the ceiling.

The temperature and humidity outside the shop was approaching the nineties; the constant opening and closing of the door, as customers left with their packages to make room for others to enter, was putting a strain on the hundred-year-old building's air conditioner, making it nearly as hot inside. Her hot pink Hex Appeal tank top was beginning to stick to Roxi's body and her hair felt like a thick dark curtain hanging down her back.

While Jaira went over to model jewelry and flirt with a trio of bedazzled males ostensibly shopping for their mothers back home—if, in fact, Swedish mothers actually wore chandelier garnet and seashell earrings—Roxi wrapped up a voodoo doll for a tall, stunningly voluptuous woman her own age who easily could've been a member of the Swedish Bikini Team.

Interestingly, none of the Vikings who were swarming around Jaira seemed to be paying any attention to her, which Roxi took as validation that blondes didn't always have all the fun.

As the blonde left the store with two more members of the team, all sporting fuchsia Hex Appeal baseball caps with its signature witch logo, the phone rang.

"*Bonjour*, Hex Appeal," she answered, tossing in a bit of her native Cajun French, which customers seemed to enjoy. "Love spells for the sexy sorceress."

The laugh on the other end of the phone was rich and familiar. "It's me," Emma Broussard said.

"I know. I recognized the number on the caller I.D., but

wanted to try out my new branding line. You're the first person to hear it. So, *chère*, what do you think?"

"I like it better than the one you've been using."

"I do, too," Roxi agreed. "I decided this morning that more people would rather be sexy than sassy."

The revelation had come from last night's hot, hot dream. The one that had her waking up with her hands between her legs. And still, dammit, unsatisfied.

"How's the creature from the deep lagoon?"

"Should I be offended that you insist on calling my unborn child a creature?"

"Hey." Roxi shrugged and grinned. "You should've known you were taking a risk when you sent me that sonogram." Her voice, and her mood, turned suddenly serious. "You and the baby are okay, aren't you?"

"Of course. I've never been better. After I started drinking that ginger peach tea you sent me, my morning sickness disappeared."

"That's what it's supposed to do." Ha! She might not be a card-carrying member of a coven, but thanks to growing up with a Cajun *traiteur* for a grandmother, Roxi definitely knew her herbal remedies. "So, what's up?"

"I have a favor to ask."

"Anything."

While they now lived a continent apart, there wasn't anything Roxi wouldn't do for her best friend. And she knew the feeling worked both ways. Plus, she figured she owed Emma for having let her choose her own maid of honor dress instead of sticking her in pink taffeta. Or worse yet, the southern belle, *Gone with the Wind* fantasy that continued to be a popular wedding theme south of the Mason-Dixon line.

"Well, actually, it's more a favor for Gabriel."

"Better yet. Tell me you've grown tired of the sexiest man alive and want me to take him off your hands."

"Thanks for the offer, but I believe I'll keep him a while longer," Emma said, proving her talent for understatement.

Roxi figured Michelle Kwan would be doing triple toe loops in hell before Emma wanted out of the marriage she'd been dreaming about since seventh grade, when she'd taken to writing Mrs. Gabriel Broussard all over her notebook.

"Funny how you can grow up with someone and not realize what a selfish bitch she is," Roxi teased. "So if you're not ready to recycle the drop-dead sexy father of the lagoon creature, what do you need?"

"It's about the Morganna, Mistress of the Night movie."

"Coincidentally, I was just talking with a local witch about that yesterday afternoon."

"Given your tone, can I deduce it wasn't a very flattering conversation?"

Emma might not be a witch, but her intuition was usually right on the mark. Including when she'd tried to break off her engagement to the dickhead. Unfortunately, her mother had laid the guilt trip of all time on her, so Emma had caved.

Bygones, Roxi reminded herself. Besides, not only had Emma overcome the collapse of a marriage that should have been declared dead at the altar, she'd emerged from the rubble a strong, bold, kick-butt heroine who could hold her own with Xena the Warrior Princess or Lara Croft, or even Morganna, any day. And in doing so, had won herself a sexy, caring man who openly adored her.

"Let's just say there's a bit of local concern about Morganna's Wiccan legitimacy."

"Would you be surprised to hear that Gabriel agrees with those detractors?"

"Really?" A faint sound, like that made when Clarence, the angel, finally earned his wings in *It's a Wonderful Life*, chimed in the back of Roxi's mind.

"Really. He just finished reading the most recent script

and is concerned the movie could come off looking like a comic book."

"Which isn't all that surprising, since it *is* a comic book," Roxi said, conveniently forgetting her earlier correction when Martha had called it that.

"True. But what a lot of people don't know is that *The Last Pirate* began as a superhero comic book type version of Jean Lafitte's life. It was only when Gabriel insisted that Sloan Hawthorne expand the concept that it became the movie everyone saw."

Everyone being the definitive word. Earnings for the film depiction of the Louisiana pirate's life had topped even Depp's *Pirates of the Caribbean*.

"Good for Gabe. So, what's the favor?"

"Gabriel thought it might be a good idea to get a witch's input on the script. And you just happen to be the only witch we know. Which is handy, because I remember you enjoying those Morganna comics."

"Actually, they're graphic novels, but yeah, I did enjoy them." And, as Emma well knew, she'd devoured them like chocolate pralines. "So, what do you want me to do? Read the script—"

"Oh, absolutely, we'd appreciate that! But rather than have Gabriel pass your opinions secondhand to Sloan, which can always result in miscommunication problems, we felt perhaps you should meet with him directly."

That niggling little chime sounded again. Louder, and a bit more insistent this time.

"I'd love to help you out, *chère*. Right now's a busy tourist season and I only just hired a part-timer helper, so it may take me a couple days to arrange things, but I'll check the flights and—"

"Oh, we wouldn't want you to have to go to all the trouble of coming here," Emma said quickly. Too quickly. The chime was now an alarm bell. "As it happens, he's coming to you."

Make that a damn siren. Like the civil defense one Paul Rigaud kept insisting on testing once a month back home in Blue Bayou.

"You're kidding. Some wunderkind movie screenwriter is flying all the way to Savannah just to get the opinion of a woman he's never met?"

"Sloan's directing the film along with writing the screenplay. He's also very hands on, which is why he's insisted scouting out shooting locations himself. He'd originally planned to shoot in New Orleans and out in the bayou, but then he lost a lot of the sites to Katrina."

"I can identify with that."

"Having grown up in Savannah, he knows the city well and thought it'd provide a lot of local color."

"It does have that," Roxi agreed.

"I can't wait to visit and see it all for myself. Anyway, given the lucky coincidence that you just happen to be living there, as well, Gabriel and I were hoping you'd be willing to meet with him."

"You wouldn't be trying to fix me up with this Hawthorne guy, would you?"

"Why would I want to do that?" Emma countered. "When we both know you're more than capable of getting any man you want?"

It did not escape Roxi's notice that Emma hadn't answered her question directly.

"Even if that were true, which it isn't, how about the fact that now that you're so happy in your little oceanside love nest, you've fallen prey to the dreaded MWS disease?"

"MWS?"

"Married Women Syndrome. Being perfectly content in your gilded institution of marriage, you now want to lock up every other woman in there with you."

"Don't be silly." The answering laugh was merry and bright. And, Roxi thought darkly, fake. Emma never had been able to tell a lie. "I seem to recall you telling me that you never went for a man with the entire package. That you just went out with men with a below-the-belt package."

"Yeah, I vaguely remember saying something like that."

She'd been lecturing about the need to separate emotions from sex. A warning that had come too late for Emma, who'd already fallen head over heart in love with Gabriel. Which had been a very good thing, given how well things had turned out.

"Well, if you truly meant it, then you definitely won't be at all interested in Sloan. Because the man defines a complete package."

"If he's such a paragon of perfection, why hasn't some woman snatched him up?"

"Perhaps because from what I've witnessed in the few months I've known him, he's every bit as commitment-phobic as you are. Which, by the way, blows any theory about me wanting to play matchmaker between the two of you right out of the water."

Unless, Roxi considered, she was using reverse psychology.

Which was crazy. There wasn't anyone in the world as straightforward as Emma Quinlan Broussard.

Emma pressed her case when Roxi didn't immediately respond. "We really need your input, Roxie. Gabriel doesn't want to back out of the project, especially since he and Sloan have a verbal agreement, and he's always felt strongly about keeping his word, but—"

"Okay." Roxi threw up her hands, both literally and figuratively. "When's this full package paragon due to arrive in Savannah?"

"Tomorrow evening." Unlike her husband, Emma Broussard was no actor. Which explained why she couldn't quite keep the satisfaction from her tone. "He's staying at the Swansea House," she said, again a bit too quickly. "I told him I'd ask if you'd be willing to meet him for dinner."

"So now you're his social secretary?"

"No. I merely felt uncomfortable giving out your number without checking with you first," Emma said mildly.

"I'm sorry." Roxi blew out a breath. "It's just been a crazed morning." After a frustratingly restless night.

"Well then, a lovely dinner with an attractive, interesting man sounds like just what you need."

Actually, if her reaction to that dream was any indication, what she needed was to get fucked, but since an elderly Swedish tourist was approaching the counter with a silver Viking dragon brooch in hand, Roxi kept that thought to herself.

Besides, as always, the quintessentially practical Emma had a point. The past few months, with her life in such flux, Roxi hadn't taken time to actually relax and enjoy herself. The Swansea House boasted one of the best restaurants not just in Savannah, but in the entire Lowcountry region. An expensive dinner on someone else's dime sounded more than a little appealing.

And if the evening ended in one of those antique four-poster beds the inn used in its advertising campaign, so much the better.

Five

"Well." Out on the raised deck of her Malibu home, which looked out over the vast blue Pacific, Emma Broussard hung up the phone and eyed the man seated across the white wrought iron table. "I've done all I can. Whatever else happens is up to you."

"I owe you, darlin'." Sloan lifted his glass to her. "Big time."

Her smile faded and a warning glinted in moss green eyes. "If you hurt her—"

"I know. You'll have Gabe rip out my lungs."

"That might be an option," she agreed mildly. "But only after I hack your balls off with a rusty knife and feed them to that shark that was spotted offshore last week."

He blew out a breath as just the suggestion of the threat had his testicles shooting up into his tonsils. "Wow. Who'd guess an expectant mother could be so harsh?"

"I like you, Sloan. A great deal. I also enjoy your artistic vision and believe that you're one of the few people who understands and appreciates my husband's complexities enough

to draw an amazing performance from him. I'd like to believe that's because, although you do appear to have a bit of
a Peter Pan complex, you're not a typically shallow, egotisti-
cal Hollywood movie prick."

"Thanks. I think."

"It was meant as a compliment. Roxi's been my best
friend since we were in kindergarten." Her expression soft-
ened and her eyes drifted back over the sun-silvered waves.
"We met the day she put a spell on a boy who'd called me
fat."

"I hope she turned him into a frog."

"Nothing that dramatic. But he did fall off his bike riding
home from school and broke his arm."

"Let's hear it for the witches," he said with a grin, then
sobered. "Kids can be mean."

Sloan knew, by some standards, especially Hollywood
standards, the adult Emma would be considered overweight,
as well. Personally, he found her lush and ripe and sexy as
hell.

"It was the truth," she said with a shrug. "I was, as my
mother insisted on pointing out, a 'butterball.' But you
should have seen the way Roxi lit into him. She was a five-
year-old warrior." She smiled at the memory. "Thinking
about it now, although the books hadn't been written yet,
she's always reminded me of Morganna."

She slanted Sloan a knowing look. "I believe you see her
the same way."

"I've never met the woman."

He'd been in the Sahara when Gabe and Emma had gotten married, and a damn sandstorm had kept him from getting to Louisiana and acting as his friend's best man.

"Yet here you are, planning a trip all the way across the
country to be with her. After asking me to lie for you."

"And I appreciate it, Emma. But it wasn't exactly a lie."

She lifted a bright russet brow, reminding him yet again that the lady was no pushover.

"More like a sin of omission," he qualified. "Number one, I really did grow up in Savannah." He began counting off on his fingers. "Second, I *am* going to be scouting shooting sites there." A third finger went up. "And finally, meeting with someone who believes herself to be a real witch will help flesh Morganna out."

Believes herself to be a real witch. That qualification did not escape Emma's attention.

"Do you believe in destiny?" he asked suddenly.

"Of course."

"I never did. I always figured we made our own destiny."

"Perhaps it's a bit of both," Emma suggested. "We all have free will, the ability to make choices, take different paths. Take advantage of opportunities."

She crossed her legs and took a sip of herbal tea. "Gabe and I knew each other back in Blue Bayou growing up," she said. "We'd been friends for a lot of years. Well, to be perfectly honest, I'd been a friend who had a major crush on him. But things didn't work out."

From the shadows in her expressive green eyes, Sloan sensed that was an understatement. "He moved to Hollywood. Then my marriage broke up, and Gabriel had his little problem—"

"His scandal, you mean."

The sunlight returned to her eyes when she laughed. "Ah, yes, let's hear it for kinky sex scandals . . . Anyway, after he decided to return home to hide out from the press until things blew over, a friend of both Gabe's and mine pulled a few strings, forcing us to spend some time alone together. The sparks were still there, so . . ."

"You lit yourself a fire."

"More like a conflagration. But yes. Either one of us

could have backed away. In fact, I tried to. But Gabe had other ideas."

"I don't blame him. Hell, sugar, if I'd have seen you first, I would've given your movie star husband a run for his money."

"That's sweet." She patted him on the knee. "But getting back to the point of this conversation, are you suggesting you believe Roxi may be your destiny?"

"That's probably an overstatement. But I gotta tell you, Emma, it's the damnedest thing. The minute I saw that e-mail of your wedding picture, I felt poleaxed."

"Roxi has that effect on men."

"It's more than just her looks. Hell, this is L.A. You can't throw a stick on a beach here without hitting a dozen women probably just as beautiful."

"Who undoubtedly wouldn't enjoy getting hit by flying sticks, but I understand what you're getting at."

"The point, and I do have one, is that the woman's been flat out driving me out of my mind. She's all I can think about. All I can dream about."

"I know the feeling," Emma said dryly. "Very well. But have you considered that it's because you've been so caught up in this new project, and she does resemble Morganna?"

If that wedding picture was any indication, she was the crime-fighting witch in the flesh. He wondered if she owned a catsuit.

"Sure I have. And that's probably all it is. But if I'm going to be able to keep my mind on work long enough to get this project in the can, I need to find out."

Surely taking Roxi Dupree to bed would get her out of his system once and for all. And let him get on with his movie. And his life.

"I can understand that, as well. May I offer a word of advice?"

"Sure."

"I've never been one to involve myself in other people's personal lives, but since it also occurs to me that if it hadn't been for Nate Callahan, Gabriel and I might not have had a second chance, I'm going to risk a bit of meddling.

"If, after you get to Savannah, you begin to suspect whatever you're feeling is more than just understandable lust for a beautiful woman, don't tell Roxi."

"O-kay." He knew his skepticism was written all over his face.

"I know what you're thinking. That deep down inside, no matter what they might say to the contrary, most women are looking for commitment."

"Far be it from me to make sweeping generalities. But just going by my own experience, that seems to be the case more often than not."

Although he'd always told women right up front that he wasn't the marrying kind, after a few months, or even weeks, most suddenly started talking about silverware patterns, and bridal magazines would magically show up on bedside tables.

"Roxi's the exception. She's always up for a good time, but if you let her think you're getting serious, she's going to run. I've seen it happen hundreds of times."

"Hundreds?"

Emma nodded. "At least. But I'll let her tell you about her rule of three herself. If things get that far."

"I know about the rule of three," he said. "It's the Wiccan code about whatever you do comes back to you threefold."

"That's one version," Emma agreed. "But Roxi's got her own take on it."

"Well now, sugar, I have to admit you have indeed piqued my interest. But if she's into threesomes, I'm afraid she's going to be disappointed."

Emma laughed. "I can't swear to know everything about her, but I'm pretty sure that you're safe there." She touched a fingertip to her lips. "But that's all I'm saying."

Emma was still smiling long after Sloan had left for the airport.

"I believe," she told Gabriel later that afternoon, "that things in Savannah could get very interesting."

They were lying in bed, bathed in the warm afterglow of passion after making love. It still amazed her that after all these months together, she still couldn't get enough of him. And, amazingly, if his behavior in the past half hour was any indication, her husband, who undoubtedly could have any woman in the world he wanted, felt the same way.

"*Mais*, yeah." He pressed his lips against her temple. Skimmed a wickedly clever hand down her side, from her shoulder to her thigh. "Sort of like nitroglycerin and a flamethrower are interesting."

She laughed, enjoying the image even as heat bloomed beneath his caressing touch. "I suppose it's only fair." She twined her arms around his neck and lifted her face for his kiss. "Why should we have all the fun?"

Emma's last thought, just before her husband took her back into the mists, was that her two favorite commitment-phobic people might have finally met their match.

Six

They'd agreed, during their brief phone call, to meet at the restaurant. Although he'd offered to pick her up, Roxi had thought that a foolish waste of time and effort, especially since he was already staying at the inn.

She'd heard the hum of jet engines during the call and wondered what it must feel like to actually be able to pick up one of those phones in-flight and pay the outrageous charges.

"Of course, when you're rolling in dough, I guess there's nothing you can't buy," she told her cat, La Betaille, who was lying on her bed, watching her get ready for the dinner date. "Undoubtedly even women."

Ignoring her with a feline elegance that belied the fact that the eighteen-pound former stray was missing one ear and had a diagonal scar across her nose, La Betaille began fastidiously washing her huge black paws.

"I wonder if the casting couch still exists?" She reached into the small enameled box on the dressing table and took out a pair of earrings shaped like crescent moons. They might be rhinestones rather than the diamonds Sloan Hawthorne was undoubtedly accustomed to women wearing, but Roxi liked the way they sparkled.

She studied the results in the full-length mirror standing across the room. "Though I'll bet a man like Sloan Hawthorne probably doesn't have to hold out walk-on roles in his movies as a carrot to get women to go to bed with him."

She'd spent the better part of the morning shopping for an outfit designed to knock off the Hollywood hotshot's socks, and if she was lucky, various other pieces of clothing.

She turned sideways and ran her hands down the front of the dress. Her breasts, which had always suited her just fine, thank you, suddenly seemed, well . . . a bit insignificant.

Since when had she started comparing herself to any other woman?

"You're an original, you," she said, looking over her shoulder at her butt, which, if she did say so herself, looked damn fine in this dress. "Besides, it'll be a new experience for him. Touching real, honest-to-god womanly flesh instead of silicone."

Apparently unimpressed by that prospect, La Betaille merely yawned.

She'd just fastened a moonstone pendant around her neck when the limo Sloan had insisted on sending for her arrived outside the small carriage house she was renting behind one of the stately homes on Chippewa Square, where Forrest Gump had sat on his famous bench and contemplated life as a box of chocolates.

"Okay," she said, as the driver rang the bell. "Showtime." Smoothing her hands over her hair, Roxi drew in a deep breath and pressed a hand against her stomach, which had suddenly gone all fluttery.

Which was just proof that she'd definitely been working too hard. Men never made Roxi Dupree nervous.

She reached down and stroked the cat's head. "Don't wait up."

As if taking her literally, La Betaille rolled over, closed her amber eyes, and immediately fell asleep.

The Swansea Inn had begun its life as an antebellum mansion belonging to a cotton broker. Three stories tall, created of the local gray Savannah brick that turned a dusky pink when bathed in the red glow of sunset, it overlooked the Polaski Monument in Monterey Square, which Roxi considered the prettiest of the city's twenty-four lush green squares.

She'd heard rumors that the inn had, for several decades prior to the War Between the States, been a house of prostitution, where wealthy planters and merchants had kept a bevy of women for their shared pleasure. There was even one bit of local lore that had General Sherman, after deciding not to torch the city, but to give it to President Lincoln as a Christmas present instead, paying a visit to the house to celebrate having concluded his devastating march across Georgia to the sea.

Like so many stories about the city, the tales were couched in mystery and wrapped in sensuality, and had been told and retold so many times it was impossible to know how much was true, and how much was the product of Savannahians' vivid imaginations.

She'd never been inside before, partly because she knew she'd never be able to afford the prices, but mostly because it was a private club. A place, yet more rumors persisted, of assignations. Even, she'd heard whispered, the occasional orgy.

She might have a liberal view of sex, but if Sloan Hawthorne had plans along those lines for tonight, he was going to be disappointed.

The moment the black car glided to a stop at the curve, the inn's glass door opened and a man came down the stone steps.

A sudden, white-hot sexual craving zigzagged through her like a bolt of lightning from a clear blue summer sky, sending every hormone in her body into red alert.

Roxi recognized him immediately. She'd Googled him yesterday after talking with Emma on the Internet, and while on all those Web sites she'd visited he'd definitely appeared to be a hunk, up close and personal he was downright lethal.

His hair was warm chestnut streaked with gold she suspected was a result of time spent beneath the California sun, rather than some trendy Beverly Hills salon. He was conservatively dressed in a crisp white shirt, muted gray striped tie, and a dark suit, which looked Italian and probably cost more than her first car.

He opened the back passenger door. His eyes, which were as green as newly minted money, lit up with masculine appreciation as they swept over her.

"Wow. And here I thought the woman was fictional," he murmured.

"Excuse me?" Her body wasn't the only thing that had gone into sexual meltdown. Sexual images of herself and Sloan Hawthorne writhed in her smoke-filled mind.

She told herself the only reason she was taking the hand he'd extended was that the car was low, her skirt tight, and her heels high.

Liar. Not only wasn't she sure she could stand on her own, she was actually desperate for his touch. Not just on her hand, but all the other tingling places on her body.

"I'm sorry." He shook his head. Sheepishly rubbed the bridge of his nose. "I tend to talk to myself when I'm bewitched."

"I see." He wasn't just drop-dead gorgeous. He was cute.

It also helped to know that she wasn't the only one who'd been momentarily mesmerized.

The butterflies settled, allowing Roxi to pick up a bit of her own scattered senses. "Does that happen often?" she asked.

"This is the first time." His gaze swept over her—from the top of her head down to her Revved up and Red-y toenails, then back up to her face again. "That is one helluva dress."

"Thank you." It was a basic black dinner dress. That was, if anything that was strapless and fit like a second skin could be called basic.

"Did you wear it to bring me to my knees?"

"Absolutely."

"Well, then." He flashed a grin that would've dropped a lesser woman to *her* knees. As it was, it had moisture pooling hotly between Roxi's thighs. "You'll be glad to know that it's working like a charm."

Like so many of the fine old homes in Savannah's historic district, the Inn had several steps originally designed to keep the dust and mud from the unpaved dirt streets outside the house.

Sloan put a hand on her back as they started walking up the five stone steps, hip to hip. Although the gesture seemed as natural to him as breathing, Roxi's knees were feeling a bit wobbly as a doorman in a burgundy uniform with snazzy gold epaulets swept the door open for them.

She would have expected Sloan to stay at one of the modern brass and glass high-rise hotels that tradition-loving Savannahians loved to complain about. It would have made it easier to dislike him. Or at least keep her emotional distance.

But the minute she walked into the inn, which epitomized sultry Savannah, Roxi was charmed by the black and white marble floors, the mahogany paneling, the pink marble pillars holding up a ceiling that soared at least fifteen feet, and the grand, sweeping staircase that made Scarlet's Tara look like a poor imitation.

"It's stunning," she breathed, gazing up at the ceiling that managed to have enough gold leaf to be elegant without crossing over to tacky excess.

"My family's always been proud of it," he said mildly, waving a hello at the concierge seated behind a cherry desk polished to a mirror sheen.

She stopped in her tracks. "Are you saying your family owns this inn?"

She'd known he was rich. His family, according to Google, owned one of the largest brick companies in the country. But having grown up with a shrimper for a father and a house-wife for a mother, Roxi found herself a bit intimidated by the idea of old wealth.

"No. I'm saying an ancestor built it."

"He was the architect?" Her heels clattered on the flow-ing black and white marble as they crossed the room.

"Actually, he laid the bricks. My family came from a long line of stonemasons. Which is how we got into the brick business."

"Ah, Mr. Hawthorne." The tuxedoed maître d' at the open doorway to the restaurant bowed as if greeting foreign roy-alty. "It's a pleasure to see you again."

"It's good to be back, Randall," Sloan said. "How's the family? Didn't my mother tell me your daughter was about to have another baby?"

"She gave her mother and I our third grandchild last week." His chest puffed up with obvious pride. "A beauti-ful little girl. Seven pounds, three ounces. They named her Elizabeth Rose."

"That's wonderful." Sloan's answering smile was, Roxi noted, every bit as warm as the ones he'd been tossing her way. She'd read a quote from Nicole Kidman, who'd called him a rarity in Hollywood, a genuinely nice man who treated everyone, from grip to catering staff to star, with equal respect.

"Give the proud parents my best," he said.

"I'll certainly do that." The maître d' beamed. If he'd had a tail, he would have been wagging it. "If you'll just follow me, we have your table waiting for you."

The restaurant floor was carpeted and the walls draped in a rich Savannah green silk, both, Roxi suspected, designed to mute the noise. It seemed to be working. Although the dining room was crowded, quiet conversation was possible.

It could have been a dining room in any other five-star restaurant. The men were all wearing suits or black tie, the women, for the most part, dressed much as she was, though she did glimpse some cocktail suits, and quite a few floaty, flowered dresses in the pretty pastels so popular in the South.

The walls were lined with banquettes covered in a rich burgundy tapestry, and as they walked across the room, she caught sight of several floor-to-ceiling draperies which seemed to close off private alcoves.

Were these rooms, she wondered, where the assignations took place?

As they followed the man toward the kitchen, she was thinking that for all the bowing and beaming, the old guy hadn't given Sloan a very good table, when he opened a door leading to some steep stone stairs.

"I'd thought we'd have dinner in the wine cellar," Sloan explained as Roxi looked up at him. "Given that the place tends to be packed on Friday night, I thought it'd give us more privacy."

He paused just a beat, long enough to let that idea and all its implications sink in. "But if you'd like to eat in the dining room—"

"The wine cellar will be fine." She hoped.

What did she really know about Sloan Hawthorne, after all? What if he was some sort of crazed sex fiend? What if the cellar was a secret S&M dungeon where members chained women to the wall and whipped them for their own sadistic gratification?

God. What on earth was the matter with her? Although Savannah, which Margaret Mitchell had referred to as "that gently mannered city by the sea," was well-known to possess an erotic, sensually adventurous side, it certainly didn't have S&M dungeons hidden away in five-star restaurants.

Besides, Emma, despite her uncharacteristic mistake with the dickhead, was a very good judge of character and never would have hooked her up with a sex maniac.

Although the walls and floor were made of the same stones she'd seen all over the city, stones that had arrived in Savannah as ballast in the holds of ships, there were no chains. No whips that she could see.

A single table had been draped in a snowy cloth, and set with gleaming crystal, china, and heavy silverware. Wall sconces cast a soft light over the room and a candle in a hurricane glass glowed. The damask napkin the maître d' had placed in her lap with a flourish had been lightly scented with lavender. Smooth and sultry jazz flowed from hidden speakers.

Perversely, although she certainly wasn't into masochism, after their drink orders had been taken—a summer melon martini for her, beer for him—Roxi experienced a twinge of disappointment that he appeared to have been telling the truth about having chosen this room solely because it allowed for more private conversation than the upstairs dining room.

"Did your ancestor lay these stones, as well?"

"He did. The cornerstone was set a hundred and sixty

years ago and you'll note the place is still standing. I'm not
sure how many modern-day buildings we'll be able to say
that about."

"I love old buildings."

"Me, too, which is one of the things I miss in California,
where it seems all the great old houses are being bulldozed
down and replaced by megamansions. When I was a kid I
used to have my birthday parties down here and show off to
all my pals."

"That's nice."

It also took away the idea of the house being used as a
sexual pleasure palace. From what she'd read of his family,
his parents were respectable Episcopalians who attended Savannah's first church, which since 1733 had been designated as
"Georgia's Mother Church." His father was CEO of one of
the largest brick suppliers in the South, while his mother
owned an antique shop on Bull Street across from the gold-
domed City Hall. They did not sound like people who attended orgies. Nor would they, she suspected, appreciate
their son dating a witch.

"My friends always wanted to go to my grandmother's
shop," she revealed.

"Was she into magic and spells and such, too?"

"She was a *traiteur*—that's Cajun for a healer. But she
also had some Caribbean heritage, so she was active in the
voodoo religion, as well."

"Religion?"

"Despite the way it's often depicted in movies, what with
people biting heads off chickens, making blood sacrifices,
and dancing naked, voodoo is a very structured religion."

"Damn." One brow lifted. "And here I was, really looking
forward to that naked dancing part."

Arousal stirred in her belly. And lower. "Oh, I've been
known to go skyclad. When there's a full moon."

She combed a hand through her hair, a time-proven gesture that lifted her breasts appealingly. Unsurprisingly, his gaze followed.

Ha! As she'd always told Emma, men were easy.

Unfortunately, despite having always insisted on maintaining the upper hand, she was proving every bit as easy. She wanted him. Here. Now. In every way there was to want a man.

"I don't happen to have a calendar," he said hoarsely. "Would you happen to know when, exactly, the next full moon will be?"

Hanging onto her ebbing control with her fingertips, she managed a coy smile as she trailed a languid scarlet nail down her throat. "Not tonight."

"Well, damn. There goes that moonlight fantasy, shot to smithereens."

He might not believe in magic and spells and things that went bump in the night, but Roxi Dupree definitely had him bewitched and as bothered as hell.

The thought of those sexy, red-tipped fingers curving around his cock was all it took to give Sloan a massive hard-on.

He was debating just ditching the Southern manners he'd been taught in the cradle and jumping her luscious, sexy bones, right here and now, when the waiter showed up with their drinks, giving him time to drag his rampant libido back into check.

Seven

"So you were sharing a religious experience with your friends by taking them to your grandmother's shop?"

"No." Her laughter was rich and warm and curled around him like satin ribbons. "To be perfectly honest, they just wanted to see all the gator heads and teeth."

"I imagine gators beat foundation rocks any old day when you're a kid."

"Perhaps. But wasn't it in Savannah that that fictional pirate gave Billy Bones the map of Treasure Island?"

"Yeah. Some of the background for that novel supposedly came from the Pirate's House restaurant, where pirates supposedly hung out."

"Maybe they hung out here, as well," she mused.

As she glanced around at the gray stones, he imagined her a captive, chained to the wall, naked. Hot. Wet. Forced to do his every bidding.

He wondered what she'd do if she knew that the cellar had been originally built to hide smuggled pirate treasure. And stories persisted of Blackbeard having spent several weeks hiding out here with a woman he'd taken prisoner who'd become one of his fourteen wives.

"So, your family's from Savannah originally?"

"No, they landed in New England in 1630."

It was proving harder and harder to carry on a civilized, getting-to-know-you conversation when in his mind, she'd climbed onto his lap, her dress up around her waist as she straddled his thighs and gave him the lap dance of his life.

"About sixty years later, a group who didn't exactly buy into Puritanism broke off and moved south. And immediately became known as the black sheep branch of the family tree."

That was putting it mildly. Though, to his mind, building brothels was a lot more respectable than hanging women falsely accused of witchcraft.

"My family's story was much the same," she said. "Oh, not the Puritan thing. Which would have been unlikely, given those people's attitude about the only good witch being a dead witch."

So, here's your chance, a little voice of reason in the back of his mind counseled as she picked up the tasseled menu and began leafing through the pages of listings. *Tell her. Now. Before you get in over your head.*

Don't be a damn fool, said another voice, which seemed directly linked to his hopeful dick. *You think she'd be willing to go to bed with you if she knew the truth?*

Trying to ignore them both, he took a long drink of Guinness.

"Your name's French," he said, shifting the conversation away from his family heritage.

"Acadian." She put down the menu and took a sip of her martini. "My father's people were kicked out of Nova Scotia in the eighteenth century for refusing to convert to Anglicanism."

"And ended up in the bayou because they figured it'd be

the last place in the country anyone would want, so they'd be left alone and finally allowed to settle down," he said.

"That's right." She sounded surprised.

"I had to read that Longfellow poem about Evangeline and Gabriel back in high school." He did not mention the family lore about Longfellow having been inspired to write the poem about the Acadian maiden and her lover torn apart on their wedding day, by a story told to him at a dinner party at author Nathaniel Hawthorne's home. "I've always thought the story would make a great movie."

"There have already been two made, back in the 1920s," she divulged after their orders had been taken. "In fact, Delores Del Rio, who starred in the second one, had a statue made of herself and placed on the site where Evangeline's supposedly buried."

"But she wasn't real."

"Try telling that to some of the people down in the bayou. The Evangeline Oak in St. Martinville is actually the third oak designated as the site where Evangeline and Gabriel were united. Tourists continue to flock there, decade after decade, which is why I strongly doubt moviegoers would enjoy having the heroine find the hero in an almshouse after years of separation, then the two of them dying in each other's arms."

"That could present a problem," he agreed. "Given that moviegoers these days mostly prefer their love stories to come with a happily ever after guaranteed ending."

"Fiction always sells better than truth," she said knowingly.

He arched a brow. "Sounds as if you don't believe in happy endings."

"I suppose it depends upon your meaning of happy." Her tone definitely closed the door on that topic.

Not wanting to press, Sloan switched gears. "What about the other side of your family?"

"They came over on the coffin ships from Ireland about a

hundred years later and ended up in Louisiana building the levees."

"With all those Catholics in your background, it's interesting you'd decide to become a witch."

"I didn't decide anything. Other than to practice the Craft. I have Druid blood from my mother's side of the family. And, as I said, my father's great grandmother was a Haitian voodoo priestess, which carried through the women's side of his family."

"Which makes you a two-fer."

"I suppose you could put it that way."

"Are you into voodoo like your grandmother?"

"No. I suppose I'm more like your ancestors in that way."

"My ancestors?" His gut clenched. And not in a good way.

"The ones you told me didn't make it as Puritans? The religious aspects were just too structured for me, which is why I'm not Wiccan, either."

"There's a difference?"

"Wicca is a neopagan religion. Not all witches are Wiccan, and not all Wiccans practice magic," she explained as the waiter delivered their dinners and discreetly disappeared.

"Anyway, though I'd been drawn to the Craft all of my life, I'd never thought about actually earning a living with it until my grandmother Evangeline died and left me her voodoo shop. I gave away all the gator heads and teeth and was planning to dissolve the business entirely, but people kept showing up at the day spa I'd opened up with Emma, wanting spells like they'd bought from Grand-mère."

She took a bite of crab cake and closed her whiskey-hued eyes, looking like a woman in the throes of ecstasy. Actually, Sloan realized, she looked exactly the way the witch had in his dream, when he'd ridden her hard and fast beneath the icy winter moon.

Although the stone walls kept the cellar insulated, and additional cooling kept the room at an optimum temperature for wine storage, air-conditioning going full blast, his internal temperature spiked.

Sloan pulled at the starched collar of his shirt and was seriously considering yanking off his tie when another, equally provocative image flashed in his mind.

A mental image of Roxi Dupree, naked, his discarded tie lashing her ankles to the legs of the chair, holding her legs open for him as he knelt on the stone floor, painting those smooth, taut thighs with his tongue, lapping up the warm cream flowing from her cunt, taking her engorged clit between his teeth . . .

"What?" she asked when she opened her eyes again and found him staring at her.

In his unbidden fantasy, she'd been writhing against his mouth, her screams bouncing off the stones.

"Nothing."

He hadn't creamed his jeans since he'd been sixteen and Danielle Davenport had dry-humped him in the backseat of his Dodge Charger one steamy summer day they'd been parked out on Tybee Island. But he'd just come damn close to a repeat performance without this woman so much as laying a hand on him.

"You were telling me about after your grandmother died," he reminded her.

She gave him a look that let him know he wasn't getting away with anything. Then shrugged her bare shoulders.

"I didn't want to turn the people down, so I dragged out all my grandmother's shadow books—they're sort of like a witch's cookbook—learned the ones she'd been doing for her clients, then started blending up her recipes for the various lotions and oils, which fit in nicely with the spa concept."

"But you don't have the spa anymore?"

"No. Katrina did it in. As Margaret Mitchell might say, it went with the wind." She took another bite. "Oh God. This is so amazingly delicious."

He'd never before realized that the ordinary act of swallowing could be so fucking sexy. "Randolph, the chef here, has always had a deft hand with seafood."

She cut off a piece and held it out to him. "You have to try it."

She might as well have been Eve, holding out that shiny red apple. Like Adam, Sloan found himself unable to resist temptation.

"May as well. Given that you've already got me eating out of your hand. But I gotta tell you, sugar, pan-fried crab is sure as hell not what I'm hungry for."

He curved his fingers around her wrist and, with his eyes on hers, he closed his mouth over the fork's tines.

Watching her closely as he was, he didn't miss the way her eyes darkened at the movement in his throat as *he* swallowed. Beneath his thumb her pulse had trebled its beat.

"Good," he decided. He kissed her knuckles. "As far as appetizers go." He trailed his fingers up her arm, allowing the back of his hand to brush against the side of her breast. "Makes me anticipate dessert all the more."

She licked her lips, which had his mutinous penis leaping in response. "I hear the key lime pie's to die for."

"It's good, sure enough. But tonight I seem to be craving something sweeter." His caressing touch slid over her shoulder. "Smoother." Lower, to skim along the crest of her breasts. "Warmer."

Her nipples were pressing against the black silk. "Maybe topped with some nice, ripe berries," he decided.

She pleased him by laughing at that admittedly over the top sexual metaphor. He was less pleased when she lightly slapped his hand away.

"You are so bad."

"Sweetheart, you've no idea." He cupped the back of her neck. "But you're about to find out."

Encouraged when she didn't back away, Sloan gave her the warm, seductive smile that had always been one of the most devastating weapons in his arsenal.

Then lowered his head.

Eight

Roxi was not inexperienced. She'd been kissed hundreds of times before. Thousands. But never had the mere touch of a man's lips against hers caused her world to tilt on its axis.

Amazingly, it was just like she'd dreamed. His mouth was firm and hot and outrageously clever, just skimming her lips, drawing forth a ragged sigh, before moving on.

His warm breath fanned her cheek. Her temple. Her other cheek.

"Sloan." Her voice sounded far away, as if it were coming from the bottom of the sea.

"What, sugar?" He nipped at her bottom lip, just hard enough to make her shiver.

"Kiss me."

"I am." He soothed the tender flesh with the tip of his tongue. "Do you have any idea how long I've been wanting to do this?"

"All of thirty minutes?" She realized she'd totally lost track of the time since arriving at the restaurant.

"Longer than that."

"An hour, then." Her breath was clogging in her lungs. Which was ridiculous, since he hadn't even properly kissed her yet.

"Longer." His tongue slid silkily between her parted lips, tangling with hers, engaging it in a slow, sensual dance.

"That's impossible."

"Nothing's impossible." His mouth skimmed down her throat, across her collarbone. At the same time his hand glided tantalizingly up her leg. "When you're talking about magic."

Her skin felt hot. Her dress, suddenly too confining.

"I fell in love with Morganna back when I was in film school at USC," he said conversationally as his fingers traced seductive figure eights on the inside of her thigh.

"If I'd known she actually existed, I would've dropped out and hightailed it down to Louisiana and proposed."

"It would've been a wasted trip," she managed in a ragged voice choked with need. How did he do it? His stroking touch was making her nipples ache and her clit pulse, yet he was chatting away as if they were having an ordinary dinner date conversation.

"You sure of that, are you?" His Georgia drawl had thickened to that of whiskey-drenched bread pudding. Roxi could've eaten him up with a spoon.

She closed her legs, capturing that roving hand between them. "As sure as I'm sitting here talking with you."

Trying to talk when what she wanted to do was strip off her dress, and climb into his lap, and have him take her aching breasts in his mouth and . . .

"Not that I'd want to go braggin' on myself or anything," he was saying as a red haze shimmered over her mind and her blood boiled and thickened in her veins. "But I've been told that I can be irresistibly charming." Those treacherous fingers crept higher. "When I put my mind to it."

"I've not a single doubt of that." She gasped when he pinched the flesh at the inside of her thigh, hard enough to leave a bruise.

At the same time her body arched toward his wicked hand.

Wanting.

No, dammit, *needing* more.

"But back when you were sitting around your dorm room, lusting after a comic book witch, I was a mere girl of fifteen."

A virgin who, despite all those erotic novels she'd hidden beneath her mattress, had no earthly idea that someday she'd actually meet a man who could have her on the verge of orgasm with such a tantalizing, feathery touch.

"And since even down in the swamp we girls didn't marry at fifteen, Daddy and *Maman* never would've allowed me to accept your proposal."

"Fifteen might have been a bit young," he allowed. "Though I'll bet you were hot even back then."

She nearly screamed when his hand, mere inches from her clit, which had begun to burn with need, reversed direction.

"Fortunately for us," he continued, "that six-year age gap doesn't make a difference anymore."

His fingers were now massaging the back of her knee, which she'd never realized was an erogenous zone.

Roxi heard a ragged whimper, only to belatedly realize that it'd been ripped from between her own suddenly parched lips.

She drew in a breath to steady her breathing. "I think it's that time of the evening where we set some ground rules."

He leaned forward again. Touched his mouth to hers. "I've never been all that fond of rules."

"Neither am I." The kiss was light. Almost tender. But it still had her lips tingling. Along with the rest of her. "But they do help keep things civilized."

"That may be. But I have to tell you, sugar, I'm not feeling all that civilized right now."

He was looking at her as if he'd like to strip her naked, drag her off to his cave, and ravish her. Once again she considered how cavelike this cellar actually was.

She wondered if that thought had occurred to him when he'd made the reservation. Wondered if he realized that if he actually dared to try to take her right here, right now, she'd help him.

"There's something you need to know before this goes any further."

He lifted a dark brow. His hand, which had been moving back up her leg, paused.

"I'm not in the market for marriage," she said.

A smile quirked. Wicked laughter sparkled in his green eyes like sunshine on a tropical lagoon. "I believe that's my line."

"It may be." She sighed prettily. "But believe me, *cher,* I've heard those words before. Yet, invariably things between a man and a woman get complicated. Especially once sex gets added into the mix."

"Are you telling me you're not in the market for sex, either?"

She tilted her head. Studied him. It would be a little hard to claim that now. Without seeming like the world's worst pricktease, but she had to ask. "Would it make a difference if I wasn't?"

"Like you said, sex always makes a difference."

He retrieved his hand, took a long drink of water, and eyed her thoughtfully over the rim of the crystal goblet.

"But I've moved beyond thinking with my glands. At least I thought I had until you climbed out of that limo. You are the most stunning woman I've seen in I don't know how long, you smell fabulous, and"—his appraising gaze skimmed over her—"until you decided to have this rules discussion, I was about ten seconds away from biting your thigh. And that was just for starters.

"But even if we back away from what we're both feeling, I'd honestly like to hear your take on Morganna. Maybe get some background on this witch business you've got going."

"Hex Appeal."

"That's it." When he smiled again, she had to restrain herself from nipping at his square, manly chin.

"The thing is," she said, trying to keep her mind on what she needed to say, "as much as I like you, *cher*, inevitably relationships get fucked up."

"Maybe you've just gotten involved with the wrong men."

"That's been true enough. On occasion."

God, could she screw things up any more? She'd come here tonight prepared to go to bed with him. There was nothing wrong, to her mind, about wanting to scratch an itch without having to deal with the time and energy of a committed relationship. So why in hell was she insisting on talking it to death when what they should be doing was fucking each other's brains out?

"But it wouldn't matter if you were Prince Charming in the flesh and the sex between us was gold medal, world class—"

"Which it's going to be," he promised with sublime self-confidence.

She couldn't argue that. The sexual vibrations between them were so strong she was surprised this entire building wasn't in meltdown.

"All the more reason to agree to call a halt afterwards. Before we get to that pissed-off point."

"So, are you saying you're only into one-night stands?"

"Of course not. I mean, I've nothing against them, and they can certainly be pleasant—"

"If we end tonight with you even thinking the word *pleasant*, I sure as hell won't have done my job."

She felt herself shudder. Knew he'd seen the involuntary response by the satisfied gleam in his gaze.

"What I meant," she said, as his hands cupped her breasts and began plumping her nipples, "was I believe they can be . . . very . . . oh God . . . empowering."

"You know, I'd applaud that idea." He tugged the dress down, exposing the black lace bustier she'd bought this morning with him in mind. "But my hands just happen to be a little busy at the moment."

As if to back up his words, he caught one erect nipple between his thumb and index finger and squeezed. Hard. She gasped at the stab of pain/pleasure, but rather than back away from the stinging touch, she arched her back, inviting more.

Much, much more.

"The waiter," she remembered reluctantly.

"Isn't going to come down here unless I call him." He bent his head and soothed the tingling flesh with his tongue.

Her hands felt inordinately heavy as they lifted to comb through his hair. "You planned this." Her head fell back. "All along."

Roxi wondered if Emma had known about Sloan's intentions.

"Let's just say I was hopeful." He drew the nipple into his mouth with a deep, wet suction that caused her pulse to beat painfully in that hot and liquid place between her thighs. "I'm also going to tell you, darlin', that female empowerment aside, one night with your sweet body isn't going to be nearly enough."

She had the same feeling. "That's why I have my three-date rule," she gasped as his teeth closed down on the flesh his tongue had tormented.

His breath was a hot breeze against her breast as he sighed. And drew his head back.

"I'm getting the feeling this isn't about that witchy Rule of Three that states three times what thou givest returns to thee."

She was surprised he knew about that, then remembered she was here tonight because he really had read the Morganna books. "No, not that one." Though she not only believed it, but practiced it.

"Nor the usual female one about putting off sex until the third date."

He was now openly frustrated. Roxi suspected he wasn't accustomed to a woman setting the rules. Especially when it came to sex.

"Actually, it's just the opposite. I never go out with a man after the third date."

"Seems that would be a bit limiting."

"Perhaps." And one problem she was just discovering was that she couldn't imagine wanting any limits where Sloan Hawthorne was concerned. "But the problem is that after three dates it's possible that someone's going to start feeling something—"

"I'm feeling something already." He leaned back in the wooden chair and spread his legs, revealing the thick weight of his erection thrusting against the zippered placket of his slacks.

"Come here." He patted his knee, his green eyes glittering with a masculine sexual challenge.

Nine

Roxi lifted her chin. "I'm not a dog you can call whenever you want attention."

A rough, harsh laugh burst out of him. "Sweetheart, that's one word that no one would ever use to describe you. But, you know, now that you mention it, tonight you're going to play my sweet, obedient pet."

"You make it sound as if I have nothing to say about it."

"So far, you've been setting all the rules," he reminded her mildly. "But here's one from my side of the negotiating table. If we're only going to have three fuck dates, tonight's will be on my terms." His penetrating gaze narrowed, burning into hers. "My rules."

She'd never been into submission. Which was, she admitted, why she'd also chosen men who were more willing to be led. Men who were, well, malleable. Controllable.

There was nothing the least bit malleable about Sloan Hawthorne. On the contrary, he was suddenly revealing a dark and dangerous side Roxi reluctantly found wickedly exciting.

"So much for Southern charm," she murmured.

He rubbed his jaw. "Now see, it's the accent that throws people off. Some people hear my Georgia drawl and mistakenly believe I'm a pushover.

"If you're looking to hook up with some mealymouthed, sweet-talkin', roll over and pee on himself Ashley Wilkes type, you've got the wrong fucking man."

The drawl hardened, like steel wrapped in black velvet. "But if you're lookin' to explore the dark side of your dreams, well, I'm your man."

Her body responded to that suggestion, becoming more aroused, even as she struggled to maintain some vestige of control.

"What makes you think I've been even having that sort of dream?"

"Of course you have," he said with an arrogance that would have annoyed her had it been any other man. "Same as I have."

"Emma didn't mention you were psychic."

"I've never claimed to be. But something happened when you got out of that car tonight. I recognized you, same as you recognized me. We've already done it in our sleep. Lots of times and lots of ways. Seems we may as well see what it feels like with our eyes wide open . . .

"I'm going to take you, sugar. I'm going to make you beg. And then I'm going to make you scream. And you're going to love it.

"Now." He patted his thighs again. "Come here."

His words—his dark and erotic threats—had her drenched. Telling herself that she really wasn't giving in, that it wasn't really surrender if she ended up getting what she wanted—a mind-blowing orgasm—she stood up and started to straddle his thighs.

He shifted her so she was sitting sideways on his lap, her legs dangling over his. "You put that sweet hot pussy against my groin right now and there's no way I'm going to be able to control myself."

He cradled her head against his shoulder and slid his hand beneath her skirt. Since he'd been gentle with her so far, she sucked in a harsh breath as his short square nails scraped a stinging path up the inside of her thighs.

"You like that?"

"Yes." It was half sigh, half moan.

"It's just the beginning." He rubbed a fingertip against the crotch of her silk panties. "You're wet." His exploring touch slipped beneath the elastic band. "And hot." He combed his fingers through the triangle of curls as if he owned them. "Is that for me, sugar?"

She flinched as that treacherous touch brushed against her clit. "What do you think?"

"I think you're the most responsive woman I've ever met. Even more than I'd imagined."

As if to prove his point, he skimmed a thumb over her clit and drew a ragged moan from between her lips.

"You are so slick." She sucked in a sharp breath as his finger penetrated her. "And ready for me."

He inserted a second finger. Opening her. Preparing her.

"That's it, darlin'." He murmured encouragement as her body clutched at him. His treacherous thumb pressed down on the tangled knot of hot nerves. "Let's see you ride." His fingers thrust into her. Withdrew. Then plunged harder. Deeper.

Her hips bucked. She drenched his hand as she rode him faster and faster, lifting her hips to press against his fingers, gyrating around his demanding touch, her hot, wet flesh making a harsh sucking sound on each upstroke.

When his fingers suddenly arched inside her, and pressed against a secret spot at the roof of her passage, she cried out, stiffened, and exploded over him.

"You definitely liked that."

It was not a question, but Roxi struggled to answer it anyway, which wasn't easy with the top of her head blown off. "Y-yes." She'd never believed the G-spot really existed. Sloan had just proved her wrong.

Her inner muscles were clenching at him like a hard, wet fist. "Oh, God, yes." *Like* didn't even begin to describe the sensation.

"Good. Let's try it this way." When his wickedly clever thumb found her clit again, she climaxed with a smothered scream, stiffened, then collapsed like a rag doll, sprawled bonelessly on his lap.

The top of her dress was down around her waist, and somehow her skirt had ended up there, as well, as he'd hand-fucked her. Her panties were drenched and his powerful erection pressing against her bottom was driving her mad.

"Sloan." Her body moved restlessly, needing more. His fingers slid slickly out of her, leaving her cunt feeling abandoned. And empty. "Please." She would have, if physically possible, split herself open for him. The climaxes he'd given her had only whet her appetite for more. "I need you."

"I know." He stroked a hand down her hair. "And you'll have me. We'll both have each other. Later."

He tipped up her face with a fingertip beneath her chin. Touched his lips to hers, at first lightly, then deepened the kiss degree by devastating degree until she trembled and moaned against his mouth.

"Amazing," he murmured again.

She could feel his satisfied smile and felt a spark of irritation at herself for making this so easy for him. "You really are a wicked, wicked man."

"Absolutely." He slid her off his lap onto her feet. "And you're about to find out exactly how wicked I can be."

Wanting to take his time, he debated tugging the dress

back over her breasts, which were so enticingly displayed by the spiderweb thin lace of that corset she was wearing, then decided to stay with the theme of the evening.

"As much as I really, really like that dress, right now I want you to take it off."

It was a test, and they both knew it. They also both knew that she wanted what was about to follow every bit as much as he did.

Which was why he wasn't all that surprised when she reached behind her back. The whispered sound of the zipper lowering sounded unreasonably loud in the hushed room.

The dress slid down her body, pooling in a black, silken puddle at her feet. She stood before him wearing that lacy corset that lifted her breasts, erotically offering them up for a man to look at. To touch. Taste.

She was—thank you, God!—also wearing a matching black garter belt, lace-topped stockings, and that drenched pair of panties that were so miniscule, he wondered why she bothered with them.

"You look," he said, drinking in the exquisite sight, "like you should be on some Victoria's Secret runway."

She folded her arms. Shook her head. "Why does it not surprise me you'd watch that show?"

"What can I say. Men are pigs." The show was admittedly one of his guilty pleasures. He figured most men in America would watch if their wives or girlfriends let them.

He started to instruct her to hold her hands away from her body, then decided to wait until they got upstairs before laying on the orders. Instead, he took hold of her hands and held them out for her.

Apparently she got the idea because when he let go, she continued to hold them out, inviting him to look.

He made a little twirling motion with his finger.

She turned around slowly, like a girl showing off a new party dress, though there was nothing girlish about either the outfit or the woman. He was also impressed as hell that she was able to move so smoothly on four-inch, fuck-me-big-boy stilettos.

"You look," he murmured, "good enough to eat."

She looked up at him through her lashes. It was, Sloan thought, the same look Scarlet had flashed at Rhett when she'd shown up wearing curtains and trying to coax him into giving her the money to pay the taxes on Tara.

"That's something to look forward to," she said.

A laugh burst out of him. He might have cast her in the role of his pet submissive tonight, but Roxi Dupree was definitely his equal. Intellectually, emotionally, and, he suspected, sexually.

"Absolutely." He scooped up the dress from the floor. "Let's go."

"Go?" He thought she paled a little at that idea.

"Upstairs. Where I intend to have my wicked way with you."

Ten

He wouldn't.

Wouldn't make her walk through an entire dining room of Savannahians in the barely-there underwear and high heels.

He wouldn't treat her like a sexual slave in front of people she'd run into on the street, in the grocery store, people who might even be Hex Appeal customers.

Would he?

No. Roxi blew out a short, head-clearing breath. Even if Emma hadn't vouched for him, she knew he wasn't into humiliation.

"There are a set of back stairs to your room, aren't there?"

For a long, suspended moment Sloan was very still. He rubbed his chin. Frowned down at her. "What if I said there wasn't?"

She smiled. Serenely. Confidently. "You'd be lying."

His lips twitched. Just a bit. "You think you know me that well?"

"Yes." Although it didn't make any sense, she did.

He gave her another of those long deep looks that made her think he could see all the way inside her heart. Her soul.

Then he put his hands on her shoulders and turned her around, pointing her toward the door.

"You'd be right," he allowed.

She let out a surprised squeal when he slapped her butt.

"Now, let's get going," he growled. "I've plans for you."

That thought, combined with the rough and hungry tone of voice, made her shiver.

At any other time she might have felt self-conscious as she walked up the secret stairway in front of him. The lingerie that had seemed so alluring in the dressing room of Sensual Essentials this morning could seem a bit sluttish while parading around in it in front of a fully dressed man, but the entire evening had taken on a somewhat dreamlike quality, just like those hot and sexy dreams she'd been having night after night, so it seemed perfectly normal.

The stone steps ended at a thick wooden door with heavy iron hinges. She glanced back over her shoulder to see what he intended to do to her now, and saw him take an old-fashioned key from the inside pocket of his jacket.

He reached past her, slipped the key into the brass lock, and turned the handle.

"Come in."

"Said the spider to the fly?" she asked.

His grin was quick and wicked. "Of course."

The walls of the room were draped in a deep burgundy silk, which wasn't unusual for older homes in Savannah. But it was the art hanging on the walls that captured the eye and stirred the senses.

While unabashedly erotic, the paintings did not feature the familiar airbrushed, vacuous girls from the pages of men's glossy magazines or porn flicks.

These women were strong, confident, powerful in their

skin, whether dressed in dominatrix black leather and wield-
ing a whip, or kneeling blindfolded on a stone floor—much
like the one in the wine cellar, Roxi noticed—hands clasped
behind her back, about to take an engorged penis, which was
only a breath away, between her parted, glossy red lips.

Another painting featured a woman seated on a table, a
dark and swarthy man pressed against her, fastening a pair of
handcuffs around the wrists he was holding behind her back.

"Well." Having to remind herself to breathe, Roxi exhaled. "We're definitely not at the Hyatt, Toto."

He chuckled as he tossed her dress over the back of a
chair covered in a dark brocade. It was only when Roxi
looked closer that she noticed the pattern was taken from
Japanese Netsuke woodcuts depicting a dizzying variety of
sexual positions. "Good guess."

"Am I allowed to look at them?" Or were they, she wondered, going to get straight down to business?

"That's what they're here for."

He took off his jacket, yanked the tie off, slipped the onyx
links out of his cuffs and put them in a ceramic box shaped
like one of Georgia O'Keefe's flower pictures, which, of
course, everyone, even people who knew nothing about art,
understood immediately were meant to depict vulvas.

"Would you like something to drink?"

"No, thank you." Her earlier orgasms, along with anticipation and the blatant eroticism of her surroundings, already
had Roxi drunk with feeling. She didn't want to risk adding
alcohol to the mix.

He unbuttoned the top two buttons of his shirt, poured a
glass of brandy for himself, then leaned against the desk,
legs crossed at the ankles. She could feel him watching her.

"It's quite a remarkable collection." And extensive. She
glanced down at the ivory chess set on the table and realized
that the depictions of the ancient gods were anatomically
correct.

"Thank you."

Surprised, she glanced back at him. "You own them?"

"I've collected them over the years. And yes, to answer your next question, this is my suite."

"Did you bring your little friends up here back when you were celebrating your birthday?"

"No, because at the time it was merely an inn and restaurant with a rather interesting past."

"As a whorehouse."

"You make it sound so shoddy," he chided. "But yes, sex was for sale here. As it was in other places. Swansea was just"—he trailed a hand over the back of the chair—"a sumptuous cut above the rest.

"When my first film hit it big a few years ago, I had some funds to invest. Since I'm a Savannahian at heart, when the building came on the market I bought it, dumped a bundle into restoring it to its former glory, with some admittedly modern touches like soundproofing the rooms and some state-of-the-art video equipment, and turned it into a private club.

"And yes, I also returned the focus to eroticism. But if money is being exchanged between consenting adults, business is taken care of before anyone arrives at the door."

"I didn't read anything about you owning a place like this."

"That's because the deed's in the name of a real estate development company I founded with friends. And my managing partners, who take care of the day-to-day running of the premises, are very discreet, which is a must given our clientele."

"I suppose it would rock the social order if people found out about all the rich, lecherous old movers and shakers swinging with their young mistresses on the chandeliers," she said dryly.

"Would it surprise you to know that approximately one

third of our memberships are owned by women? And that I'm told that many of our guests are married couples who enjoy having a place away from home where they can indulge their fantasies without worrying about mothers-in-law calling or children walking into the bedroom at inopportune times?"

"Sort of like a sexual Disneyland for consenting adults."

"Everyone needs a hobby." Amusement touched his eyes. "I prefer to think of Swansea as a five-star date destination."

"Well, it's definitely a level above pizza and a chick flick," Roxi said. "You must come to town often."

The door to the bedroom was open, revealing a lake-sized, hand-carved bed that claimed the center of the room. She was surprised as something twisted inside her. Something that felt uncomfortably like jealousy.

"Apparently not as often as I should." He sipped the brandy. "An oversight I'll have to correct."

"You're forgetting my three date rule."

"Sweetheart, I doubt there's anything I could forget about you."

"Then you're ignoring it?"

"Let's just table the topic for now." He put his glass down on a mahogany desk next to a brocade chair and wagged a finger. "Enough chitchat. Come stand in front of me and let me look at you."

This time she didn't argue. Just crossed the room and stood, the toes of her spindly black heels touching the front of his shoes as she waited for what would happen next.

"Good girl."

It was more than a little chauvinistic. Strangely, at this moment, she didn't care.

He skimmed his fingertips down her throat with tantalizing slowness, his touch leaving a trail of sparks.

His stroking fingers moved over the bodice of the corset. "Take this off."

Gladly, given that it had been hours since she'd been able to take a full breath.

Roxi reached behind her back and worked the hook and eye fasteners open, one by one. Which wasn't easy. She would have appreciated some help, had actually anticipated him taking it off her when she'd handed over her Mastercard this morning, but apparently for now, anyway, she was on her own.

She might be playing submissive, but that didn't mean she had to play dead. When the last hook was unfastened, she held the corset against her chest with one hand. Her eyes lifted to his. And held.

She waited.

He waited.

When she took her hand way, it fell to the floor.

"Nice." He took her breasts in his hands, as he had downstairs in the cellar. "A perfect handful."

Ha! So much for worrying about not owning a pair of silicone D-cup boobs.

He frowned when he took in the red indentations left by the corset boning. "As sexy as that little bit of frou-frou is, you won't wear it again when you're with me," he said.

"Not tonight," she agreed. "But we're on Cinderella time, *cher*. After midnight, you don't get to call the shots."

"Emma hinted you might not be the type of woman I'm accustomed to." He traced his fingers over the faint red lines. "She's right." Roxi sucked in her stomach as he pressed an open kiss against the skin his fingers, and his eyes, had already warmed. "I don't want anything marring this tender flesh."

He picked up the glass again. Took another sip of the brandy. "Now take off those panties."

She slipped her fingers beneath the elastic riding low on her hips, did a little shimmy, and sent them sliding down her legs.

Then stepped out of them and stood there, hands behind her back, breasts thrust out, inviting his study.

"Incredible," he murmured, seemingly more to himself than to her.

He framed her waist with his broad, long-fingered hands. Expecting him to kiss her, she tilted her head and allowed her eyelids to drift closed.

When he lifted her off her feet, her eyes flew open.

He sat her on the desk. Then used his knee to coax her stocking-clad legs apart.

"I want to see you."

She knew exactly what he meant. But because she didn't want to hand him everything he wanted on a silver platter, she pretended otherwise. "I'm right here, *cher*. Nearly naked."

"Good try." He lifted the heavy glass in a salute. "I want to see those lower lips that proved so sensitive earlier this evening. And then I want you to make yourself come."

She felt the blood rush into her cheeks. Her breasts. Across her stomach, spreading like a fever.

"I don't think I can."

"Of course you can," he said reasonably. "Unless you expect me to believe a woman who's reached the ripe age of twenty-five, a woman of your intense passions, has never masturbated?"

"Of course I have."

In fact, she'd brought herself off just the other night, while reading much this same scene in *The Story of O*, when Sir Stephen had brutally punished his new slave for not doing what Sloan was instructing her to do.

Which was scary, thinking of how she was alone here in this sex suite with a man she didn't know. While she might be intrigued by the occasional kink, she definitely wasn't into pain or humiliation.

He cupped the snifter between his palms and took another drink, eyeing her over the rim of the glass. "If it eases your mind, I'm not into hurting women."

"I know that." His aura might be blazing red, but she didn't detect a bit of danger. While she wasn't in the habit of masturbating in front of a partner, this wouldn't be the first time. But she was suddenly feeing uncharacteristically self-conscious. "I just need a minute."

"Take your time." He smiled, showing her that while the circumstances might seem similar, he was nothing like the brutal Sir Stephen. "I'm enjoying the view."

She touched her hand between her legs, in that same place it had been again this morning when she'd awakened. Then she flinched. It was still slick from her orgasms, swollen and painfully hypersensitive from the earlier deep thrusts of his fingers.

"That's it."

She lifted her head and met his eyes, which had darkened to a deep emerald flame and were watching her every movement.

"Now open yourself wider." His dark voice wrapped around her like velvet bonds. "Let me see the lovely rose bloom."

She did as instructed, parting her swollen lower lips, like separating the petals of the rose he'd suggested.

"Does that feel good?"

"A bit."

"Does it hurt?"

"Not too badly." It was getting better. Closing her eyes, she slipped into a warm, sensual fog of need.

"Tell me exactly how it feels."

"Lonely."

He chuckled. "We'll take care of that soon enough." She heard something rustle, but unwilling to risk losing the fantasy, didn't open her eyes. "Now lift that tender little bud."

It pulsed like a hot little heart against her fingertips as she obeyed.

"That's excellent."

His voice sounded as if it was coming from far away. Like right after Katrina, when a post-traumatic stress therapist hypnotized her to help her overcome the nightmares that had plagued her. The difference was, the therapist's goal had been to soothe her. Sloan's voice was doing exactly the opposite.

"Now let me see you make yourself come."

By this point, she was so turned on he couldn't have stopped her. Leaning back on her elbows, she lasciviously rubbed her fingers over her soaking clit, driving herself closer and closer to the brink.

She was panting, one hand on a tingling nipple which had turned diamond hard, the other between her legs, two fingers pumping fast and deep.

She heard herself begin to moan, and couldn't care, so caught up was she in her desperate need for release.

"That's it, baby," Sloan encouraged on a ragged groan that had her looking up at him through slit lids. He'd left the chair and was standing over her, naked and gloriously erect.

All it took was the sight of those long dark fingers curled around his sheathed, rampant penis to push Roxi over the edge.

She came with a shudder and a sound that was half cry, half sob.

But before she could come down, while she was still scattered into a million little pieces, she felt his hands against her trembling thighs and he was pushing her legs apart.

"More."

"I can't."

"Want to bet?"

She cried out when his hot and hungry mouth clamped down on her painfully sensitive clit.

"Oh, please." Her hips bucked. "Sloan." She'd fallen back

onto the desk and was writhing beneath the mouth that was sucking on the fiery nub. "It's too . . . I can't . . ."

His fingers dug into her thighs, pinning her to the glossy wooden surface as he continued to feast, devouring her with lips and teeth and tongue.

Just when she was sure she couldn't endure another moment, another orgasm ripped through her, more intense than any she'd ever experienced.

"Again," he said over her scream, not giving her a second to recover before driving her up the steep peak again, even higher this time, to where the air was thin and her eyes went darkly blind.

The entire world spun away. There was only the painful pleasure between her legs, the thrust of his tongue plunging in and out, and in and out, his teeth tugging on her swollen, throbbing clit, creating a pleasure so acute she could only scream and plead, in a voice that sounded nothing like her own, for him to stop. To never stop.

Her bare hips were slapping the desktop in a way she knew on some distant level would leave bruises. She was moaning. Sobbing. Cursing, then begging in a way she never would have imagined she, a sexually liberated woman of the twenty-first century, would ever do.

And then she was coming in a burst of heat and light, a supernova of a climax that had her shattering into a thousand brilliant pieces.

And even then, even as her screams were still reverberating in the silk-draped room, he wasn't ready to let her come down.

"My turn," he said, lifting her limp and drained body off the desk. Holding her up by her sore bottom, he plunged into her, all the way to the hilt.

Somehow, she managed to lock her legs around his waist as he carried her into the adjoining bedroom, working her back and forth from the root of his penis to the tip, her soaked pubic curls slamming hard against his groin.

Once. Twice. A third time.

She heard the groan rumbling deep in his sweat-slicked chest. Felt the shudder deep in his loins.

The bed was a four-poster, draped in the same wine silk as the walls. Bracing her against one of the posts, he thrust his hips one last time, his cock surging deep, all the way to her womb, a feral shout of release ripping from his throat as he came with a bone-racking shudder, triggering yet another deeper, longer climax that rolled over her like a tidal wave.

"Oh my God," she gasped. "I think you've killed us."

"You'll be fine." He dragged her down, his hot and heavy body pressing her deep into the mattress. "Better than fine." He kissed her, a long, deep kiss she could feel all the way to her toes. "You're fuckin' fabulous."

He pulled out of her, rolled over, and wrapped her in his arms, holding her while the tremors subsided and her breathing began to return to something resembling normal.

"Fuckin' fabulous," he repeated against her throat. "And as good as that was, things are about to get a whole lot better."

Roxi was too spent to argue with that outrageously confident statement. Which was just as well. Because, she was to discover, as the waxing white moon moved across the night sky, Sloan Hawthorne was definitely not a man given to exaggeration.

Eleven

Having grown up enjoying the tales of pirates using the underground tunnels throughout Savannah to smuggle their stolen booty, Sloan found Hex Appeal, located on the city's Riverwalk, to be an absolute treasure trove.

The small space was packed from gleaming wood floor to rafters with a dizzying array of New Age stuff. Claiming the center of the bay window that extended out onto the cobblestone sidewalk was what appeared to be a maypole, festooned in colorful ribbons, surrounded by earthenware bowls of crystals that captured the spring sunlight and bounced rainbows around the room.

Colorful glass shelves lined two of the walls and were crammed with bottles of herbs, candles, and figurines of various gods and goddesses he couldn't begin to recognize. An overstuffed couch covered with gaily patterned pillows claimed the back wall, and was flanked by two comfortable chairs. A tea set and wicker baskets of what appeared to be home-baked cookies sat on a small brass table, inviting shoppers to linger, while a pretty little sign above the sofa gently warned that unaccompanied children would be turned into toads—or given a free kitten.

The crush of customers kept Roxi from hearing the brass bell that had announced his arrival, allowing him to watch her undetected from the shadow of a display of handmade straw brooms in the corner.

Unlike the sexy witch he'd spent the night with, she was surprisingly, briskly efficient. But she certainly hadn't traded efficiency for the personal touch. On the contrary, proving herself a deft juggler, she somehow managed to pitch the eclectic merchandise, answer questions, ring up the flood of sales, and package the purchases in hot pink Hex Appeal shopping bags.

She was, as he'd already decided long before he'd dropped her back at her house a little after dawn, spectacular. And, although she might not know it yet, she was his. Not just for last night or today, but forever.

Reminding himself of Emma's cautionary words, which had been underscored by Roxi's own ridiculous three date rule, Sloan decided to keep his intentions to himself. For now.

If the lady wanted to believe their relationship was all about sex, he wasn't going to dissuade her. At least not until he'd managed to work his way around, over, or through those emotional barricades she'd erected around her heart.

As if sensing his thoughts, she glanced up. And amazingly, after all they'd shared last night, blushed.

He found the tinge of pink brightening her cheeks endearing. Found her actually dropping a pewter unicorn encouraging. She could deny it all she wanted, but he'd gotten to her. The same as she had to him.

"Well, this is a surprise," she said as she wrapped some pink tissue paper around a fist-sized piece of quartz.

He crossed to the counter. "I don't suppose you'd believe I was in the neighborhood."

She shrugged, shoulders bared by a snug pink knit halter top. "And just happened to be in the market for a love spell?"

"That's not such a bad idea." Not that he believed in such things, but so long as she did, maybe that might be the means to achieve his ends. He dipped his hand into a bowl of small tumbled stones. "I actually came in to get some perfume blended for my mother—she has a birthday coming up—but a love spell would be cool, too. What would you suggest?"

"Roxanne." A woman wearing a flowing purple tunic and ankle-length skirt shoved him out of the way. "You haven't put out any *cannariculi*."

"Those cookies need honey for drizzling and dipping, which gets messy in the store," Roxi said mildly. "Which is why I chose oatmeal. Which," she tacked on over the woman's snort, "are also a traditional Beltane food."

"Perhaps where you come from," the harridan sniffed.

"I like oatmeal," Sloan said. Then, to prove a point, he took one from the tiered plate she'd put by the register with a calligraphic little note that read: Help yourself.

"Hmmm," he said around a mouthful of oatmeal and golden raisins, "delicious."

The woman looked up at him as if noticing him for the first time, then shrieked. "You are Sloan Hawthorne."

"That's me," he agreed. "And you are?"

"Martha Corey." She glared up at him. Poked him in the chest. "A name you should know well."

"I'm sorry." Sloan exchanged a glance over the top of her head with Roxi, who shook her head and rolled her eyes. "I'm afraid it's not ringing a bell." He flashed her a winning smile. "Do our families know each other?"

"You might say that. In another life."

"I see," Sloan said, not seeing anything at all. They were, however, beginning to draw a crowd.

The woman turned toward Roxi. "This man is a Haw-thorne."

"I know," Roxi replied, appearing as puzzled as Sloan himself was.

"I wager he's changed it!" The way she was pointing at him, Sloan expected her to next say, *And your little dog, too!* "His name!"

Ah, hell. He'd known he was going to have to tell her, but hadn't wanted it to come out like this.

"It was undoubtedly *Hathorne*," Martha told Roxi, as well as the customers who were now standing around watch-ing the show. "The judge from the witch trials," she shrieked again, when Roxi's only response to that allegation was a blank look.

Roxi looked up at Sloan, clearly startled by the news, as he'd known she would be after she hadn't made the connec-tion when they'd been discussing their heritage last night. He'd been going to tell her. Really.

"*Those* Puritans?" she asked.

"I'm afraid so."

"Well." She blew out a breath. "You're just full of sur-prises, aren't you?"

"At least you can't say I've been boring."

"That's true enough."

"How about you come to lunch with me and we can dis-cuss it."

"I'm busy. This is a holiday weekend for us and—"

"Oh, for the Goddess's sake." A tall, gorgeous woman with braided and beaded black hair, smooth brown skin, and a body that could've walked off a *Playboy* centerfold spread came up to them. "You can be such a workaholic. Hello. I take it you're the famous Sloan Hawthorne."

"I don't know about famous, but that's my name," he said.

"I'm Jaira Guinard." She held out a beringed hand. "But

in case Roxi proves herself to be an idiot and turns you down again, you can call me available," she said with the sugar-coated, flirtatious female aggression that was uniquely Southern. Couldn't his own mother, happily married for forty years, charm with the best of them?

He laughed, despite the daggers being shot his way from the old woman's narrowed blue eyes. "I'll keep that in mind."

"You do that, sugar." Jaira skimmed a blood red talon down the front of his shirt. "And if you need a really hot group to sing for your soundtrack, you'll be wanting to hear the Papa Legba Voodoo Priestesses."

"Would you happen to be one of those priestesses?"

"Why, yes." She fluttered artificial lashes so thick and long Sloan was amazed she could keep her eyes open. "As a matter of fact, I am."

"The group's wonderful," Roxi said. "I don't know why I didn't think to recommend them while we were having dinner last night."

"That's all right, darlin'," Jaira said silkily, her gaze going to the little love bite on Roxi's neck. "I suspect you and Sloan got so caught up in other business, you simply forgot."

"That's pretty much what happened," Roxi agreed. "Now, although it's lovely to see you, Sloan, if you'll just give me some of your mother's attributes, we'll get started on her scent. But right now, if you don't mind, as you can see we're very busy—"

"Oh, don't be such a stick in the mud," Jaira scolded. "Let the man feed you, Roxi. I'll hold down the fort here."

Roxi glanced around. Sloan was encouraged when she was clearly torn. "Go," one of the customers said.

"Go," a second echoed.

A moment later the entire store, all except his nemesis, was chanting, "Go, go, go."

"All right!" She was laughing as her hands flew up.

"Thirty minutes," she told Sloan. "No more." She splayed her hands on her hips, which pulled the halter top across her breasts.

"It's a date."

"The second one," she reminded him.

"Actually, it's only the first," he said as they left the store for the cobblestone sidewalk crowded with tourists.

"I must have made quite an impression if you've already forgotten last night," she complained.

"I haven't forgotten a thing about last night." He skimmed a finger over a faint bruise on her collarbone. "Sorry about this." He vaguely recalled biting her the second—or had it been the third?—time he'd come.

"Don't apologize. I enjoyed it. A lot."

"So did I. In fact, if it *had* been a date, it would've been the best of my life. But it wasn't a date."

"Excuse me? I just happened to be wearing a dress that maxed out my credit card—which, by the way, I don't do for every guy who asks me out—underwear that cost more than my monthly power bill, and my best fuck-me heels. We had a candlelight dinner and hot monkey sex afterwards. Followed by dessert and champagne, which you ended up eating and drinking off me."

"I seem to recall you doing some fingerpainting with the fudge sauce yourself," he said, then wished he hadn't thought of that just now, being that he really didn't want to have to walk all the way down to the park with a boner the size of Texas.

"Exactly. So, if dinner, sex, and playing paint the penis with fudge sauce wasn't a date, I'd like to know what it was."

"A business meeting."

"Wow. It's true!" She looked up at him with exaggeratedly wide eyes. "Y'all really do things differently in California. If you call last night a business meeting, your Hollywood movie conferences must be full out orgies."

"We talked about Morganna over dinner." He skimmed a hand beneath the long glossy slide of hair, pleased with her faint tremor. Oh yes, they weren't finished yet. Not by a long shot. "So, technically it was a consultation."

"Good try. But it was a date." They'd already passed three restaurants which were starting to fill up with lunch crowds. "Do you have some place in mind? Other than Six Flags over Sex City? Because as enticing as the idea may be, I really don't have time for a nooner."

"I suspected that might unfortunately be the case. Though, I have to tell you, sweetheart, that shirt is damn tempting."

She glanced down at the script running across her chest that suggested, "Get a Taste of Religion—Lick a Witch."

"You've already done that."

"True. Which is why I intend to go back for seconds. Meanwhile, how does a picnic sound?"

"Lovely. But again . . ." She cast a warning glance down at her watch.

"I had the chef prepare a picnic. I thought we'd eat at the park." Which was less than a five-minute walk away at the end of the Riverwalk.

"You're got yourself a date."

He skimmed a finger down the slope of her nose. "Consultation."

"Date," she corrected firmly.

He'd always found that women were suckers for romance. Fortunately, having always been a sucker for women, it was easy to give them what they wanted. Which, in turn, tended to make them generous in return.

He'd had Roxi Dupree's body and it was everything he'd dreamed of, and more. Now he had to capture her heart. Which should've been a piece of cake.

Definitive word there, *should've*.

Unfortunately, whatever fickle fates or gods had decided

he belonged with this woman must've had one helluva sense
of humor because apparently Emma hadn't been kidding.

The luscious witch was definitely a hit and run artist.

It wasn't going to be that easy to convince her to see the
light. As he retrieved the wicker basket from the backseat of
the rental car parked across the street, Sloan tried to remind
himself that he'd never truly appreciated things that came
too easily.

Twelve

"I should've told you about my ancestor before that old woman had a chance to out me," he said as they sat on a bench beneath a leafy green tree on the banks of the river at the end of the short street.

"You did, in a way," she said with a shrug. "I mean, you did mention the Puritans. I just never put two and two together. I think the only reason Martha did was because she's one of those militant hard-liners who spends much of her life living in the past, suffering from ancient grievances. She took her witch name after one of the women who were hung on Gallow's Hill."

"Ouch. I can see where my ancestry might be a sore subject."

"Oh, she already hated you because of Morganna. She doesn't feel the Mistress of the Dark is a proper representation of the Craft."

"What do you think?"

She took a bite of shrimp salad on a buttery croissant that nearly melted in her mouth. "I think if I had more than three dates with you, I'd end up being the size of that tanker," she said, nodding toward the huge cargo ship making its way up the river just a few yards away.

"You'd be perfect whatever size you were."

"Flatterer."

"It's true." He took a bite of his huge roast beef sandwich. "Besides, we'll work it off."

"I'm going to hold you to that."

"I hope you do." He considered kissing her, then decided that if he began, he wouldn't be able to stop, and being that they were in a public park, that probably wasn't the hottest idea he'd ever had. "By the way, did you happen to notice that that Corey woman filched a candle?"

"A candle and a vial of dragon's blood," Roxi said. "She's a kleptomaniac. Her niece always pays up at the end of the month."

"Maybe she's just smart. Getting someone else to pay for her witch supplies."

"That thought has occurred to me."

They continued eating in a surprisingly comfortable silence.

"So," she said, gesturing toward a nearby statue with a crunchy sweet potato French fry, "do you think she was really waving for her lover?"

The statue, portraying a woman in a simple dress waving a piece of cloth, with a collie by her side, represented one of Savannah's most endearing legends. The daughter of a lighthouse keeper on the nearby coastal island of Elba, Florence Martus, who'd become known as Waving Girl, had lived a quiet and uneventful life until one day she began communicating with sailors by waving a white handkerchief as they passed. At night, she'd wave a lantern, and it wasn't long before sailors around the world began to signal her back.

Over the decades she became a beacon of the city, daily offering a joyful welcome or fond farewell.

That story in itself would have been good enough for most cities. But Savannah, staying true to its colorful self, had chosen to add speculation that Florence had fallen in love with a sailor who'd promised to return, but had vanished into the ocean's vast horizon.

"I think it's a nice story," he said. "And perhaps it began that way. But while most women are probably willing to stick a relationship out for more than three dates, forty years seems like overkill. I suspect it's more likely she lived a lonely life and waving to the ships not only gave her a connection with someone besides her father and brother, but also gave her something meaningful to do, given how, if the thousands of letters addressed to Waving Girl she received are any indication, the sailors seemed grateful."

"I suppose. It's sad either way."

"Granted." He balled up the waxed paper and tossed it back into the wicker basket. "So, I guess you're not going to stand out at the airport waving off planes until I come back?"

"Sorry. I wouldn't hold my breath if I were you."

"I figured that'd be your answer. And I've decided what kind of spell I want."

She arched a brow.

"A binding spell."

She laughed. Reached out and ruffled his hair. "That's what you say now. Trust me, *cher*. That's one helluva powerful spell and not to be used casually. If I gave you the power to bind me to you, by this time next week you'd be so sick and tired of constantly having me around, you'd start hating me."

"Think so?"

"I know so."

He knew differently. But reminded himself that patience was supposed to be a virtue.

"So," he said, deciding it was time to change the subject,

"remember that scene where Brianna uses her charmed sword to behead the evil gods of Hades?"

"Of course. It was the first time she ever went over to the dark side."

"You don't think audiences will have a problem with that? She is, after all, the 'good' twin."

"They were holding her sister hostage. Of course she'd save her. I have seven sisters and brothers, and if anyone threatened them, I'd do whatever was in my power to save them.

"But you know, as much as I really like the books, pagans don't view light and dark, good and bad, the dualistic way Western society does. Western thought, being deeply rooted in the Christian view, tends to view dualism as a battle between the good, or light, versus evil, which is dark.

"While paganism is based on monism, where light and dark exist, but as polarities, two opposite, yet complementing aspects of a whole. So, in reality, Morganna and Brianna should be equal parts of the whole. If you want to stay true to the belief system. But," she said, "I can understand how that doesn't work well when you're telling it to an audience steeped in Western thought."

"Plus there's the little matter of Gavin Thomas having written the characters that way."

"Well, there is that," she agreed with a smile. "And what a unique concept. A moviemaker actually attempting to stay true to an author's vision."

"I try," he said modestly. Not mentioning that Thomas's witch wife had threatened to turn him into a toad if he didn't treat her husband's work—and witchcraft—with respect.

"That's one of the reasons I came to Savannah," she revealed. "After Katrina blew away the Every Body's Beautiful day spa and spell shop, since I had to rebuild anyway, I was looking to spread my wings. Savannah had always interested me because, like New Orleans, it's a city that embraces its dark, midnight side right along with its light. And, as I said, that balance is what the Craft is all about.

"This time, though, without Emma to handle the spa stuff, I decided to stick with the magic aspect, and the concept seems to be working. I suppose, if the box office for your Morganna movie comes even close to *The Last Pirate*, my business should get a nice boost from all the moviegoers who leave the theater wanting to embrace their inner witch."

"I'm all for Morganna making buckets of bucks," he said. "But how many people do you believe are actually harboring an inner witch?"

"I believe everyone's born with the power of magic. It's just that not everyone learns how to use it."

"Now you remind me of Morganna again."

She stood up, folded her arms, and looked down at him. "Let me guess. Despite making this movie, you don't believe in witchcraft. Or magic."

"You're not talking about an illusionist making a seven-forty-seven disappear, are you?"

"No."

"Then, I guess I have to say no. I don't. But don't take it personally, sugar. I don't believe in the Easter Bunny or Santa Claus, either."

She didn't respond. Just gave him a long, steady look. He could practically see the wheels turning inside that gorgeous dark head, but had no idea what she was thinking.

He wondered idly if Gavin's wife was actually telling the truth about that toad thing. Thought about the sign on the wall in Hex Appeal.

Nah.

"What are you doing tonight?"

"I was hoping to spend it making love to you."

"It's customary to ask a woman for a date ahead of time. I have a thing tonight."

"A thing. Is that like a date? With some other guy?" Like that was going to happen.

"A date. But not exactly with another man. It's Beltane. You might know it as May Day."

"Ah." Comprehension belatedly sunk in. "So I guess you'll be doing some sort of ritual thing with your coven, or whatever you call it."

"Martha would call it a coven. As it happens, I'm a solitary witch. I'll be doing my ritual at home."

"May I come watch?"

"I would have thought you had enough of a show last night."

"I'm serious. I'll admit that I'm not a believer in what you call the Craft, but I'd really like to see how a witch celebrates a sacred festival."

"For research."

"No." He thought they ought to get this point perfectly clear. "Because I want to know you better. I want to try to understand what's important to you."

She gave him a narrowed, slit-eyed look. "That's probably a mistake. The more people know about one another, the more likely they are to get involved. And I've already told you I'm not into commitment stuff."

"Are you saying you don't want to know anything about me?"

She flushed again, just as she had back in her shop.

"No." She shook her head. Dragged her gaze out toward the river where another tanker was heading into the harbor. "I mean, sure. Of course I'm interested, *cher*. It's just that I . . ."

"Dammit." She turned away and began marching back down the cobblestone roadway. "You're confusing me."

The admission, Sloane thought, was a start.

He let her get a little ahead of him, enjoying the sexy sway of her tight butt in those white cotton pants that stopped right below her knees. The back of which, he'd discovered last night, were directly, erotically, connected to her pretty pink clit.

Catching up with her in two long strides, he grabbed her arm, spun her against his chest, and little caring about the tourists crowding the sidewalk, kissed her, a long hard kiss that sent a jolt of heat shooting through them both.

"Static electricity," she murmured, sounding as staggered as he felt.

"That must be it." He opted against pointing out that he couldn't recall any science class teaching about receiving electrical shocks from cobblestones.

"Are you going to let me come with you tonight?"

She shook her head. Not in denial, but resignation. "You may as well."

"Thank you, darlin'."

He'd received more generous invitations over the years, but wasn't going to quibble. Leaning forward on the balls of his feet, he brushed a lighter, gentler kiss against her tightly set mouth, encouraged when her lips parted on a soft sigh.

They continued walking back to the shop, his arm around her shoulders, hers around his waist.

"Beltane," he said, "that's a fertility festival, right?"

"It celebrates the divine union of the Lord and Lady."

Sloan grinned. "Hot damn."

Thirteen

After she went back to work, Sloan researched Beltane on-line and discovered it was the one festival people had been most unwilling to give up, no matter how much the Church had fought against the holiday.

Which made sense, he thought, given that it was definitely the kinkiest of all the pagan holy days, revolving around lust and passion as the celebrants honored not just the mating of their goddess and her consort, but their own bodies and the male and female physical relationship, a necessity if they wanted the human race to continue.

In ancient times they'd burn fires on hilltops, couples would make love in freshly plowed fields to ensure the success of the crops, and any child resulting from this night was considered a chosen one. A blessing from the goddess.

A nice thought, Sloan thought, at the same time making sure he stocked up on enough condoms to ensure there wouldn't be any surprise blessings from this Beltane celebration.

The moon was a silver sickle, slicing through a deep purple sky. Fog was drifting in from the sea, obscuring the stars and wrapping the silent night in a soft, misty shawl of white. Thunder rumbled in the distance.

They were sitting outside, sipping red wine in her postage-stamp backyard which was surrounded by a tall green hedge that provided privacy.

She was filling in the bits and pieces of the Shabbat he'd learned about today.

"In Celtic society," Roxi explained, "not only did the woman own all the land and cattle, she also chose who she'd marry. The handfasting contract lasted a year. At the end of that time, if she or her husband were unhappy with each other, they'd just walk away."

"No harm, no foul," he said.

"Exactly." She nodded. "It was actually a very sensible system."

"This from a woman who'd insist on renewing every three days," he reminded her.

"Times were different then," she said mildly. "Relationships were all tied up with land and property and survival. Not to mention that being tied to the earth as they were, an agrarian society, there was so much more opportunity for powerful outside forces to rule your life."

"I know how it feels to have outside forces rule my life every time one of my movies has its opening weekend," he said.

"I believe it would have been a bit more serious."

"Hey, they're both about survival. If Morganna goes bust, I don't eat."

"At least not caviar and champagne," she said dryly. "My point is that Beltane would've been the one time a year when people could let loose and celebrate the future instead of dwelling on all the things that might have gone wrong in the past."

"And fuck like bunnies."

She dimpled prettily in the light from the candles she'd placed around the yard.

"I was going to say it was when they'd make wishes for the year ahead, because their lives would be forecast by what they saw at dawn the next morning. But that fucking thing works for me, too."

As they laughed together, her eyes warmed with something richer than lust. Perhaps he was only fooling himself, but Sloan didn't think so. Despite what she might think she believed, he knew that by inviting him here tonight, by allowing him to share in something so important to her, she was opening not just her body to him, but her heart, as well.

"You know when I said you reminded me of Morganna?"

"It would be difficult to forget. Being that it was only last night."

"I was wrong."

"Oh?" Her luscious lips turned down in a little moue.

He skimmed a hand down her hair, which she'd woven with a riot of fresh flowers that smelled like a night garden. "You're worlds above that fictional witch." He touched a palm to her silky smooth cheek. "In fact, I may just be beginning to believe in magic."

She smiled, openly pleased, and covered his hand for a moment with hers.

Although he had never witnessed a ceremony in real life, he'd read enough books and seen enough movies to recognize the casting of the sacred circle, the calling of the elements. In lieu of a maypole, she'd woven ribbons of traditional white and red together and had hung them from the branches of a sweet gum tree in the center of the yard. A CD of a Celtic harp played softly.

The wide sleeves of the red robe she was wearing slid down her arms as she lifted a silver chalice in a toast.

"Behold the chalice, symbol of the Goddess, the great Mother who brings fruitfulness and knowledge to all."

Putting the chalice onto the table, she lifted a knife, the handle formed into the shape of a Celtic crane, the blade glinting in the slanting moonlight. Although Sloan knew it was only his imagination, he could have sworn he saw a shimmering blue energy swirling around the sharp steel tip.

"Behold the Athame, symbol of the God, the all-powerful Father who brings energy and strength to all."

The distant storm was growing closer, lifting her hair, tossing it in a tangle around her face. Heat lightning shimmered behind churning dark clouds as she picked up the chalice again and slowly and deliberately lowered the Athame blade into the wine.

"Joined in holy union together, they bring new life to all."

Impossibly, the wine began to bubble, smoke pouring out of the chalice like the dry ice his mother used to put in the Halloween punch.

"Blessed be."

She took a sip of the wine, then held the chalice out to Sloan, who couldn't have resisted if his entire fortune—his life—depended on it.

The wine was warm, like deep red velvet against his tongue. After he'd taken a drink, he handed it back to Roxi. Instead of taking it from his hand, she placed her palms on top of his hands and together, with her leading the action, they poured the remainder of the wine onto the ground, which immediately swallowed it up.

Returning the chalice and knife to the table, she went through the rite of closing the circle, then turned toward Sloan.

With her eyes holding his, she lifted her hands to the silver brooch holding her cape together, unfastened it, and let it slide down her shoulders to the ground.

She was an enchantress. Circe. Lorelei. Morgan La Fey.

Brigid, goddess of eternal fire. She was all the goddesses of all the ancient myths in one stunning package and he wanted her more than he'd ever wanted anything in his life.

Smiling a sorceress's smile she went up on her bare toes, splayed her fingers at the back his head, and pulled his lips down to hers.

Fourteen

Sloan heard the low, threatening rumble of thunder and couldn't tell if it was coming from the midnight dark sky or inside himself as he kissed her in a deep, tongue-thrusting, branding kiss.

He felt the four winds whipping her hair across both their faces, and although he knew it was as impossible as the blue light he'd thought he'd seen bubbling in that chalice earlier, he felt as if they'd been swept into a tempest and were being dragged across the night.

She tasted of sex. Of temptation. Of magic.

As the sky opened up in a hot, drenching rain, they dragged each other to the ground, rolling on the wet grass, greedy mouths devouring raw, painful breaths, hands tearing at his clothes.

The storm broke with a clap of thunder directly overhead that shook the earth beneath them. As Roxi ripped Sloan's shirt open, sending buttons flying across the garden, neither noticed.

Lightning forked across the sky; as he sat up and yanked the ruined shirt off, neither cared.

Her shaking hands struggled with his belt buckle, but she managed it, whipping it through the loops of his slacks. There was a clang of metal as it landed somewhere on the brick patio.

Bending over him, her face shielded by her thick fall of hair, she lowered the zipper then released his rampant erection from its confinement. It jutted from the whorl of dark hair, thick and long and heavy. And for tonight, it was hers.

She curled her fingers around the suede-smooth girth and began stroking him.

"Harder," he instructed through clenched teeth. Covering her hand with his, he tightened her grip and increased the strength as he began to pump their joined hands up and down, spreading the slick fluid from root to purple-hued tip.

"That's the way, sugar." Sloan couldn't remember the last time he'd shaken from need. "That's right." He couldn't remember because he fucking never had before tonight. Before Roxi. Not even when he'd been a hormone-driven kid.

"God, you're good at this." He bucked into her clenched fist and tangled his hands in her hair. "Faster."

She did as instructed, stroking, pumping him hard and fast, her own breathing getting harsher as she got into the rhythm.

"More," she said. Dragging her head away from his grasp, she scrambled up onto her knees and bent over him, her long wet hair draping over his chest.

She kissed the tip with that same gentle touch she'd first used, making him fear she was going to drag this out. But once again she proved herself to be perfectly in sync with him sexually as she took him in her mouth, swallowing him deep, all the way to the back of her throat.

Her tongue was doing amazing things, stroking up and down and around while her head bobbed, and the slurping as she sucked him was one of the sexiest things he'd ever heard, right up there with the way she'd screamed.

"Oh, yeah. That's it, baby." He could feel the pressure building in his balls, at the base of his spine. "But you'd better pull out now because—"

"Mmmph." Her jaw was stretched wide so she could take him all in, which only allowed that mumbled protest, but she had no trouble making her intentions known.

Stubbornly shaking her head, she dug her fingers into his hips and kept pumping.

His stomach clenched. His thighs were trembling. And then he lost it, pistoning his hips violently as he exploded with a long, shuddering moan.

And still she kept sucking and licking, her lips closed tightly around his throbbing cock until he was semi-flaccid. Then, and only then, did she allow herself to collapse upon his chest.

Sometime during that world-class blow job, the driving rain had lessened to a soft drizzle that should have, in theory, cooled them off. But as the water hit their overheated flesh, Sloan imagined he could hear a sizzle, like water on a hot griddle.

"Thank you," she breathed, pressing a kiss against his wet skin.

He managed a rough, hoarse laugh. "I think you've got that backwards."

"No." A lingering bit of lightning illuminated her face as she smiled up at him, and Sloan knew he'd remember the way she looked tonight for the rest of his life. "I love your body, *cher*. All of it. Especially"—she trailed a finger over the tip and made it jump in response—"this delicious super-sized cock."

"You realize, if you keep talking to me this way, you're not going to get any sleep tonight either," he growled as he felt himself growing hard already.

Her laugh as she kissed him was sexy and wicked and probably would've gotten her hung on Gallows Hill if she'd lived in old Judge Hawthorne's time.

"Promises, promises."

"I've got a proposition for you," he said, much, much later as they lay in her bed, arms and legs entwined, riding the golden afterglow of a night of passion. A soft predawn light was beginning to slip through the slats of the plantation shutters, casting a lavender glow over the room.

"I don't think there's anything we haven't done," she said. Her fingers were idly trailing through the arrowing of hair on his chest.

"Oh, I'm sure we can think of a few things." Sloan ran a lazy finger down her spine.

He glanced around the room, taking in the crystals with their glittering magic from the earth waiting to be released, the candles on every flat surface, the bottles of lotions and potions, and the frilly pillows that had been on top of the bed and were now scattered all over the floor.

The scarred, one-eared cat, who looked as if it had gone ten rounds with a junkyard dog, had huffed off somewhere.

"If we take some more time to put our heads together."

"How much time?" She leaned up on an elbow and kissed his flat nipple.

"Oh, I don't know. Maybe forty, fifty years."

She stiffened as he untangled himself from her sweet embrace.

"You can't be serious."

"Actually, I've never been more serious in my life." He reached into his pocket and pulled out a black velvet box. "I'd intended to give you this earlier, but I got a little distracted."

Sitting upright now, she was looking at the box as if it were a water moccasin about to strike. "What is this?"

"You'll probably be able to see better if you open it," he coaxed mildly.

The pendant hung on a platinum chain was a stylized Celtic silver dragon on onyx set with garnets. "It's yin and yang," he said into the thundering silence. "Jaira told me it signifies the duality of Morganna, and also of the equal forces of male and female."

"You spoke with Jaira? About us? When?"

"This afternoon."

"You weren't in the shop."

The mattress echoed his sigh as he sat down on the edge of the bed. "There's this new invention. You may have heard of it. Called a telephone? We discussed what I wanted and she had it sent to the inn."

"I remember her wrapping it up," Roxi said. "But I had no idea . . . if I'd known . . ."

"You would have refused to sell it to me?"

"No. Yes. Dammit, Sloan, I don't know." She ran a finger over the dragon's silver wings. "You're confusing me again."

"If you don't like it—"

"No, I love it. I loved it when I ordered it from that jewelry dealer at a southeast Atlantic craft show. But it was too pricey for me."

"Fortunately, I'm rich. It seems a little strange buying something for you from your own shop, but Jaira assured me it was perfect."

"It is."

She didn't look pleased by that idea.

"The dragon, of course, is a fire sign for Beltane. I figure can get you a different one for each Shabbat we celebrate together. It'll become our tradition."

He'd never had to beg for a woman before. Sloan feared

he might have to for Roxi. Which wasn't a problem. He'd crawl naked on his knees through broken glass down Bul' Street in front of the entire town if that's what it took to ge' his sexy witch to agree to spend the rest of her life with him but he feared she wasn't going to make it that easy.

"That wasn't . . . it couldn't have been a proposal?"

"I believe it was. Though if you have some rule agains' marriage—"

"Of course I do! Oh, not for other people. Emma and Gabe certainly seemed happy when they left for Califor-nia—"

"They're even happier now."

"I'm glad. Like I said, maybe it's okay for other people But it's not for me."

"We're back to that ridiculous three date rule?"

He liked that she tossed up her chin. On some perverse level he even liked that she was making this difficult. He'd always preferred a challenge.

"I'll have you know that rule's always worked before."

"That's because you hadn't met me before." The calm controlled tone cost him.

"You mean I haven't met anyone crazy enough to propose after two dates."

"That's exactly what I mean. Are you saying you don' believe in love at first sight?"

"Of course not."

"You didn't feel anything last night?"

"Well, sure. Lust."

"I recognized you. You recognized me."

"You thought you were looking at Morganna," she in sisted.

"And what did you think?"

"Okay." She yanked the sheet, which had been down around her hips, up to cover her breasts, and folded her arms

t may have crossed my mind that you reminded me, just a
t, of Damian. Morganna's lover."

Sloan arched a brow at her sudden show of modesty, but
cided against getting sidetracked off topic. "And partner
crime-fighting."

"Sloan. Listen to me. They're fictional characters!"

"I know that. Just as I know we've done this dance be-
re."

"You don't believe in magic," she reminded him.

"I didn't. But that was before. This is now." He forced a
nile to encourage one in return. It didn't work.

"It's only chemistry."

"Hey, don't knock chemistry. It's what makes coal into dia-
onds and dead dinosaurs into oil."

"It also doesn't have anything to do with love."

"Try telling that to my parents. My father proposed to my
other the day he wandered into her antique shop looking
r an anniversary gift for his parents. They've been married
rty years."

"That's lovely. But—"

"And my grandparents, for whom my father bought that
a set from my mama, have been married sixty-five years.
ey had one of the longer courtships in our family. Gramps
oposed to Nana on their second-week anniversary. He was
pilot in World War II. She came to his base in England
ncing on a USO tour and broke her ankle when she
pped over his big feet. He likes to say she fell for him on
e spot."

"Clever," she said dryly.

"He and my grandmother Anna seem to think so, given
at they still tell the story every anniversary. They couldn't
t married right away, because of that little complication
garding the German army, but they made up for lost time
er. My dad's one of six kids. And my great-grandparents—"

"That's my point," she broke in, holding up a hand like a traffic cop. "Not the part about your great-grandparents, but your grandparents having six kids. I grew up in a family of eight kids. I watched my mother not have a moment's freedom. Her life totally revolved around us kids. I swore I wasn't ever going to fall into that trap."

"Interesting that you'd think of children as a trap, but I don't recall asking you to procreate."

"Are you saying you don't want children?"

"I'm saying I want you. However I can get you."

"This is crazy." She jumped out of the cozy bed and began to pace. "Just because the men in your family have this crazy tradition, or habit, or whatever the hell you want to call it, of proposing to a woman as soon as they meet her—"

"Not just any woman. The *right* woman." He caught her in midstride, linked their fingers together, lifted them, and brushed his lips over her knuckles. "How about we make this a little easier? We'll table the *M* word. And just focus, for now, on living together.

"Now, as long as I show up in California from time to time for meetings, I can work anywhere. You've already been displaced once in the past year, and I've been getting homesick anyway, so we can buy a house here in Savannah and—"

"I'm not living with you, Sloan."

"How about going steady?" he asked. His voice was calm; his eyes were not. "Think you'd be up for that? I believe, if I ask my mother, she may still have my old high school class ring in a cigar box somewhere in the house."

"You're making fun of me."

"No." He pulled her closer and pressed his lips against her hair. "I'd never do that. However . . ."

With a deep sigh, he released her and began putting on the clothes they'd thrown onto a wing chair covered with dancing fairies. "If your mind's made up—"

"Set in stone."

"Okay." He pulled on his knit boxer briefs and slacks. "You know where to find me when you change your mind." Which he had not a single doubt she would.

"What? You're leaving?" She scooped her hair back with a frustrated hand. "Just like that?"

"Since you insist on counting last night as a date, we only have one more anyway. By your rule of three."

"So you're just going to cut your losses." *And not even try to change my mind?* She didn't say the second part of that sentence, but the words were hovering between them just the same.

"No. I'm going to go back and prepare for a preproduction meeting with some studio execs that's been scheduled for two months. Then I'm going to sit in on some casting auditions. And while I'm doing that, maybe I'll pay a visit to Venice Beach and get one of those fortune-tellers to weave me that binding spell we were talking about earlier."

He touched a hand to her cheek. Her lovely, lovely cheek. "I really do love you." Which was why walking away was the most difficult thing he'd ever done. But he'd already determined that Roxi Dupree was one hard-headed lady. The more he pushed, the more she'd back away.

Better, he'd decided, to let her be the one to make the next move.

"You can't possibly."

"Why not? You happen to be a very lovable woman."

"It's too soon."

"There you go. With that counting thing again. So how many dates do we need before it's real? Four?" He bent his head and touched his lips to hers in a light kiss. "Five?" Another kiss. "A dozen?"

Her lips clung, sorely tempting him to stay. Keeping his eyes on the prize, he forced himself to back away. Now, while he still could. "If it's not love, I guess the only answer is that you put some kind of love spell on me."

He touched a fingertip to the lips whose taste he hoped would hold him until she saw the light.

"Thanks for that Beltane party. Who knew paganism rocks? Last night's going to make a great story—censored, of course, for the PG family audience—to tell on our sixty-fifth anniversary."

"You're crazy." Moisture pooled in her whiskey brown eyes and almost broke his heart.

Hold firm, he told himself one last time. "Crazy about you," he agreed.

He kissed her again, a hard, possessive kiss that ended too soon for both of them. "Call me when you change your mind."

He did not look back as he walked out of the room, out of the carriage house. But if he had, he would have seen Roxi—who hadn't even cried after Katrina had blown away both her home and her business, and had certainly never cried over a man—standing at the window, tears streaming down her too pale face.

Fifteen

Five days later, Sloan was sitting on the deck of Gabe and Emma's Malibu home, watching the waves roll onto the impossibly golden sand.

"You sure you know what you're doing?" said the man who had, during the filming of *The Last Pirate*, become Sloan's best friend.

"I sure as hell hope so." He took a long pull on a bottle of pale ale. "Emma seems to think it's the way to play it, and if I'd stayed in Savannah and let the woman play her three date game, I'd be gone now anyway."

"What if she decides to stay single in Savannah?"

"She won't do that."

"You're that sure of her?"

"No. I'm that sure of us." He leaned forward, dangling the green bottle between his thighs with two fingers. "The thing is, she has to want this. I figure if I put on a full court press, I could convince her. But then there's an outside chance that she'll always wonder if she'd made the right decision. No." He shook his head, firmed both his jaw and his resolve. "It'll be better if she comes here to me. Without any lingering reservations."

"And if she doesn't?"

"Then I'll go back to Savannah, and tie her to my bed at Swansea until she changes her mind."

Gabe lifted his bottle in a toast. "Works for me."

Sloan's office bungalow, located at the far reaches of Baron Studios' sprawling properties, belied his skyrocketing fame and fortune. It was a small, white stucco building designed for efficiency rather than boosting the ego.

As the golf cart carrying Roxi approached, the door opened. She wasn't surprised to see Sloan. Although Gabe had gotten her a studio pass, the ancient guard had insisted on calling the office so Sloan could utter whatever magical command would open those high, wrought iron studio gates.

"Hello, sugar," he greeted her in a neutral tone that threatened to destroy the last of her already tattered nerves.

It had been two weeks since she'd last seen him. Two weeks during which she'd tried to convince herself that he was just like any other man. That all they'd shared was some blanket bingo that had, admittedly, been more earth-shattering than most. But sex was just sex.

She'd told herself that over and over again. But after two long and unbearably lonely weeks she'd decided that she'd badly miscalculated and it was time to put her heart before her pride.

The fear of commitment that had been such a deeply imbedded part of her for so long was gone. She'd never been forced to examine it until Sloan had dragged it out into the bright light of day, where, she'd discovered, it had as much substance as morning mist beneath a hot Savannah summer sun.

When just the sight of him, standing in the doorway of

the building with its red tile roof, caused her previously barricaded heart to turn over, then settle back into place, as if it had finally found a proper home, she knew she'd made the right decision.

One tanned hand was braced against the doorframe, the other was stuck in the pocket of a pair of faded jeans so worn through her mother wouldn't have even saved them for dusting. The stance drew Roxi's eyes downward, to where the denim cupped his penis. The memory of him fucking her mouth while the rain poured down from a stormy sky caused heat to curl in her belly.

"Hello, *cher*." As she climbed out of the golf cart, her legs felt uncharacteristically wobbly.

He stayed where he was, watching her, his gaze narrowed against the slanting afternoon sun, which kept her from reading his eyes. There was a coiled, dangerous intensity around him that frightened her just a little. And excited her a lot.

"I hope I haven't interrupted your work?"

"Nothing important." He moved aside, inviting her in. "And I'll always have time for you, Roxi."

She glanced around, getting a vague impression of bold colors and bright movie posters, but her nerves were too knotted for her to concentrate on any one thing but her reason for having come here today.

"I brought your spell. The binding one," she said when he didn't immediately respond.

Had he forgotten? Oh God, even worse, had he changed his mind? Wouldn't that be ironic? If she came crawling to a man only to end up being the one who got dumped?

"Ah. I hadn't realized Hex Appeal had delivery service." He sat down in a chair behind a glass-topped desk, braced his elbows on the arm of the chair, and observed her over the top of his tented fingers.

"You had this delivered to the inn," she reminded him,

lifting the dragon pendant from where it had been nestled between her breasts ever since May Day morning.

"So I did. But it was two blocks from your shop to my suite. This is a bit more of a trip."

He wasn't going to make this easy on her. He hadn't even asked her to sit down. So much for her midnight fantasies of him dragging her down onto his casting couch and ravishing her the moment she walked in the door.

"True. But being a firm believer in the value of service, I've always been willing to go the extra mile to keep a valuable customer."

She took out the small, black silk drawstring pouch containing a vial of rose water made from petals picked while they were still wet from morning dew, seven vanilla beans, a lock of her hair tied with a red ribbon, and a small seashell she'd picked up on the Tybee Island beach and charged beneath the full moon.

"I've written the spell on a piece of paper. It's best that after you do it you place the package beneath your lover's bed for seven days and seven nights."

"That presupposes that I'll be anywhere near my lover's bed for the next seven days and nights."

"Well, all magic has its challenges." She echoed his neutral tone, which was beginning to make her last nerve screech.

Deciding that, having tried subtle, it was now time to pull out all the stops, she went around the desk and settled herself in his lap.

He might have been able to keep his desire for her from his voice, but the enormous erection pressing against her bottom was proof that he was no more immune to her than she was to him.

"What are you doing here, Roxi?" he asked. "Really?"

"That should be obvious, *cher*." She began unbuttoning his shirt. "I've come to seduce you."

He sucked in a sharp breath when she pressed a wet, openmouthed kiss against his chest. "I do so love the taste of your skin." Her lips skimmed over him, reveling in the rich male flavor she'd been dreaming of ever since he'd been gone. "It tastes so dark. And warm." She circled his nipple with the tip of her tongue and felt his penis leap. "And forbidden. It's the dark side of the dream."

He thrust his hands through her hair, burying his face in the sleek black strands. "You've changed your scent."

"Because I've changed. I blended it up special to help me seduce you." She pressed her lips against the hollow in his dark throat, thrilled that his pulse echoed the trip-hammer beat of her own heart. "Is it working?"

He caught hold of her waist, shifting her on his lap. "You know damn well it is."

His hand slid up her bare thigh, slipped beneath the sherbet pink, yellow, and green skirt, and discovered hidden delights.

"Damn, sugar. You must've been in one hurry this morning, leaving Savannah without your underwear."

"I haven't worn panties since you left," she revealed. "I've been walking bare-crotched all around Savannah, feeling the river breeze and the heat on my pussy, imagining your hands and your mouth on me there, remembering how you felt inside me."

"I've been thinking the same thing." He dipped a finger into the moist cleft, causing a secret thrill. "Doing the same damn thing and it's been driving me fuckin' nuts."

He shifted her slightly again, giving him access to the fly of his jeans, opening the metal buttons with hands that were not nearly as steady as Roxi remembered them.

Her eyes went dark and warm as she took his freed cock in one silken hand, brushing her thumb over the drop of precum.

Her gaze, when she lifted it to his, shone with a heady

mix of lust and what he knew to be love. "I've never felt this way with any man," she murmured wonderingly. "Oh, I've had sex before. Good sex. Even great sex."

"Well, that does a helluva lot for my ego."

She laughed like the sexy, seductive witch she was, then anointed the thick and throbbing head of his penis with her lips. "It's another world with you." She looked up at him again, her heart in her eyes. "You've got a dark and dangerous aura at times that both scares me and thrills me. But at the same time, whenever I'm with you, I feel totally safe. As if I'm exactly where I belong."

"I've felt the same way. From the first. The dark and light." He skimmed a finger over the pendant he'd bought to symbolize it. "All in one."

"Yes." She smiled. Lifted her face for a long, deep, soulful kiss. "I thought it would be hard."

"It is."

"No." This time her laugh was merry, reminding him of sunshine on water. "I meant submitting. Not sexually, which is exciting on occasion, but giving myself—all of me—to another person." She framed his face in her hands. "But once I made the decision, it was not only easy but exactly right. Because Beltane was all about looking ahead, not back, and I realize that whatever the future brings, you'll be there with me."

"I know the feeling." His own laugh was one of pent-up relief. "Very well."

Her nerves settled, she glanced around the room, her gaze settling on the black leather sofa.

"Is that your casting couch?"

"Why?" He arched a sardonic brow. "Do you feel like auditioning for a part?"

"Actually, I do." She slid off his lap and pulled her dress over her head. Then stood before him wearing only a pair of strappy pink Manolos and perfumed and powdered skin. "I want to audition for the part of your wife."

Desire. Lust. Gratitude. And love. She could read them all on his beautifully sculpted face.

"That's a very important role," he said. "It's important I choose right."

"Oh, Mr. Movie Director, I so agree," she said in a breathless little Marilyn Monroe voice she'd practiced back in junior high. It had worked then. It worked now. "I'll do anything to get the part." She trailed a hand across the crest of her breasts. Around her taut and tingling nipples. "Absolutely anything."

He stood up, crossed the room and locked the door. Then scooped her into his arms.

"I hope you didn't have any other auditions scheduled for today, sugar," he said as he carried her over to the couch. "Because this may take a while."

A full moon rode high in sky, casting a warm and benevolent white light over the Southern California coast, illuminating the man and woman.

"Mine." He needed to say the word out loud. Needed to hear her response.

She didn't hesitate. "Yours," she agreed on a soft, shimmering breath.

For all time.

Clinging to him, her body bowed, her slender hands racing up and down his back while she chanted words from an ancient time, the witch opened completely. Utterly.

As the man opened to her.

And together, moving to music only they could hear, they surrendered to the magic of the night.

DEAR SANTA

———

One

The deer came flying out of nowhere, a flash of dark brown in a swirling white-on-white world.

At least it seemed that way.

One minute Holly Berry was driving on the winding, two-lane road that snaked through Washington's Cascade Mountains at a crawl, straining her eyes to see through the wall of white snow piling up too fast for even her furiously working windshield wipers to handle. The next minute she was fishtailing into a series of dizzying spins that a gold-medalist Olympic skater would've envied, sliding helplessly toward the edge of the cliff.

That's when she realized that it was true—your life really did flash before your eyes just before you died.

"You're *not* going to die," she insisted, as if saying it out-loud could make it true.

After what seemed a lifetime, but in real time was only a few seconds, her SUV slammed into an ice-encrusted snow-bank.

Then pow!

While her heart was pounding like an angry fist against her ribs, the airbag exploded from the center of her steering wheel in her face.

Which wasn't exactly like getting hit by a marshmallow.

Actually, it hurt. A lot.

It also filled the car with acrid smoke and a fine powder she'd managed to suck into her lungs as she'd shouted out a string of curses that turned the smoky air even bluer and would've made a sailor on shore leave proud.

Unfortunately, as soon as she'd opened her mouth, she'd sucked the stuff in, which triggered a coughing fit as she fought against the bag that was—thank you God!—quickly deflating.

That, and the fact she was alive, was the good news.

Once the huge white bag was out of her face, she could see that not only had it cracked the windshield, her dashboard looked as if a maniac had attacked it with a sledgehammer. And steam was rising from beneath the snowbank, hinting at a burst radiator.

Which was, she feared, just the beginning of even more bad news.

"And wow, isn't this just what you need?"

The rain that had been falling when she'd left her downtown Seattle apartment had turned to sleet as she'd crossed the bridge into east King County. She'd thought things were looking up as she began driving into the mountains and the sleet was replaced by a scattering of downy white flakes.

Unfortunately, by the time that deer had leaped in front of her, the damn snow had escalated into something close to a blizzard.

Dammit, she never should've swerved. Then again, if she'd continued to drive straight ahead, she would've risked hitting the deer, which could've resulted in it flying through her windshield onto her lap.

And wouldn't have that just been fun?

Since her electrical system seemed to have been killed, the windows wouldn't go down, so, shoving the deflated nylon bag out of her way, she cracked open the driver's door to let out some of the smoke. Which, in turn, let wind-driven snow come swirling in.

Retrieving her purse from where it had fallen onto the floor, she took out her cell phone and flipped it open. Unsurprisingly, given her remote location in these mountains, her screen showed no signal bars.

"And isn't this a fine mess you've gotten yourself into," she muttered as she wiped the air bag talc off her face with one of the wet wipes she always carried with her and tried to decide what to do next.

Holly had always prided herself on her practicality. Oh, she was aware that creative people were considered by many to be flighty. Unpredictable. Impulsive. Even undependable.

But just because she told stories for a living didn't mean that she didn't plan every single detail of her books. She'd plot the stories for weeks, even months beforehand, each and every scene carefully detailed on Post-its, color coded by character, and stuck onto the huge board that took up a major portion of her office wall. She never wrote so much as a first line without first knowing her characters' goals, motivation, and conflict. And each and every scene in each and every chapter was totally completed to her satisfaction before she moved on to the next.

Real life, to her mind, was no different. Which meant that her goal was to get herself out of this mess and her motivation was to do so before she froze to death—which was, needless to say, the ultimate conflict of man (or in her case, woman) against nature.

She knew the conventional wisdom was to stay with the vehicle so search teams could find her. The problem was that it could take several days for anyone to even realize she was missing. Oh, sure, the hotel in Leavenworth was expecting her this evening, but if she didn't show up, the desk clerk would undoubtedly just shrug it off as yet another undependable guest, and, since she'd given them her AMEX number to guarantee the room, they'd just run her card and not give her another thought.

Since the crash and subsequent air bag explosion had also disabled her dashboard GPS, Holly had no idea of exactly where she was. Actually, she'd begun to suspect that the calm female voice directing her over the mountains may have made a mistake, because although she'd never driven this way before, it seemed the highway should be four lanes, not the two that had, because of snowplows, narrowed down to about one and a half.

Unfortunately, the Washington state road map she'd bought as a backup was still sitting on her kitchen counter. The totally uncharacteristic oversight had her grinding her teeth even as she assured herself that just as she'd gotten her last heroine away from that serial killer, she could plot her way out of this predicament.

Holly's idea of exercise might be walking to Starbucks down the street from her apartment, but surely she could hike to wherever the next town was. And wouldn't movement keep her warmer than if she stayed here, shivering inside her disabled vehicle, like a damsel in distress waiting for a white knight in a shiny suit of armor to show up?

Of course, the flip side of that was that trudging through the snow could expend energy. Which wouldn't be good. Also, the sun was sinking lower and lower behind the mountains and no way did she want to risk becoming dinner for a mountain lion or bear.

Since this was, after all, supposedly a major road, surely the state would have the snow plows out working to stay ahead of the storm. A storm that hadn't even shown up on the weather channel. She'd checked the forecast before leaving her apartment.

Forty-five minutes later, as the snow kept falling and the sky darkened to a deep purplish blue, and her fingertips, even inside her leather gloves, had begun turning to ice, and Holly was beginning to get seriously concerned, she thought she heard the low drone of a car engine.

Of course, that could just be a hallucination.

Or a dream.

Didn't people fall asleep as they were freezing to death? She was sure she'd read that somewhere.

Using her gloved hand to wipe the steam off the window, she saw a fire engine red Ford Expedition, which dwarfed her stuck Highlander, come chugging out of the storm and pull to a stop.

Even as she could have sworn she heard a chorus of angels singing the "Hallelujah Chorus" from Handel's *Messiah,* the Expedition's door opened and a pair of long legs, clad in jeans and a pair of heavy PAK boots, swiveled out.

The rest of him, wearing a dark blue parka, followed. Despite those angel voices of joyous relief ringing in her mind, all the research over the years she'd done for her mystery novels had left Holly more distrustful than the average woman.

Still, while it was difficult to tell through the swirling snow, he didn't look like a serial killer.

Of course, neither had Ted Bundy. Who, now that she thought about it, just happened to have been from Washington state. As had the Green River Killer, along with several others, including the never apprehended Snohomish County dismemberment killer she'd used as a model for the villain in her first novel.

He was getting closer, his stride long and purposeful as he crunched through the snow.

Feeling as if she was in some woman-in-jeopardy movie, Holly retrieved her Zeus Lightning Bolt stun pen from her bag and slipped it into her jacket pocket.

Two

It was amazing how much a guy's life could change in twelve months, Gabriel O'Halloran considered as he cautiously made his way around the twisting switchbacks of the icy mountain road. This time last year, he'd been in Iraq, patrolling streets, dodging insurgent gunfire, praying like hell that he and his fellow Marines wouldn't get blown to pieces by an IED.

On a sixty-five-degree Christmas morning, while on patrol, his team had nearly walked into an ambush. Fortunately, one of the bad guys had gotten trigger-happy and begun to shoot as the first Marine entered the alley. Even better was that his "pray and spray" gunfire hadn't managed to hit anyone.

The battle, which was a long way from the peace the season was supposed to celebrate, lasted less than five minutes. The insurgents, knowing when they were outgunned, faded away, undoubtedly to fight another day.

As leader of the patrol, Gabe could have ordered the team to go after them. Deciding he didn't want to be responsible for any deaths on Christmas Day, they'd returned to camp in time for a traditional feast of prime rib, turkey with cornbread stuffing, mashed potatoes, and pumpkin pie, served up by a two-hundred-and-fifty-pound master sergeant wearing a red, white, and blue Santa Claus hat.

Now, here Gabe was, plowing his way through a frigging blizzard, tires crunching beneath the snow, the radio reporting road closures and accidents throughout the mountains, his eyes burning from trying to focus on the road as he doggedly made his way in near whiteout conditions home to a town that had boasted the teeming population of six hundred and twenty-five.

Six hundred and twenty-seven now that he and Emma had settled in.

Having spent his teenage years trying to escape his hometown, then intending to be career military, becoming a Christmas tree farmer and running an inn and bar wasn't the future he'd planned. Not by a long shot. But having seen a great deal of the world, despite the twists and turns his personal road had taken over the last few months, he had begun to enjoy himself.

Hell, he even had a dog, who was currently curled up in the backseat, snoring away like a souped-up chainsaw.

Couldn't get much more damn domesticated than that.

He'd just cautiously maneuvered around a particularly nasty S-curve, his studded tires crunching on the icy pavement, when he viewed an SUV partly buried in a snowbank. Pulling as far as he could off the road, he set the emergency brake.

The dog, having been born into a war zone, immediately sensed trouble. Choosing flight over fight, he scrambled off the seat onto the floor, where he somehow managed to curl up into a remarkably small ball, considering that the last time he'd been weighed at the vet, he'd come in at one hundred and thirty pounds.

"Stay," he told the dog as he retrieved the first aid kit—just in case—from the floor.

The dog looked conflicted. On one hand, or, more accurately, paw, he obviously wanted to stay hunkered down out of danger. On the other, he'd spent nine months of Gabe's thirteen-month second tour on patrol loyally sticking close to the squad of Marines who'd adopted him.

"Stay," Gabe repeated, holding up a hand. "Everything'll be okay."

Gabe hoped.

He'd no sooner jumped out of the Expedition when a woman stumbled out of the disabled Highlander. She was tall, leggy, and wearing a scarlet ski jacket, snug black jeans, and sheepskin-lined boots that rose nearly to her knees.

"Looks like you've gotten yourself in a little trouble," he said. "Are you all right?"

"I'm fine. Well, mostly," she allowed as his gaze swept over her, looking for injuries. "I swerved to miss hitting a deer." Before he could respond to that, she held up a hand. The red leather glove was thin, fitting her hand, well, like a glove, and while a nice look with the coat, wasn't all that practical for this kind of weather. "I know you're not supposed to do that, but it was all so sudden, and . . ."

She paused, as if picturing the moment he figured had been indelibly scorched into her mind. Emotions—especially fear—could do that to you. God knows he had memories that still, even after a year stateside, occasionally, when he least expected it, played in his mind.

Her hair—which fell in a trendy, expensive-looking cut that just skimmed her shoulders beneath a red knitted cap—was a strawberry blond, more gold than red. Her slightly slanted catlike eyes were moss green, her complexion, the part of it that wasn't already turning red and splotchy, which he suspected was the beginning of what could be some serious bruising, was as smooth and pale as top cream.

A sprinkling of freckles across the bridge of a cold-reddened nose, and a mouth that was a bit too wide, but eminently kissable, along with the way her diamond face came to a point in a slightly stubborn chin kept her from being perfect.

"And?" he prompted.

"This is going to sound crazy, but although I'm admittedly no expert, it didn't look like an ordinary deer. More like a—"

"Reindeer?"

"Exactly."

Which was, of course, ridiculous, Holly told herself. Adrenaline, caused by the stress of the moment, must have caused her brain to fritz out, overlaying the actual event with other pictures in her memory. Pictures from the storybooks her father had read her so long ago.

He nodded. "That'd be Blitzen."

Leaving her staring after him, he strolled around to the front of the car and studied the hood buried deep in the snowdrift. The steam had quit rising from the radiator several minutes ago, but it didn't take a mechanic to know the poor Highlander wasn't going to be driving anywhere soon.

"Good thing the guard rail was there under the piled-up snow," he said. "Or you could've gone right over the edge and might not have been found until spring."

"Well, isn't that a lovely thought?"

She slipped a hand into her pocket and curled her fingers around the stun pen. Although he certainly looked normal enough (actually he was obscenely handsome, with slate gray eyes beneath black brows, a face that was all masculine planes and angles, and a jaw shadowed by a day's worth of dark beard wide enough to park his Expedition on), from that casually issued comment about the reindeer, she feared he might be a 5150, which a cop she'd once interviewed for research had told her wasn't merely an old Van Halen album but police code for a crazy person on the loose.

"And what do you mean, Blitzen?"

"He's a reindeer."

"So I've heard."

"Well, this one happens to belong to a friend of mine. He escaped from his pen yesterday." He opened the driver's door, looked into the car, and frowned. "Wow. Who'd have guessed an airbag could do that much damage?"

He looked down at her, eyes narrowed as he scrutinized her face. Then frowned. "You're going to have some bruising. And maybe a black eye." He skimmed a gloved finger beneath the eye in question. "But you're damn lucky you weren't burned."

That was, admittedly, one positive. "I guess I am."

Some people were touchers. Holly was not. Backing up a few steps, she flicked the cap off the marker-size stun pen, just in case. The salesman at the spy store had assured her that the electric arc that pulsated across the top of the pen would create a sharp, crackling sound, intimidating most would-be attackers.

And if that wasn't enough, the 800,000 volt output would drop a guy to his knees. Although it was supposedly able to zap those volts through clothing, Holly wondered how effective it'd be through all those layers of down parka.

"You seriously have a friend who owns a reindeer?" Her tone radiated her skepticism.

"Not just one. Eight."

"Next you'll be telling me he uses them to pull his sleigh."

"Actually he does." He gave her a slow, easy smile that was too charming for comfort and sent something turning inside her. Steeling herself against its charm, she told herself that Ted Bundy had probably used much the same smile to lure unsuspecting victims into his Volkswagen. "But Blitzen is the one who always seems to get antsy this time of year."

He had to be putting her on. Wasn't he? Feeling like Alice

after she'd fallen down the rabbit hole, Holly wondered if she was hallucinating. Maybe she'd knocked herself out in the accident and was dreaming this entire conversation.

Because if she was awake, he could be seriously unbalanced. She took another step backward and, considering her escape options after she'd tasered him, hoped he'd left the keys in the Expedition.

"You know," he said, his midnight deep voice breaking into her tumultuous thoughts, "it's obvious that your rig isn't going anywhere anytime soon. And, as you've undoubtedly discovered, cell service here is pretty much non-available, so why don't you let me give you a ride into town, then we can arrange to have your SUV towed to a garage in the morning?"

That was obviously the logical thing to do. The *only* thing to do. But accepting that didn't stop every FBI serial killer profiling book she'd ever read for research to go flashing through her mind.

"Look." He folded his broad arms and seemed to be holding in a sigh when she didn't immediately jump at his offer. "If it makes you feel any better, I'm a former Marine."

The proud. The few.

And wouldn't he just look dandy on a recruiting poster?

While his service record was moderately encouraging, if it were true, it also could mean he was armed. Not that he'd need a gun to kill. From the size of those big, black-gloved hands, Holly suspected he'd be able to snap her neck before she knew what was happening. Before she could even turn off the safety switch on the stun pen and find a down-free place to jolt him.

She'd taken a self-defense course taught at the police station just last year. One of the basics she'd learned was GET— to go for the groin, eyes, and throat if attacked. Holly was considering the logistics of that when she realized he'd caught her checking out the G part of that acronym. Which was covered up by the heavy parka he was wearing, but given his size . . .

Heat flooded into cheeks that only moments earlier had been turning to ice.

"Sorry," Holly muttered, wondering about the chances of an avalanche coming down the side of the mountain to bury her and save her from further humiliation. "Suspicion comes with the job."

The humor in his gaze faded as he took a longer, more judicial look at her. "You a cop?"

"No. A writer. Mysteries." And just because she wrote about serial killers and psychos didn't mean she couldn't tell fiction from reality. At least most of the time.

She waited for him to ask if she'd written anything he'd read. Instead, his cheeks creased as he flashed another of those devastating smiles—who knew Marines had dimples?—and said, "Cool."

He held out his hand. "Gabriel O'Halloran. But most people, except my mother, call me Gabe."

"Holly Berry."

She waited for the inevitable joke about her name. It was especially difficult to escape this time of year.

Instead, he tilted his head. "The Holly Berry who wrote *Blood Brothers*? *Deadly Deception*? *Power Play*?"

"My publisher's fond of alliteration."

She was currently plotting her sixth book. The previous had garnered good reviews, even landing on some prestigious bestseller lists, and while she was no John Grisham, she was making a nice enough living.

"I thought you looked familiar. I've seen your photo on the back of your book covers. You're a lot better looking in person, by the way. Not that it's a bad photo. In fact, it's pretty cool, with you in that kick-ass long black leather coat, glaring at something in the distance, looking like you eat bad guys for breakfast, lunch, and dinner, then either shoot them or send them up the river for life plus ten.

"But . . . Shit." He shoved back the hood of the parka and dragged a hand through his wavy black hair. "Why don't you do me a favor and just shoot me and put me out of my misery before I dig this hole I'm sinking into any deeper?"

"I'm not armed." Holly figured the taser pen didn't really count and wasn't prepared to tell him about that yet. Just in case. "Besides, you're right. That's exactly the look the photographer was going for."

"Well, it worked. My mom's a huge fan."

"That's nice to hear."

A breath she'd been unaware of holding came out on a puff of ghostly white. He'd actually been kind of cute when he'd gotten all embarrassed. And that he had a mother—who made him smile when he talked about her—was a positive sign.

Until Ma Barker came to mind.

"Some moms read romance." The smile in his gray eyes echoed the one on his sinfully chiseled lips. "Mine is into murder and mayhem."

"Well, thank her for me."

"I'll do that. So, now that we've introduced ourselves, and hopefully you've decided I'm not going to slit your throat once I get you alone with me in my vehicle, are you ready to get going?"

"I didn't think that," she lied as she recapped the pen and reached into the backseat of the disabled Highlander to retrieve her suitcase and computer bag.

"It's good that you're not a cop," he said conversationally, as he took the suitcase from her hand and began walking toward the Expedition.

"You don't like cops?"

"My dad's a cop and I like him just fine. He's sheriff of

Cascade County. Which is where you are," he tacked on, in case she didn't know. Which, admittedly, she didn't. "He was an L.A. cop. I was in eighth grade when he turned in his shield and moved up here."

"That must've been a big change for all of you."

"My sisters—I have three—bitched for a long time about missing all their girlfriends."

"Totally understandable."

"I suppose." He shrugged. "But there was sure a lot of door slamming going on around the house for the first year or so. I missed the surfing. And the Cineplex, and, given that my hormones had just begun to kick in, all the girls in their itsy bitsy teeny weeny bikinis."

"I can see how that would be a loss," she said dryly.

Doing the math, since he seemed in his early to mid thirties, she guessed she hadn't quite made it into bikinis by the time his family had left California.

"But the change seemed to suit my mother and him, which was the idea. She transferred to teaching English at Cascade County High until she retired last year."

He opened the back of the Expedition, tossed in her case, and held out his hand for her computer, which she handed over.

"Dad says he never minded working the hard streets—burglary, murder, that sort of thing. It was the domestic disturbances that really got to him. Up here he mainly deals with tourists who don't realize that tossing back tequila shooters at a mile-high elevation has a helluva more effect on your bloodstream than it does at sea level."

He retrieved a black box, opened it, and took out some red plastic highway flashers. "There's also the usual barking dogs, mailbox bashing, and the occasional tree snatching. Pop's always said it's sorta like retirement, but he doesn't have to spend all his time fishing or playing golf."

Holly had climbed up into the Expedition and was just

beginning to relax when a head that could've belonged to a small horse suddenly popped up over the top of her seat. She couldn't stop the slight sound—not quite a shriek, but close enough—from escaping her lips.

"Damn. Sorry about that." Gabe unzipped the parka, reached into an inner pocket, and pulled out a Milk-Bone the size of a dinosaur thigh, which he tossed at the animal, who snapped it out of the air. "I should've warned you about Dog."

Huge yellow canine teeth made short work of the cookie.

Holly, whose writer's imagination had kicked back into gear, immediately thought of Cujo. She also wished she'd left the cap off the taser pen.

"He's certainly large."

"Yeah. But you don't have to worry, because he's about as vicious as a newborn kitten." He climbed into the driver's seat and rubbed a hand over the dog's huge head. "Say hello to the lady, Dog."

The dog sat on his haunches and lifted a gigantic brown paw between the seats.

"Hello, Dog." The beast's furry tail began pounding the floor like a jackhammer when Holly shook his extended paw. She glanced up at Gabe. "That's his name?"

He shrugged. "I didn't want to get too attached to him. It seemed naming him would make it harder to leave him behind."

"Behind where?"

Wiping the dog drool onto her jeans, she looked back at the animal, who'd crawled up on the backseat and was now sprawled over what appeared to be a camouflage-colored sleeping bag.

"Baghdad. He was a stray pup running the streets. At the time he was about a tenth the size he is now and it was obvious he was on his own, so my squad started giving him food. Which, of course, had him adopting us back."

"I imagine that's not uncommon in such a situation."

"Not at all," he agreed. "A lot of the troops had camp dogs. Not only did it lift morale, some served as additional force protectors."

"Still, I'll bet those other troops didn't jump through whatever hoops it took to bring them back to America."

"No. But Dog was special. Although you could tell gunfire— and just about everything else—scared the hell out of him, he still insisted on going on patrol with us. He sniffed out an IED one day, which saved I don't know how many lives. No way was I going to leave him behind after that."

"Well, that's quite a story." She couldn't imagine the paperwork that it would have taken to get a stray dog from Iraq into America. "Sounds like you were lucky to have met each other."

"Yeah. That's pretty much the way I look at it, too."

"What kind of dog is he, anyway?"

"Beats me, but my best guess is a cross between a Great Dane and a Hummer."

After flashing her another quick grin, he crunched his way back through the snow and set up the flashers in both directions from the disabled Highlander.

"They'll go for thirty hours before the batteries run out," he told her when he returned. "Give us plenty of time to get a tow truck out here in the morning."

"I appreciate that. Of course, that leads to the problem of where I'm going to spend the night. Is there a town nearby?"

"Yeah. About forty-five minutes away in this weather."

"I guess I won't have any choice but to get a motel room there."

"That might be a little tricky this time of year," he said. "Given that it's a really small place and high tourist season. But we'll work something out."

She had an idea of what that *something* might be. If he was thinking she was going to spend the night with him, he as going to be disappointed. But, weighing her options, olly decided she'd wait until they got to town to face that scussion.

"Were you serious about the tree snatching?" she asked, eciding to change the subject.

"Yeah. The timber industry's taken a hit these past years, it there's still some good money to be made in stolen ees."

"Really?" She looked up at the towering fir trees packed gether beside the road. "How much money?"

His laugh was deep and rich and took a bit of chill from er blood, making her feel as if warm brandy had begun owing in her veins. "Enough."

Sensing that he was laughing at her, she folded her arms. omething funny?"

"Not about timber theft. A full grown old growth cedar n bring in five thousand bucks at a sawmill, and a larce-us guy could make a hundred thousand with a few days' rd work, so it's not as benign a crime like it sounds. But, e I said, it's a good thing you're not a cop, because your ce gives away your thoughts."

He twisted the key in the ignition. The engine roared to e and began blowing blessed heat through the dashboard nts. "I could practically see the wheels of a possible murder-r-tree plot turning in your head."

"It has its possibilities," she allowed on a voice as chilly the outside temperature. An intensely private person, olly wasn't wild about anyone reading her so well. Espe-lly since Gabriel O'Halloran was the first person to ever ve accused her of being that easily read. "Though at the oment I'm working on another idea. A black widow murder."

"Ah." He nodded as he pulled the Expedition back onto e narrow road. "The chirpy, white-haired owner of Black rest Cookies who's accused of having poisoned six hus-nds."

"You've heard of the case?"

"Sure. Leavenworth's just on the other side of the mountains," he reminded her. "Maybe you could call it *The Cookie Caper*."

She was about to inform him that his suggested title was more suited to a cozy mystery when she realized he was joking, playing with her alliterative title idea. Again, not exactly serial killer behavior.

"I'll take that under advisement."

Three

Having already had one accident that day, Holly was relieved when he kept the Expedition at a safe crawl, the yellow beam of the headlights bouncing off the wall of white stuff that continued to fall.

"We'll be in the town in another twenty minutes or so," he told her after they'd been driving approximately twenty-five minutes.

He'd turned the radio down, but she'd listened to a steady stream of road closures throughout the state. His voice sounded deeper and richer in the intimacy of the snow-shrouded silence.

"Okay, here's where I admit I have no idea what town that might be."

"Santa's Village."

"You can't be serious." Maybe he wasn't a stone-cold killer, or even 5150 insane, but once again Holly began to worry about him being delusional.

"It's the town's name, all right. Population six hundred

twenty-seven." He glanced over at her. "It's also not on the way to Leavenworth."

She definitely would've noticed that town on the map while planning her trip. "Damn GPS."

Not encouraging was that she'd bought the faulty navigation system from the same guy who'd sold her the purse-size Zeus Lightning Bolt taser pen. What if it turned out he was pushing fake Chinese stuff on an unsuspecting public? How many lives could that put at risk?

"Ah." He nodded as she filed the idea of a faulty taser away. She couldn't see it working in her black widow cookie killer story, but perhaps, like all the other bits and pieces of criminal behavior she had tucked away in her mind, it could prove useful down the road. "It told you to turn right at that crossroad outside Skykomish," he guessed.

"Exactly." Which was where she'd obviously gone wrong. "How did you know?"

He shrugged. "It seems to be a glitch in some programs. We've gotten lost drivers before."

"Who suddenly find themselves in Santa's Village."

"Yep."

Damn. "That's certainly a colorful name. Is it one of those cutesy theme towns?"

Leavenworth, where she'd been headed, had re-created itself from a dying timber and railroad town into a faux Alpine Bavarian Village, which reputedly drew two-and-a-half million tourists a year.

"It pretty much is." He glanced over at her. "Sounds like you're not a fan of cute."

"Cute has its place. Like puppies and kittens. Johnny Depp. I just don't celebrate Christmas."

"So, is that a religious thing? Or were you at some time traumatized by a department store Santa?" Easy humor laced his voice.

"Let's just say the rampant commercialism gets to me." Her tone, chillier than the snow falling outside, strongly suggested they drop the entire subject.

Holly hated Christmas. The whole Christmas season.

She hated the tinsel, the trappings, the decorated trees, the wrappings, and most of all, she hated Santa Claus, whom she'd quit believing in when she was seven years old.

"And here I would've guessed the season would be a big deal for you. Given your name and all."

"My father named me. *He* liked Christmas." Which was putting it mildly.

She couldn't remember all that much about her father, but she could recall him taking her to see them light the tree at Rockefeller Center every year.

They'd been living in New York City, and, although she couldn't remember it, she'd been told that she was a year old the first time she'd attended Macy's parade, dressed in an elf green snowsuit, perched atop her father's shoulders. The next year he'd put her on double runner skates and taken her ice skating for the first time.

Christmas, especially Christmas in Manhattan, had been nothing short of magical.

Then, the night Holly turned seven, while she was at home frosting sugar cookies for Santa with her mama, while out doing his annual Christmas Eve shopping, George Berry had been shot dead by a mugger who'd gotten away with three credit cards, forty-five dollars in cash, a Timex watch, and a Josephine Irish Cabbage Patch Kid with a pink dress and cranberry-colored pigtails.

Her mother had gone into what Holly now recognized as a deep clinical depression. So dark that she packed up what was left of their little family and moved them to L.A.

But despite the bright sun that was always shining above the palm trees, a dark cloud had settled over the house. And the next year, when Christmas rolled around again, there was no tinsel-draped tree. No presents. No trips to Macy's to sit on Santa's lap.

That was when Holly, in an attempt to bring some small ray of happiness back into their lives, had written to Santa.

She could still remember the letter. *Dear Santa,* she'd written in her very best second grade printing with a red pencil in the hopes the bright color would help it stand out from all those other millions of letters he probably received at the North Pole. *My mama cries all the time since Daddy died. She says you can't bring him back to life. But this year, the only thing I want is a happy family. Like I used to have. Thank you and Merry Christmas to you and Mrs. Claus and all the elves and reindeers. Especially Blitzen.* For some reason, whenever her daddy had read her *The Night Before Christmas,* Blitzen had been her favorite. *Love, Your friend, Holly Berry.*

P.S. In case you didn't notice, being so busy with your toy factory and all, I'm living in California now.

Whatever she was thinking wasn't good, Gabe thought. Her lips were pulled into a tight line and she'd encased herself in enough ice to cover Mount Rainier. The lady was a touchy one. He also suspected there was a story there. One he intended to discover for himself.

Meanwhile, with her Highlander stuck in a snowdrift and the roads closed all throughout the mountains, it wasn't like she'd be going anywhere soon.

And neither was he.

Four

She stayed silent for a long time, seeming lost in thought as she watched the woods out the passenger window.

The only sound was the crunch of the snow beneath the tires, the slight scraping noise of the wipers as they struggled with the snow that was rapidly turning to ice, and the low drone of the voice on the radio announcing yet more road closures.

Her scent—reminding him of a vacation his family had taken to Vashon Island, where they'd gleaned fruit from a peach orchard—bloomed in the heat blasting from the dashboard vents.

He wondered if she smelled like that all over. Wondered if she tasted as good. Which had him imagining her lying on hot, tangled sheets while he ran his tongue down her smooth white throat. Across her collarbone. Then lower, over her pink-tipped breasts that he'd make wet with his kisses . . .

Fire shot, along with his blood, from his obviously fevered brain to his groin.

"I don't understand," she said as he shifted to adjust his

suddenly too-tight jeans. "This storm wasn't even on the radar. I checked. The forecast was sunny, with temperatures in the high forties."

"Things change fast in the mountains."

"So I've heard."

"So, you're not from around here?"

He was hard and ached and short of pulling over to the side of the road and somehow getting her out of those tight jeans and boots so she could ride him hard and fast—which, unfortunately, wasn't an option, especially since he didn't exactly run around with a condom in his pocket these days— there wasn't a helluva lot he could do about it.

At least not for now.

Although it might not make a lot of sense, Gabe suddenly wanted to know everything about her—her favorite food, her favorite color (though he'd guess, from the coat, hat, and gloves, that would be red), whether she was a morning person or night owl, whether she liked her sex hot and fast, or slow and dreamy.

He wanted her both ways. First fast, then, once they got that out of the way, he'd take his time, touching her all over. Tasting her everywhere. Drawing out every sensation, warming every bit of her fragrant peach-scented flesh until she was begging for him to finish her off.

Then, what was really scary, was the absolute certainty that he'd want her again. And again.

"I've been in Seattle the past six months," she said, her voice breaking into a fantasy of being deep inside of her, feeling her contracting around him. "Before that I lived in L.A."

"Now there's a coincidence. Us both coming from the same town."

It didn't suit her, he decided. With that white as cream skin, she was the least likely California girl he'd ever seen.

"So, is your family back there?"

Significant other? Fiancé? Lover?
Or, oh hell, how about a husband?

"My father died when I was a kid."

"That must've been tough. I'm sorry."

"So was I." She exhaled a slight breath that told him she still hadn't quite gotten over it. "My mother's spent the past few years traveling."

"Lucky her." Having joined the Marines to see the great big wide world, Gabe wouldn't mind if he never left these mountains again. "But where's her actual home?"

"She doesn't have one. I mean she *really* travels. She works as a croupier on a cruise ship. So mostly she sails around the Caribbean. And occasionally along the Mexican Coast, what's called the Mexican Riviera."

"Sounds like an interesting gig."

And lonely, Gabe thought. Even though you'd be surrounded by people, wouldn't they mostly always be strangers? That was one of the things he'd liked about being a Marine. Semper Fi wasn't just some snazzy military slogan. It was a way of life. Once you got that service emblem pin at graduation, you became part of a family for life.

Not that he didn't love his own family. But after having grown up with three older sisters, it had been cool to have brothers.

She moved her shoulders in a small shrug. "Mom seems to like it."

Her tone didn't exactly ring with enthusiasm.

"Although you might not celebrate Christmas, to a lot of people it's a pretty big deal," he said. "So, can I take the fact that you're traveling to a murder trial over the holidays to mean that you don't have some guy waiting for you back in Seattle?"

She glanced over at him. "No. Why?"

The NO TRESPASSING sign was up and flashing in bright Day-Glo neon letters. A sensible man would back away. But, dammit, Gabe had been unrelentingly sensible for the past year. And more amazingly, celibate for two.

Maybe it was high time—hell, past time—to take a few risks.

Having never been one to play games, he decided to just lay his cards on the table.

"Because you're a good-looking, obviously intelligent woman and you pretty much had me from the moment you stepped out of that SUV. So, I just wanted to know if there's some guy out there I'm going to have to fight for your favors."

Her eyes widened. The smudge around the right one was growing darker. Yep, the lady was definitely going to have one helluva shiner.

"Well, that's certainly direct and to the point."

"I've never been one to beat around the bush. Or waste time playing games."

"I'm not one to play games either. But has anyone ever told you that you're a very unusual man?"

"Because I admire a woman with brains and looks?"

"No. Because, along with supposedly having a friend with eight reindeer and a sleigh, and living in a town called Santa's Village, you don't know anything about me."

"That can always be changed. And, for the record, about the town? It gets worse. Santa's Village bills itself as 'The Most Christmassy Town in America,' and you happen to be looking at the guy who not only owns an honest-to-God Christmas tree farm, but the Ho Ho Ho Inn."

"You have got to be kidding."

She was, unsurprisingly, less than impressed. He figured the usual guys she went for in the city were lawyers and stockbrokers who wore Armani suits and lived in penthouses overlooking Puget Sound.

"Hey," he said, "it's not like I named it."

Of course, admittedly, he hadn't changed the name either.

He'd told himself that was because it was, in a way, a historical landmark. But it was mostly because Emma loved it.

After having been absent for so much of his young daughter's life, Gabe was willing to give her whatever she wanted. Within reason. And hey, his ego was strong enough not to feel the need to change the name to something his former Marine buddies wouldn't have ragged him to death about.

"I returned home last year and bought it from this couple who'd run it for the past thirty years and decided it was time to go lie in the sun and catch marlin and sun fish in St. Petersburg, Florida."

He could tell she thought he was crazy. And, hell, maybe he was. But he'd been starting to get crazy more and more back in the sandbox. And to Gabe's mind, the admitted wackiness of his hometown was a helluva lot better than the insanity of a war zone.

Five

_____

"When do you think he's going to get here?" the five-year-old girl asked for the umpteenth time in the last hour.

"It's been snowing to beat the band," Beth O'Halloran reminded her granddaughter yet again as she took the basket of sliced potatoes out of the deep fryer and dumped them onto a plate next to a half-pound of Angus beef burger. "It takes time to get back up here from the city."

"I know." Emma O'Halloran's frustrated sigh ruffled her bright bangs. "But it's just taking forever!" She began pacing again, the heels of her pink cowboy boots clicking an impatient tattoo on the heart-of-pine plank floor of the Ho Ho Ho Inn.

"I know," Beth said sympathetically, stepping around the little girl to get the coleslaw out of the commercial refrigerator.

With three of her four children being daughters, Beth was accustomed to the amount of passion that could simmer inside even the youngest feminine body.

Emma stopped in front of the kitchen window again, pressing her nose against the double-paned glass, peering into the gathering purple darkness. "Do you think he's bringing my present?"

"He probably did some shopping," Beth hedged as she added the slaw to the plate.

"No. My real present!"

Beth sighed. They'd been through this before. Too many times to count. Although Gabriel had been, in some ways, easier than her girls, Emma was definitely her father's child when it came to tenacity. Once either one of them got something into their heads, it was nearly impossible to shake loose.

"Even if your father does decide to give in and get you that pony, I doubt he'd risk pulling a trailer up the mountain today."

"Not *that* present." The pink ribbon Beth had tied the unruly red-gold curls back with this morning loosened a bit as Emma emphatically shook her head. "I changed my mind. To something more special. Something I'm going to ask Santa for."

Beth sighed again as she thought about the palomino Welsh pony currently residing at Lucas Nelson's stable waiting to be delivered on Christmas Eve night. Although she'd personally thought the gift had been a little extravagant, she understood why Gabriel had bought it for his daughter. And it was a sweet little animal, she allowed. And docile enough for a child to handle.

Now, if Emma had changed her mind this close to Christmas, with the roads being closed, even if they could order a new present on the Internet, the delivery trucks wouldn't be able to reach town.

Well, no point in borrowing trouble, Beth decided. Whatever else her granddaughter had her heart set on now, Beth knew Emma would be over the moon when she got up on Christmas morning and saw the pony grazing in the small pasture behind the inn.

She held out the plate. "Here. Take this over to Ben Daughtry. He's sitting in the back booth."

"That's where he always sits."

"It's called tradition. Some people believe it's a good thing."

Heaven knows, until this past year, Emma's life had been unsettled enough. There were times Beth blamed herself for that. She and Will had visited their granddaughter three times a year and had never witnessed any signs of domestic trouble, but if they'd left the mountains and moved back to California, perhaps they might have been able to provide the stability they hadn't realized the little girl had been missing.

Then again, had she known about her daughter-in-law's illicit romance with her wealthy property developer boss while Gabriel had been overseas, Beth wasn't sure what she would or could have done. Surely e-mailing her son about his wife's adultery would've just given him one more thing to worry about during a time when he'd needed to keep focused on staying alive.

Unfortunately, life was a great deal more complicated than it appeared in those mystery books she liked to read, where problems were presented, then, in four hundred pages, neatly solved, with the bad guys behind bars and the good guys living happily ever after.

She watched the little girl carry the plate across the wood floor with the care that suggested she was walking on eggshells. Her teeth were worrying her bottom lip. Better fretting about a dropped cheeseburger than her daddy having an accident, Beth decided.

There may be state laws against child labor, but the way Beth saw it, this was a family business, Emma was most definitely family, and besides, having the child help out now and again made her feel useful, kept her out of trouble, and most important, tonight would hopefully keep her mind off her father's trip up the mountain.

Emma had reached Ben Daughtry's booth without incident. The sixty-something artist had moved here after being priced out of Seattle's Capitol Hill neighborhood, which, he'd complained, was having its bohemian roots overtaken by Starbucks and sushi joints. He'd never married, apparently choosing to direct all his energies toward his art, which, when he'd arrived had been—to her mind—disturbingly dark.

These days, rather than painting landscapes of a school of sharks attacking kayakers in Puget Sound, or King Kong atop the Space Needle fighting off attacking fighter jets, Daughtry earned a comfortable living creating seasonal watercolor greeting cards that all tended to make Santa's Village look like, well, a Hallmark card.

Beth suspected his former artist friends in the city would be amazed at the transformation of the man who'd arrived depressed and argumentative, but she wasn't surprised. She'd seen it happen many times, and although there were those few detractors who suggested that the town council was putting something in the water, she liked living in the kind of small town epitomized in old black and white movies and the Sinclair Lewis stories she'd enjoyed teaching to high school English classes.

Ben was good with children, she'd give the man that. After chatting easily with Emma for a moment, he took a pencil from the pocket of his red and green plaid shirt and quickly sketched something on a white paper napkin.

Emma studied it with a seriousness way beyond her age, then bobbed her head and beamed.

As the little girl returned back toward the kitchen, the napkin in hand, Daughtry dug into his dinner. Which was also the same thing he had every night, except on Wednesday, when, for some reason Beth couldn't fathom, he'd switch out the coleslaw for baked beans.

Her gaze drifted out the window. Although she would never admit it out loud, she was a bit concerned by the delay as well. Gabriel had blessedly escaped injury during all his years in the military, including two tours in Iraq and another in Afghanistan, but that didn't mean that a mother ever stopped worrying about her child.

Six

From high atop the town, bathed in the rising moonlight that cast a bluish glow over the snow, the small town of Santa's Village looked like the set of a model railroad. There appeared to be one main street—strung with, natch, bright red and green flashing lights—then a handful of others going off at ninety-degree angles. It was admittedly charming, if you liked the *It's a Wonderful Life* approach to the season. Taking the moonlit scene in, she decided the entire village couldn't be more than nine blocks square.

Winter-bare trees in front yards were strung with fairy lights and electric candles flickered in windows.

"Cute," she murmured dryly as they passed by a giant statue of Santa welcoming visitors to "Santa's Village, The Most Christmassy Town in America."

The part of her accustomed to editing her manuscripts wondered if *Christmassy* was even a word. The right arm, which had to be at least six feet from fingertip to shoulder, was automated to wave a manic greeting. It was, hands down, at the same time both the ugliest and scariest thing she'd ever laid eyes on.

"Granted, he takes some getting used to," Gabe said as he turned onto—what else?—Rudolph Road. "After about three months I just quit seeing him."

Holly figured it would take longer than that for her to stop seeing the oversize jolly old elf. As it was, she feared the scarily grinning Santa was going to appear in her nightmares. Looking a lot like Freddy Kruger wearing a pillow beneath a tacky red velvet suit.

The sidewalks were lined with lighted pine trees, and more lights, which flashed merrily, had been strung across the streets. Every storefront seemed to be trying to outdo its neighbor.

"Is the town decorated like this year round?" she asked.

"Pretty much," he allowed. "Though people do tend to crank things up a bit come Thanksgiving. Tourism has become a major industry here, especially since the timber business dropped off. Along with the Christmas junkies, we do get a lot of sportsmen and cross-country skiers."

"That's nice."

Holly had never understood the appeal of strapping sticks to your boots and trudging through miles of snow, but she figured it took all kinds to make a world. After all, not everyone enjoyed murder mysteries either.

They passed what she supposed must be the town square, boasting a white Victorian bandstand decorated in yet more white fairy lights. A towering Douglas fir blinked in multicolors, a crèche topped by a star and lit by a floodlight shared space with a menorah that had to be eight feet tall, with flickering red bulbs atop the candles.

"Nice to know Santa's ecumenical," she murmured.

"We try." When he made a left turn on Dasher Drive, Dog sat up and began paying attention. "Fortunately, the pagans signed on to the tree as their symbol and I've got a committee working on what to put up for Kwanzaa for next year."

"*You* have a committee?" Holly absently petted the huge head looming up through the space between the seats.

He shrugged. "I'm mayor. Which isn't any big deal," he told her before she might suggest it was. "The previous owner of the inn had the job, so I sort of inherited it along with the mortgage."

"Well, that's one way to avoid paying for a new election."

"There's not that much to do," he said. "Between the council, the school board, and the tourism bureau, the town pretty much runs itself. The main business has always been Kris Kringle's Workshop."

"Okay. Now you've got to be pulling my leg."

"Although it's a very fine leg—which seems to go all the way up to Canada, by the way—and there are a lot of things I'd like to do to it . . . beginning with starting at the ankle and nibbling my way up it . . . actually, I'm not."

"You're going to be disappointed regarding the nibbling," she said firmly. Just because he'd saved her from possibly freezing to death didn't mean she was going to show her gratitude by getting horizontal with him. "As for the workshop, if you are telling the truth, I'm starting to wonder what Kool-Aid you all are drinking here in this charming little hamlet."

His chuckle was deep and rich and stirred places in Holly she'd forgotten could be stirred. "Sam Fraiser's the seventh-generation owner, and although he's never actually laid claim to the title, a lot of people, and kids, in town believe he's the 'real' Santa Claus.

"Anyway, the workshop had been facing some lean years, make that decades, but all the problems with imports have made the shop's more traditional toys—like wooden planes, trains, and cars—more in demand. In fact, he got written up in the *Wall Street Journal* and *Business Week* last month."

"Okay." She gave the so-called Santa reluctant points. "That's admittedly impressive."

"A lot of people think so. Though the Fraisers have never been in the business for fame. In fact, my sister Rachel, who works as his accountant and business manager, says producers from *Ellen, GMA,* and *CBS News Sunday Morning* have called in the past few weeks, wanting him to appear on their shows, but he's turned them all down."

Holly had met writers who would run over their dear old grannies for such an opportunity.

"So, what is he? Some sort of hermit? Or another Unabomber in hiding?"

"Gotta love a woman with a twisted mind." Again Holly found his deep chuckle way too appealing for comfort. "Actually, he told them it was his busy season."

"Of course it is," Holly said, not bothering to keep the sarcasm from sharpening her tone. "After all, he's got a big trip coming up."

"That's what he reminded them."

Forget about falling down the rabbit hole. Holly had just decided that somehow she'd gone into another dimension and landed in the Twilight Zone when he turned one more corner and the Ho Ho Ho Inn came into view.

You couldn't miss it. With those flashing red ten-foot-tall letters. But she'd been expecting some sort of tacky little motel-looking place. The type where you'd expect to find animal heads hanging on cheap paneled walls. Granted, the inside could still meet expectations, but the exterior was a surprise.

It was actually a compound of log and stone buildings nestled in a grove of fir trees. The lodge itself had a roof that soared two and a half stories high. The front was all glass and jutted forward like the prow of an ancient sailing ship. Perhaps a dozen smaller cabins were scattered around in the woods. Close enough to give a sense of a community, but far enough apart to allow privacy, if that's what a guest had come here seeking.

"Okay, I'm impressed."

"You were expecting, perhaps, the Bates Motel?" Rather than seeming to take offense, his voice held that humor she was beginning to find all too appealing.

"Something like that," she admitted.

"According to old-timers, the original main inn was more along those lines. But it burned down two years ago after it was hit by lightning. The owners had plans drawn up and had begun construction when they decided they didn't want to make that much of a commitment at that point in their lives. So, they put it up for sale just when I got out of the service and was looking to make a lifestyle change. The top two floors are living area. I had soundproofing put in between the floors that allows me to live above the store without getting any of the downstairs noise."

"Lucky you." A warm, welcoming yellow light gleamed forth from the windows. "And it's stunning. But you've got to admit the signage is a little tacky."

"More than a little," he agreed. "The thing is, it fits the town's building code. I could've left the flashing lights off, but decided to put them back up because my daughter loves them."

"Your daughter?"

"Yeah." He pulled up in front of the lodge, parking between an ancient VW bus that had been painted in geometric squares reminiscent of the Partridge Family tour bus and a trendy Lexus crossover. "Emma's five. Needless to say, she finds all the kitsch in the town to her liking."

"I can imagine." Memories of her own childhood Christmases in New York, which she'd buried deep inside her long ago, stirred. From habit, Holly rigidly tamped them down. It figured that the first guy she'd found appealing in months was not only married, but a player. "How does your wife feel about it?"

"Wife?"

He cut the engine and turned toward her, a quick spark firing in eyes that had turned to flint. The easy humor was gone and the mouth that had been so quick to smile was drawn into a hard, tough line. For the first time she could see the warrior dwelling inside the friendly Good Samaritan inn owner.

"What the hell would I be doing hitting on another woman if I had a wife waiting for me at home?"

She shrugged. "People cheat all the time. You wouldn't be the first married person to fool around."

In fact, although she wasn't prepared to share the fact, she'd lost her virginity her freshman year of college to her English Lit professor, who'd neglected to mention a wife who'd just happened to be away on sabbatical studying the Brontë sisters at University College, Oxford.

The ironic thing about that whole sad affair was that at the time the Brontës had been her favorite authors, and the dark, broody, and overly temperamental professor had reminded her of Heathcliff.

"Other people may cheat." Something else came and went in Gabe's eyes. Something Holly couldn't quite read. "But not me. No way. No how."

He was suddenly looking at her as if she were a stray dog. No, worse than a stray, given the story of him having adopted that oversize mutt who was currently whining impatiently to get out of the SUV—he actually *liked* strays.

"Okay." She held up a hand. Obviously she'd misread the situation. "Since I just met you, I'll have to take your word for it. But may I point out that you're the one who hit on me. Talking about nibbling on ankles and such." Just the thought of all the other body parts representing the "such" was enough to make her blood run a little hotter. "Then, out of the blue, you brought up your daughter."

"You've never heard of a single dad?"

"Of course. I've just never actually met one."

The line of his jaw hardened. "Well, you have now."

Apparently he'd had enough of the conversation because after muttering a rude curse, he opened the door and climbed out. Not quite understanding how the mood had taken such a drastic turn, just because she'd made an understandable mistake, Holly didn't wait for him to come around the front of the Expedition, but jumped out and placed a hand on his arm.

"Look," she said. "I'm sorry if I offended you. That wasn't my intention." She offered a smile of contrition. "Especially after you rescued me from turning into a popsicle."

He looked down at her hand. Then cursed again. It might've been mild for a Marine, but it still wasn't a word Holly had said more than once, okay, maybe twice in her life.

"Hell. While we're sharing apologies here, let me offer you one for overreacting. My only excuse, not that I have much of one, is that you hit a hot button I didn't realize I had."

As they stood there in the snow-covered parking lot, Gabe looking down at Holly, her looking up at him, something stirred in her. More complicated than lust, it felt uncomfortably like need.

"Okay," she said through lips that had gotten suddenly dry. "So, we're even. No harm. No foul."

As quickly as the winter storm had swooped down over the mountains, his grin was back, quick and, dammit, sexy as sin. "Gotta love a woman who can use a sports metaphor. I don't suppose you eat meat?"

"I've been known to eat a bloody steak from time to time."

"How about carbs?"

"A steak without a baked potato or fries is like a day without chocolate." She shrugged. "What's the point?"

The air was biting, the snow continued to fall, but Holly was feeling warmer and warmer inside as his eyes swept over her face.

"I don't suppose you've watched ESPN on occasion?"

She tossed her head. Flashed him a flirty smile she didn't even know she had inside her. "I'll see your ESPN and raise you. I happen to subscribe to the NFL network."

"Be still my heart." He patted the front of the parka with that wide gloved hand that she was no longer worrying about breaking her neck. No, it was the other things she was imagining it doing that could prove really dangerous. "I'm not absolutely positive, but I think I may have just fallen in love."

"Don't get overly worked up," she said as he opened the back of the Expedition and got out her things. "I only signed up because I was thinking about writing a book about a crazed fan who killed off players from rival teams.

"Although that concept didn't quite work out, I kept the network, because, while I couldn't tell you an option play from a quarterback sneak, what's not to love about hunky guys in shoulder pads with tight butts running around in spandex?"

"I'd never thought of it that way."

"Now there's a surprise." Although the single former Marine Corps dad was certainly no Rambo, the testosterone he oozed was definitely of the heterosexual variety.

Toughening herself against it—and him—she turned and began walking down the narrow path someone had shoveled from the parking lot to the front door.

Seven

The sweep of headlights flashed in the window.

Over the sound of the wind in the tops of the trees, Beth heard a truck door open and shut. Then, surprisingly, another.

The door to the combination inn/restaurant/bar opened a moment later and Gabriel entered with a woman who looked vaguely familiar.

"It's her!" Emma hissed.

"Who?" Beth looked closer.

"My present!"

"What present?"

"The one I decided I wanted more than a pony," Emma insisted on an impatient huff. "My new mom!"

"What?"

"See." The little girl shoved the napkin at her grandmother. "I had Mr. Daughtry draw her for me, so Santa would know exactly what she looked like."

Beth studied the pencil sketch, then looked back at the

woman stamping the snow off a pair of calf-high chocolate-hued Uggs.

Daughtry's sketch wasn't as detailed as a photograph. But there was no mistaking the resemblance. The artist had captured the pointed, stubborn chin, the wide mouth, which was smiling in the sketch, unlike the real woman whose intelligent green gaze was sweeping over the room.

It was only a coincidence, Beth assured herself, as her granddaughter ran across the wooden floor to greet them. Just random luck. Just as it was only the chill of the night air that had caused the goosebumps to rise on her skin.

Revealing a speed that belied his size, Dog streaked past Gabe into the inn just as Emma came barreling toward him.

Then she skidded to a stop in front of Holly Berry, staring up at her with the awe that the adolescent boy Gabe had felt upon his first sight of a *Playboy* Playmate of the Month foldout.

"Hi." Her little voice was breathless, her face beatific.

"Hi, yourself."

The woman won huge points with Gabe when she returned his daughter's smile. Meanwhile, Dog came screeching to a halt with the scratching sound of claws on the wooden floor, rolled over, and waited for Emma to start scratching his stomach, as she always did.

"I'm Emma."

"I'm Holly."

The little girl's eyes lit up as Dog began wiggling on the floor, trying to get the attention he'd grown used to receiving. "Like Christmas Holly?"

"Exactly like that. I was born on Christmas Eve, so although my mother was pushing for Caroline, my father, who was a huge fan of Christmas, won the argument."

"That's cool." Emma's beaming smile could have lit up the town of Santa's Village for a month. "Maybe your daddy would like to live here. This is the most Christmassy town in America."

"So I read on the sign." When Dog, tired of being uncharacteristically ignored by his small owner, let out a deep rumbling bark, Holly absently began scratching his belly. "Unfortunately, my father died when I was young."

"That's too bad." Rosebud lips pulled into a pout Gabe recognized all too well. Even a five-year-old female, he'd discovered, could be every bit as capricious as the older variety, and Emma's emotions could swing in a wide arc. "My daddy almost died in Afghanistan. But he saved a bunch of people in a big battle and got a medal."

"Well." Holly glanced up at him. "That's very heroic."

Gabe cringed inwardly. He hated talk of heroism. "I was just doing my job," he insisted as he always did when either his mother or daughter brought it up. His father—having been a grunt in Nam—was wise enough to let sleeping dogs lie. So to speak. He took off the parka and hung it on the rack on the wall. "Same as any other Marine would've done."

"Hmm."

He could tell Holly wasn't exactly buying that, but was grateful when she didn't push for details. Instead, she stood up again and swept an appraising glance over his daughter. "I like your outfit."

Emma preened like a Junior Miss Cascade Rodeo Days finalist as she skimmed a small hand down the front of the pink fringed faux suede skirt. "It's my cowgirl outfit." She stuck out a small foot. "See, I have boots to match."

"I've never seen pink cowgirl boots before." Holly gave them an admiring appraisal.

"They're special. My aunt Julie sent them to me from Calgary. That's in Canada."

"I know."

"She went up there to compete in the barrel race in the

Calgary Stampede, which is this really big, famous rodeo. But she fell off her horse and broke her arm."

"That's too bad."

"Not really. Because she fell in love with the doctor who put her cast on."

Holly won additional points with Gabe by smiling. Not just a phony patronizing one for show, but a real one that crinkled the corners of her green eyes. "Sounds like a lucky break."

"That's what Aunt Julie says. Especially since she'd never, ever"—red curls danced as Emma shook her head—"fallen off her horse before. My uncle Jeremy—he's the doctor she married—says it was kismet. That's kinda like magic. Like Ariel saving Prince Eric from drowning, and falling in love with him."

"Sounds like it to me," Holly agreed, exchanging a glance with Gabe, who rolled his eyes. She suspected the family had very few secrets with this pint-size Paul Revere living among them.

Not that she'd pump a little girl for information about her father. Even if she was interested in the man. Which she wasn't.

Liar.

"Did Daddy bring you back from Seattle with him?" Emma asked.

"Part of the way." He'd shoved his fingers into the front pockets of his jeans, his thumbs arrowing downward, drawing her attention to his 5-button fly. "I had an accident, and he came along just in time."

"That's what heroes do," the little girl said, as if she were an authority on such matters. "Like Aladdin did when he rescued Princess Jasmine when she was about to get her hand cut off for giving an apple to a poor beggar."

"The world according to Disney," Gabe murmured, once

again sounding more than a little uncomfortable at being stuck atop that pedestal his daughter had created for him.

"Nothing wrong with fairy tales," Holly murmured back, even though her own mother had never allowed her to read them. Or go to Disney movies.

Better, she'd said, for little girls to grow up believing in reality. Of taking charge of your own life. Because waiting around for knights in shining armor and expecting happily ever after endings could only lead to heartbreak.

Still, Holly hadn't needed to spend a bundle talking about her childhood with some Freudian shrink to make the connection between her father's murder and her having grown up to be a mystery novelist.

Perhaps NYPD had never managed to catch George Berry's killer, but in Holly's stories, the bad guys were *always* captured by the final chapter, justice prevailed in the end, and the good guys—and women—went on to live happily ever after.

It was, in its own way, every bit a fantasy as the one those romance novels her best friend, Jeanine, who ran the Body Beautiful Day Spa next to the Starbucks down the street from her apartment, gobbled up like chocolate-covered coffee beans.

"Which is why they call it fiction," Holly had been quoted as saying just last week during an interview on Seattle's KOMO's *Northwest Afternoon* program.

Since selling her first book the same week she graduated from college, for the past seven years crime had been Holly's business. And fortunately, since people seemed to be endlessly fascinated by murder and mayhem, business was good.

Still, she was intrigued by the idea of this hottie Marine sitting in a theater, or even on a couch in his living room, watching *The Little Mermaid*.

"Ms. Berry has had a long day," he said on a mild tone that nevertheless brooked no argument. Holly figured the quiet authority must have served him well in the military. "We need to see about getting her a room for the night."

"She could stay with us," Emma volunteered quickly. A bit too quickly, Holly thought. "We've got lots of room."

"I think Ms. Berry might feel more comfortable with other arrangements."

His fingers curved around Holly's elbow as he led her across the room, which she was surprised to find tastefully decorated for the season. The fragrant green fir had been draped in white fairy lights, its branches adorned with what appeared to be hand-carved ornaments. Fresh wreaths hung on the windows, and the staircase was wrapped with pine garlands.

There were no animal heads on the walls, no inflatable snowmen or waving Santas.

Unfortunately, there was a juke box from which Lonestar was promising to be home for Christmas.

Yeah, right, Holly thought.

Great group. Stupid song. In fact, it was, thanks to her own personal history, her least favorite song ever recorded. Unfortunately, this particular one seemed to have been covered by anyone who'd ever picked up a microphone and it was impossible to get through the holiday season without being bombarded by various versions.

At least the country edge to this rendition kept it from being as saccharine as the one by The Carpenters, which had come onto the Highlander's radio as she'd left Seattle.

The kitchen had been built with a large window, allowing diners to watch their meals being made. It also, Holly thought, enabled the kitchen staff to keep an eye on their customers, thus allowing better service. The smells emanating from the room outfitted with what appeared to be state-of-the-art equipment made her mouth water. Then again, all she'd had to eat since that bagel this morning had been a thermos of coffee and a package of M&M's.

The fire he'd told her about probably made it impossible for the long check-in counter to be original, but it certainly looked antique. Perhaps an old bar from an 1880s saloon. She ran a finger over the crease in its polished surface and imagined a bullet skimming by during some long-ago gun-fight.

A woman, with fashionably silver hair cut in a short bob, wearing a white chef's apron over jeans and a blue Seattle Seahawks sweatshirt came out of the kitchen.

"It's about time you got home." She wrapped her arms around Gabe's wide shoulders, went up on her toes, and kissed his beard-roughened cheek. "I've been a little worried."

"I was delayed." He ran the back of his hand down the side of her face, the gesture easy and natural, demonstrating yet again that he was a man comfortable with physical displays of affection. "Holly, this is my mother, Beth O'Halloran. Mom, this is—"

"Holly Berry." Twin dimples that echoed her son's creased in her cheeks as she smiled. "I'm a huge fan."

A slender gold ring flashed in the twinkling white lights of the Christmas tree as she held out her hand. "Welcome to the Ho Ho Ho Inn."

"Holly had an accident on the road," Gabe revealed. "She swerved for Blitzen."

"Sam said he'd gotten out again," Beth agreed. "But, thank heavens, he's back home now." Hazel eyes swept over Holly's face. "Let's get some ice on that eye while I fix you some dinner."

"I was thinking perhaps, since we're booked solid, she could stay with you and Pop until her SUV's fixed and the roads open again," Gabe suggested.

"Well, now, of course you'd be welcome," Beth agreed.

"But as it turns out, we've a lovely one-bedroom cabin that just opened up today. The Davidsons' daughter went into labor early," she informed Gabe. "Even if they could get over the mountains, which they probably can't, since your father's been out putting up road closure barricades all day, they understandably decided to stay in Portland."

She smiled at Holly. "They've been regulars since their daughter, Madison, was about Emma's age. We'll miss them, of course, but it's a lucky timing for you."

"It seems to be." Holly decided her luck had definitely been mixed the last few hours.

"Is Madison okay?" Gabe asked.

"Better than okay. The Davidsons are now proud grand-parents of twins."

"That's good news."

The genuine warmth in his tone suggested he knew the new mother. Which only made sense. Of course, there could also be a history there, Holly considered. She couldn't imag-ine many teenage girls not noticing Gabriel O'Halloran. Es-pecially in a town this small. As the idea of a Christmas vacation fling with a hunkier younger version of the Marine single dad came to mind, Holly felt a little twinge of some-thing that felt uncomfortably, ridiculously, like jealousy.

"Fabulous news," Beth agreed. "Anna sounded over the moon about being a new grandmother when she called to cancel. Why don't you take Holly's things over to the cabin, Gabriel," she suggested, "while I fix her something to eat."

"I'll help," Emma chirped up. "Do you like gingerbread?" she asked Holly.

"Doesn't everyone?" Holly responded, suspecting that was the answer the little girl wanted to hear.

"Good. Because Gramma makes the best gingerbread in the whole world. I helped her make it this morning."

"Emma's quite the little helper," Beth agreed, her smile

once again reminding Holly of her son's. "I don't know what I'd do without her."

Five minutes later, Holly was sitting at a small table in the kitchen, a bag of frozen peas wrapped in a dish towel against her eye, while Beth whipped up a serving of the daily special—gravy-smothered chicken fried steak and mashed potatoes.

Even as she could practically see the dinner attaching itself to her hips, Holly, who was more accustomed to nuking a Lean Cuisine or takeout Chinese, couldn't deny it smelled heavenly.

If she was going to get stranded somewhere, a town called Santa's Village definitely would've been her very last choice. Well, at least right above hell.

Still, as Emma chattered on like a little red-haired magpie about her various aunts and uncles' adventures, and Beth hustled around the kitchen with an ease a finalist on *Top Chef* would've envied, Holly decided it was actually rather pleasant.

When Gabe's mother put the white plate in front of her and she discovered the calorie-laden dinner tasted even better than it had smelled, she decided she could have done a whole lot worse.

Eight

The cabin, which was stone and wood on the outside, wa warm and cozy, with overstuffed furniture covered in sturdy fabric designed to take a lot of abuse. The furniture was a eclectic mixture of pine and other woods, the plank coffe table wide enough to encourage visitors to put their feet up

Someone—it had to have been Gabe—had lit a fire in th stone fireplace while she'd been eating dinner. There was powder room and large but cozy combination living roor and kitchen separated by a granite-topped counter dowr stairs. Upstairs, in the loft, was a bath with separate showe and oversize whirlpool tub that looked out onto the dark ex panse of forest, and a bedroom boasting a king-size fou poster bed created from logs.

Yellow plank pine walls glowed like warm butter beneat the wrought iron chandelier. A second fireplace, this or gas, flickered in the corner and a Native American print qui and pillows covered the bed.

A smaller blanket, bordered in deep brown and blu woven petroglyphs, hung on the wall opposite the bed.

fanciful figure in colors ranging from red to bright yellow stood in the center of the blanket.

"It depicts a spirit quest," Gabe told her as she paused in front of it, "symbolizing a young brave seeking his destiny. The petroglyphs were designed after those found near the Columbia River. They've been dated back to over ten thousand years. The ones on the stones," he said. "Not the blanket."

"It's lovely," she murmured. The woven wool was incredibly soft to the touch. "It must've been nice. To believe in such a thing."

"Nice?" He tilted his head and looked down at her.

"That's not exactly the word I mean. More life affirming. The idea of a quest to follow your fate."

"And you don't believe in that idea?"

"I believe we all make our own fate. . . . What?" she asked, after a long, humming moment when he didn't respond.

"I was just thinking how I used to believe that, too. When I left town on, I guess you'd have to say, my own spirit quest."

"Which led you into the Marines."

"Yeah. Where I learned that despite all the training, despite being a member of the strongest military in the world, fate has a helluva lot more to do with life than most of us want to admit."

Suspecting that he'd seen a lot during his years in the service, Holly didn't want to argue. Besides, if she was going to get technical, she suspected fate had played more than a little part in that Manhattan murderous mugger being on the street corner that long-ago Christmas Eve.

"Well." She blew out a breath. "Thanks for rescuing me. And for the place to stay. And the dinner."

"The Ho Ho Ho Inn prides itself on its hospitality."

She couldn't help smiling.

"What?" His chiseled masculine lips quirked just a bit in response to her smile.

"I was just thinking how amazing it is that a big tough Marine can say the name of this place with a straight face."

His rich, warm laugh was every bit as intoxicating as the buttered rum Beth O'Halloran had insisted on sending with her in a foam to-go cup, along with a plate of ginger spice molasses cookies.

"Believe me, it took a while." His eyes warmed like gleaming pewter in the glow from the wrought iron chandelier's candelabra bulbs. "Nearly as long as it took me to get used to the idea of being an innkeeper."

"It seems a little—" She paused, taking time to find the right word. "*Staid* for someone who's obviously accustomed to more action."

"Which is precisely why I'm happy with staid for the time being. Plus, there's Emma to think of."

Holly wondered how he'd ended up in America's most Christmassy town the single dad to a little girl. Where was the former Mrs. O'Halloran? If there'd even been one.

"She's darling. And going to be a heartbreaker when she grows up."

"Oh, Lord. I don't even want to think about that." He'd unzipped the parka he'd put back on to walk her to the cabin, and now rubbed a hand against his chest. "I'm thinking about locking her in a closet at puberty and letting her back out at thirty. Or seeing if I can talk her into a convent."

"Well, those are two possible solutions." She wondered if her own father would've felt the same way. Felt a tinge of the sadness at the idea she'd never know.

"Probably not the most practical," Gabe allowed. His lips were still smiling, but his heavily lidded eyes, as they moved slowly, intimately over her face, were not.

"What?" she asked, her voice uncharacteristically soft after another long, drawn-out pause.

"I was just thinking about fate." Thoughtful little lines appeared at the corners of those unreasonably sexy eyes. Once again demonstrating he had no concept of personal space, he ran a hand down her hair. This time Holly did not—could not—move away.

"What about it?"

"How if all of the events of the past few years hadn't conspired to bring me back to this place I always swore I wanted to escape, I wouldn't have happened to have been on that road today." He combed the long, dark fingers of his left hand through her hair, which was still a bit damp from having walked out into the snow again from the inn to the cabin. "Just a few minutes after you'd run into that snowdrift."

"It was more like forty-five minutes," she managed through lips that had gone ridiculously dry.

"Then I guess I'm damn lucky that fate kept some other guy from getting there before me."

At this moment, Holly was almost hoping that some other man had. Someone like, perhaps, Sam Fraiser, the owner of Kris Kringle's Workshop, out searching for his runaway reindeer. If only she'd been rescued by the village's own personal Santa, she wouldn't be so tempted by those lips that were getting closer to her own.

And she definitely wouldn't be going up on her toes to help him close the gap.

"Gabriel." His name came out on a ragged breath.

"That's funny." His free hand slid beneath the back of her sweater, roughened fingertips warm against her flesh.

"What?"

"The only person who's called me that since sixth grade is my mother." He drew her closer. "But it sounds really, really different coming from your lips."

He lowered his mouth and brushed at those lips with a feather-soft touch that was more temptation than proper kiss. The hand on her back was both gentle and confident as it pressed her even closer against him.

"Say it again." His breath was warm against her lips. He tasted of coffee, and cinnamon gum, and desire. A desire that was ribboning through her own veins.

"Gabriel." The archangel's name came out on a shuddering breath. "Please."

"Please yes?" His lips continued to drift over hers in a slow, lazy seduction that was as enticing as it was enervating. "Or please no?"

Although her taser pen was back inside her bag, which was currently lying on the coffee table in the other room, Holly knew she could stop him. She had, after all, taken that protection course at the police station, and while she might not be able to break bricks with her bare hands, she knew moves that could have him writhing on the floor gripping his wounded balls.

But she knew that she wouldn't need those GET skills with this man. Knew that she could simply step away and he'd stop.

But, oh God, his mouth was so amazingly clever. The almost kisses so tempting, drawing her into complacence, even as they excited.

Telling herself that it was only because it'd been a very long time since she'd been with any man, that this hot, intoxicating pleasure had nothing to do with Gabriel O'Halloran himself, or the admittedly unusual circumstance that had landed her in first his SUV, then his arms, Holly twined her arms around his neck.

"Yes, dammit."

Nine

She closed her eyes, expecting the former Marine to ravish, to take what she was so willingly offering. But instead, she felt the curve of his lips against hers.

"Well"—his voice, husky with lust, but tinged with humor, had her toes curling in her Uggs—"since you put it that way."

Needs. Hunger. Lust. They surged through Gabe, battering away at his hard-won self-control, demanding satisfaction.

In response to her demand, he crushed her against him as his lips turned hard. Fueled by his own burning hunger, driven by her uninhibited response, he wanted to devour her—her warm, ripe mouth, her hot, peach-scented skin, which was practically melting beneath his now roving hands.

His tongue was in her mouth, his hands were beneath the sweater on her breasts, and as he pressed against that soft, womanly place between her thighs, he felt about to burst all five metal buttons beneath his fly.

Too fast, he told himself as her mouth clung to his and her silky soft hands dove beneath his sweatshirt. Too soon.

Although his aching body was shouting at him to take her the hell to bed, now, when he did make love to her, and Gabe had every intention of doing exactly that, he wanted to be able to take his time. To give, as well as take.

When her greedy touch went lower, her fingers slipping between denim and skin, he grasped hold of her wrists.

Not yet ready to quit, he pinned her hands to the wooden post of the bed and slowed the pace, lips plucking at hers again, rather than devouring, his tongue leaving the lush hot moistness of her mouth to skim a slow, tantalizing circle around her parted lips.

"Dammit." His breath was rough. Ragged. His body ached and his damn heart hadn't pounded against his ribcage this hard since the last time he'd been on a battlefield. "Do you have any idea how much I want you?"

And because he did want her, more than was either reasonable or safe, he let go of her and backed away.

"I think that was fairly evident." Her eyes were wide, and just a little unfocused, which was sexy as hell, as she rubbed her wrists.

"You didn't say no," he reminded her.

"Would it have mattered?" On a flare of heat, she tossed up that stubborn, pointed chin.

"Hell, yes." She might as well have slapped him. "I've never been into forcing women."

"Like you'd ever have to," she muttered.

The mood was disintegrating. Like morning mist that rose from the lake each summer, only to be burned away by the sun. But her tone, rather than sexy warm, or even annoyed hot, had turned as chilly as the icicles hanging from the cabin's eaves.

Women, Gabe thought. From five to twenty-eight—and he knew exactly how old she was because he'd taken the time to Google her while she'd been in the kitchen with his mother—they could all be as capricious as the damn weather.

"You met my mother."

Because it was impossible to be this close to her and not touch, he linked their fingers together and led her out of the room and down the stairs, away from the temptation of that king-size bed.

Not that the lack of a bed would stop him if he put aside principles and just went for what he wanted. Especially since he was really, really tempted to drag her down onto the rug in front of the stone fireplace.

But hadn't he learned the hard way that people could get hurt when you only thought about your own sexual needs?

"Do you think she'd have raised a guy who didn't respect women?" he asked.

"No." Holly blew out a breath as they reached the front door. "And it's not just her. I watched you with your daughter. You're a nice guy, Gabriel O'Halloran."

"Terrific." Because his body still wanted her, still ached with the need for her, and because she'd just reminded him that Emma was waiting in bed for him to read the Grinch story to her, Gabe laughed. A harsh, rough sound from deep in his throat. "Kittens are nice. Boy Scouts and TV weathermen are nice. Believe me, sweetheart, a lot of the things I want to do with you don't begin to fit into that category."

He skimmed a finger beneath the eye that, despite the ice pack his mother had given her, was still blossoming into one hell of a shiner.

"You've had a stressful day." His mother's response to stress came to mind. "Why don't you take a long, hot bubble bath and relax?"

Hell. The words had no sooner come out of his mouth than Gabe regretted them. Because they stirred up images of being naked with her straddling his legs in that oversize tub. And afterward, smoothing lotion the scent of ripe peaches over every inch of her porcelain-pale skin.

"Get some rest." He plowed forward before she might

just go insane and invite him into that bathtub with her. "Since breakfast comes with the cabin, and you obviously haven't had time to go shopping, I'll see you in the morning."

He skimmed a finger down her nose. Then, before he could change his mind, he turned and walked out of the cabin into the dark and snowy night.

Ten

Holly stood at the door, watching him walk out of the yellow circle of light from her own porch back to the inn. White flakes continued to fall, shawling silently over the land, and once he'd been swallowed up by the snow-swirled darkness, she could have been the only person in the world. Which was all it took to kick Holly's imagination into high gear.

She hadn't been all that wild about the cookie murders, anyway, having already written a black widow killer. But six weeks ago, although she'd never allowed herself to believe in writer's block, she'd run smack into it.

She'd always read three newspapers a day looking for story ideas. Desperate, and with a deadline approaching, she'd added two more papers and more magazines than anyone could read in a lifetime.

She began taking tabloids home with her frozen dinners from the supermarket. Okay, her audience might not want to read about bat boy being found on a melting glacier at the North Pole, or the *Titanic* being discovered by a lunar rover in a previously uncharted sea on the moon, but there were a lot of crimes profiled between those newsprint pages. Unfortunately, none had gotten her balky muses—who seemed to have gone into permanent PMS—to cooperate.

Neither had Court TV. Nor any of the other true-life crime shows that seemed to run 24/7 on cable. It had been desperation, and a need to be anywhere away from home on Christmas, that had had her driving over the Cascades to Leavenworth.

And that same desperation had landed her in the arms of a hottie ex-Marine who had her feeling things she'd forgotten she *could* feel. Tingling in places she'd never known she could tingle.

But now, as she closed the heavy wooden door, she thought about all the things that might be lurking out there in the dark winter night.

Mountain lions, perhaps? Although bears were supposed to hibernate, surely once in a while a rogue one might come out of its den to go searching for food. Or wolves, which, thinking about it, the wind in the top of the trees sort of sounded like. Did they have wolves in Washington?

But even as that idea caused the hair to rise on her arms, she didn't write about killer animals. Well, actually she did, but Holly had always thought human animals could be far more terrifying due to their propensity for evil.

What if a woman was alone here in this very cabin while a serial killer lurked outside, armed, with a huge hunting knife—with a serrated edge and ugly blood groove—hidden in his boot?

But what was the woman doing here, out in the middle of nowhere? Perhaps her car had broken down?

No.

Holly shook her head as she took the plastic lid off the takeout cup and sipped the buttered rum, which while no longer exactly hot, was still warm. That was too close to real life. It wasn't always easy keeping fact and fiction separate, and bringing her own experience into her story could very well blur the line.

So . . .

She began to pace the wooden plank floor, her mind spinning with possibilities. What if it just wasn't a lone woman at risk—which brought to mind all those Halloween slasher stories—but a young mother? With a small son.

No. A little girl. With hair the color of a newly minted penny, who was clever and funny and chattered like a magpie.

Although Holly hated putting children in jeopardy, even in books, there was admittedly something visceral about the idea. Something that her readers could connect emotionally with.

"But what would they be doing out here in the middle of nowhere?" she asked herself out loud.

Running from something. Or someone. Hiding out. Perhaps to keep the little girl safe?

Holly felt a stirring in the far reaches of her mind and realized that she'd just hit on something that had appealed to one of those bitchy muses who'd been refusing to cooperate.

"That's it. She's running from her husband." A dangerously possessive psychopath who'd do anything, stop at nothing, to get her back.

Of course, she considered as she took another sip of the cooling rum, even if her beleaguered heroine knew every martial art in the world, and was armed to the teeth, she'd still be in danger.

Unless . . .

"There's a hottie sheriff in town." That worked, she thought. So long as he was self-assured enough not to overpower the heroine's autonomy. "Maybe former military."

She nodded, liking that idea. "A former Navy SEAL."

Which was a possibility, but she'd also written SEALs in her second and fourth books, which had been set in San Diego and Virginia Beach.

"Maybe a former Marine." Her mind immediately spun up an image of thick black hair and steely gray eyes. "Who's come back to his hometown and taken on his father's job as sheriff."

That worked, Holly decided.

She went over to the kitchen table, where Gabriel had left her laptop, took it out of the case, and sat down to work.

As the words started flowing, like water from a magical well, and her muses finally began to cooperate, Holly decided that she wasn't the only one who found the hunky inn owner an inspiration.

Eleven

It was the knock on the door that woke her. Sitting up, Holly looked around the unfamiliar surroundings.

It took her a moment to realize where she was. Aha! The inn out in the middle of the Cascade Mountains, where she'd landed after wrecking her Highlander. She squinted, trying to read her watch.

"Ten in the morning?"

She never, ever slept past seven. Except that time two years ago, when despite having a shot, she'd come down with the flu. Or, when she'd been writing madly until deadline. Which is exactly what she'd been doing last night.

She vaguely remembered saving her story. Then e-mailing it to herself, just in case some crazy electrical storm surge might come along to fry her laptop.

Then she'd dragged herself upstairs where, because even with the central heat there was a chill in the air, she'd put on her flannel pajamas, after which she'd fallen into bed.

Then crashed. That had been, what? Two hours ago?

She thought about ignoring the knock, rolling over, burying her head in the thick cloud of down pillow, and going back to sleep. But what if it was something concerning her Highlander? What if the tow truck driver had already arrived with it?

Rubbing the grit out of her eyes with her knuckles, she padded in sock-clad feet downstairs, opened the front door, and found herself looking a long way up into Gabriel O'Halloran's apologetic gaze.

"Sorry. It looks as if we woke you up."

"I worked late." She ran a hand over her hair, which, if it was behaving in its usual bedhead fashion, was undoubtedly stuck up in all directions, looking as if she'd put her finger in a light socket.

A small bright head peeked around his jean-clad thighs. "Wow." Bright eyes swept over Holly's face. "Does your eye hurt as bad as it looks?"

Amazingly, she'd forgotten all about that. Lifting a finger to her face, Holly couldn't quite refrain from flinching as she touched the bruised skin beneath her eye. "I don't know how bad it looks," she said, even as she feared the worst. "But it's okay."

"That's good. I had a black eye in September, after I got in a fight with Jimmy Jones—he's one of the big kids, in second grade—on the playground because he said Santa wasn't real." Pink lips turned down in a moue. "He's not a very nice boy."

"Doesn't sound like it, hitting a girl," Holly agreed.

"Oh, I hit him first," Emma said casually. "Daddy said I was wrong, even though he told a fib about Santa." She glanced up at her father, who nodded resigned confirmation. "Gramma was worried you'd be hungry. So we brought you breakfast. So you can eat before we go out and get your tree."

The scent of fresh brewed coffee rose enticingly from the brown paper bag Gabe was holding. As uncomfortable as she was, letting the former Marine see her in her flannel jammies and spiky hair, not to mention whatever her eye must look like, there was no way she could resist a morning jolt of caffeine.

"That's very considerate of your grandmother." She moved aside, allowing them into the cabin, and folded her arms across her breasts. "What's this about a tree?"

"It's an inn tradition." Gabe put the bag on the butcherblock counter, took out a tall cardboard cup, and handed it to her.

"Thanks." She took a sip and nearly wept.

"My pleasure." He skimmed a look over her, and amazingly, instead of cringing, if the light in his eyes was any indication, actually appeared to like what he saw. "As for the tree, like I said, it's an inn tradition. Everyone who stays here gets to choose their own from the farm."

"Thanks," she repeated as she took another, longer drink. It was hot, dark, sweet, and caused a much-needed jolt to her system. "But as soon as my Highlander gets fixed, I'll be on my way."

But not on to Leavenworth. After the nearly twenty pages she'd written last night, Holly had committed to her runaway wife and psychotic, possessive husband story. The cookie-baking black widow would have to wait.

"Ken Olson, of Olson's Auto Repair, took his tow truck out to bring in your rig a bit ago," Gabe said. "You've probably got at least a couple hours until he's got it back to town and checked it out."

"Well." Holly supposed she couldn't expect things to move as quickly up here in the mountains as they might in the city. "I appreciate your help with that. But I'm really not into the whole tree thing."

"You don't like Christmas trees?" When Emma's eyes widened to saucers of disbelief, Holly felt like the Grinch who stole the little girl's Christmas.

"I like them just fine," she said. "It's just . . . well, I've never had one."

Emma gasped. "Never?"

"Well, not since I was seven."

Gray eyes, replicas of her father's, narrowed as they skimmed over her face. "Wow! That was a really, really long time ago."

"Sorry," Gabe said as Holly choked on her coffee. "We're still working on the concept of tact."

"It's okay." Holly wiped her lips with the back of her hand. When Gabe's gaze followed the gesture, she knew they were thinking the same thing. Of that hot kiss they'd shared last night.

She could also tell that she'd hugely disappointed his daughter.

"Daddy grows the very bestest trees," Emma said fervently. "We could find you the neatest one ever. To make up for all the Christmases when you went without one."

"I think maybe Ms. Berry would just as well forgo the tree hunting experience," Gabe told his daughter gently.

"But, Daddy, everyone else at the Ho Ho Ho Inn has a tree." The little girl's voice rose perilously close to a whine.

Something occurred to Holly. "Don't you have school today?" she asked. Surely she hadn't worked through an entire weekend?

"I'm in kindergarten," Emma confirmed. "Which is just half days until I get to first grade next year. But we had a snow day. Which is even more special because now I get to go with you to pick out the most perfect tree."

Although the child was only five years old, it was like trying to stand up to a velvet bulldozer. Holly exchanged a look with Gabe. He shrugged, letting her know that it was her call.

"Let me get dressed," she said. "And we'll go see what we can find."

"Awesome!" A small fist pumped into the air. "We brought you doughnuts, too. Since you missed breakfast."

She held out the brown paper bag. There was a bear claw, a filled doughnut, and a flaky croissant.

"If I lived here, I'd be the size of Mrs. Santa within a week," Holly said. Then, seeing the frown lines on the small forehead, she managed a reassuring smile. "They smell delicious."

Emma nodded, the worry lines smoothing. "The lemon-filled doughnut is my favorite. That's why I picked it for you."

Holly lifted her gaze to Gabe again, who was watching her carefully. As if she'd hurt a little girl's feelings? Holly didn't know what the father and daughter's backstory was, but she did know how it felt to be a child and have your life pulled out from under you. As Emma's must have been.

"Lemon-filled are my very favorite kind," she said, then watched him blow out a breath she suspected he'd been unaware of holding. She didn't care what he'd said. Gabriel O'Halloran *was* a nice guy.

Holly took a knife from the drawer, cut the doughnut in half, and put one of the halves on a small plate from the open shelf over the sink. "But I don't think I can eat them all myself. So why don't we share?"

"Okay." The cheerful child was back as she shrugged out of her coat and mittens and happily carried the plate over to the table.

"I'll be right back down," Holly said. "As soon as I get dressed."

She'd just started up the stairs leading to the loft, when Gabe caught hold of her arm.

Holly glanced back over her shoulder.

"Thanks," he said, with a heartfelt appreciation that didn't surprise her as much as it might have only a day earlier.

That he loved his daughter was more than a little obvious.

Although she wasn't about to envy Emma for having the father she herself had always dreamed of, Holly nevertheless found herself warming to him. And not in the sexual way she'd experienced last night. But something deeper. And, oddly, more unsettling.

"I've never gone tree hunting before," she said. "I'm looking forward to the experience."

The oddest thing was, the words that were meant to reassure both father and daughter were absolutely true.

Across the room, Emma was licking lemon filling from a small thumb, oblivious to the look Gabe was sweeping over her.

"You look good enough to eat," he said.

She refrained, just barely, from running her hand down the front of the cream pajamas covered with deep red cherries. "If you're hungry enough to eat flannel, there's a bear claw in that bag with your name on it."

His deep rumbling laugh followed Holly up the stairs and into the shower, staying with her while she quickly blow-dried her hair and tried to cover up the purple and blue pouch of swollen skin around her eye.

And his laugh was still there, warming her blood in a not unpleasant way after she'd dressed.

There had to be some kind of mind-altering Kool-Aid in the water, Holly decided as she headed back down the stairs to willingly go on a Christmas tree hunt.

Twelve

Emma was bundled up like a snow princess in her Hello Kitty pink hooded jacket lined with white faux fur, matching pink snowpants and boots, and fuzzy pink mittens, when Holly came downstairs. The expectation on her face was so bright Holly felt she needed to put on her sunglasses.

"Emma," Gabe said, not taking his eyes from Holly, "why don't you go check on Dog. Ms. Berry and I will lock up and be out in a minute."

"Okay." She obediently went outside.

"Now that she got her way, she'll be sweet as a sugar plum for at least the next ten minutes," Gabe said. His wry grin creased his cheeks in a way that made Holly want to lick those dimples.

"She's darling." To keep her hands out of trouble, Holly turned her back and slipped her arms into the scarlet ski jacket she'd hung on the wall hook last night. "And you're good with her."

"It's taken some adjustment on both our parts," he surprised her by admitting. "But we're getting there."

His fingers brushed the back of her neck as he lifted her hair from beneath the collar. Like everything else about the man, the casual touch proved unnervingly seductive.

"I don't mean to pry, but did your wife die?"

Emma's mother would have been young, but having written a serial killer who targeted soccer moms in her fifth book, Holly knew that youth wasn't always enough to keep that old boogie man Death from claiming another victim.

"No." His tone was curt, but in the short span of time it took for her to turn back around, his face had set in a not unfriendly, but unreadable mask.

"Sorry," she said as she plucked her knitted hat from the rack. "As I said, I didn't mean to pry. Besides, it's none of my business—"

"I'm beginning to think it just might be." He seemed nearly as surprised to hear himself say that as she was to hear it. "But, the thing is, it's not a pretty story. Not all that unusual, either, unfortunately. But definitely not something I want to talk about when I'm headed out on a beautiful winter day with an even more beautiful woman."

"Oh, that's good." She drew in a short breath. "Do you practice those lines? Or do they come naturally?"

"I don't know, since, having grown up with three older sisters who never let me get a word in edgewise, I've never exactly been the talkative type." He tilted his head and studied her, the same way he had last night. Slowly. Silently. Intimately. "Come here."

Holly could no more have resisted that husky invitation than she could have sprouted gossamer wings and flown to the moon.

"I thought about doing this all night," he said as he enveloped her in his arms. She felt her body melting. Degree by enervating degree. "About holding you again." He brushed his lips against her temple. "Tasting you again." His mouth skimmed down her cheek. Nuzzled her neck. "You smell like sugar cookies this morning."

"It's the vanilla in my lotion." She tilted her head, giving his lips access to that little hollow in her throat where her pulse was beating so hard and fast she wouldn't have been surprised if he could hear it. "I have a friend who runs a day spa. She creates personalized scents."

"I'm sure she does a dynamite business. But I have the feeling you don't need any extra embellishment." His tongue slid silkily up her throat, from that wild bloodbeat to brush the line of her jaw before encircling her lips. "Though I have to admit, sugar cookies are one of my favorite things."

"I dreamed of this," she said, as her hands stroked his shoulders.

They were wide and strong and capable of carrying heavy burdens. Just like the small-town sheriff in the story she'd stayed up all night writing. There was no point in denying that Gabriel had been her inspiration for that gentle, but tough, defender of women and children.

"Of you. And me. Together."

It had been after she'd pictured the sheriff shooting the psycho husband dead. Oh, she hadn't gotten to that scene yet, but she could see it as clearly as if it was running on her HDTV. She'd had it in her head when she'd fallen into bed, thinking of the abusive bad guy's scarlet blood staining the pristine moonlight snow.

Once again, justice had prevailed. As it always did in a Holly Berry mystery.

But her muses, and her unconscious mind, had a different ending. As she'd discovered when she'd dreamed of the hero making slow, amazing love to the heroine, in front of a fire blazing in a stone hearth, while the little girl slept the safe, protected sleep of innocents in her pink canopied bed upstairs.

She could feel his lips quirk against hers. "Was it a good dream?"

Holly tilted her head back. "What do you think?"

"I think"—his lips plucked at hers, punctuating his words as he made her blood sing—"that there's no way you and I couldn't be spectacular together."

And then, as if to prove his point, his mouth swept down and took hers. Hard and fast, the sudden punch of heat literally rocking her back on her heels, warming all the cold, empty places inside her.

It was the strangest thing, she thought, as the amazing kiss went on and on and on. His mouth was still on hers, but somehow she could feel it in every cell of her body. Shooting out her fingertips, her toes, curling in her stomach, making her nipples tingle and that hot, needy place between her thighs ache.

"If we were alone," he groaned into her mouth, one large hand holding her intimately against his lower belly, where he was rock hard and swollen, "we'd finish this."

"Yes."

Somehow, as he'd dragged her into the heat, both arms and one leg had wrapped around him. Reality had receded as he'd made love to her with only his wickedly clever lips, teeth, and tongue. At this moment, Holly would have said *yes, yes, yes!* to anything, everything, Gabriel had in mind.

As he'd done last night, he backed away. His hands on her shoulders, his eyes on her face, which, she feared, was not only bruised, but flushed the crimson color of her jacket.

"Unfortunately, right now, we have a tree to hunt down." He bent down and kissed her nose. Then her lips again, the brief flare of heat ending too soon. "So, hopefully you'll be issuing me a snow check."

"I think you mean a rain check." Although she'd never been the type of woman to go to bed with a man she'd just met, Holly was definitely issuing one to this man.

"Maybe that's what you call them in Seattle." He grinned, took away the leather gloves she was about to put on, and replaced them with a pair of insulated blue gloves covered with white snowflakes.

"My sister Rachel is a serious skier," he explained. "She was on the Olympic team that went to Japan in '98 and her closets look like an REI warehouse. Since your own gloves didn't look that warm, I stopped by her house this morning before coming over here."

"That's very thoughtful." They might not go with her coat, but they definitely looked warmer.

"We do our best to keep our guests comfortable here at the Ho Ho Ho Inn. And, getting back to my plan of nibbling every fragrant inch of your sugar-cookie-sweet body, here in Santa's Village, it's a snow check." He picked up the conversational thread. "We're a little different from the rest of the planet."

As she walked out into the bite of an icy winter's morning and saw the huge sleigh pulled by—count them!—*eight* reindeer, there was no way Holly was about to argue that claim.

"Blitzen, I presume?" she asked with an arched brow.

"Back left, right in front of the sleigh," Gabe said without a touch of irony in his tone.

She narrowed her eyes at the brown, antlered reindeer who'd caused her accident. In turn, he returned a blank, brown-eyed stare.

"So, what happened to Rudolph?" Holly asked.

"He's make-believe," Emma volunteered from the backseat of the huge red, gold, and black sleigh. Dog sat beside her, long tongue gathering in snowflakes that continued to fall like feathers from a patchy blue and gray sky. "From the song. 'Rudolph the Red-Nosed Reindeer.'"

"Of course. I'd forgotten that."

"I can sing it for you." Without hesitation, she began to do exactly that.

"There's still time to change your mind," Gabe murmured.

"No." Between the coffee and the mind-blinding kiss, she was already too awake to go back to sleep anyway. "Besides, I'm looking forward to seeing an actual Christmas tree farm."

The weirdest thing was, it was true.

Five minutes later, Holly was snuggled beneath a pile of blankets next to Gabe, who was actually driving the sleigh.

"You're very good at this," she said. Even Blitzen seemed to be obeying the light flick of the reins.

"I've had a lot of practice. Sam Fraiser, that'd be—"

"The village's very own Santa Claus," Holly said.

Although she couldn't quite keep the wry tone from her voice, there was no way she was going to question the reality of the man the little girl singing in the backseat had gotten in a fistfight over.

"Yeah. That's him. Well, he's been loaning the rig out to the inn for a long time. It sorta adds to the appeal, and bringing the tree back on that rack at the back of the sleigh is more colorful than strapping it to the roof of the Expedition. Also, back when I was in high school, I picked up some extra Christmas bucks driving tourists around during the holidays."

Picturing the teenage boy he must have been, Holly had no problem at all imagining long lines of high school girls waiting for rides.

"How does this tree hunting thing you've got going work during really bad weather?" she asked.

"I don't know, since this is my first winter running the place and we haven't had any so far this season. This storm might have closed the roads because of the snowpack and ice, but it's still nowhere near the blizzards the place can get. I suppose, if the weather got really nasty, most guests would prefer to stay inside by the fire and let me bring their trees to them."

That was probably the case, Holly thought. But as the harness bells jingled merrily, the metal runners crunched against the snow, and Emma segued into "Frosty the Snowman," she decided they'd be missing something special.

"Oh, they really do look just like Christmas trees," she said on a little appreciative intake of breath as they approached the acres of fir and spruce trees lined up like little blue-green conical soldiers.

"That's the point," Gabe said. "And I don't want to burst any bubbles, especially since you're not a real fan of the holiday in the first place, but although they're trained to grow into a more pyramid shape than, say, pine trees, they still need to be trimmed and shaped at least once a year."

"They're still lovely." Again, she meant it. "The only thing missing are lights, glass balls, and angels for the tops."

He bent his head toward her, lowering his voice for her ears only. "The angel's sitting right here."

"Flatterer," she said. When she turned her head, their lips brushed.

"It's not flattery if it's true."

He pulled up on the reins, clucked lightly, and the reindeer came to a stop next to a big gray barn. A huge fresh wreath made up of spruce boughs hung above the closed double wooden doors of the barn, and trees, wearing red bows fashioned from outdoor velvet ribbon, flanked either side. A hand-painted sign offered sleigh rides, cocoa, hot apple cider, free disposal bags, and the loan of saws and axes for the do-it-yourselfers.

"We closed down this past weekend because the previous owner always gave his employees the last week of December

and all of January off to spend with their families," Gabe
said. "But if anyone in town wants a tree, they know they're
free to come cut one."

"Doesn't that invite tree theft?"

"I suppose it could, though there's not as much profit in
second- or third-growth trees," he said as Dog jumped down
from the backseat and set off across the field, snow flying,
chasing after a squirrel.

"Poor guy never catches them," Gabe said with another of
what she was beginning to think of as his trademark grins,
"but that never stops him from trying."

"Maybe the fun is in the chase," she suggested.

"There is that."

Taking Holly's word that she could certainly climb out of
a simple sleigh herself, he lifted Emma down.

"How can anyone ever decide?" Holly asked.

She had a vague memory of going to a neighborhood lot
with her father, and him carrying a tree back to their apartment, but there couldn't have been more than twenty or
thirty to choose among. Here the forest of conifers seemed
to stretch on for miles.

"You have to look and look and look," Emma informed
her. "But all Daddy's trees are the best. You can't pick a bad
one. Do you know Nordstrom?"

"Of course." Part of the appeal of Seattle, when she'd
been looking for a new place to live, had been the fabulous
downtown flagship store.

"Well, one of Daddy's trees is on the front of their catalog
this year."

"I'm impressed."

Gabe shrugged broad shoulders. "We're local. It only
made sense."

Holly knew men, both in L.A. and Seattle, who'd be
broadcasting such a coup through a bullhorn.

"Good try," she said. "But I'm still impressed."

As perfect as every tree appeared to Holly, Emma seemed determined to find the "most bestest" tree. This one was too skinny. Another too tall. A third's branches were too close together. A fourth's were too far apart.

"How about this one?" Holly asked finally, after the search had stretched on for an hour.

Emma's lips drew together into a thoughtful line as she looked a long, long way upward.

Holly, who was holding her breath, realized that Gabe, standing next to her, was doing the same thing.

Emma let out a long, happy breath of her own.

"It's perfect," she pronounced. "Better even than the one that lady from Nordstrom picked."

Not bothering to hide his relief, Gabe took the hatchet and saw he'd retrieved from the barn, and, after making sure Emma and Holly were standing out of the way, lay down on the ground and began to saw.

Less than three minutes later, the tree toppled to the snow. While he was wrapping the snowy branches in netting, Emma gathered up a handful of snow and, giggling, stuffed it down the back of Gabe's jacket. Which had him, in turn, expertly packing a snowball that he then threw at his daughter.

"Holly!" the little girl shouted as she ran a zigzag retreat through the trees. "You have to help! It's girls against boys."

Holly had never, in her memory, taken part in a snowball fight. But as Gabe chased after his daughter, Holly chased after him, throwing herself at his legs, causing him to crash to the ground, with her sprawled on top of him.

"Damn, you're pretty good. For a city girl." Wrapping his arms around her, he rolled over, so she was lying beneath him. "But guess what, sweetheart, you and half-pint over here just happen to be outmanned."

Laughing, and a little out of breath, Holly shoved against him. "Let me up, you big bully."

"In a minute." His body was warm against hers, his eyes

hot. Holly wouldn't have been surprised if all the snow on
the mountain melted from the way he was looking at her.
"Your nose is red."

"So's yours." Reaching out, she grabbed a handful of
snow and washed his face with it.

"You realize, of course," he said, using his superior strength
to press her deeper into the snowdrift, "that you're daring to
take on a United States Marine."

"Yeah, yeah," she responded breathlessly, as she wrestled
beneath him. "The few." She scissored her legs around his.
"The proud." Using the instructions the Seattle cops had
taught her during that class, she managed to flip their positions so she was now lying on top of him. "The oversexed."

"Got that right." When he cupped her butt with his gloved
hands and pressed her against him, she realized that he'd allowed her to overpower him. "As I intend to prove to you
tonight."

Before she could respond, Emma had returned and was
standing over them. "The girls won," she decided.

"They always do," Gabe agreed. "At least in this family."

"Why don't you kiss Holly?" Emma suggested. "To show
you surrendered."

"From the mouths of babes," he murmured. "I hereby
surrender to the superior super power of females." Lifting
his head, he brushed his lips against hers. While still cold,
they managed to send a burst of heat through her veins.

"Okay." Before she got into more trouble, Holly stood up.
"On behalf of the female forces, I accept your surrender."

"Consider this lone, lowly male your prisoner. Do with
me as you please," Gabe said.

"Funny you should mention that," Holly shot back just as
Dog, looking like the abominable snow beast, came loping
up to him and swiped a huge tongue down Gabe's face.

"God, I knew I should've left you back in the sandbox."

Laughingly pushing the ball of wet fur away, Gabe stood up and began brushing the snow off the front of Holly's jacket.

She did not immediately brush his hand away.

Unable to remember the last time she'd felt so carefree, Holly laughed as they walked back toward the sleigh.

Memories danced through her mind. Of hot roasted chestnuts and gaily decorated store front windows, and holding the hand of a man she suspected she'd gazed up at in exactly the same way Emma was looking up at Gabe.

And, although it didn't make any sense at all, Holly oddly felt as if having landed here in Santa's Village, she was catching a glimpse of what her life might have been.

Thirteen

The excitement of the day had obviously gotten to Emma, who fell asleep in the back of the sleigh on the ride back to the inn.

"Blessed silence," Gabe murmured.

"I think she's darling," Holly said.

"You're not going to get any argument there," he agreed. "Sometimes, like out of the blue, it'll dawn on me that she's actually my child, you know, the seed of my loins, all that sort of thing, and I'll just feel knocked flat."

"She's fortunate to have you."

He shrugged. "We're both lucky."

Gabe knew Holly was curious. Knew he was going to have to tell her what happened. But since his mother had already warned him about Emma thinking that this newcomer to Santa's Village had been sent to be her new mother, he feared his daughter might just be pretending to sleep. She had, after all, proven herself to be a fairly good little actress.

He was going to have to talk with Emma about Holly. Explain that while Santa had many great qualities, and while maybe he might be able to fit a pony in this sleigh, which turned magical when he drove it, he wasn't in the habit of delivering actual *people* to good little girls and boys. He wasn't looking forward to the conversation. It seemed kids grew up way too fast these days, and his daughter was already five going on twenty.

"After I take her back to the inn and we drop off your tree, I'll take you over to Olson's, so you can talk to Ken about your Highlander," he said to Holly.

"Thanks. I'd appreciate that. I also have some shopping to do."

"If you want to make a list, I can pick some things up for you," he offered. "Consider it part of the service."

"That's nice. But since I have a feeling I'm going to be here for a while, I might as well check out the town."

"Your call," he said agreeably.

Twenty minutes later, he'd carried his daughter—who actually did appear to be sound asleep—upstairs and tucked her into bed.

"An advantage of living above the store, so to speak," he said as they drove the short distance to the center of town in the Expedition, "is that there are always a lot of people around willing to watch out for her. It makes it like a large extended family."

"That's lucky. Especially with your mother working there."

"Not just my mother, but one of my sisters. Janice, who graduated from Washington State in Hospitality Business Management, is in charge of the rentals. From keeping housekeeping on their toes, to arranging for repairs, decorating, the whole nine yards. Even mostly the kitchen stuff, though Mom's beginning to take that on more and more now that she's retired. Which allows me to concentrate on the farm.

"I'd like to make it a year-round destination. Maybe hav
some classes on conservation, invite the school kids to hav
field trips during planting season, and since it's located c
the other side of the lake, maybe even get into boat rental
bait and tackle, that sort of thing."

"Sounds as if you're really settling in."

"Yeah." Gabe was surprised about that. He hadn't bee
sure the move from California to this small mountain tow
would work out. But at the time, not wanting to leave Emm
with sitters while he worked some 9-to-5 job, or worse ye
become a cop like so many ex-military, and like his own da
had done, hadn't been an option, either.

"Her mother left us," he said, deciding the best way
handle those questions she'd been too polite to ask was th
same way he'd done everything else in his life. Just straig
out.

"I'm sorry."

"I guess I was, too. For a while. But it was most
wounded pride. And it wasn't as if we'd had what anyon
could consider a real marriage. I met Lila while I was st
tioned at Camp Pendleton. She was a civilian secreta
working on base. I thought she was pretty, which she was.
also thought I was the hottest Marine ever to come down th
pike."

"I don't know much about the military. But from all tho
commercials I see on TV and in the theaters, I'd suspe
that's pretty much the Marine mindset," she said mildly.

He chuckled at that all too accurate appraisal. "Car
argue with that. Neither one of us was looking for anythir
serious. Then she got pregnant."

"I see."

Gabe wasn't certain anyone actually could understand h
and Lila's relationship. Since he hadn't understood it himse
at the time. Not even after it had crumbled down aroun
them, leaving a vulnerable little girl amidst the rubble.

"She didn't really want to be a mother. Had never planned to be." He remembered the conversation as if it'd happened yesterday. "Said she liked kids okay. Other people's kids."

"Not every woman feels the need to define herself by motherhood," Holly said quietly. He could tell she was walking on eggshells.

"How about you?"

Although he knew he was getting way ahead of the game, he'd wondered about that long into the night. As much as he wanted to take Holly Berry to bed, once his mother had told him about his daughter's belief that this woman was destined to be her new mom, he hadn't wanted to risk hurting Emma.

As Lila had told him when she'd greeted him at their house with her suitcases already packed, he'd already spent too many years thinking only of himself. Of his own wishes and needs.

Well, that had certainly changed. And although he wasn't going to deny that he missed sex—a lot—and there were a lot of women in town who'd been more than open about their willingness to let him put his boots beneath their beds, if only for a night, he'd screwed around with too many of those sex candidates in the backseat of his Camaro IROC-Z back in high school. And although those days and nights parked out by the lake had been fun, he wasn't really in a mood to relive them.

And then, as always, there was Emma. From what he'd been able to glean from their conversations, there had been more than one man in his wife's life while he'd been away keeping the world free from terrorism. No way was Gabe going to put a revolving door in his bedroom.

Although celibacy definitely wasn't a natural state, he'd been doing just fine. Until he'd driven around that S-curve and come across Holly Berry, who was causing all his good paternal intentions to pretty much fly out the window.

"If you'd rather not talk about it . . ." Her voice broke int
his thoughts.

"No." He shook his head to clear it. "You'll probably hea
different versions of the story anyway, if you're going to sta
here for any length of time. You might as well know th
truth. I talked Lila into having the baby. I promised that it
be good. That we'd be a family."

"Like the one your mother and dad made with you an
your sisters."

"Good guess. Being a male and pretty clueless about th
nuances of relationships, I didn't realize that my parents' re
lationship hadn't come easy for them. That they'd worked
it every day. And that part of the reason for them moving u
here had been because Dad had gotten so stressed out
work it was impacting the rest of their lives."

"Admittedly, I don't have any experience with a close-u
and personal view of marriage," Holly said quietly. "But
suspect no child really understands what's going on outsic
his or her own self-centered world."

"That's probably true." He sighed. "So, Lila had the bab
I was in Panama at the time. During Emma's very short lif
time, I've done two tours in Iraq, and another in Afghanistan

"That doesn't allow much time for being a husband. C
father," Holly allowed.

He slanted her a look. "Good point. And one Lila mac
right before walking out the door. She's now married to h
former boss. A property mogul who builds shopping center
They live in some McMansion in a seaside development ou
side San Diego. He's a nice enough guy. But he doesn't wa
kids. Especially one who isn't biologically his."

"That's his loss."

God help him, he didn't just *want* Holly Berry. He like
her. A lot. Liked her intelligence, her tenderness, and h
matter-of-fact way of cutting to the chase. She might prove

challenge, but a guy would always know where he stood with her.

"Yeah. I remember standing there, thinking that here I was, a tough battle-hardened Marine who'd been on the front lines against al-Qaeda and the Taliban, but I had no idea how to take care of a little girl. Hell, the only thing in the house turned out to be Chunky Monkey ice cream and Lucky Charms cereal and since either my mother or the Marines had fed me all my life, I didn't even know how to make out a grocery list."

"So you came home."

"Not at first." He remembered those early days. "I didn't want to run back home to my parents because I think it would've been too tempting just to hand Emma over to my mother and sisters, who were certainly more than willing to help out. I'd missed out on most of her life. I wanted, needed, to build a bond between us before I brought others into our life."

"Well." She blew out a long breath. Her eyes, including the one she'd put a little powder on while he'd been in the inn putting Emma to bed, were bright with a suspicious moisture. "That's very impressive."

"No." Gabe might not be an expert in parenting, but of this one thing he was very sure. "It's not. Because women do it every day. All over America. The world. Hell, look how well your mother raised you, and I'll bet there weren't any people handing out single mother medals."

"She did the best she could," Holly agreed. "Under difficult circumstances."

Haltingly at first, she told him about her father's murder. Although he'd seen death, killed bad guys himself, Gabe found the circumstances of George Berry's death even more terrible. Especially given the way it had obviously shattered his daughter's small family.

"So," she wrapped up, "my mother moved to L.A. and, well, with all the palm trees and sunshine, we sort of just let the Christmas season slip away."

There was a lot more there she wasn't telling. Having spent the first thirteen years of his own life in southern California, Gabe knew that while it definitely wasn't anything like here, most people still celebrated the holidays. Hell, each December his mother had put a tree in every room, created crafty, handmade ornaments, and directed the kids' pageant at church, while his father would fill up the front yard with the plywood reindeer, snowmen, angels, and wise men he and Gabe would spend the summer making on the table saw in the garage. Thinking back on it, Gabe suspected their electricity bill between Thanksgiving and New Year's probably doubled from all the lights.

Speaking of lights . . . Gabe was tempted to suddenly look up and see if a lightbulb had just lit up over his head.

"What?" Holly asked, sounding defensive. And no wonder. Here she'd just opened up and shared a story he suspected she didn't tell often, if at all, and he'd laughed.

"I just realized why, of all the towns in America, my parents moved to this one. They've always been Christmas junkies."

"I'm beginning to think that may not be such a bad thing," she admitted.

"Well, you're definitely going to be making up for lost time."

They shared a laugh, putting their individual difficulties behind them as they enjoyed the moment. And each other.

Fourteen

"A week?" Holly blew out a frustrated breath. Dragged a hand through her hair.

"At least," Ken Olson, of Olson's Auto Repair, repeated. "Sorry. But this isn't the city. It's hard to get parts over the holidays. Especially with all the roads closed."

"But surely you have radiators." She looked around the garage that was packed concrete floor to ceiling with car parts that Ken, a major packrat, had collected over more than fifty years in the business. "Maybe a refurbished one that'll get me back to the city?"

"Well, now, I might be able to find one that'd fit your vehicle," he allowed, the unlit cigarette Gabe had never seen him without bobbing between his lips. "But the thing is, you've got more trouble than a radiator. Your fuel level float's flat busted, and the flange on your alternator's cracked, plus, your power steering pump's leaking fluid, the front struts don't look good, and I sure wouldn't want to send you back down the mountain with those brake linings."

He took off his red and green plaid wool cap with the

shearling earflaps and scratched his head. "No telling what might happen. And without you having an airbag anymore. Well, shoot, I'm sorry, ma'am, but my conscience would just eat away at me like battery acid if anything happened to a pretty young thing like you."

Holly dragged a gloved hand down her face.

Then turned to Gabe. "I don't suppose there's a car rental place in town."

"There's a small Avis outlet," he allowed. "Out at the airfield. But they ran out of cars two days ago. And right now . . ."

"I know," she huffed, "with the roads closed, they can't bring any more in."

"That's pretty much it," he said sympathetically. "If you need transportation, the family's got enough vehicles to lend you one."

"That's very generous. And I might take you up on that," she said. "But that doesn't get me back to the city."

"What happened to Leavenworth?"

"I've changed the story. I don't need the cookie lady anymore." She drew in a deep breath. Let it out. Repeated. Remembering when his sister Janice was studying yoga, Gabe figured she was trying to find her center.

"Why don't you let me take you shopping," he suggested. "Whatever happens, you're going to want some coffee and chocolate, at least."

Her eyes narrowed. "How did you know about the chocolate?"

He shrugged. "Hey, I have a mother and three sisters. Plus, I may not write mystery novels, but the M&M wrappers stuffed into your Highlander's ashtray were sorta a clue."

Despite her obvious frustration, more, he suspected because she'd lost control over the situation, than the actual problems with her SUV, she laughed at that.

"You're right. It's the obvious solution. And I appreciate the offer."

After she'd settled back into the Expedition, Gabe said, "I just remembered. Mom asked me to give Ken a message to take home to his wife about the inn's Christmas Eve party. I'll be right back."

"I'm sure not going anywhere," she said.

He walked back into the garage where Ken was standing beneath the lift, changing the oil on an old Dodge Charger Gabe's brother-in-law Jack had spent two years restoring to its old muscle car–days glory.

"Thanks," he said. "Appreciate it."

"No problem," Ken said, the cigarette clenched between his nicotine-yellowed teeth. "Glad to be able to help out by keeping the little lady in town a bit longer. Writes books, the missus told me. About murders and such."

"Yeah. She's good, too." Gabe had stayed up most of the night reading *Blood Brothers,* a story about good and evil twins.

"Doesn't look like she'd write them kind of stories," Ken said. "Figure that's more along the lines of a guy job. She's a looker, that's for damn sure."

"You're not going to get any argument from me about that."

Gabe was halfway to the Expedition when the older man called out, "Good luck."

As he headed off to the North Pole Mercantile, drinking in the scent of sugar cookies and very desirable woman, Gabe figured that thanks to Mother Nature, he'd already gotten pretty damn lucky.

The market was a surprise. Although there were fresh trees and wreaths, which Gabe confirmed were from his

farm, for sale in front of the store, and the expected towering
pyramid of poinsettias inside, it was as well stocked as the
neighborhood grocery store around the corner from her
apartment. In fact, Holly thought, as she put a bag of pebbly
Clementine oranges into her cart, it seemed to have even
more fresh fruits and vegetables.

Gabe, it seemed, was particularly popular. They couldn't
get down an aisle without some female stopping to chat.
Most often that chat included an invitation.

"Sorry," he said, after the third such interruption, this one
by a brunette wearing ski pants so tight she must've had to
lie down to zip them up, a sweater beneath her open coat that
looked as if it'd been sprayed onto her double-D silicone-
enhanced breasts, and a pair of high-heel boots that were
admittedly good-looking, but ridiculously impractical. If she
wasn't careful, she could slip on the ice and break her neck.

And wouldn't, Holly thought acidly, remembering the
way she'd put her hand over Gabe's on the cart handle, that
be a terrible shame.

"Must be tough, being the town's hottest bachelor," Holly
said dryly as the brunette sashayed away.

"It's a dirty job," he said with a quick grin.

"And how fortunate for all the women of the town you're
willing to do it." She turned and reached for a blue box of
pasta.

"It's not that way." He leaned over her, his chest pressing
against her back as he reached over her head and plucked the
box from the top shelf. "Actually, until you came along, I
was living a pretty much celibate life." He tossed the box
into the cart. "Let me be more specific. *Entirely* celibate
life."

Holly glanced around. She'd never, ever thought she'd be
discussing such things in public, let alone in the pasta and
tomato sauce aisle of the North Pole Mercantile, but she had
to ask.

"For the entire time you've been here?"

He nodded. "And the year before that."

"Wow."

"Yeah."

"I don't want to get personal." She lowered her voice. Leaned toward him. "But since you brought it up—"

"No, I definitely don't have a problem in that regard."

She hadn't thought so. "Still, that's a long dry spell." Even longer than her own.

"I was out of the country the first year," he reminded her. "And, like I said, I don't cheat."

Having learned about his wife's affairs, Holly understood the flare of heat he'd displayed when she'd accused him of hitting on her when he had a wife at home.

"The last year has been complicated. And, like you said, it's been a long dry spell." His pewter eyes swept over her face with all the impact of a caress. "One I'm hoping to change."

"You never know." She tossed her head in a flirtatious way that was so not typical for her. "Play your cards right and I might invite you over to dinner tonight. If you think you can get a sitter."

"Sweetheart, all it would take is for the women in my family to know I had a date and they'd be standing in line to have Emma spend the night with her cousins."

"Well, then. How do you feel about lasagna?"

"My favorite thing," he said promptly. "So long as we're having sugar cookies or peaches for dessert."

Because it had been too long since he'd kissed her—at least since he'd parked the car in the lot twenty minutes earlier—he bent his head and brushed his lips against hers.

Mindless of the fact that she was in a public store, Holly allowed her own lips to cling. And cling. Until the unmistakable sound of a throat clearing behind them broke through the silvery mist clouding her mind.

"Sorry." If he was at all embarrassed, Gabe didn't reveal it. He moved aside. "Merry Christmas, Mrs. Whetherton," he said with a friendly smile.

Beady black eyes as sharp and dark as a crow's took in the two of them. "Merry Christmas, Gabriel," the woman, who looked to be at least in her eighties, said. "And it's about time to see you spooning with a woman. Your poor mother has been despairing about you ever giving her another grandchild."

Her gaze swept over Holly, as if checking out her breeding credentials. "You'll do," she decided before continuing down the aisle.

Rather than be embarrassed, or offended, Holly surprised herself by breaking into laughter.

Because she wanted some time to herself to explore the town, Holly asked Gabe to take the groceries back to the cabin for her.

"It's less than five blocks," she pointed out. "I walk a lot farther than that in the city. And it's stopped snowing."

His forehead frowned. "If you have any trouble—"

"Gabe." She touched a hand to his cheek. "You're not a Marine any longer. You don't have to save the entire world. Besides, I'll be fine. Really."

"I need to split cord wood for the inn. I guess I'll just work off some of my sexual frustration on some logs."

"Don't work it all off."

He laughed, a rough, harsh sound edged with need. "Sweetheart, where you're concerned, that's not possible."

Holly knew exactly how he felt.

Fifteen

The town was surprisingly charming. Oh, overdone, certainly, if you weren't a fan of Christmas, but still, once you looked beneath the tinsel and trappings shouting out from the storefront windows, there were really lovely locally handcrafted items inside the shops. Many that would easily belong in the trendy galleries of Seattle's Fremont and Pioneer Square neighborhoods or even Kirkland, known as the Monterey of the West, across Lake Washington.

Telling herself she wasn't really becoming a Christmas shopper, that she was just paying back a kindness, she bought a lovely cashmere scarf, woven by a local artisan, in soft shades of cream, moss green, and gray, for Beth O'Halloran.

Once she'd done that, well, of course she needed to find something for Emma. Which was when she decided to check out Santa's Workshop.

The building was housed in what appeared to be an old brick warehouse at the end of North Pole Lane. The minute she walked into the gift shop, Holly decided the place definitely lived up to its name. The floor-to-ceiling shelves were filled with dolls (cloth and baby dolls, with not a Barbie or Bratz to be seen), stuffed animals, and what, although she was no expert, even she could see were beautifully crafted wooden cars, trains, airplanes, and boats.

"Welcome to Santa's Workshop." A woman, wearing a red wool blazer over a cream ribbed turtleneck and an ankle-length, slim green and red plaid wool skirt, greeted Holly with a remarkably familiar smile.

"You're Rachel O'Halloran."

"Got it in one." The dimples that had been a dead give-away deepened. "And you'd be Holly Berry."

"News travels fast."

"Honey, around here, it's like lightning. By the time you got back from cutting that Christmas tree this morning, everyone in Santa's Village probably knew your height, weight, hair color, and what you did for a living. Speaking of which, I like your books, by the way."

"Thank you."

"No, thank you. Sometimes life is just so damn cheery here, I enjoy diving into a good, gory murder. Especially on those days I feel like murdering my own kids. I have three, all boys, which can be a challenge, just like their uncle."

"Gabe was a challenge?"

"Since everyone already knows about you, including, now that you've gone shopping, that you prefer the yellow packet artificial sweetener over the blue, and that you're cooking my brother lasagna tonight, and it's obvious that he's taken with you, it's only fair that we women stick to-gether. God knows, he's never been all that talkative, so I doubt he's shared that much with you."

Holly was beginning to understand exactly why Gabe wasn't all that chatty. Especially if his other sisters were at all like this one. "He told me about his marriage breaking up." The minute she'd heard the words leaving her mouth,

Holly wished she could have called them back. Although obviously his family knew at least some of the circumstances, she felt as if she'd betrayed a confidence.

"Did he now? Well, that shows Mother's right. As usual. The boy's definitely serious."

Holly was equally uncomfortable that she and Gabe had been a subject of discussion. One of the things she liked about being a writer was it allowed her to live a very private life.

"He's not exactly a boy," she felt obliged to point out on his behalf.

"Well, that's certainly true enough," Rachel allowed. "Going into the Marines really changed him from that hell-bent for trouble kid who wrecked that car he'd borrowed from Kendall motors when he was fifteen—"

"Gabe stole a car?"

"Well, he was planning to take it back," Rachel assured Holly. "It wasn't exactly his fault Margaret Whetherton was such a horrible driver. She's always been a menace. You've no idea how relieved everyone in town was when her doctor grandson came down from Bellingham and took the keys to her Caddy away. Now we all take turns driving her around so she won't feel tempted to get back behind the wheel.

"Anyway," she continued, amazing Holly when she didn't so much as pause for a breath, "Gabe wasn't a bad kid. He just wasn't happy about leaving L.A.—not that any of us were, but at least we girls had each other—and having your dad be town sheriff, as bad as it was for us, because of all the boys who were afraid to try to so much as get to second base for fear of Daddy shooting them, had to have been worse for Gabe because there was so much expectation put on him. Like what they say about being a preacher's kid. If you know what I mean."

She stopped. And flashed another of those smiles. When the pause lasted longer than a second, Holly decided she'd just been invited to respond.

"I can see how that would be the case. I was an only child. So I always felt like I had to be perfect at everything."

"That's exactly how I felt." Rachel nodded her dark brunette head. "Although, of course, I wasn't an only. But birth order has onlys and eldest, which is where I fall in the family, pretty much fitting the same model. So, are you here to visit? Or to buy something?"

"I was hoping to find something for Emma."

"What a lovely idea." She flashed another of those Gabe replica smiles. "Especially since she believes you're going to be her new mama."

"What?"

"Uh-oh." Gabe's sister had the grace to flush. "I guess I let that cat out of the bag. So, Gabe didn't tell you about her Christmas wish?"

"No. It didn't come up."

Holly couldn't decide whether she was glad or not that he'd neglected to share that little bit of information. Then decided it could've only made this morning's tree hunting expedition uncomfortable. But it did explain why the little girl had been so eager for Gabe to kiss her. Obviously she'd been doing a little matchmaking.

Which wasn't all that surprising, Holly decided, remembering how many of the men she'd tried to set up her mother with over the years. Including her fifth grade teacher, her pediatrician, and the guy who came by their house every month to read their electric meter.

"Well." Rachel tilted her head. "I guess, staying at the inn as you are, you would've figured it out pretty soon. Let me show you some of the stuffed animals Emma was looking at when she visited last week."

Holly was trying to decide between a fluffy panda bear and a pink and purple polka dot elephant when the door at the back of the room, which she guessed led into the actual workshop, opened, and a tall, lanky, silver-haired man wearing cowboy boots, jeans, and a western snap-front shirt entered the gift shop.

"Well," he said on a western drawl that possessed just a bit of twang. "If it isn't Holly Berry, come to pay us a visit."

She'd begun, just a bit, to buy into the tourism aspect of the town, but if this was the guy they were putting forth as Santa Claus, someone obviously needed to call Central Casting.

"And you must be Sam Fraiser?"

"That's me." He held out a huge hand that was nicked and scarred from a lifetime of carving wood. "Welcome to Santa's Workshop." He glanced down at the two stuffed animals she was holding in her hand. "Go with the elephant."

"I guess you know that because, deep down, you're Santa Claus?"

"That and the fact that the colors match her bedroom," he said.

"And you'd know that how?"

"Because she's one of those little girls who wakes up at the crack of dawn and can't wait for her family to come over before checking out her Christmas presents. So, she and Gabe worked out a deal. Instead of hanging her stocking on the family room fireplace mantel, they put it in her room. That way, she's allowed to look through it on Christmas morning while she waits for the adults to get things ready."

He winked. "Last year I put in a coloring book and a set of crayons that kept her busy for a while. This year I'm thinking about a Game Boy. They come in pink now, you know. And there's a Powerpuff game I think would keep her occupied until Gabe gets up."

"Whatever happened to handmade wooden toys and baby dolls?" Holly waved a hand toward all the shelves.

He slipped his hands into the front of his jeans. Rocked back on the heels of his Tony Lamas. "Do you have any idea how many children there are in the world?"

"No." She folded her arms. "Why don't you tell me?"

"A bunch. So, sometimes the only choice is to outsource."

"Of course." She gave him a long look. "You know, you don't exactly look like a jolly old elf." In fact, now that she thought of it, he was a dead ringer for Paul Newman. The older, still sexy one, not Hud.

"Yeah, I know." He rubbed a shaven jaw that was nearly as broad as Gabe's. "My wife put me on a low carb diet a few months ago. Said that with obesity becoming such a serious problem among not just adults, but children, it's important for Santa to set a good example."

"Your wife sounds very wise."

"She's smart as a whip," he agreed. "Has kept me on my toes all the years we've been together. And while I occasionally miss potato chips, and still have cravings for Mrs. Fraiser's apple cobbler, I've gotten used to it. For the children's sake."

It was a good act. But that's all it was. An act. And for some reason she couldn't quite understand herself, although she felt a little ridiculous arguing the subject, especially in front of Gabe's sister, who was watching with undisguised interest, Holly couldn't just let his claim go unchallenged.

"You're not really Santa Claus."

Blue eyes narrowed even as the friendly smile stayed on his lips. "You're sure of that, are you?"

"Of course." Oddly, since it didn't make any difference in the grand scheme of things, she was beginning to get frustrated. "I'm an adult. I know Santa doesn't exist. That he's merely a lovely myth told to children. Partly to get them to behave."

Fraiser rubbed his chin. "That sounds vaguely familiar. Maybe you've watched *Miracle on 34th Street* recently?"

"I don't watch Christmas movies."

"Actually, I know that," he said. "Which is a shame. But I was merely pointing out a similarity."

"Look," Holly said in an exasperated breath. "I think it's lovely that your family has run this toy shop for so many generations and that the things you make here bring children pleasure. I also think it's great the way the town reinvented itself to bring in tourism."

"Is that what you think we did?"

"Winnie Jenson, the clerk at the checkout at the market told me that the post office does a huge business postmarking Christmas cards with the Santa's Village, America's Most Christmassy Town postmark."

"That's true," Rachel entered into the conversation. "But it doesn't bring in revenue. It also causes more work, which is why—"

"So many people in town volunteer to help out," Holly interjected. "Mrs. Jenson already told me that. And, as I said, I think it's a great marketing idea. But I don't play games, Mr. Fraiser. I'm a realist."

"Yet, you tell tales for a living," Sam Fraiser pointed out.

Damn. He had her there.

He smiled. "Take the elephant," he suggested gently, effectively declaring the topic closed. "She'll love it. Meanwhile, it's been lovely finally meeting you in person, Holly Berry."

It wasn't until the elephant had been rung up and wrapped in paper with a smiling, red-cheeked bearded Santa printed on it, and Holly was a block away, that his words sunk in.

"What did he mean, *finally*?"

The question puzzled her until she'd turned onto Dasher Drive, headed back to the inn. From what Gabe's sister had said, the gossip line worked at lightning speed in Santa's Village. Obviously Fraiser had heard about her arrival in town.

That settled to her own satisfaction, Holly began thinking ahead toward the evening.

Sixteen

Anticipation, Holly thought, as she bathed in the oversize tub—after stealing a nap so she'd be rested for the evening ahead—then smoothed on the peach-scented lotion Gabe had first mentioned wanting to taste, could be a bitch. It wasn't as if she were some virgin bride getting ready for her wedding night. She'd had sex lots of times before.

Okay, probably not nearly as many as he'd undoubtedly had. But how hard could it be? She not only wanted his hot, rock-hard Marine body, she liked him. Which was, to her mind, even more important than chemistry. So why were her nerves so tightly tangled they felt on the verge of snapping?

Her cheeks were flushed, more from emotion than the warm bath, and her hands were shaking so hard she'd nearly poked her eyes out with her mascara tube.

Somehow they made it through the dinner, which hadn't been that much of a problem. Anyone could throw together some lasagna, after all. She'd learned to make the dish when she was only a few years older than Emma, during a time when her mother's depression had kept her in bed for days at a time.

"If you want," he said, as they sat in front of the fireplace, sipping on the brandy he'd brought over with him, "I can come over tomorrow and help you trim the tree." A tree that was currently sitting in his garage because he'd warned her that if she'd taken it inside with all that snow and ice on it, she'd end up with it snowing inside the cabin.

"I'd think Emma would want to help."

"She's the one who brought it up."

"Ah." Holly nodded. Took another sip and wondered if bringing up the topic of Emma's Christmas wish would ruin the sex part of the evening.

"Rachel told me she told you about Emma." He'd put his arm around her shoulders and now smoothed a hand down her hair. "I hope it isn't going to make things uncomfortable for you."

"No." She'd thought about it a lot while soaking in that bubble bath. "I'll be careful that she doesn't get her hopes up and make it clear that you and I are merely friends—"

He lifted a brow. "Is that all we are?"

"Well, friends with benefits, which she doesn't need to know about. Don't worry, Gabe. I understand how vulnerable she is. And how much she wants a complete family."

"Yeah." He brushed his lips against the top of her head. "I can see how you would understand that."

They sat there, listening to the music he'd brought over that was playing on the CD player. It was something classical, familiar, but Holly couldn't quite identify it. She'd been grateful, after having the carols blasted to her from the loudspeakers all over town, that he'd left the holiday music at the inn.

"I read one of your books last night," he revealed. "*Blood*

Brothers. You kept me guessing until the end which brother was going to turn out to be the evil prostitute serial killer."

"My take on Jack the Ripper." She smiled a bit. "With a touch of Dr. Jekyll and Mr. Hyde thrown in."

"Well, like I said, you kept me turning pages. My mother's obviously got terrific taste in authors, because you're really, really good."

"Thank you." The compliment, which, if she were to be brutally honest with herself, was just one person's opinion, should not have given her so much pleasure. But it did.

Silence fell over them again.

"This isn't as easy as I thought it was going to be," she said finally as she stared into the flickering orange flames of the fire he'd built when he'd first arrived.

He put a hand beneath her chin. Gently turned her head toward his. "I'm not sure it should be that easy," he said.

Gabe had figured out that nothing about Holly Berry was going to be that simple. Which was fine with him, really, because he'd never trusted things that came too easily.

"Admittedly, some people might consider this rushing things," he said, his eyes echoing his encouraging smile. Wanting to soothe, as much as he wanted to arouse, Gabe kissed her, a satiny meeting of lips, a mingling of breath. "But it doesn't seem too fast to me. And it damn well isn't going to end up a one-night stand."

"Not for me either," she admitted throatily.

He smiled. Took both their brandy snifters, placed them on the coffee table, then stood up and held out his hand.

As if it was the most natural thing in the world, she put her hand in his and together they walked, side by side, up the stairs to the loft. The storm that had brought all the snow that had landed her in the village had moved on, leaving the sky a vast canvas of black satin studded with icy crystal stars.

Silver moonlight streamed across the sheets as she pulled

back the comforter while Gabe turned on the gas fireplace, causing sparks to flare.

Then he took her in his arms and lowered his head until their lips were close, not quite touching. "I want you to know, absolutely, that this is important to me."

"I do." Her breath shuddered out as he stroked her throat with the pad of his thumb. "It's important to me, too."

Those gorgeous creases in his cheeks deepened. Just when she thought he was going to kiss her, really kiss her, Gabe tilted his head so that his lips grazed her cheek. Her mind spinning, she moaned softly as his firm, but snowflake-soft lips skimmed around the curve of her jaw to her other cheek.

She turned her head, trying to capture those tantalizing lips, but his mouth deftly evaded hers, gliding up her bruised face, where she feared the heat raging beneath her skin had burned off the mineral powder concealer she'd applied so carefully earlier this evening.

His breath warmed the hollows of her cheeks, her temples. When it whispered gently over her eyelids, they fluttered closed and she forgot all about worrying about how her black eye might look.

She couldn't think. Couldn't breathe. Every fiber of her being was so brilliantly, radiantly alive, concentrating on the drugging feel of his clever hands as he undressed her, piece by piece, then following the blazing trail those broad hands made with his mouth.

Finally, it was her turn. Holly took her time, as he had, pulling his sweater over his head, allowing her mouth to drink in the taste of his heated skin. Her blood pounded in her veins as she stripped away the rest of his clothes.

Then somehow—was it possible to float?—they were lying on the moon-spangled sheets, hands touching, lips exploring, soft sounds of desire filling the air as they became lost in each other.

When Holly would have hurried, Gabe slowed the pace, as if intent on savoring every moment. Her body felt as if it had been turned to liquid, flowing heatedly beneath his touch, which promised erotic delights. When his fingertips plucked at her sensitive nipples, she arched her back. But already his hands had moved on, leaving only a lingering sense of pleasure and a steadily rising need.

His hand spanned her stomach, causing a weakening warmth there before continuing downward. When his tantalizing touch skimmed up the inside of her legs, and his thumb flicked against that damp, ultrasensitive place between her thighs, her entire body began to tremble.

Just when she felt on the verge of shattering, wanting, needing to treat Gabe to the same sensual pleasure, she shifted, so she was lying next to him, exploring his body as he had hers, entranced by the contrast of his surprisingly soft skin pulled taut over steely muscle.

She skimmed her lips down his damp chest and drew a shaky groan. Dipped the tip of her tongue into his navel, and had his fists knotting the sheets. The sheer masculinity of him was both powerful and beautiful at the same time, and suddenly, Holly wanted nothing more than to feel him inside her.

As if reading her mind, he caught hold of her shoulders and flipped her over, taking a moment to sheathe himself in the condom he'd placed on the nightstand after lighting the fire.

Bracing himself over her, he looked deep into her eyes.

"Now," he said.

"Now," she whispered.

He surprised her. Dipping his head for a soft, tender kiss that for some reason seemed more intimate than everything else they'd shared.

Their hands linked. Watching each other, they joined. Bod

ies. Minds. Hearts. He began to move, driving her deeper into the mattress, plunging into her hot slick heat until she cried out his name. When he felt the rippling waves of her climax, Gabe surrendered the last of his control. With one last mighty thrust of his hips, he filled her completely, giving in to his own release.

He could still feel her inner tremors as they lay there together on the hot, tangled sheets, pulses of passion continuing to spark between them.

"I wanted this." He lifted his head and brushed the damp hair away from her face. She still had a few red scrapes from the airbag and her poor swollen and discolored eye looked as if she'd gone ten rounds with Evander Holyfield, but he'd never seen anyone so beautiful. "From the minute you stepped out of that Highlander."

"I know." She smiled beneath his thumb as it stroked her love-swollen lips. "At least I sensed something spark. I wanted you, too." She smoothed a hand down his damp back. Over his butt. "That is, once I got over worrying about you being a serial killer. Or a 5150."

"A 5150?"

"A crazy person." She sighed as he kissed her again. "On the loose."

"I am crazy." He deepened the kiss. "About you."

Not wanting to go into the local drugstore and buy rubbers for tonight, which would've allowed every damn person in town to know that he'd been about to get naked with Holly Berry, Gabe had been grateful that his brother-in-law Jack, who'd been trying to get him laid since he'd first come back to town, had shown up two weeks ago with an invitation to dinner and a box of Trojans.

The double date his sister had ambushed him with hadn't worked out. The third grade teacher had been sweet and pretty and had, with a few little hair flips and a lip-licking thing that women did, let him know that if he wanted to get lucky when he took her home, she'd go along with the program.

But there hadn't been any chemistry. Not so much as a twinge on his part, and if she'd been totally honest, he suspected she hadn't really been all that hot to jump his bones either. Just lonely. Or more likely, tired of being alone.

Which he could goddamn understand. And identify with. Just not enough to do anything about it with someone he didn't want to have to talk to over a breakfast table the next morning.

Rachel had complained he was too picky. That it was time to move on. Jack had suggested he just drive into the city, pick up some hot chick in a bar, and go for it without over-analyzing it. That, Jack had decided, was the best way to get over whatever mental block against sex his cheating wife must've saddled him with.

As much as he'd appreciated them caring about him, Gabe had ignored both their advice. But as the moon rose higher in the star-studded sky, and he and Holly Berry made love all night long, Gabe was damn grateful for the condoms.

Seventeen

It was a time of mistletoe and magic. Of cocoa, and carols, and walking hand in hand down snowy lanes. Although she'd spent twenty-one years of her life avoiding Christmas, over the next five days, as if determined to make up for all she'd missed growing up, Holly allowed Gabe to coax and cajole her into experiencing the joy and fun to be had during the holidays in "The Most Christmassy Town in America."

Although it had been obvious that Emma's sacrifice to forgo helping decorate the tree had been a matchmaking attempt, Holly insisted the little girl help, and as the three of them hung the wooden ornaments they'd picked out together at Sam Fraiser's shop, when Gabe had lifted Emma high to put the red-haired angel on top of the fragrant blue spruce, Holly felt as if they were becoming a family.

A feeling that intensified as she attended the school's Christmas pageant, sitting in metal folding chairs with the entire O'Halloran clan. They watched Emma, clad in a long white nightgown Gabe's sister Janice had sewn for her and angel wings Holly, Beth, and Rachel had spent an entire evening gluing sequins and tinsel onto, sing "Hark the Herald Angels Sing" and "Away in a Manger."

"I didn't forget my lines," she said as she flung herself into Gabe's arms after the play.

"You were perfect," he said.

"Better than perfect," Holly seconded. "In fact, when you were singing, I felt as if I was listening to a real, live angel."

Emma beamed. "This is," she said on a long, happy sigh, "my bestest Christmas of my whole life."

Gabe met Holly's eyes over the top of his daughter's bright head. "Mine too," he said, his voice roughened with the desire that seemed to grow, rather than diminish, each time they'd made love.

The auditorium was filled with parents and children. The scent of cedar mingled with the happy buzz of holiday conversation and snatches of carols as students continued to sing, not as a performance, but for their own enjoyment.

But all that faded away, and once again, as always happened when he looked at her that way, Holly felt as if they were the only two people on the planet.

"I'll make that unanimous," she said.

The annual Ho Ho Ho Inn Christmas Eve party, unsurprisingly, given that Gabe's sister Janice appeared capable of being CEO of a Fortune 500 company, went off without a hitch and was a smashing success.

By the time the evening had come to an end, Holly figured she'd danced with just about every male between the ages of fifteen and ninety in town. Including Daniel O'Halloran, a tall, rugged, still handsome man who looked, Holly guessed, exactly as Gabe would look in his fifties. He was also even less talkative than his son, which wasn't surprising, given that he'd spent so many years living with a wife, three daughters, and now a granddaughter who was showin early signs of someday claiming Rachel's conversational crown.

No longer bothering to pretend that their relationship was casual, after the last guest had drifted out the door, Holly went upstairs with Gabe and Emma, who, after a day of ice skating on the lake, snowwoman building, topped off by the party, had fallen asleep the minute her head had hit her pink Powerpuff Girls pillow.

It was like a scene from Currier & Ives. Outside the soaring window, fat white snowflakes floated down from the moongilded sky, turning the forest, and the lake beyond, into a winter wonderland.

Inside, a red and orange fire crackled in the grate and two stockings—one for Gabe and another for Holly—hung from the mantel. Emma's own stocking was, as Sam Fraiser had claimed, hung in her bedroom.

Holly was sitting on the leather couch in front of the fire, her feet up on the coffee table, sipping brandy, as she had their first night together, gazing at the Christmas tree that was decorated with the same wooden ornaments that hung on her own tree and the one downstairs, along with blown-glass balls Gabe had told her had been handed down from his mother, and red and green construction paper chains. She'd never felt more content in her life.

"It was a good party," he said.

"The best," she agreed. "That was nice of you to eat Mrs. Fraiser's pork rinds. I think you and your mother were the only two people who actually tried them."

"I didn't want her feelings to be hurt. They're pretty gross, by the way. Gotta feel sorry for Sam, being on that low-carb diet."

"Speaking of Sam, I noticed he wasn't at the party."

"Never is," Gabe said.

"Because it's his busy night."

"Exactly."

Holly was in too good a mood to argue something that no longer mattered. If Sam wanted to pretend to believe he was Santa Claus, what harm was there in the entire town going along with the idea?

"It's perfect," she murmured.

He followed her glance to the tree. "The construction paper was definitely the final touch."

Holly smiled. She and Emma had made those chains together at a table downstairs in the restaurant two days ago. "Definitely. But I was talking about my life. Right now, at this frozen moment in time, it's positively perfect."

"You know," he said, with what she could feel was studied casualness, "if you were to hang around here a while longer, we might manage to work our way up to absolutely, positively perfect."

"Why should I leave?" she asked with a feigned casualness she, too, was a very long way from feeling. "I can work anywhere. Everyone's so friendly and welcoming." She ran her finger around the rim of the brandy snifter. "And, of course, there's Emma. And Dog." She smiled down at the huge dog who was currently snoring away in front of the fire. But as soon as the lights went out and the adults went to bed, Holly knew he'd sneak into Emma's room. "And, of course, you."

"I saw this interview you did on YouTube the other day," he confessed. "While you were over at the cabin writing."

"Ah." She nodded. "I know which one you're talking about." She'd been nervous, as she always was when the spotlight was turned on her, but she'd thought it had come out well enough. "About life imitating art after that strangler appeared to be using one of my books as a how-to guide."

"That's the one. Anyway, you were talking about how you plot everything out beforehand, with all the Post-its and index cards and notebooks."

"That's the way I always worked," she agreed.

Until coming here. Every afternoon she'd spend two or three hours writing, and without any forethought, the words had been flowing as if from some magic well. Not wanting to send her muses back into sulk mode, Holly hadn't questioned the change in process. Just welcomed it. Although she did occasionally wonder if again, it had something to do with the magic of this place. Or, perhaps, just how Gabe had her opening up to so many new experiences and ideas.

"This past week I've been more of a go with the flow kind of girl."

"Then you won't panic if I give you something you might not have planned for? Something personal?"

"Well, I was really hoping for a George Foreman grill," she said on an exaggerated sigh.

Surprisingly, he didn't smile. In fact, he seemed unreasonably nervous. "Next time."

He bent down, and from behind the stack of packages beneath the tree, took out a small, gilt-wrapped box.

Holding her breath, Holly slipped the ribbon off it. Carefully took the tape and paper off. Inside the black velvet box, an antique diamond ring, set in white-gold, glistened like a glacier.

"It's my grandmother's," he said. "If you'd prefer something more modern, that's cool, too, but I knew if I bought a ring here in town, you'd hear about it before I could get it home, so I figured that perhaps, this could stand in as a promise, and later, we can go to the city, and—"

"Why would I want to do that?" she asked. "When this is so perfect?" Not just because she honestly found the filigreed ring lovely. But because of its history. A history that connected Holly with Gabe's family.

She slipped it onto her finger. "It fits." Perfectly.

"I'm glad." His shoulders, which had looked as stiff as if

he'd been standing at attention on a Marine parade field, loosened, revealing his relief. "I love you, Holly. More than I ever thought was possible."

"I know the feeling." She reached into her bag and took out an envelope. "I didn't buy you a gift either, for the same reason," she admitted. "But I wanted to give you something. So, I wrote you this."

She'd poured her heart out for nearly a dozen pages. Sharing the years of sadness, some she hadn't even realized she'd been suffering. And how, since meeting him, her entire life had changed. All because of the wonderous joy of loving this very special man. And his equally special child.

She watched him, her heart in her throat, as he read the deepest secrets of her heart. Her yearnings. And her conviction that despite everything she'd been brought up to believe about fate being merely an appealing myth, her entire life had been leading her here.

To this place.

To this man.

When he lifted his head, his eyes were bright with suspicious moisture. "Thank you."

Simple words, but she'd already come to accept that Gabe was a man of few words. It was the emotions behind those words that counted.

He drew her into his arms. Kissed her long and deep. Then drew back. "Every time I look at you, every time I kiss you, I fall in love all over again."

She smiled. Touched her hand to his cheek. "Then don' stop looking," she suggested. "Or kissing."

"Don't worry. I plan to keep on doing it for the next fift years."

"And then?"

"And then we'll just continue kissing our way to our cen tennial anniversary."

"Oh, I do like how you think," she said on a breathless laugh.

She was about to suggest they move into his bedroom where they could move beyond the kissing part of the evening, when he drew back.

"That's funny."

"What?" She followed his gaze to beneath the tree.

"That box wasn't there when I arranged all the packages before the party."

He left the couch again and picked it up. It was wrapped in green paper with Santa's smiling face. The same paper Rachel had wrapped Emma's elephant in.

"The tag says 'To Holly. From Santa,' " he read.

"Good try." She smiled even as she shook her head.

"I swear." He lifted his right hand. "I've never seen this box before."

Holly didn't believe him. But, because she loved him, she played along with the game, opening the package.

Inside, lying on a bed of red satin, was a yellowed envelope, addressed in red pencil to Santa Claus, postmarked twenty-one years earlier, from Los Angeles, California.

"It can't be," she said. When her fingers began trembling too much to open the envelope, she held it out to Gabe, who pulled out a folded piece of lined filler paper.

" 'Dear Santa.' " He read the all too familiar childish printing out loud. " 'My mama cries all the time since Daddy died. She says you can't bring him back to life. But this year, the only thing I want is a happy family. Like I used to have. Thank you and Merry Christmas to you and Mrs. Claus and all the elves and reindeers. Especially Blitzen.' "

"He was always my favorite," Holly murmured.

"Helluva coincidence," Gabe said.

"That's one word for it."

Gabe continued reading. " 'Love, Your friend, Holly Berry.' "

There's a P.S. 'In case you didn't notice, being so busy with your toy factory and all, I'm living in California now.' "

"How on earth?" Her mind was spinning with possibilities. Dazzling, gilt-edge possibilities that were as wonderful as they were impossible.

"There's more. I think you'd better read this for yourself." Gabe handed her the letter.

Below the careful printing Holly remembered laboring over was a note, written in a big, bold, masculine scrawl. *My Dearest Holly. Please forgive the delay in answering your letter. Some Christmas wishes just take a bit longer to fulfill. Merry Christmas back to you and, of course, your own special happy family, Gabriel and Emma. Love, Santa Claus.*

Books by Bestselling Author
Fern Michaels